The Shepherd's Moon

List of Novels Published:

A Race for Glory Run
The Bride Price
The Chording of T. O. Malone
Up the Hill, Through the Long Grass

The Shepherd's Moon

A novel sequel to:

Up the Hill, Through the Long Grass

Barclay Franklin

iUniverse, Inc.
New York   Bloomington

The Shepherd's Moon

This is a work of fiction. All of the characters, names, incidents, organizations, and dialogue in this novel are either the products of the author's imagination or are used fictitiously.

iUniverse books may be ordered through booksellers or by contacting:

iUniverse
1663 Liberty Drive
Bloomington, IN 47403
www.iuniverse.com
1-800-Authors (1-800-288-4677)

Because of the dynamic nature of the Internet, any Web addresses or links contained in this book may have changed since publication and may no longer be valid. The views expressed in this work are solely those of the author and do not necessarily reflect the views of the publisher, and the publisher hereby disclaims any responsibility for them.

ISBN: 978-1-4502-2569-4 (pbk)
ISBN: 978-1-4502-2570-0 (ebook)

Printed in the United States of America

iUniverse rev. date: 5/5/10

This book is dedicated to all my female friends,
each a strong woman in her own way,
and to those few males who treat such women with respect.

Acknowledgements:

I would like to thank:

Mrs. Stephenson, 10th grade Sharon, Pennsylvania High School English instructor, who got me started down the writing path.

Virginia V. Chanda, Yavapai College creative-writing instructor, who nurtured my hopes and made me believe I could become a published writer.

Dr. Allen Woodman, Northern Arizona University writing professor, who welcomed me into the graduate-degree program and taught me not only writing skills, but the value of humor and fair play.

Moraine Benny for creating such beautiful hearts and for giving me permission to use a reference to them in this novel.

Joan Bourque, once again, for creating the cover for this novel.

John Potts, iUniverse Publishing Service Associate, for facilitating the production of ***The Shepherd's Moon***.

Becky Cranmer for her willingness to read all 18 of my novel manuscripts and catch the typos and errors.

Carole J. Greene, literary agent, for her Christmas Day (2009) validating gift to me, and for her patience and wise advice on revisions.

All the readers who take the time to drop a note to say how much they enjoy my novels. In the dark of night, when the words come hard, I remember your notes and they give me the courage to sit down again and write.

Chapter One

Nearly every window in the AmeriBasque's ranch house was ablaze with warm yellow light. The open barn doors of the shearing barn spilled the same warm glow as Rory and Bernardo hitched two horses to the wagon full of straw in anticipation of a full-moon hayride for all Rory's nieces and nephews and the children of his drovers.

Rory was sliding on the twin hames and buckling straps when a small voice spoke from behind him.

"Whath hith name?" It was Bailey's almost four-year-old son, Todd, that Rory affectionately called the lisping inquisitor.

"His name is Domino," Rory told him.

"Can I thit on hith back, Uncle Rory?"

"Only if you hold onto the horns really tight and promise not to fall off."

"Okay."

Rory boosted Todd up. His legs stuck out at ninety-degree angles to his short, stubby body, so broad was Domino's back.

"Hold on now. Your mama would boil me in oil if you fell off and got hurt."

"Whath hith name?" Todd asked, pointing to the other horse in the hitch.

"Her name is Jemima." She's a girl horse.

"Jemima like the thurup on pancakth?"

"Yep, like the syrup on pancakes. Do you like pancakes with syrup?"

"Yeth. And thauthageth, too."

"Good, I like that for breakfast myself. Do you think we could maybe ask your Aunt Marta to mix up a batch of pancakes with syrup and sausages for breakfast tomorrow?"

"Yeth."

Rory, the four drovers and nearly 600 sheep had been up on the mountain meadows late into October, taking advantage of a warmer-than-normal fall. Only after two nights of heavy frost, followed by a couple of rain squalls with winds that tore the remaining gold and yellow leaves from the quaking aspens, had they started the long drive down to the ranch again.

Marta was overjoyed to have her husband back in residence. All summer she'd ferried frozen meals up to the meadows and sometimes spent the night with Rory in the camper on the back of the truck. It had been a long separation for a new bride, especially when she found out she was pregnant. The first three months had been hard, with daily bouts of morning sickness not helped by the smells of casseroles being constructed and then frozen.

She'd found a part-time position working for a lawyer in Butte in the afternoons, Tuesdays through Fridays, so that meant she'd had to make the supply runs up the road to the meadows on Mondays, for weekends had been devoted to thoroughly cleaning and painting the many rooms of the ranch house.

When the last of the sheep were safely installed in their various sheepcotes, Rory had come in through the mudroom door to a kitchen now sporting bright yellow walls and cheery café curtains sprinkled with roosters and hens.

Each room he entered wore a new color with coordinating drapes or curtains. The furniture had been polished to a high sheen and the whole place looked much warmer and more inviting than when he'd departed for the meadows in late June. Upstairs, he opened doors on the several bedrooms and found there were colorful spreads and sheets on the beds, and new towels in all the bathrooms.

His and Marta's bedroom was done up in browns with chocolate walls and tan and brown bedding. It remained predominately on the masculine side in its colors and appointments and he was happy she hadn't done it up in lavender and ruffles.

He jumped in the shower and relished the feel of clean *hot* water cascading over him. The last month he'd not come down once from the meadows to enjoy the comforts the ranch provided, being wary of an early snowstorm which might require all their efforts to get the sheep down safely. The hot water was a welcome treat.

He'd just wrapped the towel around him and was wiping the steam's moisture off the mirror so he could comb his hair when the door opened and Marta flew into the room. She didn't say anything, just wrapped her arms around him from the back and laid her head between his shoulder blades.

"Hello, wife," he said, catching her reflection in the mirror. He grinned, and slowly turned around.

"Hello, yourself, husband mine."

"I like what you've done with the place. It looks great! Maybe you ought to become an interior decorator."

"Do you really like it?"

"Yes. You've managed to turn a house into our home. It's warm and inviting and color coordinated. I'm truly impressed."

She glowed in the praise he was dishing out. "I was afraid you'd be angry because I didn't ask you about the colors or anything."

"What do I know about colors? Left to my own devices, I'd have purchased 17 gallons of some putrid shade of green and painted all the rooms the same color. It would never have occurred to me that you could do all the rooms in different shades. It gives them each a different personality—which is much better. Thank you for all your hard work."

"I wanted to get it done before you came home for the winter. I thought maybe we could host Thanksgiving this year. Invite all your brothers and sisters and your Mom and Walter and even Jack and Connie."

"Missing your old boss?"

"Sometimes. It's not that Ron Harrington is a bad boss, but he's laced up tighter than Jack. I miss the easy, breezy fun of Jack. He was always giving me advice or counseling me on some of the aspects of my life. Or telling some tall tale or funny joke."

"Yeah, I remember. He was the one who told you I'd break your heart."

"Oh, Rory. That was when he thought you were still in love with Kelsey."

"The whole family, huh? You're sure you want to inflict them on us?"

"I am so proud of you and of this ranch. I want them to see how well you have prospered."

"Long as nobody is looking at the balance of the checkbook."

"The balance is a bit better. I've been putting in my checks—all of what was left over after I bought paint and stuff."

He pulled her into his arms and kissed her, the intensity of his kisses telling her how much he'd missed her over the last four months.

"So, are we rich enough to host this big family gathering and include the drovers and their families, too? And Kelsey?"

"I think we can swing it. Why not invite them for the Tuesday before Thanksgiving? Then you can show your relatives around the place while we women work on baking pies and stuff. And you know the kids will all want a tour and maybe a hayride, too.

"They can gather old branches and leaves and some of the gourds from the garden and make the centerpieces for the holiday table and play games and if you tell all your family to bring sleeping bags for the kids, we'd have enough bedrooms to give all the adults a bit of privacy."

"Sounds like you've been giving this a lot of thought."

"I have. I didn't like the way things went the last time we all were together. I'd like to promote more harmony within the family. So can I call everyone and invite them?"

"Let me think about it tonight."

In the morning, Marta's plan won out over Rory's small set of reservations. The Tuesday before Thanksgiving, cars and motor homes began arriving late in the afternoon. Soon, kids were everywhere, climbing the rock walls of the sheepcotes and running pell-mell through the fields around the house. Sleeping bags for the kids were stacked in the corner of the den and Marta had assigned a bedroom to each of Rory's brothers or sisters and their respective spouses. Maire and Walter got a quiet room on Consuela's end of the house, and she'd assigned Jack and Connie separate rooms on the same wing.

"Nice of you to put us close to each other," Jack confided. "If I want to slip in for a little afternoon delight, maybe nobody will notice."

"If you'd rather share the same room, I'm sure nobody will care, Jack. I just didn't want to presume anything."

"I think it's best the way you arranged it. I know you wouldn't be carrying tales back to Boise, but I'm not so sure Sean or Maeve might not be willing to spread a bit of gossip. Where's that husband of yours, anyhow? After he met us at the door, I've not seen him since."

"He and Bernardo went down to the barn to fill the wagon with hay. There's an almost full moon tonight, and Rory thought the kids might like to have a hayride."

"Only for the kids? Connie and I might want to go, too."

"We thought we'd take the kids first and then the little ones can get to bed at a decent hour. If some of the adults want to go for a hayride, I'm sure Rory won't mind making a second trip."

Rory took the lead rope and walked Domino and Jemima up the hill to the front porch of the house with Todd hanging onto the hames horns for dear life.

"Okay, cowboy. Time to get down and sit in the hay with your cousins."

"That wath fun, Uncle Rory. I like hortheth. Can I ride more later?"

"We'll see. Maybe I'll saddle my horse and let you ride with me on that one. But for now, you need to get down and go in and ask all the kids who want to go for a ride in the hay wagon to come out."

"Okay."

A minute later all the kids came rocketing down the stairs. The bigger ones climbed up the spokes in the wooden wheels and plopped into the hay. Rory and Bernardo handed up the smaller ones, cautioning the older kids to each hang onto a little one.

"Can I ride shotgun?" Jack asked.

"Get aboard. Bernardo, will you please take the back end and make sure nobody falls out?"

"Okay, boss."

Rory made a loop of the yard picking up Enrique and Juan's kids, too. They set off down the dirt road toward the highway just as the yellow moon rose above the mountains to the east, lighting the way. Bernardo snatched up his guitar and began to strum it, playing "Clementine." Fifteen kids of the twenty-one that had come to the ranch were soon singing along. The other six, considering themselves too old for such nonsense as a hayride, were battling it out with each other playing video games.

By the time they went out to the highway and back, a few of the younger kids were nodding off. Rory left Bernardo in the driver's seat as he lifted sleeping children from the straw and carried them inside to snuggle them into sleeping bags in the den. Holding his finger to his lips to shush the older kids, he told them they could play any of the games in his game closet, but they had to be quiet. Marta put out some nachos and cans of soft drinks and soon the room was busy, with games of checkers, Monopoly and Sorry going on in various corners.

Kelsey, who was very pregnant, offered to stay at the house and maintain order rather than try to climb into the wagon. Consuela volunteered to keep the snacks coming, freeing Marta to join Rory and the others for a hayride.

"Okay, Bernardo, let's see if you drive well enough to keep the wagon on the road. Stop and see if your mom and dad and Juan and Dulce want to go, too."

Manuel and Ricardo and their girlfriends had already piled in the back. Even Walter and Maire joined in. Connie had a sneezing fit until Rory offered her a bandana to wear over her face.

"Makes it kind of hard to steal a kiss, Rory," Jack complained. "Don't they make some sort of synthetic hay so people don't get all watery in the eyes?"

"Not that I know of, Jack, but they do make antihistamines. Hold up, Bernardo and I'll get a couple of them for Connie."

He jumped down from the wagon and returned with the tablets and a plastic cup of water.

"Here, Connie. Try these."

"Thanks," she managed to squeeze out before another round of sneezes erupted.

Bernardo drove while this time Juan plied the strings of his guitar. Rory added his harmonica to several tunes as the moon rose higher in the sky.

"Can you play 'Moon River,' Juan?" Rory asked his drover.

"*Sí*, I play that."

Marta snuggled closer to Rory in the hay as "Moon River" echoed down the road. He stopped playing the harmonica long enough to kiss her tenderly twice. When they got to the bottom of the road, Bernardo said he might need help turning the team and the wagon around, so Rory stuffed the mouth organ in his pocket and claimed the reins and the seat in the front of the wagon, geeing and hawing to the team until they were headed back toward the house again.

"Anyone else want to give driving a try?" he asked.

"I'd like to," Jack said.

"Me, too," Walter chimed in. "I haven't driven a team since I was knee high to a grasshopper."

"I wouldn't mind taking a turn, Rory," Connie said. "I think my sneezing has subsided."

"It's getting late. Let Walter take his turn tonight and tomorrow afternoon, I'll hitch up the wagon and let you and Jack have a go at it, Connie."

Rory halted the horses until Walter could climb over the seat to sit beside him, then handed Walter the reins. Walter gave the horses a smart slap with the reins and they moved out, stepping high. Juan picked up the rhythm of the horses' hooves and played a flamenco tune while Rory noticed several of his siblings and their mates taking hold of the sideboards of the wagon.

"Hey, Walter, you might want to ease up a bit on the speed. Some of the passengers are looking a trifle nervous back there."

Walter collected the horses into a more sedate walk. "Bunch of tenderfoots," he complained under his breath to Rory. "In my day, what I was going *was* slow. This is like the way you'd tote a coffin to the cemetery. This speed is for funeral processions."

Rory had to grin. "I'll hitch up the sulky early tomorrow if you want and we'll go down the lane at warp speed behind my horse."

"Not too early. It was damn chilly here this morning, and it's fixing to be another cold night. Part of my reason for going fast was to get home to the fireplace sooner. My old bones don't enjoy the cold anymore."

Everyone got out at the front porch and Rory and Bernardo drove the team down to the barn and unhitched. They brushed both horses and turned them into their stalls giving each a big flake of hay.

"Thanks, Bernardo. You're turning out to be a right dependable hand with all the animals. Good job with driving, too. We'll practice turning some this winter until you get onto it. And the kids all enjoyed your music. Another few years, you'll play better than Juan. But don't tell him I said so, okay?"

"I won't say a word, but I don't think I'll ever be able to play flamenco like he does. The easy songs, maybe, but not that fast stuff."

Manuel and Ricardo sat down to breakfast the next morning, joining Sean, Clancy, Colton, Rory, Jack and Todd, who'd demanded the promised pancakes and sausages with syrup at that early hour. Marta and Consuela were manning the range, Marta flipping pancakes while Consuela broke a dozen eggs to scramble in an iron skillet.

"Aunt Marta, may I have more pancakth, pleath? And two more thauthageth, too?"

"Coming right up, Todd." Marta flapped two more of each onto Todd's plate.

"Uncle Rory, can you pour more thurup?"

"I'm sure I can. You want the Jemima or the Karo?"

"Jemima, like your horth."

Shortly after breakfast, Manuel and Ricardo excused themselves and went to tend to their sheep, telling Rory in Spanish that they'd feed for him, too, so he could enjoy his guests.

"I confess, Rory, I don't understand you," Sean said, as they each drank another cup of Consuela's coffee.

"Oh? What don't you understand, Sean?"

"Here you have a house full of guests and you let the hired help eat at the same table with the rest of us."

When a frown knit Rory's eyebrows together and his jaw muscles clenched, Marta feared the worst. She knew he was furious at Sean's putdown of his drovers. For what seemed like ages, he studied his coffee cup. When he finally looked up, Marta held her breath. She laid her hand on his shoulder, hoping to forestall an explosion.

"Marta, will you round up all my family and their mates?" he asked quietly. "Jack, will you excuse us for the moment. You and Connie could to take a short walk."

"I can think of better things to do with Connie this morning, Rory. Marta, if you'll pour me a cup for Connie, I'll go see if she's up yet." Jack gave Rory a wink and took the cup Marta proffered.

Marta soon had the rest of the family seated at the table. She continued to make pancakes and fry sausage patties, still hoping Rory was not about to go ballistic and spoil Thanksgiving. As she poured orange juice for them, she caught Rory's eye and raised her eyebrows in question.

"It's okay, I'm cool," he told her.

"Mom, Walter, all of you," he began, sliding back his chair at the head of the table and rising to address them. "We invited you all for Thanksgiving. But there is something I need to make clear to all of you. The drovers and their families or their girlfriends will be sitting down to eat with us—at the same table as all of you are invited to eat at— tomorrow night. Their children will be sharing the tables in the den with your kids.

"In our home, we don't exclude anyone based on their heritage or their stations in life. In this house, the drovers are as welcome to join in a meal as are all of you."

"You gather up deadbeats from skid row, too?" Sean asked. "They're your hired hands, for God's sake."

"You're wrong, Sean. They're my *partners*. AmeriBasque is not *my* ranch, it's *our* ranch. Those four drovers have stood beside me through good times and bad for seven years. They've sweated the same sweat I shed at shearing time and frozen their tails off when mine was freezing, feeding sheep in a blizzard. We may not be related by blood, as I am with most of you, but in every way that counts, they are my brothers, too. And as such, I expect all of you to treat them with respect. They've earned it.

"They would never think of speaking about any of you in the manner you speak about them, Sean. They're Basques. They're equally as proud of their ancestors as you are of yours. So, from this moment on, I expect you to treat them as your equals.

"When Marta and I first came as man and wife to this ranch, I promised her this would be a place where love and harmony prevailed. And it will prevail, beginning now. If you think you can't manage that, then I invite you to pack up and head on home in the next hour. In this house, there will be no discrimination. Not now. Not ever. *Everyone* is welcome here."

Rory sat down again and there was a period of silence. He wasn't sure what to expect from his oration. It was Todd who came to his rescue.

"Aunt Marta, more pancakth and thauthageth, pleath," came Todd's small voice. The tension melted as everyone turned to smile at him.

"And more Jemima syrup, too, Todd?" Rory asked.

"Yeth, more thurup, too."

Marta filled his plate for the third time and Rory poured more syrup on. "Todd, where are you putting all those pancakes, buddy?" Rory asked.

"In my tummy. I like them. Yeth I do. Aunt Marta makth them tathe good."

"Yep, she does. That's one of the reasons I married her. She makes everything taste good."

Chris glanced around the table. Everyone was staring at his or her plate. Only Todd seemed oblivious to the undercurrents as he dove into his pancakes and sausages.

Once again, it was Chris who came to Rory's defense.

"Good for you and Marta, Rory. I like the idea of promoting harmony and love instead of the constant bickering we all seem to have fallen heir to in this family. Sean, this is Rory and Marta's home, so I think they have the right to set the agenda in it and it's up to us to respect their wishes.

"Rory is correct. We have no business looking down our collective noses at those some of you consider 'beneath' you. Enrique, Juan, Manuel and Ricardo *are* like Rory's brothers. They're out there right now feeding for Rory so he can enjoy time with all of us. Let's honor his request and welcome them into this McCrea family circle. Let's make the drovers and their families feel welcome at the holiday dinner and at every instance in between."

"I second my wife's request. I know that some of you did not look with favor on me, too, when I asked Christina to marry me. I, too, come from a different culture. I also am proud of my heritage, though it is different from yours. But I think all peoples can open their hearts and respect the differences—appreciate them, even.

"My country, Italy, has given this America the pizza and I see that you all like that very much. So perhaps you can stretch yourselves to like also the peoples that have given you this food you love so much. No? The men who help your brother Rory are good and honest men—hardworking, with many hidden talents. Did not Juan serenade us all last night on his guitar? Did not Bernardo drive the wagon so you could enjoy the moonlight and Rory could steal some kisses from Marta? Was it not Juan's wife who gave Rory his haircut Tuesday morning before the rest of you arrived?

"This is what families do. They give equally to each other. And I think I will be very happy to have everyone together at the table on this American holiday called Thanksgiving. We should all give thanks for Rory's drovers and their families. Without them, I think Rory and Marta would not be in such good shape to offer us their hospitality and a fine repast come tomorrow, no?"

"Amen to that, Ernesto," Rory told him.

"Okay, Rory. For the sake of your *harmony* we'll try it your way."

"Thank you, Sean. Hey, guys, soon as it warms up, I'm up for pitching some horseshoes. Any takers?"

"Did you say, horseshoes?" Walter asked, turning up his hearing aid.

"Yep, sure did. Marta said the women want us out from under their feet while they bake pies for tomorrow, so maybe we can have a tournament. Make up teams until we finally arrive at the best two of the bunch."

"How many teams?" Colton asked.

Rory counted off on his fingers. "Well, there are eleven adult men. Maybe I can persuade Bernardo to make it twelve—six teams of two each. The winners of each round go on to play the next two until we crown the champs. You think any of your kids would like to participate?" he asked of his various siblings.

"I don't think that's a good idea," Maeve said. "Paul is big enough, but if you ever watched him pitch a baseball, you'd think twice about handing him a horseshoe. Better leave my kids alone with the video games. No concussions will result from their participation in that."

Behind the shearing barn, Bernardo raked out the sand in the pits evenly. Sean and Enrique took up the gold-painted shoes while Walter and Colton picked up the silver ones.

"What are the rules?" Clancy asked.

"I don't know what the official rules are. We usually give three points for a ringer, two for a leaner and one if the peg at least an inch inside the tips of the shoe. Twenty-one is game," Rory told them. "We'll keep track on the chalkboard here. Golds are team A, silvers are team B."

Walter proved to be a pretty fair pitcher and the silver team won, 21-16. Next up, Juan and Clancy stood Walter and Colton. That time, Walter's knees got the better of him and Juan and Clancy took top honors.

Juan and Clancy beat Manuel and Ricardo, then absolutely demolished the team of Ernesto and Jack.

It came down to Bernardo and Rory against the team of Juan and Clancy. It was a hotly contested game, the lead going back and forth until Juan scored a ringer and Bernardo's shoe sailed into the shearing barn, ending up in an empty stall.

"C'mon, Bernardo. Tell me you aren't going to let that bunch of wimps win. Try to keep the shoes in the pits, kiddo."

"Sorry, boss. I'll do better."

With that, he gave his all and got one point for his effort, but the next shoe Juan tossed was a dead-on-center ringer.

Juan and Clancy spent all of ten minutes gloating before Jack made a suggestion.

"I think, gentlemen, we should draw straws for partners next time. Six sets—all six sets different lengths. And to make it more interesting, let's all put in a couple of bucks. Winners take all."

"Okay," Rory agreed. "Bernardo, get some straw from the barn and make two of each set the same size."

"Todd. Can you help us out?"

Todd, who'd been sitting on the bench beside the barn said, "Yeth."

When Bernardo came back with the sets of matched straws, Rory asked Todd to open up his hand. He placed all the straws in Todd's mitt with the tops being even.

"Now close your hand, Todd, and don't let anyone peek at the straws."

Each of the men came and drew out a straw from the batch, then went around measuring against what everyone else had drawn. Sean ended up with Juan, Enrique with Ernesto, Walter with Rory, Jack with Colton, Bernardo with Clancy and Manuel with Ricardo. They all pulled a couple of dollars out of their pockets to add to the kitty.

"Todd, can you keep the money in your pocket?" Rory asked.

"Yeth. Ith it for ithe cream?"

"No, but if you keep it safe in your pocket, I'll have Aunt Marta give you ice cream with your lunch, okay?"

"Yeth. Lunch ith thoon? I'm hungry."

"Oh, Todd, how could you be hungry after all those pancakes this morning?"

"I runned all the way down to here."

"Okay buddy. We'll try to make this quick so you can eat lunch soon."

"Shortest pairs start. Bernardo and Clancy, you're up against Jack and Colton."

Walter and Rory played Jack and Colton next. Walter seemed like he'd gotten a second wind or else the money enticed him to ignore his sore knees. He and Rory came out on top. Enrique and Ernesto almost caught them in the next game but Walter's leaner decided that match. Manuel and Ricardo took them on next and lost.

"Hey, Walter. Keep up the good work and I'll hike up into the hills for some old gnarled wood you can turn into one of those fancy lamps at your workbench. Okay, Sean and Juan. Get up here so we can send you back up the hill crying cause you lost the pot."

"You're kind of impressed with yourself, Rory. Juan and I will have to take you down a peg."

"Put your horseshoes where your mouth is, Sean."

Back and forth it went until Juan clinched the victory for himself and Sean with another ringer.

"Now whose shoes are in his mouth, Rory?"

"Mine," Rory admitted. "Todd, give your Uncle Sean and Mr. Juan the money."

Todd fished in his pocket and pulled out the dollars, one-by-one to hand to Sean. Sean divided the pot with Juan, then hugged him, thumped him on the back and told him he wanted the Basque on his team every time.

Rory was glad Sean seemed to be mellowing out a bit toward the drovers. *Nothing like winning some money to enhance a relationship*, he thought.

"C'mon, Todd, I'm hungry, too. Let's go get that ice cream. Want to ride on my back?"

"Yeth. Ith it okay if I pee here firth?"

"Yes, sir. Pee here first. I don't want you peeing on my back. Water those weeds over there near the wagon."

A long stream of urine ensued while all the men watched in amazement.

"Makes me damn glad he decided to pee before he got on for his ride up the hill," Rory commented. "I'd have been drenched."

The guys all laughed, then put on their straight faces as Todd returned to their circle. Rory helped him zip up his zipper then swung Todd onto his back.

"Hold on tight, I'm going to trot."

Rory took off, with Todd bouncing on his back, and laughing all the way to the house. He backed up to the porch so Todd could step down on it.

"You are a good horth, Uncle Rory. You go fath."

"Sure do. Now I need some oats for my lunch."

"Whath oath?"

"It's like ice cream for horses. Tonight, when I go to feed Domino and Jemima you can come with me and give them their oats."

"I love you, Uncle Rory."

"Love you, too, Sport. Let's see if Aunt Marta can rustle us up a sandwich."

"Yeth."

Pie construction was well under way in the kitchen, so Marta laid out the ingredients for sandwiches in the dining room and invited all to build their own. Rory spent the better part of an hour making peanut butter and jelly sandwiches for the smaller kids, and stirring up chocolate milk to wash them down with. Once the thundering herd had been fed and watered, he collapsed in his chair with the few shards of lunchmeat still on the tray and began to construct a sandwich for himself.

Marta leaned over his shoulder and put a double-decker sandwich down in front of him.

"Bless you. I don't think I have the strength to make one out of what's left on the tray. The calories I'd expend would vastly outnumber the ones I'd take in with these few wafers of ham."

"Pretty slim pickings, I'd agree. What's on your agenda for the afternoon?"

"Maybe I'll take all the kids that can walk and we'll hunt up some of those leaves to decorate the table with tomorrow. And if I find some wood that Walter can build into a lamp, I'll tote some of that back, too."

"Take your brothers in case some of the kids need a piggy-back ride home. And see if you can entice your sisters to go with you, too. They all want to help in the kitchen and we're tramping on each other. Leave me Kelsey and Chris, but take the others, please?"

"They have something to say about my spiel this morning. They get on your case?"

"No, but Consuela has her way of doing things in the kitchen and your sisters don't know her ways. Chris is fine, and Kelsey just sits at the table cutting out leaves from the dough to decorate the pies with, but the rest want to help in ways that don't help. So take them, will you?"

"Yeah, sure. I'll need some extra eyes with all the kids. Sure smells good in there. Any chance I could get you to slip me a piece of pumpkin pie now?"

"Not a chance."

"Well, how about some ithe cream? Todd and I want ithe cream."

"Isn't he just the dearest thing? He's so cute and man can he put away the pancakes. I think there should be about eight gallons of ice cream in the basement freezer. Maybe some of the other kids want some, too. There are cones in the pantry down there."

"How do I get stuck with all this work? Where's Bailey? It's her son that's hot for ithe cream. Give her a scooper. I'm not doing the whole blessed crowd by myself."

"Oh, poor soul. I'll see if I can line up some help."

Chris and Rory ended up filling cones after which Rory told all the kids to go out on the porch and eat them.

"You don't want to find ice cream in the couch and chair cushions?" Chris quizzed.

"No, it's because I want to fill up my bowl to the max and pour chocolate sauce and peanuts on it, that's why. The little blighters see that and they'll all be clamoring for the good stuff."

"Soo-eee! Rory."

"Yeah, right. I am a pig when it comes to ice cream with all the toppings. But you knew that from a long time ago, didn't you?"

"I certainly do remember you hogging the ice cream, yes."

"Nothing has changed in the interim." He grinned at her and then got serious. "Hey, Sis, thanks for what you said this morning. Ernesto, too. Do you know that Sean actually hugged Juan when they beat us at horseshoes?"

"Really?"

"Yeah. I wasn't sure if it was because he'd decided to treat the drovers with respect, or because he liked winning the twelve bucks when they split the pot. More the latter, I suspect . . . but whatever works."

"Give me some of those peanuts, Ror."

"Not a chance, Chris. There's only a pound left. Hardly enough to coat my ice cream."

"Think of it as saving your arteries."

"My arteries are just fine, thank you."

"Ernesto. I could use your help."

Ernesto came into the dining room. "What do you need me to do, Cara?"

"Hold Rory down while I steal the peanuts."

"I don't know if that's possible."

"Sure it is. Get behind him and I'll move in from the front."

Rory tried to stand up with his bowl and the peanuts, but Ernesto was quicker. He pinned Rory to the chair back. When Ern locked his hands together, Rory found he couldn't budge. With a glint of victory in her eyes, Chris snatched the peanuts.

"Marta, come quick. I need help!" Rory bellowed.

Ernesto was laughing so hard by that time that he lost his grip. Rory jumped up and chased Chris into the living room, finally snagging the peanuts back. "Damn it. Don't git between me and my peanuts, woman or I fear I'll have to fetch me my six-shooter and plug ya a good one."

"Not if I git my six-shooter first. You're one ornery polecat." She made another lunge for the peanuts.

"Children, children. Let's not quibble. Rory, share your peanuts with your sister. This is a house of love and harmony, remember?" Marta chided. "You don't need a pound of peanuts, Rory McCrea."

"I get three-fourths of them. This is my house and these are my peanuts. I'll share, but she doesn't get more than me."

He gave Chris and Marta his best petulant look then burst out laughing.

"Chris, in March, it looks like I'll have two children to look after. The baby and Rory. I'm not sure I'm up to the challenge."

"You're pregnant?"

"Yes. I'm a little more than four months gone."

"Why didn't you say so? You're hardly showing. I never would have guessed. You should be sitting down and taking things easy, not standing up creating all those pies."

"Oh, I'm fine. The doctor said I'm healthy as a horse and that exercise is good for me."

"Congratulations, Rory. Sheep aren't the only things you breed well, so it seems."

"I could probably manage twins next time, but only if I can eat the peanuts."

Chris opened the lid and dumped most of the nuts on Rory's ice cream.

"Never let it be said that I stood in the way of procreation, Rory."

"Thanks. If it's a girl next time, we'll name it for you."

He dug into the ice cream, savoring every peanut-covered bite.

"Got to keep up my strength for the afternoon hike," he told them, smirking, and licking his lips. "Mmm. Really good Chris. You should try some."

"No pie for Rory tomorrow, Marta. Not unless he wipes that stupid grin off his face this minute. I'm a sore loser, Ror. You should remember that from a way back. I don't get mad, I get even. You'll get yours."

"I already did, Chris," he told her, raising his spoon on high.

Chapter Two

Thanksgiving Day arrived with wind and much colder temperatures. Most of the outside activities were curtailed in favor of inside games. The men got up an impromptu poker game while the women played gin rummy or bridge. Kids got along surprisingly well, with only an occasional squabble. Older kids read to smaller ones, while the teens and nearly teens challenged each other to video game matches. Todd and his age group were busy building all sorts of things with buckets of Lego blocks.

Rory and the drovers had their usual chores that not even major holidays disrupted. Once done with the feeding of the sheep and horses and the mucking out of stalls, Rory came in through the mudroom just as Marta and Kelsey were finishing stuffing the two enormous turkeys. Pies were lined up on the counters, and Consuela was paring potatoes.

He washed his hands at the sink and gave Marta a kiss good morning.

"I hope there will be enough meat to eat," Marta quietly worried.

"Two big roasts of beef in the grill outside and two huge turkeys in the ovens in here? And you're worried about enough to eat?"

"Well, there are so many. . . ."

"Yeah, but most of them are kids."

"You saw how many pancakes even someone Todd's size can eat."

"Yeah." Rory laughed. "Maybe I should butcher a sheep and put it on a spit. No, Marta, with all the other stuff, they'll all get filled up just fine."

They sat down at four to dinner and as was predicted, with all the food on the tables, nobody went hungry. Enrique's wife had made a huge pot of cowboy beans and Dulce, Juan's wife, had produced a big pan of tamales wrapped in cornhusks.

Conversation ebbed and flowed, with laughter erupting as jokes were shared. Rory sat at the head of the table and Marta at the foot, and every so often he'd catch her eye and nod—a silent approval of the feast and all her hard work in producing it. Even Consuela, who usually shunned large gatherings, preferring the privacy of her room, joined in the conversation. Ricardo and Manuel had supplied the wine, and as the evening wore on, people got mellower and mellower.

The sun sank in the western sky and soon it was dark enough to light the twin chandeliers that hung above the long table where the adults had eaten. Marta, with the help of Maire, Consuela, Chris, and Bailey began to gather the dishes from the table and stack them in the kitchen.

When Marta suggested pie and coffee, everyone protested they were still too full for any more of anything, so the good-natured ribbing and talk went on for another hour. Marta got up to turn on the urn and heat the coffee. As she passed Rory, he reached out and took her hand.

"Marta, hit the lights off when you come back and tell the kids to come into the dining room, too, can you?"

"Sure, but why?"

"You'll see."

The big picture window at the east end of the dining room looked out on the mountains rising in the distance. Outside it was as black as the face of a Suffolk sheep.

Marta went to the doorway of the den and invited the kids into the dining room. When they were all inside, she flipped the light switch and it was dark.

"Are you going to tell us a scary story, Uncle Rory?" Clancy's son, Gordon, asked.

"I'm going to tell you a story, but it's not a scary one."

He was quiet and the kids were restless with anticipation.

"When are you going to start?" Sean's daughter, Sabrina, asked.

"Any minute now."

"What are you waiting for?" Mariah quizzed.

At just that moment, a warm orange glow appeared above the mountains.

"I was waiting for the shepherd's moon to rise, and there it is. Watch."

Inch-by-inch the moon rose until it loomed, huge and round and yellow above the peaks of the mountains.

"Why is it a shepherd's moon, Uncle Rory?" Jayce asked.

"That's the story I want to tell you. You know that there's a full moon every month, don't you?"

Several heads nodded in the glow of moonlight cascading through the window.

"Well, most of them have names. There's the blue moon, when two full moons come in the same month, for instance. I won't go through all of them, but you all know that the October moon is called the harvest moon, because it gave farmers enough light to finish collecting the food that grew in their fields and gardens. In the old days, before tractors with lights, lots of things were harvested by hand or by using horses and wagons.

"Farmers worked long hours back then and with winter coming, they used every spare minute to collect corn and wheat and tomatoes and other stuff. They didn't want to be hungry in the winter. After all the ears of corn were pulled, they made silage of the corn stalks and fed that to their cows, because happy and full cows give lots of milk. Sometimes, the farmers ran out of daytime to collect the corn stalks and other things, but when the October moon rose and was full, it gave them extra light and extra nights to finish harvesting their crops.

"So, October's full moon is called the harvest moon, and the November full moon is called the shepherd's moon."

"Why?" came the question from a half-dozen children.

"You remember when the baby Jesus was born?"

"On Christmas, Uncle Rory. Everyone knows that," Ciara said.

"Right. In Bethlehem. In a stable. And who came to see the new baby?"

The kids were warming to the tale Rory was spinning. Brows furrowed as they thought about the answers to his questions.

"Wise men," Thomas offered.

"And shepherds," Nate added.

"Right. And how did those wise men and shepherds know where to go?"

Riley, Sean's son, said, "A star led them to the right place."

"Good," Rory said, "looks like you've all been paying attention to your Bible lessons."

"But you still didn't tell why the November moon is the shepherd's moon," Annette and Susanna complained almost in unison.

"I'm getting there. So, it seems like the shepherds and the wise men were a long way away from Bethlehem. The wise men were on their camels way off in the deserts of Asia. The shepherds were far away, too, because near the bigger cities like Bethlehem, there wasn't much grass left for the sheep to eat. Just like you can't find many sheep in Boise. They're all out in the hills and mountains and on big ranches like this one where there's lots of grass.

"But God knew the baby Jesus was about to be born in that Bethlehem stable, and God said to his favorite angel, 'How am I going to get the wise men and shepherds to the stable?' He gave her that puzzle to solve, you see. All God told her was that the birth would happen in December, but he didn't say what day Jesus would be born. Maybe he didn't know Himself.

"Well, the angel thought a long time about that—all through September and the first part of October the angel pondered God's question. How could the wise men and shepherds come to the stable in time for the birth of Jesus?

"Then the harvest moon came up in October, and the angel said, 'AHA!' She had one of those moments when a light bulb went off in her head you see. She said to the other angels, who were like her cheerleading squad, 'When the moon is full in November, the wise men and the shepherds could travel all day and long into the nights to get to Bethlehem because the moon would light their way.'"

"But they didn't go to the stable in November, Uncle Rory. They went there in December."

"Right, Marian. But the angel had a plan and she whispered it into God's ear and God thought the plan was a good one. See, the angel didn't know if the birth of Jesus would happen when the moon was full, so she couldn't count on the December moonlight for enough light to let the shepherds and wise men travel. That's why she chose the November moonlight."

"God knows everything. He would have known if Jesus was going to be born when the December moon was full," Paul challenged. "Why didn't God tell the angel if the moon would be full?"

"Well, God gave the angel the task of coming up with a plan, so even if He knew about the moon phase when Jesus would be born, He didn't think it was fair to the angel to scuttle her plans just because He had more wisdom. God wanted his angels to think for themselves and puzzle stuff out.

"You know that you take more satisfaction if you read a mystery book and find out 'who done it' on your own than if your mom or dad tells you they read the book long ago and it was the butler who stole the candlesticks."

"Yeah, okay," Eagan prompted, anxious to get on with the story.

"Just before the November moon came full, the angel did a fly-over. First she whispered to the wise men because they had more miles to go, then she hit the sheep camp and told the shepherds, too."

"What did she say to them?" Annette asked.

"She said, 'There will be a birth in December. The Son of God will be born in a stable in Bethlehem, and you are to go there. She told the wise men that they should bring gifts—what were they?"

"Gold, frankincense and myrrh," Jayme volunteered.

"Right. And she told the shepherds to come to sing the praises of the new baby, because Jesus was supposed to be the Good Shepherd of all God's flocks of people. So you see, the shepherds, though they weren't nearly as wealthy as the wise men, had just as important a role to play, if not the most important one.

"The shepherds and wise men set off on their long journeys, in the full-moon time of November, and they were kind of discouraged when they still had some miles to go when it got darker and darker as the moon went to its last quarter. By then there was no moonlight to be seen in the dark-of-the-moon phase. But they'd made amazing progress toward Bethlehem, and to dispel their worries, the angel came to both groups again and said, 'Remember how big and bright was the shepherd's moon of November?' And the shepherds and wise men nodded and said they did remember, but now it was dark and how could they find their way in the dark?

"It was then that the angel said they should follow a star. But the shepherds and wise men looked up into the night sky and scratched their heads because, as you all know, there are thousands of stars in the sky. But the angel told them to remember the brightness of the shepherd's moon and look for the one star that would shine as bright as that moon, and so, it was the shepherd's star—as bright as the shepherd's moon—that led them to the manger where the baby Jesus lay.

"You all go out on the porch or in the front yard and look at the shepherd's moon. Remember how bright it is. Then if you ever lose your way in life, look for a guiding star that's as bright as the shepherd's moon and you'll find your own way again."

"Ah, Uncle Rory, how do you know that?"

"I'm a shepherd. An angel whispered it in my ear," he told them in a serious voice.

Twenty-one nieces and nephews and all of the drovers' kids got up and went to the front door. Rory went out with them and all faces turned upward. Awe was what suffused their faces, along with the light of the shepherd's moon.

"It really *is* bright, Uncle Rory."

"Yep, sure is. Now you all better hustle back inside. It's cold out here."

The lights were back on when they went in and after pie and whipped cream, kids went willingly to sleeping bags and moonlit dreams. At the table, the drovers and their wives got up to leave as the chores of the next morning started early. Dulce hugged Rory with tears in her eyes.

"You tell beautiful stories. Makes me proud to be married to a shepherd. I will pass on your story to my grandchildren. Thank you."

"*De nada*, Dulce. Thank you for your *tamales*. I know how much work they are to make. Everyone enjoyed them—the pan was empty in minutes. And for your *frijoles*, too, Melinda. I can't think of anyone who makes them better than you. Sleep well, and thanks to all of you for making our first Thanksgiving at AmeriBasque such a fine affair."

Rory shook hands with each of his drovers and finally closed the door on the chill wind from the west. Most of the McCrea family was still lingering over coffee and second pieces of pie when he sat down again at the table. A huge chunk of pumpkin pie with a tall mound of whipped cream graced the table in front of him.

"Wow!" he said, glancing around the table. "Did any of the rest of you get *any* pie?"

"We all got some, Rory. You just got the huge piece for telling the most beautiful story I've heard in ages. I'll never look at the full November moon in the same way again."

"Thanks, Kelsey lass."

"I agree, Rory. Jack said you were an Irish poet at heart," Connie told him. "Magnificent story. Very well told. You should be on Garrison Keillor's Christmas show."

"As the Grinch?" he asked, picking up his fork. He dug in, savoring the richness of the pie and the sweetness of the cream. "I'd be totally tongue-tied," he mumbled around a mouthful of pie.

"No you wouldn't, Rory. Anyone who can tell a story that keeps my four on the edges of their seats is a natural," Chris told him. "And I'm not afraid to admit you had Ernesto and me both fumbling for a tissue."

"It was a good story, Rory. There's Irish poet in you, sure. If it wasn't total *bullshit*."

"Sean!" Maire said. "Get upstairs this instant and wash your mouth out with soap, then take a day-long time-out sitting in the corner. How could you say such a thing? I was looking around while Rory was telling the story and all the kids were giving him their rapt attention, and several of us oldsters were dabbing eyes right along with Chris and Ernesto. For you to hint that the story isn't true—you deserve coal in your Christmas stocking for even suggesting that."

Rory was grinning openly now as Sean squirmed in his chair under his mother's tongue lashing.

"Mom, didn't you ever notice how all Rory's stories end up glorifying sheep or shepherds? Why didn't the angel call it the wise man's moon? Or the sheep moon? Or the camel moon? NO! None of that for Rory. Even when he's spinning a yarn so full of blarney it would make St. Patrick blush, somehow the sheep man always comes out the hero," Sean said in his own defense.

"I don't know, Sean. It just wouldn't have the same ring to it if the angel had called it the restaurant-owner's moon. Or the car-dealer's moon," Rory said, having a hard time suppressing a laugh.

Marta came and stood behind his chair. "I don't know about the rest of you, but I'm *really* tired. Can I get some help to do up the dishes so we'll have plates enough for breakfast? Then, I suggest we make an early night of it."

"Hey, guys. We've been pitching horseshoes and playing poker while the women sweated in the kitchen to produce this really nice dinner, so I propose we do our good deed for the day and handle the cleanup in the kitchen. C'mon, Sean, you can work off your penance for your bullshit remarks by rolling up your sleeves and washing some dishes."

"Okay. Guess that beats standing in the corner for two days. Does that meet with your approval, Mom?"

"Yes, Sean. But only if you put on Marta's big ruffled apron and I can take a picture."

"Ah, Mom. Why would you make that part of my absolution? Blackmail is not your style. You just want to have a picture like that so you can threaten me. If I don't behave, you're going to hang a huge blowup of the shot in the restaurant, aren't you? Isn't that what you were planning to do with the picture?"

"Yes, son, the thought did occur. Now that Aidan's gone, you seem to feel the need to fill his shoes. Everyone else is thinking what a nice story Rory told and you're the only one thinking of it in terms of fecal material. You're too old and I'm too old for me to ply my rod, so I think the picture would be a good stand-in to keep you in line."

Rory held out two of Marta's aprons.

"Blue one or the yellow, Sean?"

"Jesus Christ! Neither. I *am NOT* wearing an apron." Sean stomped over to the sink and turned on the faucet, pouring in liquid soap, then piling the first stack of dishes in the water. "Well, Rory, are you going to dry or does telling your story absolve you from the household chores tonight?"

"I always do my fair share, Sean. But it might be better if Clancy and Colton and Jack dry. I'll put the dishes away, seeing as I know where they go."

"Oh, so you're on KP even when there aren't tons of dishes to wash?"

"Sure, Sean. Lots of nights."

"Does Marta make you wear an apron?"

"I have on a few occasions."

"Why? You'd never get me into one of those."

"If you want to take your girl out for a show after dinner and you don't want beet juice on your dress shirt, an apron makes it possible to help with the dishes and still stay clean. And I've never felt my masculinity was dependent on what I wore. Is yours?"

"Son of a. . . ."

"Ah, Sean . . . best not to go there. We both share the same one of those."

"Well, shit!"

With that, Sean shut his mouth and washed all the plates, cups and glasses. Then he turned the sink over to Jack who volunteered to take on the pots and pans. Rory told the rest of the guys to call it a day and he'd help Jack finish the rest of the cleanup chores.

"Rory, a tip of our hats to you and Marta. This was one of the best Thanksgivings I ever enjoyed."

"We're glad you could join us, Jack. Marta was just saying the other day how much she misses working for you. Guess her new boss has a little tighter ass than you. She said he never opens up and laughs or tells a joke."

"I miss Marta, too. Not that Amanda doesn't do a good job—she does. But at least when Marta worked for me, I got to see you now and then. Now, it's too damn long between visits."

"We were up on the meadows late this year and as soon as we came down it was time to begin fall breeding. I've been busy. Even Marta laments that I'm not around much. But between now and shearing next spring, maybe we can get away for a couple of weekends in Boise. For sure, we'll be there for Christmas."

"Following a shepherd's star? You almost had me believing in Jesus."

"If you'd convert to Catholicism, Jack, I could invite you to share Christmas with us, too."

"Wouldn't that send my temple's Torah spinning in its ark?"

"Maybe we can get together for a night out over the holidays, spinning Torah or not. Sometimes I need to get away from the clan for a few hours."

"I notice they're a lot less caustic toward you here, than they are at the old homestead."

"Oh? Who's been filling your ears with tales about life on the ranch in Idaho?"

"Umm, a couple of times Marta seemed kind of upset. She'd confide in me because she knew it wasn't going to be in the tabloids the next day. She told me some of it. Has it more to do with being here on your turf, that they've been better this week, or more to do with Aidan's death, do you think?"

"I think it's because when I asked you and Connie to take a hike—literally take one—I told the whole crew that AmeriBasque Ranch was going to be a place where harmony and love prevailed and if that didn't suit them, not to let the door slam them in their collective asses on their way out through it.

"It's part that, and maybe it's part of being out of their element a bit here, too. Sean, I think, has already taken over where Aidan left off. But here, I'm not going to let him shift his nastiness into high gear. At the homestead, I'm low son on the totem pole. Here, I'm top dog."

"How are things, generally? If you don't mind me asking."

"Oh, we're not out of the woods by a long shot, but the fleece sale brought in more than I expected, and Marta's checks have helped a bit. I've been to a few sheep meetings and some of the smaller outfits have been paying for the use of a few of our rams for their breeding programs. We'll soon cull the older ewes and sell the meat from those, so funds keep dribbling in. I can just about keep our heads above the lapping waves of the lake if I'm very careful and tread water 24/7."

"This weekend must be about to pull you under, then. Can I offer you a couple of Franklins for all your hospitality to me and Connie?"

"Certainly not. How many times did I eat at your trough on legal things? I'd have to invite you to Thanksgiving dinners well into the next century before I'd feel maybe I'd squared my obligations to you."

"Rory, don't *ever* feel you owe me. Every time I pull my socks up over those scars, I'm reminded again that you were willing to lay down your life to save mine. We're friends—and good ones, too. Our friendship isn't a ledger affair. I'm not keeping track of your visits to my office."

"No, I know that. And I'm not keeping track of how much pie and turkey you ate today either."

"Can we let this last roaster pan soak? I'm tired and I slept in this morning. You must be at exhaustion's doorstep, Rory."

"Sure. Consuela will finish it in the morning. She likes her kitchen neat. I think the rest of them will be heading out for Idaho tomorrow—all but Chris and her family. Can you and Connie stay? Marta and I would be pleased if you could."

"I'll talk to Connie. If she's not got a big banquet scheduled, I'd love to stay. No phones. No clients. No mean-assed judges. You're living in paradise, my friend."

"I'll invite you back in April for the shearing. Then we'll see if you're of the same opinion."

"Pretty rough, is it?"

"Worse than that. Go ahead to your room, I'll turn off the lights once you get there."

"Goodnight, Rory. And thanks."

"You, too, Jack."

When he stole in between the flannel sheets, Marta reached over to hug him.

"I think that Thanksgiving went really well."

"Yep, it did. Everyone enjoyed the day and all the good food. Thanks, wife—for suggesting it in the first place and for everything you did to pull it off and make it so successful."

She snuggled tighter against him and said, "Your story about the moon touched my heart and made me want to cry. And I wasn't the only one. I could have clobbered Sean for what he said. It was a beautiful story—one I'll never forget and one I'll tell all of our children when November rolls around. Did you do research? Is it really a true story? Is the November moon really the shepherd's moon?"

"Nope, it's all bullshit, just like Sean said."

"Oh, Rory. Don't tell me that."

"I don't know if it's true or not, Marta. I've always heard November's moon referred to as a shepherd's moon, so maybe there's a reason it's called that. Maybe it is a true story and I know about it because up there on the meadows in the full moon of October, an angel came by when I was sleeping and whispered it in my ear. Maybe she spun the story and that's how I came to know it and be able to tell it. Angels work in mysterious ways. Or so Father Leahy always said when I was in school."

"Well, true or not, angel delivered to your ear or not, I love the story. Almost as much as I love you."

She kissed his ear and that started them both down the road to a fitting closure of a day filled with harmony and love. After making love, she dropped into dreamland and left Rory filled with tender feelings for her and the child she carried, and suffused with gratitude toward her for pulling off the best family gathering he'd enjoyed in years. As often as he'd noticed Kelsey's eyes following him in the last two days, he was sure he'd made the right choice when he married Marta.

Chapter Three

"Rory and Marta, thanks so very much for inviting us. It was a very nice Thanksgiving," Maire told them as she and Walter stood on the front porch getting ready to leave. "I think you have the beginnings of a wonderful life here at your new ranch."

"Yes, indeed," Walter echoed. "And Rory, I really appreciate your rising early to fetch me some of those gnarled branches of wood. They'll keep me busy through the winter. I got a little heater for the garage so I can use my workbench on the warmer afternoons. When you and Marta come for Christmas, I hope to have you a brand new lamp for your living room."

"Super, Walter. I really like your stuff. If you get any extra time, maybe you could make one for our bedroom, too. When the baby comes and we have to get up for those 2 a.m. feedings, I won't be stubbing my toes on the way to the crib with a lamp there."

"I'll do my best, Rory."

Marta went back in to help the ones who were leaving collect their belongings. Kids and parents and assorted treasures gleaned from their walks piled into the various cars. Jack came out carrying Kelsey's suitcase for her as she waddled through the door.

"Looks like you're about to pop, Lass. Do call us when it happens—day or night."

"Oh, I bet you're just panting for a 3 a.m. call from me saying the new lamb is on the ground and taking teat."

"Wouldn't have said it I didn't mean it, Kels. I worry about you all alone in that big house. Who's going to take you to the hospital when the time comes?"

"Sue Caswell said she'd drive me and stay until I delivered or until Maeve can come to be there. Sue's been my Lamaze coach for the last few weeks, but she can't be away too long. She has Alex to contend with. I'm hoping it happens after Alex goes to school in the morning and is all over by the time his bus gets home in the afternoon. Alex is a handful. You'd think Max could supervise for a day, but I think Alex has Max buffaloed."

"Sue could stick Alex in that boarding kennel in Boise so she can still coach you."

"Right. Like that'd ever happen. Maeve looks like she's ready to head out, so give this old walrus a kiss and I'll be on my way."

Rory hugged her to him and kissed both her cheeks, and whispered in her ear, "You're no walrus, Lass. You're as beautiful as anything Rubens ever painted. You're like the Madonna, and I don't mean the singer."

"If my boobs get any bigger, I might need to borrow some of her pointed metal bras just to hold them up."

Rory threw back his head and laughed just as Marta came through the doorway carrying Todd. Marta handed the lisping inquisitor to Rory and gave Kelsey another round of hugs and kisses.

"Do come back soon, Kelsey. And thanks ever so much for all you did to make those pies special. You've got a real artistic flair. No wonder you do so well in the boutique."

"Thanks Marta—thanks to both of you. I was glad to finally get to see this place and now that I have, I feel assured that you made the right choice, Rory. It's beautiful here. I know you'll both do well and be happy. See you come Christmas. By that time hopefully you'll both have a new niece or nephew to spoil."

Todd's mother, Bailey, and his baby brother, Eric, were next in line for hugs as Michael, Bailey's husband, loaded their car.

"Hey, Todd, I hate to see you leave. Who will I have to eat pancakes with in the mornings?"

Todd turned to his mother and said, "Mama, can I thay with Uncle Rory? I want to feed hith hortheth more oath."

"Don't you think Eric would miss you if you stayed here with Uncle Rory and Aunt Marta?"

Todd's nose wrinkled up and he frowned, then finally said, "Yeth."

"I think he would miss you, too. You make him laugh. Give Uncle Rory and Aunt Marta a hug and kiss good-by. We need to hit the highway, Todd."

Rory gave Todd a hard squeeze and then tilted him toward Marta for her hug. "I'll miss you, Todd." He set Todd down on the porch.

"I will mith you too. And the horthes. Can I take one home, Uncle Rory?"

"Todd, Jemima would be lonesome without Domino, just like Eric is lonesome without you. But come back next summer and I'll let you ride more, okay?"

"Yeth." He spun around to Bailey and asked, "Mama, when ith next thummer?"

"It's not so far away. First comes Christmas, then your birthday and Valentine's Day and Easter when the rabbit hides the eggs, then it will be almost summer. When we get home, I'll make a calendar so you can cross the days off and when they're all gone, it will be summer."

"Okay. I love you Uncle Rory. And Aunt Marta."

"Love you, too, Todd. Be good to that baby brother."

"Yeth, I will."

Finally it was down to Chris and Ernesto and their kids and Jack and Connie.

"Whew! I don't know about you and Rory, Marta, but the quiet that just descended is wonderful. Family is fun, but all those kids get to be a bit overwhelming."

"I thought they were all pretty well behaved Chris. I loved having everyone here, especially Todd. He's so cute I just want to love him to pieces."

"Yeah, you're right, they were very well behaved. They've all loved Rory for years and I think they're beginning to love you, too. You made quite a hit, Marta, sending Rory down to the basement for the fixings for those ice cream cones."

"Did you ever hear such bellyaching about having to make a few cones? You'd have thought I'd asked him to dig his way to China using an ice cream scoop."

"Hey, wife. I still have frostbite of the right hand. A few cones? Count again—Chris and I must have made forty."

"Well, I don't hear her complaining."

"That's because she only made five."

"Rory McCrea, God's going to strike you dead telling such lies, or else your nose is going to grow a foot."

"Say, Rory, maybe we guys ought to go down to the barn if the women are going to gang up on us that way," Jack suggested. "You're always saying how hard shearing sheep is, so maybe you could show Ernesto and me how that goes. I'd like to know if it's harder than making ice cream cones."

"I don't think any of my ewes would like to shed their coats this close to winter."

"You don't have to actually clip one, just give us a demonstration."

"Oh. Okay. And when you see how it's done, I'll let you wrestle one of the ewes so you can get a real appreciation for the chore. You coming, Ernesto, or is Jack the only glutton for punishment today?"

"I come, too. It is good to learn new things, no?"

"Depends. Some things I think I'd have been better off not learning."

Outside, the men went around the house to the sheepcote and Rory whistled for Punk, Sophie and Speedo. Using hand signals, he directed the dogs to cut out a particular sheep and take her to the shearing barn.

"It is amazing how the dogs know what to do without any words being spoken," Ernesto observed. "They must be very well trained."

"Yep, they are. Mostly because of the drovers."

Once the sheep was in the shearing pen, Rory gave the all the dogs a treat from his vest pocket and a signal to lie down and be quiet. He got down a pair of shearing clippers and went through the whole procedure, including working the shears, but instead of actually cutting the wool, he air clipped.

"That doesn't look too hard, Rory. I think you've been playing up the difficulty so we'd all feel sorry for you," Jack said.

"Really? Ready to give it a try?"

"Yeah, sure."

"You might want to put on an apron. You don't want to mess up your good pants."

"You have a washer, I take it?"

"Yes."

"Then I don't see the problem. The pants get dirty, they get washed."

"Suit yourself."

Asking questions as he proceeded, Jack made the round of the sheep air clipping just like Rory had. He had some problems positioning the sheep and Rory would now and then help boost the ewe into the right position and show Jack where to place his feet and knees. At one point, Jack, engrossed in getting the procedure right, didn't look before he went down on a knee and managed to kneel directly on a bit of sheep droppings that the ewe had defecated when Jack had boosted her off her rump.

"Oh, Jesus H. Crap!" he cursed as the smell hit him.

Rory looked at Ernesto and both of them broke out laughing.

"Laugh, you idiots. An apron wouldn't have prevented that."

Rory kept glancing at his watch and Ernesto thought maybe they were keeping him from something he had to do at a certain time, but when Jack finished his round of air clipping, Rory said, "Slightly more than half an hour."

"Is that good or bad?"

"Pretty fair for a first-time effort."

"How long does it take you?"

"About twenty minutes, but when you're actually cutting wool, it's harder."

"Yeah, right!" Jack said, smirking.

"Okay, big-britches lawyer, c'mon over here."

Rory motioned Jack to an open room where there were piles of pelts that they'd skinned from some older ewes they'd slaughtered for meat.

"Bring your clippers," Rory instructed.

Once inside the room, Rory threw one of the pelts over a sawhorse. "Now, I want you to clip for thirty minutes, separating the fleece from the hide without tearing the hide."

Jack started in with a big grin on his face, but after twenty minutes, rivulets of sweat were coursing down his face, the clippers were going slower and slower, and his cocky grin had disappeared into an intense frown.

"Not quite as simple when you're actually cutting off the fleece, is it?"

"Oh, it's not so bad." Jack was unwilling to admit he was giving out.

After another ten minutes less than half of the wool had been clipped off and the shears hung down from Jack's limp hand.

"Getting tired, Jack?" Rory teased.

"A little. I guess it *is* a bit harder when you're actually trying to mow though this stuff."

"Let me throw about thirty more up for you to clip—then you might have some idea what a shearing day entails."

"So, okay. It's hard work. I'm willing to concede that. You can do thirty in a day?"

"Sometimes more."

Jack put down the shears and rubbed his hand. The fingers skewed at odd angles. "It's all cramped up."

Rory walked over to the stalls where Jemima and Domino stood and picked a bottle of liniment out of a tack box.

"Give me your hand, Jack and I'll rub a little astringent into it. It works wonders on sore horse muscles, so it ought to do the trick for you. Otherwise, you might end up having to eat dinner tonight left-handed."

Jack turned his head to the side as the strong odor from the liniment saturated the small enclosure. "Shit! Bad as this stuff smells, I wouldn't want *it* under my nose either. I'll still have to eat left-handed. Maybe Connie will have to feed me."

"Why don't you guys head up to the house? I'll be up as soon as I feed the sheep and the horses."

At a short whistle, the dogs sprang to their feet and hustled the practice sheep back to the cote while Rory threw sheep feed into a wagon hitched to a garden tractor. The drovers appeared at the barn door as if Rory had whistled for them, too, each of them looking at Jack and grinning. It soon dawned on Jack that they'd been watching the show and were now laughing at his paltry efforts at shearing.

"Where were you watching from? I know you were watching," Jack accused. "I bet the first time you tried it, you didn't do any better than me."

Rory pointed up to the hayloft where the drovers had lain. It was a good observation point with a wide view of the whole barn.

"How'd they get up there? I didn't see anyone go up the stairs."

"There's a hoist outside, to lift the bales of hay with."

"Oh. Did you know they were there?"

"Sure did. They don't get many amusements here. Thought I'd let them have their fun."

"You're a real dog, Rory."

As soon as the men returned to the house, Jack asked Marta if he could wash out a few things.

"I should hope so, Jack, starting with your pants. Rory, did you have anything to do with that? Did you let him kneel in sheep poop on purpose?"

Rory's grin confirmed her suspicions. He thought she looked like she wanted to box his ears, but refrained in front of Jack. "Why?" was all she asked.

"He wanted the shearing experience, Marta, so I let him enjoy it in spades."

Connie entered the kitchen and took one look at Jack, then wrinkled her nose in disgust.

"Jack Strauss, I thought you came here to relax and have a pleasant weekend, not so you could roll in 'eau de barnyard.' Yuck! Get out of those pants this instant and let me have them. Marta, do you have a washboard?"

"Connie, I'm not about to shed my trousers in front of you and Marta."

"For land's sake, Jack. Tell me you don't intend to go all through the house dispensing that wonderful aroma. I'm sure Marta has seen men in boxer shorts before and it wouldn't be the first time I've seen you in them either, so shuck out of them and let me see if I can get the stain out before it sets for life."

Red-faced, Jack gave in. He pried off his shoes and unbuckled his belt and stepped out of his pants with as much dignity as he could muster. As he pulled his wallet and keys from various pockets, Marta noticed his legs. She'd never seen the scaring on his legs before and had to forcibly restrain herself from sucking in a shocked breath.

"Well, don't just stand there like a deer in the headlights. Go shower and put on some clean pants," Connie directed.

Jack beat a hasty retreat down the hall, only to run headlong into Consuela who clucked her tongue and shook her head. When she got to the kitchen she was still muttering under her breath.

"Mr. Rory, my employment no say you will have naked men running the halls," she complained. "I not in favor such behavior."

"Mr. Strauss had a little accident and soiled his pants."

"He sick? He eat too much turkey and pie. I see what he eats yesterday. Not two helpings, no. Three helpings he eats. No wonder he no can hold his bowels."

"Consuela, Jack didn't. . . ." Marta began, but Rory cut her off.

"If he's still having problems tomorrow, I'll run into town for some medicine to stop them up."

"Maybe you go *now*. I no like sheets full of you know what."

"Rory," Marta said, giving him a look that made him grin even wider, "tell her what happened."

"I doubt Consuela wants the vivid details, Marta."

"No, I no want listen more." With that Consuela went muttering to the refrigerator to see what she could make for a late lunch.

"But. . . ." was all Marta managed before Rory wrapped his arm around her shoulders and steered her out of the kitchen. Chris fell in behind them.

"Marta, I told you he's got a really warped sense of humor," Chris said as they all went into the den. "Mean and miserable and low-down dirty. Consuela will likely be sniffing Jack like a dog to see if he's having more accidents in his pants from now until Jack and Connie drive out of the driveway. And checking his sheets in the mornings, too."

"It *was* mean of you, Rory. Chris is right. You're nasty and low-down. Poor Jack."

"Ah, wife, it's a bit of innocent fun. Jack's a big boy. He can take a joke. If the crap were on my knee, not his, he'd be having just as much fun at my expense."

He pulled her into his arms and kissed her to still any more protests. That garnered some snickers and finger pointing from the Giacolini children. Finally, Thomas found his voice.

"Uncle Rory, will you play Sorry with us?" he asked. Caroline and Mariah had helped him set up the game board on the table under the window. Rory Jon was playing with Lego blocks because the others decided he was too little to play the board game.

"Sure, but only if I can be green."

Thomas pulled a frown because he liked the green pieces, too, but decided he'd rather have Rory play than insist on having the green pieces for himself. Caroline wanted blue, and Mariah liked red, so that left Thomas with the yellow ones, which he thought of as a girl's color or a sissy one.

Rory got a 'one' card that allowed him to move his piece out on the board before the others did. Once Caroline got out, she drew a Sorry card and sent him back to his starting circle. The second time he got out of start, it was Thomas who sent him back into the circle again.

"Ah, so that's how it's gonna be. You're all going to gang up on the old man are you? You're going to reserve every Sorry card to send me packing? Okay, from now on, I'm no Mister Nice Guy."

They all giggled and when the game ended, three of Rory's green pieces were still in his starting circle. That made them laugh even more.

"Okay, Mariah, you sit this one out. Ernesto, come over here and sit down. I need someone on my side so the little blighters don't embarrass me like that again. If you get a Sorry card, or if I do, we'll send Thomas's yellow ones or Caroline's blue ones back to start."

As the game proceeded, Mariah came to stand between Rory and her father and pulled down her father's head to whisper in his ear. Ernesto nodded. Then Ernesto proceeded to Sorry Rory home to his start circle.

"Hey, Ernesto. I thought you were with *me.*"

"Mariah reminded me that she, Caroline and Thomas are my children and as their father, I shouldn't be helping you win. *Sorry* about that—no pun intended."

After they trounced him three more times, Rory conceded, saying he'd had enough.

"What do you want to do now, Uncle Rory?" they asked.

"I was thinking about making a swing in the big sycamore tree in the side yard. I might need some help with that project. Anyone game? We can start right after lunch."

"Sure, what do you want us to do?"

"Well, I'm going to climb up on my big ladder and when I get to the good branch, I'm going to hold the end of my measuring tape and let the other end fall down. You have to tell me how many feet and how many inches the tape says, so I'll know how long to cut the ropes. Think you're smart enough for that?"

"I can do it," Thomas said. "When Mom was measuring for new curtains for our family room, I helped her."

"Okay, and maybe Caroline and Mariah and R-Jon can stretch out the rope and untie any knots that might be in it. Then we can measure off the right amount and fix up the swing. I've got a piece of 2 x 12 down at the barn we can use for the seat and we'll drill two holes on each end of it to make a nice wide one for the swing. We might have to sand the edges so they're round or plane them down a bit. Have any of you used a plane?"

"Like the ones that fly?" Mariah asked. "We came here on a plane."

"No, the plane I'm talking about has a handle on the top and a sharp blade on the bottom—it's like a razor for wood. After lunch, I'll show you."

"Did I hear someone mention lunch?" Jack asked, back from his shower and dressed in jeans so new they crackled when he walked.

"Consuela said you might want to watch how much you eat, so you don't have to change pants again," Rory told him.

"What does one have to do with the other?"

"Jack, Rory told Consuela you'd had an accident in your pants. She thought it was because you ate too much yesterday."

"She thinks I crapped my pants?"

"Yes, Because Rory didn't set her straight on what happened to them."

"Rory, no more free law advice for you, bud. You all . . . none of the rest of you said anything, either?"

"Marta tried, but Ror cut her off and wouldn't let her say anything more," Chris told him.

"Right after lunch, I challenge you to a boxing match on the lawn."

"Can't. The kids and I are building a swing. Maybe if you come and help, I'll tell Consuela what really happened."

"You climb up that ladder like you were telling them, and I might just be tempted to yank it out from under you."

They spent the rest of the afternoon building one humdinger of a swing. By pumping his legs, Rory could go so high he could see the highway from the top of the upward arc of the swing. The rope was as thick as Mariah's legs and had no problem bearing the weight of adults, but the kids needed a series of pushes before they could build up enough momentum to reach the heights Rory had reached. All afternoon, Rory, Ernesto and Jack took turns pushing the three older kids and when Rory Jon wanted his turn, Rory would set Jon on his lap, facing him and tell Jon to hold onto his belt loops or his belt.

By the time dinner was announced, all the kids were tired from an afternoon of measuring and cutting the ropes, drilling the seats and using the plane on the edges to make them rounded and smoother.

Sitting down to eat, Rory took the bowl of beets Consuela was serving and finally told her that Jack had knelt down in sheep dung and that he hadn't soiled his trousers himself, which caused Jack to blush again.

"Good. I no like cleaning up after babies who mess in their diapers. I no like even more cleaning up for grown men. I work part time in old-age place before you ask me to come and cook for you here, and I see many times the diaper messes of old folks—enough to last me a lifetime." She gave a shudder. "Anything more you need, Mr. Rory? I go to eat in my room—watch 'Men in Trees.'"

"No, if we need anything more, Marta or I will get it."

Shortly after dinner, the kids called it a day, each of them taking a bath and climbing into their pajamas. With all the rest of the family gone home to Idaho, the girls shared one upstairs bedroom and the boys bunked in another with Chris and Ernesto's room between them.

That left the adults free to play Trivial Pursuit. They played into the wee hours of the morning before Marta complained she was long overdue for some shuteye. The game broke up about 2 a.m. and all of them scattered to their rooms. Within ten minutes, the house was quiet.

Chapter Four

Rory and the drovers were up early to feed, and when he got back to the kitchen, Marta was pulling a large quiche out of the oven. Rory took the opportunity to give her a hug and kiss.

"Nobody else up yet?" he asked.

"Did you expect them to get up at dawn after we played until 2 a.m.?"

"If we have to get up, everyone should have to. We're just as tired as they are."

"Why don't you go back to bed for a bit? They'll probably all get up by ten and want to eat."

"I've got some stuff to go over in the office. Yell when you're ready to eat, okay? Are you going back to bed?"

"No. I thought I'd pull the sheets off the beds and round up the towels that everyone used and start a wash. It looks like it may be a clear day, so I can hang them out."

"Shouldn't Consuela be helping with that? I don't want you toting those heavy baskets up from the basement."

"I won't make them be too heavy."

He gave her a look that said he doubted her words.

"I won't. I promise."

"Give a holler if you need me to carry them up. Can't have you straining your back or losing our baby."

She took his hand and pressed it to her stomach. A few mild thumps pinged against his hand.

"He's kicking?"

"Yes. Since right before Thanksgiving."

"Why didn't you tell me before now?"

"I know you, Rory McCrea. You'd have been insisting I sit in my chair and not make pies or make beds or do anything other than lie around. So, I didn't tell you because I had too much to do to have to endure your worried looks."

About ten, Rory heard the rest of their guests beginning to stir. He shut the ledger and went to the kitchen where he found Marta on the phone. Through the window he could see Consuela hanging out a batch of sheets on the clotheslines.

"Oh, Mrs. Strauss, I'm so sorry to hear that. I don't think Jack is up yet, but give me your number and I'll have him call you right back."

She jotted a number on the pad beside the phone and turned to Rory with a stricken face.

"Jack's father has had a massive stroke and his mother is quite concerned. She wants Jack to come home immediately. I wonder how she knew to call here?"

"He probably left a notice on his answering machine. Where's home?"

"Chicago. Can you go and wake him and tell him—gently—that his mother needs him to get there as soon as he can?"

"Of course. I think everyone is already stirring."

Rory went down the hall and rapped on Jack's door. There wasn't an answer, so he opened it and looked in. The bed was made up and Jack wasn't anywhere in the room or in the adjoining bath. Next he tried Connie's door, knocking again. Connie opened the door a crack.

"Jack in there?"

"Yes, but he's not awake yet."

"Tell him he needs to get up. His mother called this morning. His father has had a stroke and she wants him to fly to Chicago as soon as he can."

"Oh, no. Poor guy can't even enjoy a long weekend. I'll send him right out."

"Thanks."

Back in the kitchen, Marta asked, "What did he say?"

"Nothing. He was still asleep in Connie's bed. She said she'd send him out."

"Is there something we can do to help him out?"

"You're good at phoning up for airline tickets. Call the airport in Missoula and see if you can get Jack on a plane to Chicago."

Marta picked up the phone and dialed as Rory went down the hall again toward Connie's room. Jack was just crossing the hall to his room. He halted at the door.

"Rory, what did Mom say?"

"Said your father had a massive stroke and was in the intensive care unit. I think she'd be comforted by your presence."

"That'll create a massive logistical mess. I only brought casual clothes and my parka. It'll take me hours to get back to Boise for my suit and my good topcoat. Then, I'll have to wait until Monday to go to the courthouse and cancel my pending cases for the week or see if I can get continuances. I'll have to get the files together if the judges won't grant continuances so someone else can litigate if I'm in Chicago."

"Marta is getting you a ticket out of Missoula to Chicago right now."

"How? I can't go looking like this."

"I can lend you a suit and my topcoat, Jack. And I can drive you to Missoula, too. Go while you can still see your dad before he. . . ."

"Dies?"

"It could happen."

"You wouldn't mind me borrowing your clothes?"

"No, of course not. I don't have any silk shirts, though, just permanent-press ones."

Jack was too stressed to even smile over Rory's attempt at humor.

"You have a decent suitcase, too?"

"Yes. C'mon up to my room and take whatever you need."

Jack tried on Rory's good black suit and although the pants were a trifle snug at the waist, he managed to fasten the button. The jacket, because of Rory's broad shoulders, fit just fine on Jack's slightly larger frame.

"You want the white shirts or the lavender ones?" Rory asked.

"White. Lavender won't do a thing for my eyes."

Even the good loafers with the tassels on the top fit, and Rory laid out his garment bag to contain Jack's casual clothes and his parka and added a small suitcase for Jack to pack the dressier shirts and ties in.

"What about Connie and my SUV? I don't want her to have to drive home alone. How will I get her and the car back to Boise?"

"I'm pretty familiar with the roads between here and Boise, as you well know. Leave me the keys and I'll get Connie back to Idaho."

"Good, that'll solve one problem. When you need to come back to Montana, rent you a car and tell them to bill it to me or better yet, have Amanda call them with my business credit card. And can you go by the courthouse on Monday and tell Judge Henry and Judge Fowler that I've been called away for a family problem? See if you can get my three cases for the week postponed?"

"I can. If judges will do that on my say-so."

"I'll write you a note for both of them."

"Okay. Let's go see if Marta could book you a flight."

Marta was making rapid notes on her pad when Rory and Jack got to the kitchen.

"A 3:30 seat on Northwest Airlines to Minneapolis and then a transfer to American from Minneapolis to Chicago O'Hare? Yes, that's great. Reserve those tickets for Jack Strauss. He'll be there by 2:45 to pick them up and check in. Thank you so much."

"You'll just have time to eat breakfast and get on the way to Missoula. Your tickets will be at the Northwest Gate #4. It's a direct flight to Minneapolis and then you switch to American for the rest of the way to Chicago."

"Thanks for all your trouble, Marta. How did Mom sound?"

"Worried, scared."

"Rory, we'll take my car to Missoula and then when you get back, you and Connie can decide when to drive back to Idaho."

"I can drive your car to Idaho, Jack," Connie said. She was still in her long robe and slippers. "Marta, is some coffee brewing?"

"Yes, certainly. All of you sit down and I'll make a quick breakfast so Rory and Jack can get on the road to catch the plane."

Marta slid a casserole dish out of the refrigerator and turned on the oven. Shortly, the smell of a re-warmed quiche with eggs, ham, tomatoes and cheeses overlying a flaky crust made mouths water. Marta dished up squares of the mixture and popped slices of toast into the toaster, pouring coffee into mugs.

"Connie, I'd rather have Rory drive you home. He's familiar with the routes and I need him to take care of a few matters while he's there."

"You just don't trust a woman behind the wheel of your SUV."

"No, I'd trust you, but I don't like to think of you on the road all alone. Beautiful woman like you—well, I'd hate for you to have a problem and be at the mercy of the riff-raff that inhabits the highways these days. I'm going to have enough on my plate with Mom and Dad without worrying about your safety, too. I'd just feel better if Rory drove you. Unless you object, Marta . . . do you?"

"Of course not, Jack. It's not like he's not been gone for more than a day lots of times. If it will ease your mind, I'm sure it's fine with me."

"See how much she wants to be rid of me? Then she can lie on the couch and watch soaps and eat bonbons. When I'm gone, it's like a mini-vacation for her, right wife?"

"Rory, now is hardly the time for lame jokes," she admonished.

After breakfast, Jack and Rory lit out for Missoula and it was late in the afternoon before he got back to the ranch. Everyone was just sitting down to dinner.

"Well, looks like I timed that right," he said as Marta set out another plate at his end of the table.

"Did Jack get off okay?" Connie asked.

"I guess. He got the tickets okay and then told me to head on home, so I got him a couple of magazines to read and left."

"What time should we leave for Boise tomorrow?"

"Sunday traffic is usually heavier than some weekdays. I'd say the earlier, the better. About nine in the morning okay with you?"

"You're driving, so whenever you say."

"Nine, then."

"When will you be back, Rory?" Marta asked.

"Depends how long it takes me to contact the judges about Jack's cases. He told me he'd phone Amanda and have her assemble the right files early Monday morning. If she's on the ball, maybe Tuesday late, or Wednesday about noon, depending on how soon I can get out of Boise. "When are you and Ernesto leaving, Chris?"

"Tomorrow morning early. We're flying into Portland, and catching a connecting flight to San Diego. Unless you need us to stay with Marta, Rory."

"Don't be silly, Chris. I know Rory worries, but I'll be just fine. I have to work on Tuesday afternoon and Wednesday afternoon, too. I won't have time to be lonesome. Besides, Consuela is here and the drovers. It's not like I'm a thousand miles away on a deserted island."

That night in bed, Rory again laid his hand on her stomach to feel the kicks of his unborn child.

"You will be careful, won't you? Now that I can feel the baby moving, I'd not want you to do anything to endanger him. If it snows or the roads are bad, call in sick and don't go to work, okay?"

"It's not going to snow. The 10 p.m. report said clear and dry for the next several days. Are you going to stay at our house with your mom and Walter?"

"Yes, probably, unless they have guests."

"Now what guests could they possibly be having?"

"Walter was saying something about an old army buddy and his wife while he was here. I don't know when they might be coming, but if the coast is clear, I'll stay there. Or if I can't, and you need to reach me, call Mom and leave a message. I'll check in with them every eight hours or so."

"Well, if you're going to get an early start, you'd better get some sleep."

He pulled her to him, spooning her back into his front, and kissed her ear. His hand again strayed to her stomach, trying to feel more kicks. It wasn't long until another series of thumps rippled the surface of her belly.

"Doesn't that kid ever sleep?" he asked.

"Yes, he does. Most of the day, so he can be up all night doing the rumba. Doesn't bode well for those future midnight feedings."

"I'll have to get him a pony and send him out to herd lambs so he'll be worn out enough to sleep all night."

"Oh, please. Promise me you won't try to make a drover out of our child until he or she reaches at least the age of ten."

"We'll see. I started with my first 4-H lamb when I was not quite eight. I set up such a squall that the club admitted me even though the age limit was nine. Aidan was showing calves and steers already and I wanted in on the action. I couldn't show until I turned nine, and that ticked me off because I sure could handle my lambs better than Aidan could handle his steers. But I'd be willing to let you mollycoddle our child until at least nine, when he can join 4-H."

"That's big of you. What if it's a girl who prefers Barbie dolls and tea parties to the rough and tumble life of a sheep woman?"

"I'd have to disown her."

"Oh, Rory."

"Whatever our children want to be, it's fine with me, Marta. If they want to spend all their days on the couch watching soaps and eating bonbons like their mother, I'd be okay with that, too."

That comment elicited Rory a sharp jab from Marta's elbow to his ribs.

"Ow! For a sedentary woman, you've got a hell of a jab. Goodnight, wife."

"Night, Rory."

Chapter Five

"Hello, Walter, is Rory there?" Marta asked.

"Eh? I don't hear so well. Let me get my wife."

It was 5 p.m. on Monday night and Marta was trying to find out if Rory had left Boise for Montana yet, because she wanted him to bring her winter fur-lined boots if he wasn't leaving until the morning.

There was a long pause and finally Maire picked up the phone. "Hello?"

"Hi, Maire. This is Marta. I was trying to reach Rory. Is he around?"

"No, not at the moment. He's out to dinner with Kelsey, I believe."

"Oh. Is he starting for Montana later tonight?"

"No, he said he still has Judge Fowler to see early tomorrow morning."

"Can you ask him then if he'll bring back my black boots with the fur inside when he comes? I think they're in the garage in a box on a shelf on the left side labeled 'winter.'"

"How about if I leave him a note to call you and you can ask him? With all the activity around here, I might forget."

"Sure, I'll be up until at least 10:30. Have him call when he comes in."

"I can do that. It's too bad about Jack's father."

"Yes. It put a damper on his Thanksgiving vacation, that's for sure."

"Well, Walter sure enjoyed himself and I had a good time, too."

"I think everyone did. I'm so glad we invited you all. Well, I won't keep you—it must be about time for your dinner. Don't forget to tell Rory to call me."

"I've made the note already and I'll put it on his pillow."

"Thanks, Maire. Goodnight."

Marta sat down to dinner with Consuela, Ricardo and Manuel while keeping one ear cocked to listen for the phone. An hour later, she helped

Consuela clear the table and the drovers went up to their rooms. The two women finished doing the dishes and still the phone sat silent. Marta finally went to check that she'd replaced the receiver on its base correctly.

At ten, she turned on the television to listen to the news and check the weather report. At least the weather was cooperating. No rain, sleet or snow predicted. After the news, she was tempted to call again in case Maire had forgotten to tell Rory to call, but decided not to. She figured the older generation might already be heavy into dreamland.

By eleven, he still had not phoned, so she went up to bed, worry and a small hint of resentment sitting like twin vultures on her shoulders. She carried the phone up with her, plugging it into the jack beside her bedside table.

She was startled out of a sound sleep at 1:30 in the morning.

"Marta, are you okay? I found the note to call you. There's nothing wrong, is there? Is the baby okay?"

It took her a few seconds to shake the sleep from her mind. The delay caused a new note of worry to creep into Rory's voice.

"Marta, please tell me you're okay."

"I am. I was just sound asleep."

"Sorry. Why did you call Mom? The note only said to call you when I got in."

"Oh, I wanted you to bring my tall winter boots back. They're in the garage along the left wall in a box marked 'winter.' They're black and have fur inside, and they're warm. I'd like to wear them to work to keep my feet cozy as Mr. Harrington believes in being frugal when it comes to office heat. He sets the thermometer at 68°, even when it's cold and rainy out."

"Sure, I can do that."

"Why didn't you call earlier?"

"I just got in."

"Oh." There was a long pause. "Are you coming home tomorrow, er . . . today?" she asked, glancing at the clock

"I'll try. I have to see Fowler at 11:30 so I may not be able to leave until later in the afternoon. I'll probably go part of the way and come the rest of the way on Wednesday. Should be home by dinner Wednesday night."

"Well, whenever. Just drive safely."

"Call me again about two in the afternoon to remind me about the boots. With all the running around for Jack, it'd be like me to drive off without them."

"Okay. I will. Night, Rory."

"Goodnight, wife."

She wore two pair of socks to the office on Tuesday afternoon, and called at two just like Rory said. Maire answered the phone that time as well.

"Maire, I hate to be such a bother, but Rory told me to call him to again remind him about the boots. Is he around?"

"No. I think he took Kelsey to lunch after meeting with Judge Fowler this morning, but I know he put your boots in the rental car so he wouldn't forget them. I saw him do that before he left the house at ten."

"Thanks, Maire. Tell him I called, okay?"

"I surely will."

All afternoon, a niggling voice said he'd been out to dinner with Kelsey and hadn't gotten home until long after midnight, and now he was having lunch with her as well. It made it hard for her to keep her mind on the briefs she was typing up. What could he possibly have to talk about for 8-10 hours with Kelsey? They weren't in business together anymore, and she'd just spent most of the week at their place, so what did he need to discuss with her that he couldn't have discussed over Thanksgiving? She wasn't totally ignorant that there was still some attraction to Rory on Kelsey's part. She'd also noticed how often Kelsey's eyes followed Rory over the holiday. She tried to put it out of her mind, for Rory had assured her often and she believed, sincerely, that he no longer harbored anything for Kelsey, but still . . . 1:30 in the morning?

She was glad when it came time to quit. She hurried to the market in Butte and picked up some garlic bread to go with the lasagna Consuela was promising for dinner, before hitting the highway for home.

The hours after dinner ticked by and she half expected him to come driving in at any minute, but after the news, she was tired and he still wasn't home, so she went to bed alone again. In the morning, she pulled on heavy pants and a sweater and her parka and went to do Rory's chores of feeding his cote's worth of sheep. After feeding sheep, she picked up the pitchfork to clean out horse stalls but Enrique took it from her.

"I do this. You are with child. Not good to be lifting heavy things. You go to the house and get warm. I do."

"Thanks, Enrique. I'm sorry you all have been forced to shoulder Rory's work, too. He should be home this afternoon."

"No problem, Mrs. Marta. He has done much for me and the others, so we don't mind helping him."

Another long afternoon at work and there was still no word from Rory. If he'd arrived at home, she expected he'd have called her to tell her that, but the day dragged on to its early darkness and, except for a call or two from clients, the phone hadn't rung all afternoon. He wasn't home yet as they sat down to eat, and she was beginning to be seriously concerned. She was torn between waiting and calling the highway patrol in both states to inquire about any accidents.

At 7 p.m. the phone rang and she jumped up from the sofa to answer it.

"Rory?"

"Yeah, it's me."

"Where are you? I was about to call highway patrol."

"I'm still in Boise. I'm still at the hospital."

"Why?"

"Kelsey went into labor this afternoon. I took her out to lunch and as I was driving her back to the boutique about one, her water broke. So I drove her to the hospital. The doctor did an exam when she arrived and thought it might be 5-6 hours yet. She was only dilated to about a four he said. Sue had to go home to mind Alex at three, and Maeve was in a big insurance conference with the owners of the new mall she's handling the insurance for, so Kelsey kind of begged me not to desert her. I'm really sorry, Marta, but I couldn't just walk off and leave her all alone."

"No, of course not. But will you please call back and let me know when you're leaving for here? So I know when to expect you?"

"I will. Soon as I'm sure she's okay or Maeve can stay with her, I'll be on my way. I love you and I miss you."

Sure you do, she thought. *That's why you've been so faithful about letting me know what's happening.*

He pulled into the ranch at noon the next day, looking like something the cat dragged in. After giving her a perfunctory kiss, and handing her the boots she'd asked him to fetch from Boise, he sat down at the table with a cup of strong coffee and tried to keep his eyes open.

"Is Kelsey okay?"

"Yes. Tired and sore. It was a big baby. Nine pounds, two ounces."

"Boy or girl?"

"A boy. Daniel Aidan McCrea."

"I'm surprised it wasn't Daniel Rory McCrea."

He closed his eyes and she thought maybe he really had fallen asleep sitting up. Finally, he shook his head and stood up.

"I'm too tired right now, Marta. I need some sleep."

He went up the stairs and collapsed on the bed and was out as soon as his face landed on the pillow. She pulled the blanket that was folded up at the foot of the bed over him and got dressed for work.

He was just stirring when she got home that night. She entered the bedroom, closing the door and locking it behind her.

"Are you awake enough now, Rory?"

He rubbed his eyes and sat up, stuffing two pillows behind him as he leaned back against the headboard of the bed.

"Yes, I am. Go ahead and have your say. You've evidently been storing up some hostility for the last couple of days."

"Well, what would you expect? Every time I called your mom, you were out with Kelsey. And out quite late, too. I'm getting up at dawn to do your chores so you can spend hours wining and dining Kelsey? You don't bother to call and tell me anything about your changes in plans, so I'm left wondering if you've been in an accident or if you're still so engrossed with her that you've forgotten everything you ever knew about common courtesy. I was beginning to wonder if you even remembered you had a wife."

His initial reaction was one of anger at her words—she could see that in the clench of his jaw and she braced for an angry retort. For a long time, he looked at her and said nothing. When he finally spoke, his voice was quiet.

"You're right, Marta. I deserved everything you just said. I still care what happens to Kelsey. I don't love her like you seem to think I do, but I still care about her. I've always found her easy to talk to, so when we went out to dinner, the hours just melted away.

"When I took her home Monday night, she seemed more depressed than usual, that's why I asked her to lunch on Tuesday. Wednesday morning, I still had one more judge to see, so we went to lunch again. I know that seems like a lot, but I felt bad for her.

"Women sometimes go a little off center with all those hormones when they're pregnant. And then, when labor set in and Sue had to leave at three, I didn't have the heart to just go. Maeve promised me she'd be there in a few minutes, but she didn't arrive until after 6 p.m. By that time Kelsey was fully dilated and in the delivery room. I sat behind her head to remind her to breathe until she delivered at 6:30.

"As soon as I knew both Kelsey and the baby were okay, I did call you. Then, I got in the car and drove. I was really tired, so I had to stop a bunch of times for more coffee. I got home as soon as I could safely do that. And I apologize for not keeping in touch better. That was really not very considerate of me. You're right. I owed you the courtesy of a call when I changed the plans. I'm sorry, Marta."

Tears trickled down her cheeks.

"I'm sorry, too, Rory. Sorry for having doubts about your relationship with Kelsey. Sorry for not having enough faith in what we share that I could banish the doubts."

He patted the bed beside him and she crawled over to sit next to him. He hugged her hard against him with his right arm while his left hand turned her face toward him. He looked into her eyes for a long moment, his eyes bright with unshed moisture. Then, he pulled her across his lap and wrapped both his arms around her. He crushed her to him and kissed her hard enough to bruise her lips.

"I don't love any woman but you, Marta. It saddens me that you still doubt that. Thank you for doing my chores and for being considerate of me when I wasn't being very considerate of your feelings."

"Well, I know you had a lot on your mind. . . ."

"No. Don't." He shook his head back and forth. "You don't need to provide me with an easy way out. I feel bad about treating you that way. I *should* feel bad about it. So hang tough, and let me sweat a bit. Pull on those winter boots and give me a good swift kick in the ass. I deserve it."

"Oh, Rory." She planted a small kiss on his cheek. "C'mon, let's go eat dinner."

Downstairs in the dining room, he picked up his plate and silverware from his spot at the opposite end of the table from Marta's place and asked Consuela to move down a chair. He sat down next to Marta and after they'd both filled their plates, he took her left hand in his right one under the damask cloth and held it tight all through dinner, eating with his left one. A few peas fell on the tablecloth as he wasn't accustomed to eating left-handed, but he refused to let go of her fingers. Finally he solved the pea problem by mixing them into his mashed potatoes so they had less opportunity to roll.

"Manuel, Ricardo, after dinner go tell Enrique and Juan that they have the next four days off. And you can both have the same vacation. I appreciate all of you taking care of things while I was gone. I'll feed and muck stalls the next four days. *Gracias, por todos.*"

"*De nada*, Señor Rory."

"Consuela, would you like four days off, too?"

"No. But I would like no do dishes this evening."

"Okay. I'll do them. Take off as soon as you finish your dinner."

"You must be in hen house," she said.

"Dog house, Consuela. I'm in the dog house."

She grinned. "I thought so. I no see you leave the big chair at the table's end many nights—only when you are in the dog's house. When you sit here I think you have more than potatoes and meat on your plate—*problemas*, too, no?"

"Yes, but it wasn't meat and potatoes on my plate tonight. It was more like crow and humble pie."

"Well, Mrs. Marta, they say you no can teach stubborn donkey new tricks, but maybe you have new tricks up your shirt for Mr. Rory. I think he learns quick when you teach. He learn all of sudden eat with wrong hand tonight."

He did the dishes—both washed and dried them—making her sit at the little desk in the corner of the kitchen. "That Consuela doesn't miss a trick," he told her, hanging up the dishtowel. "Will I still be in the hen house when we go to bed, wife?"

"No. I think you've eaten enough crow and humble pie for one night."

"I appreciate the early pardon. I'd like to show you my gratitude, if you're agreeable."

"I'll think about it."

"Don't take too long. I feel a powerful need to atone for my behavior by making love to you about a dozen times."

"I don't think a dozen times will cover it, husband mine. I think twice a day for the next month might be a more fitting atonement."

"I like that better than being assigned all those Hail Marys."

"How about four Stations of the Body? My body?"

"Only four?"

Damn, he thought. *Dawn already.* Couldn't be dawn already, and he had 600 sheep to feed and horses to care for. *You're getting too damn old to be burning your candles at both ends, old man. Can't keep this up on four hours of sleep—all that sweet loving until the wee hours—not when you have all the dawn duties for the next four days.* He groaned and Marta stirred.

He was sorely tempted to get back under the covers and do another Hail Marta atonement, but the increasingly urgent bleats outside the window propelled him to his feet for the start of his long day. Looking down at her, sleeping like an angel, he once again rued his thoughtlessness. She was a good and kind woman who deserved all his consideration, not just when it was convenient for him to offer it to her. Six months of marriage almost and she still had her doubts about Kelsey. And his behavior of the last three days hadn't done anything to dispel her worries.

Still, he wouldn't have changed his behavior. The Lass had needed him. It was almost like he felt honor bound to offer her comfort. He knew there was no legal requirement that he give her his shoulder to lean on, but maybe if he'd been able to keep on better terms with Aidan, Aidan would have been there to offer Kelsey what he'd felt obliged to offer.

Despite Father Leahy's absolution, there was that lingering feeling that the current situation with Kelsey was, to a large degree, his fault for praying for Aidan's demise on so many occasions. Yanking on his boots, he tiptoed from the bedroom, taking one more loving look at the sleeping Marta.

Outside, the wind was sharp and cold. It hinted of snow and the lowering clouds didn't dispel the thought that by tomorrow, he would likely regret giving the drovers those four days off.

He was late getting in for supper and his hands felt like twin mini-icebergs as he tried to defrost them under some warm water in the kitchen sink. Manuel and Ricardo were already seated at the table and flashed him a grin, letting him know they were glad it was his turn to feed and freeze. The wind howled and rattled the windows, making him shiver and stomp his feet to increase circulation to his toes.

Marta was just coming in the front door as he entered the dining room. Consuela took that as her cue to begin slicing the roast. She pulled seven baked potatoes from the oven, and arranged them on the meat platter that she bore to the dining room to join the yams and broccoli already sitting on the warming tray at one end of the table.

"Brrrr!" Marta said, unwrapping her scarf and unbuttoning her heavy coat. "Listen to that wind. There'll be ice on the water troughs tomorrow."

"No, there won't be. I just hitched up the inserts that keep that from happening," Rory said. *"Inserciónes de calor."*

Ricardo said something in Spanish to Rory and when Marta raised her eyebrows in question, he told her that Ricardo wanted to know why he hadn't provided those inserts when they were feeding for him the last few days.

"Why didn't you?" Marta asked. "I would have liked not to have to chop ice, too, while you were gone."

"I was afraid you might electrocute yourselves," he said in Spanish and then in English.

The drovers both rolled their eyes.

"Her, yes. Us, no way." Ricardo told him, trying his English out.

"Well, don't get so cocky just because you can say a few things now in English. You still can't read the *directions* in English," he rattled off in Spanish. *No leer instrucciónes en Inglés.*"

After dinner the drovers went up to their rooms and Consuela cleaned up the dishes. Rory built a fire in the fireplace and settled down in his easy chair to read.

"I hope the roads aren't bad tomorrow," Marta said, picking up the afghan she was working on.

"I'll be happy to drive you if they are."

She shook her head and frowned.

"In case I need to put the chains on," he amended when he saw she was irked that he didn't think she could manage a snowy road. "Don't want you out there installing them in sub-zero weather. You might freeze Junior."

"Oh, so you don't care if I freeze, just don't freeze the baby?"

"I do care. That's why I offered to drive you. Tell me wife, is it the pregnancy that makes you so testy? I feel like I'm negotiating a minefield lately. You read things into everything I say."

"No. I don't think it's hormonal. It's you that makes me that way. You alternate between seeming not to worry about me at all, and worrying about me way too much. There has to be a happy medium someplace in that head of yours. I'm not helpless. I've driven on bad roads all my life. I know how to put the chains on. I can also change a tire, jump the battery, and fill up the oil and water. I'd like you to accord me due respect for the scope of my car-related knowledge."

"Yes, ma'am. I so accord you that respect. Are you saying you'd rather I didn't drive you, then?"

"I'm saying I'd be happy if you drove, but not if it's because you think I can't handle it. I admit it would be more of a chore putting on chains with this bulge in my midsection, but I *could do it* if I had to."

He raised his magazine so she couldn't see his grin.

"And don't think I don't know you've got that smirk on your face, Rory McCrea."

The phone rang and he got up to answer it.

"That's too bad. I'm really sorry to hear that."

Marta was hoping it wasn't something with the new baby—something that would require Rory to make another trip to Boise to comfort Kelsey.

"You know the time and place?

He moved the telephone pad so he could jot information down.

"By sundown? That quick? So there's no place to send flowers?"

Rory noted an address on the pad. "Sure, we'll be glad to. When are you coming back? Not for another week? Okay, I'll call them in the morning. You'll let Amanda know? Yeah, sure, Jack. Just you take care, and call again if I can do anything else to help out on this end. Bye."

"Jack Strauss?" Marta asked after he hung up.

"Yeah. His dad died yesterday morning. They buried him before sundown. Jewish custom, I guess. Seems sort of abrupt, but I don't much fancy the circus the Irish put on when someone dies, either."

"So we can't send flowers?"

"No. But there's a fund set up in his name at Sinai Hospital at this address here, so maybe we should send a check."

"He has to stay in Chicago?"

"I guess at least another week. He's got to relocate his mom to an assisted-living facility and close up the house. He's eventually going to sell it, but he'll have to go through everything before he can put it on the market. The accumulations of a lifetime he said. He also said houses don't sell well in the winter in Chicago anyhow, so he's planning to take a couple of months off next summer to go back and finish stuff up."

"Is his mom okay?"

"Yeah, I guess, but she's pretty frail and he doesn't want her living alone in that big house."

"Must be hard to give up the home you've lived in so long. I feel sad for her, and for Jack."

"I know. Anyhow, I have to make some calls to judges again in the morning and postpone a few more court dates. Maybe I'll put the chains on when I get up tomorrow to feed, so if I can't drive you, they'll already be on."

"Like you don't have enough to do since you told the drovers to take a break."

"Yeah, but some things are more critical than others—your safety for instance."

"Turn on the television and see what they're saying about the weather."

He picked up the remote and hit the power button. When the news came on, the forecast was for 6-8 inches of snow with blowing snow and the possibility of drifts.

"Maybe you ought to stay home, Marta."

"Let's wait until morning to see what it's like. How about a cup of hot chocolate? The sound of that wind makes me cold even though the fire is about hot enough to blister my skin."

"Sit still, I'll make it."

Morning found the promised six inches on the ground. It took Rory longer than usual to feed, and when he got in and finally sat down with Marta for breakfast, it was nearly 11 a.m.

"Rory, I want to get an early start to Butte so I can take my time. You have to call those judges. I'll be fine if you got the chains on. Did you?"

"Yes, but I don't want you out there all alone. That's one cold norther this morning."

"I'll take my cell phone so I can call if anything happens. You promised Jack you'd take care of the court dates."

"Yes, and I promised you I'd drive if the roads were bad."

"Well, it doesn't look like you can do both. Stay and make the calls. I'll call you if I get into a bind, okay?"

"If you're sure."

"I am. I'll call when I get to the office, or sooner if I run into trouble."

"Toss your sleeping bag in the car, and take some peanut butter and crackers and a gallon of water so if you slide off the road you won't freeze before I can come and haul you out."

"Water? You want me to be well hydrated so I can use my yellow urine to write SOS in the snow for the whirlybirds to spot? I don't need a gallon of water, I can eat snow to make moisture."

"Damn it, Marta. Don't joke around about that. Take the damn water and be sure you keep the cell phone on 'charge.' You're gonna turn me gray-headed by the time I'm 30 if you don't stop skating on the edges of danger like that."

She bent over and gave him a kiss. "I love you, you know, even when you fret like some old man. If your hair gets all white, they'd have to stop calling you black Irish. I'll call you when I get there."

"Be careful. It's not you that worries me so much, it's the idiot four-wheelers on the road. They think they can go 70 on icy roads because they have all four wheels in drive mode. I've seen hundreds of them upside down in the ditches. I don't care if they want to kill themselves with their stupidity, but too often it's the other guy—the one driving at a speed dictated by the conditions—that they wipe out. First big snow, they'll be out in force with their ski racks and a few hot toddies on board."

After Marta left, he turned on the TV to low to keep abreast of changing conditions on the roads, then sat down at his office desk to phone Amanda for the list of upcoming cases so he could call judges for Jack. He wanted to be off the phone in short order so if Marta called, the line wouldn't ring with a busy signal.

She needed to be to work by one, so he finished up at 12:30, leaving messages with judges' secretaries if their bosses were out to lunch or in court already. He was very relieved when Marta called at 12:52 to say she had made it to the office in one piece and to tell him the roads were snow-packed, but not icy.

"Thank you for calling, Marta. Call me when you're ready to head home."

"I will. Bye."

Rather than sit around stewing all afternoon about Marta driving home in the dark, he went into his office and made out a check to Sinai Hospital in the name of Jack's father, then ran it down to the mailbox at the end of the ranch road where his lane met the highway. There were two bills in the box, so he gathered them up and went back up to make out two more checks. The ranch accounts were in pretty fair shape with help from Marta's contributions and what he and the drovers had cleared from the sale of mutton at the slaughterhouse. Save for heating oil, which would cost them dearly over the long winter months, they were actually doing pretty damn well. And on these cold afternoons, he might find time to strip the sheep pelts of their shorter wool. Some of the locals would be glad to have it to spin into strands for knitting or crocheting, especially when it went for a fraction of the cost a spring shearing would sell for.

Consuela came in to ask him what he'd rather have for dinner, mutton or chicken.

"You out of dog house now?" she asked. "I can make peas and chicken and you no spill peas all over my clean cloth because of left-hand eating?"

"Yes, Consuela. Make chicken—and peas, too. We ate mutton twice last week."

"Mrs. Marta is over her mad? She no like you to spend time with your old *chica*. She gets *loco en la cabeza*."

"Were you ever that way? Loco? When you were carrying a child?"

"Yes. Many times. Once, he roll eyes at young girl with good shape and I was huge with twins. I pick up big rock and bash his ear. His ear never the same. Hang funny all rest days of his life."

"Gee, Consuela, you might have killed him."

"No. His head harder than rock. Only ear tender."

"So maybe I should be sure there aren't any big boulders around the house here?"

"No let her get near pile of stones for building sheepcotes, that for sure. But you have work to do. I go make chicken ready to cook."

Marta called at five.

"Rory?"

"Yep, it's me."

"I won't be home for dinner."

"Why? Harrington has you on overtime?"

"No. I've been invited out to dinner."

"Oh. Anyone I know?"

"I don't think so. When I was in junior college in Boise in the paralegal program, there was this guy in my class. He was from Butte. We used to study together before tests, and after a bit we started dating. We went out together for a little more than a year. I never went any further than my AA degree, but Kurt went on to law school.

"He graduated last June from the Arizona State University law program and he's in Butte interviewing for a position in a law office. I guess his family still lives near here. Anyhow, I was having coffee at Lu's about 3:30 and he came in. I couldn't believe my eyes. It's a small world. He came over and invited me out for dinner and I'd like to go if you don't mind."

"And if I said I did?"

"I'd come home."

"But you wouldn't be happy, would you?"

"No, probably not. It's been forever since I've seen him and I'd like to hear about his adventures in Phoenix and about how he enjoyed law school."

"Then I guess it's chicken and peas with Consuela tonight for me. Have a good dinner, and call me when you set out for home."

"Thanks, husband mine. I will."

"You're welcome, wife."

It was after 11 p.m. when she called to say she was on her way, and another hour before she arrived. He was still sitting in the living room reading. The fire had burned down to a few glowing coals and a chill was creeping back into the place. She sat down on the arm of his chair and gave him a kiss on the cheek.

"Rory, you didn't have to wait up for me. You've got to get up so early, you should have gone to bed."

"Wanted to be sure you got home safely. How was dinner?"

"Very nice, actually. Steak and salad and baked potatoes, and deep-dish apple pie for desert—with ice cream. Kurt said he wished he could have looked for a job in Arizona. It's nice and warm there, but he said his dad wasn't very well and he wanted to be nearer to his parents so he could help his mom if she needed it. He said it would likely take him a year or two to make his blood thick enough to endure the cold and the altitude in Butte again.

"He's such a nice guy, and smart, too. He was second in his graduating class, so he could likely have his pick of places to work. But I'm glad he came to Montana. It was good to talk to him."

"Has he found a job yet?"

"No. He's got a couple of prospects, maybe even one with Ron. It'd be great if Ron hired him. Kurt might bring in more clients and more business. I might have more to do and that'd be nice. Most afternoons I get finished with the work by about three and then have to look busy doing nothing much. I'd rather be busy than bored."

"Is Harrington looking for a partner?"

"I don't think so. Just an associate. Ron's kind of holding the partnership place open for when—or if—his son passes the bar."

"Ron's kid is in law school, too?"

"Yes, but he's not very good at it. He was on academic probation last semester. When I started in the office this summer, they had quite a row about Richard's grades and his affinity for parties. Ron threatened to cut off his tuition money if Rich didn't settle down and get at least Cs."

"Wouldn't this Kurt guy be a threat to Rich's future hopes for a position? If he's as good as you say, he'd bring in lots of clients and it'd be hard for Ron to pass him over in favor of a lazy son. Once the big bucks come rolling in, most folks get used to spending at a higher rate and aren't willing to go back to less. If Rich wasn't as gung-ho a lawyer, the money would get curtailed. Might not be in Ron's best interest to hire Kurt."

"Sure you aren't just saying that because you're a tiny bit worried about Kurt working in the same office I do?"

"Should I be?" He gave her a look that said he might be worried even if she said he shouldn't be.

"No, of course not. I just like him as a friend. He and I speak the same language—lawyerly stuff—legal stuff. Like you and Kelsey talk about sheep."

"Well, I'm glad you had a good time, but I'm going to bed now that I know you're home safe."

"You don't want some hot chocolate before you go up?"

"I don't think so. If you want some, go ahead and make yourself a cup. I'll probably be asleep in two shakes of a lamb's tail. I'll leave the bathroom light on so you can see, but don't hit the overhead. It's too bright, okay?"

"Sure. In fact, I don't think I need chocolate this late. I'll just go up with you now."

He followed her up the stairs and they each undressed, Marta pulling on a flannel nightgown and some woolen socks to keep her feet warm. He stripped down to his undershirt and put on some plaid flannel pants but left his feet bare. She got into bed and yanked the comforters up under her chin, turning on her side as she always did. Usually, he got in and spooned her to him, but tonight, he turned his back to her and crammed two pillows under his head. It wasn't long before his breathing evened out and she knew he was asleep.

Now, you know how I feel when you go out to dinner with Kelsey and don't invite me, she thought. She smiled in the darkness. She was aware that he'd tried really hard not to let on how he felt, but not offering to cuddle spoke volumes about how much it had bothered him that she'd gone out with an old flame.

At five she got up to make him a hot breakfast against the chill of a frigid morning. He didn't say much more than 'good morning' but she could feel his eyes following her while she cooked oatmeal and scrambled his eggs. *He's wondering,* she thought, *about how he compares to Kurt, just like I wonder sometimes, how I rate next to Kelsey.*

She dished up his oatmeal and eggs and poured him a cup of coffee. Each time she faced him, he was busy spooning the hot cereal into him, or buttering a piece of toast, but when she was facing the stove and glanced up at the glass-fronted cabinets she could see he was still watching her with a slight frown between his eyes. Once he realized she could see his reflection in the glass he dropped his speculative gaze to his oatmeal bowl and didn't look up again. She had to bite her lip to keep from laughing.

"Let me run up and get dressed and I'll help you feed since it's Saturday and you don't have any help."

"Hell, no, Marta. It's cold out there. Stay in where it's warm."

"I don't mind the cold. It's invigorating. Couldn't you use some help?"

"Yeah, sure, but I don't want you doing any heavy lifting. And I'd be worried you might slip and fall."

"That's not quite all you're worried about this morning, is it?"

"What do you mean?"

"You know exactly what I mean. You've been watching me all morning trying to decide how you measure up against Kurt."

"Oh, really?"

"Don't deny it. I could see your eyebrows all knitted together. I know you well enough to know what you were thinking."

"And how *do* I measure up?"

"You're the man I love, Rory. I like Kurt, but I don't love him. Not in that way, anyhow. Does that have a ring of familiarity to it? It should. It's what you always tell me when I worry about you and Kelsey. Not so much fun, is it, when the shoe is on the other foot?"

"So, you're saying you had more than a dinner with an old friend in mind when you accepted his invitation? You thought it was a good opportunity to instill some doubts in my mind about you?"

"Don't you have a few this morning?"

"Yes. And I'm not sure if your assurances will do much to dispel them. Big lawyer. Smart, rich, destined to rule the world in the near future as opposed to a sheep man up to his eyeballs in debt. Even I don't think that's much of a contest."

"You might consider that when you're out with Kelsey and forget to call me when you know I'm worried about you."

"Didn't I apologize for that? Is it something you're going to bring up every day this month?"

"No, I won't bring it up again."

"Good. I'm tired of hearing about it. I'm glad you had a pleasant dinner with your friend. I accept your word that that's all he is to you. I'm going out to feed now. I think it's best if you stay in. Maybe out there in the -10° cold the heat I'm starting to feel over this whole asinine conversation will get a chance to cool off. I'd rather not have a huge debate over get-even tactics if that's the game you're playing, Marta, so I don't want your help this morning."

He went out through the mudroom letting in a blast of frigid air while closing the door softly. He went down the hill to the barn and soon had several bales of hay in the wagon to feed sheep with.

She sat at the table watching his methodical movements. There were no wasted efforts when it came to Rory McCrea. Clip the wires of the bales, separate off flakes about a hand's width in thickness, toss them into all areas of the sheepcotes, wrap up the wires and pitch them in a garbage can. Open the next bale and repeat the procedures. So it would go until all the sheep were fed.

Then it would be back to the barn to mix warm feed of half barley, half soybean meal to put into the creep feeders so every ewe got a fair opportunity to consume some of the higher protein feed to warm her against the cold of winter. And last, he would clean the stalls of all the horses, spreading new straw to absorb the urine and fecal material to prevent thrush in the horses' hooves.

She'd followed in his footsteps more than once and was amazed at how quickly and efficiently he operated. The drovers were more disorganized, but she thought Rory could feed in his sleep, so well choreographed were his movements.

Marta got up and washed the breakfast dishes. Consuela was stirring and would soon take over the kitchen, laying out meat and other items for their dinner's preparation. She liked her kitchen clean in the mornings. When the counters were wiped down and the dishes done up, Marta went upstairs to make their bed and then moved on to the room adjoining their bedroom that she was planning for a nursery.

She was sitting in the rocker there, thumbing through several catalogs of wallpaper samples when he finished feeding. He appeared in the doorway still looking a bit somber and miffed. Putting the catalog down, she stood up and walked to face him. He made no attempt to embrace her even when she slid her arms around his waist and laid her head on his chest.

"I'm sorry, husband mine. It was a childish thing to do. You don't have anything to worry about as far as Kurt goes. He's nice, but you're everything I ever wanted in a man. You're devilishly handsome. You've got incredible eyes. You're smart about so many things. You're kind and funny and almost always considerate. You have good manners and the ability to control your anger even when goaded. You work so hard.

"Kurt on his best day couldn't hold a candle to you for strength of character, or match your stamina for hard work. I love you, Rory. I don't want us to fight. It turns my world all akimbo when you're angry with me and I don't like feeling like that. Forgive me?"

It was only then that his arms found their way around her.

"I'm sorry, too. I don't like fighting, either. All the time I was out there feeding I felt like part of my heart was missing."

He smiled down at her and when she smiled back he sought her mouth, kissing her tenderly several times before using his tongue to deepen the kisses. He backed her into the room, closed the door and locked it. He kept kissing her as he navigated a path through the bathroom that separated the proposed nursery and their bedroom. When he reached their bed, he picked her up and laid her across the covers where the kissing intensified again.

Leaving her, he locked their door as well before lying down beside her on the bed. He didn't say a word as he slowly undressed her. When she was naked, he pulled the covers down and tucked her under them, then quickly got undressed and joined her.

He was gentle and slow in his lovemaking, waiting for her to reach her pleasurable moment before he gave thought to his own.

"I've never loved anyone else the way I love you, Marta. I'll never love anyone but you. Please, please believe me."

"I do, Rory. I really do. The first time I saw you, you stole my breath and my heart away. Both of them. I don't think that feeling will ever change. You could line up millions of men for me to look over and I'd pick you again every time.

"I was watching you feed and you're all muscle and rhythm when you work among the sheep—as much as you're hard and efficient out there— you're always tender and soft when you're with me. I love you and I trust you to always love me."

"I couldn't love anyone else. There isn't room in my heart for anyone else. You fill it completely. Let's not fight anymore. I don't like fighting with anyone, but most of all, I don't want to fight with you."

He pulled her head onto his shoulder and fell asleep holding her close. Though she had a million things to do that day, suddenly none of them seemed important. She kissed his nipples and he groaned in his sleep. Neither of them stirred until it was time for the evening feeding.

Chapter Six

It was 4 p.m. on Sunday afternoon. Rory was on his knees on the bottom step of the stairs leading up to the porch. The step above the one he knelt on had split and he was in the process of replacing it when a car drove up to the porch. He glanced briefly over his shoulder at the low-slung sports car and then turned back to the work at hand. The driver exited the car and came crunching up the gravel to stand behind him.

"Are you Rory McCrea?"

"I am." He put a screw into the pre-drilled hole and drove it home with a whine of his power drill. He pulled another screw from his vest pocket and slotted that into a second hole.

"And you are?" Rory asked between screws.

The guy moved to one side, more into Rory's sideways line of vision. He was tall, at least six-foot-two, and he had the deep tan of the idle rich who spend all their time on a golf course. His hair was brown, streaked with gold. *Maybe I ought to get up*, Rory thought. *The guy has the look of an IRS auditor or an FBI agent, but there are only four more screws to insert in the step to finish the job.* He put them in before rising.

"I'm Kurt Bancroft—a friend of your wife. I was in the neighborhood, looking at some of the smaller ranches and I saw the sign for AmeriBasque Ranch. Marta told me that was the name of your place, so I took a chance and came up the lane to see where she lived."

Rory, finally on his feet, turned and faced the newcomer, saying, "I'd shake your hand, but mine are sticky with pine pitch from the wood."

At that moment, the front door opened and Marta came out onto the porch.

"Hi, Kurt," she greeted him. "Welcome to AmeriBasque Ranch. I see you've met my husband."

"Yes."

"Rory, dinner will be ready in about 30 minutes. Why don't you show Kurt around and then maybe he can come in and eat with us?"

"I still need to feed, Marta."

"Couldn't you feed after dinner?"

"I don't think the sheep and horses would appreciate the disruption to their mealtime schedule."

"Could I help? Would that be quicker, so you could sit down to eat on time?" Kurt asked.

Rory looked Kurt up and down—the preppy loafers, the cashmere sweater, the new cords and the leather bomber jacket. "Don't think you're dressed for the occasion, Mr. Bancroft. But go on inside. You're welcome to sit at the table and eat.

"I'll be up as quick as I can, Marta. Have Consuela make me up a plate and keep it warm in the oven. Should be done by six or so."

"We'll wait for you. Hurry."

He gathered up his tools, placing them in the toolbox, then went in the direction of the barn while Kurt and Marta entered the front door. Down at the barn he mixed buckets of grain and stacked several bales of hay on the cart behind the garden tractor. Starting with the sheepcotes farthest from the barn, he worked his way backwards until he had only his own cote's worth of ewes to feed. Through the dining room window, he could see Marta entertaining Bancroft, mixing him a drink from the liquor cabinet on the south wall. He was glad to notice she refrained from mixing one for herself due to her pregnant state. Consuela hove into view, placing some snack items on the table, which Kurt dove into like he hadn't eaten in days.

Rory fed both the horses and his sheep before going back up the hill. Entering the mudroom, he came into the kitchen and went to the sink to wash up.

"Will there be another dog house tonight for you to live in, Mr. Rory?" Consuela asked, giving him a grin. "Whew! You step in something? Are you going to go up and change?"

"No. I'm going to sit down and eat."

"You no smell like lavender the same as Mrs. Marta's friend. Maybe you should go up and shower."

"I smell like honest work, Consuela. Something I doubt Marta's friend has much experience with. Am I really that ripe?"

"Pretty bad."

"Okay, hold dinner ten minutes more. He's stuffed his face with your snacks enough he shouldn't be keeling over if he has to wait another ten minutes."

Consuela gave him another grin. "He like to eat, Mr. Rory. I see that for sure. Maybe he have trouble with his bowels tomorrow, like Mr. Jack."

Rory gave Consuela a small hug. "Think you could arrange that? A few of those fiery habanera chilies mixed into his meatloaf?"

"You very bad, Mr. Rory. You be in dog house until *el Año Nuevo*, I do trick like that."

He took the back stairs from Consuela's wing of the house up to his bedroom where he took a two-minute shower and scraped the stubble off his chin. He splashed on some Old Spice Lotion and pulled on clean jeans and a plaid shirt. He traded his work boots for some low-top hiking boots and combed his hair. He went down the back stairs again and told Consuela to 'dish it up.'

"You smell good now. Good man smell, not like girly smell. Lavender for woman's underwear drawer, not for man in public."

"Do me a favor and don't be making faces when you're serving or I'll likely not be able to keep from laughing, then it will be dog-house time for sure, Consuela."

"Okay, Mr. Rory. I keep face like on *el Día de los Muertos*. You go in now. I bring food."

"Sorry for keeping you waiting," Rory apologized, taking his chair at the head of the table. Ricardo and Manuel rolled their eyes and told Rory in Spanish that he could have asked for their help.

He rattled off something in Spanish in reply and both drovers laughed.

"You speak rather fluent Spanish, Mr. McCrea," Kurt observed. "Have you been abroad?"

"No. I learned it in high school—basic stuff, but I honed it in the last seven years working with my drovers. They speak Basque and I only know a few words of that. Mostly they're kind enough to speak Spanish for my benefit as they don't have much in the way of English yet."

"Marta says you have about 2500 acres here."

"Twenty-six hundred and thirty, to be exact."

"That's a good-sized operation."

"Yes, it is."

"Must have cost a pretty penny to buy. I can't believe the prices places here are going for. When I was growing up, land was dirt-cheap. Now it's very dear."

"The white-eyes have discovered the beauty of Montana. The Blackfoot Indians warned this land would be overrun with ski lodges."

"How many sheep can you run on that many acres?"

"Close to 1500, I guess. Depending on the weather and the grass cover."

"And you currently have how many sheep?"

"Almost 600."

"Do you intend to eventually run 1500?"

"No, likely less than that. The range will support 1500, but in the winter, when the range is covered in three or four feet of snow, I have to be able to afford the hay to feed them, and that comes at a pretty penny, too. As I reduce the mortgage on the place and have the wherewithal to buy more winter feed, I can increase the herd size, but that's a long way down the road yet."

"Rory is also limited by the incredible work it takes to shear them in the spring. I hardly saw him last May because of the shearing."

"You do all your own shearing?"

"Yes, the drovers and I."

"What's wool sell for?"

"We got $50,000 for just under 300 fleeces last spring."

"That much, huh?"

"Yes. Targhee wool is prized wool. It has longer strands than most other breeds. It's easier to spin and mill. We sold the whole lot to a wool mill in Scotland and I'm hoping, since Mr. McDougal was so pleased with the quality of our fleeces, I can do business with him again. Word-of-mouth might get us other buyers, too. Our wool is top-notch. I think the market will only grow because we produce good wool."

"You employ how many men to work for you? These two and how many more? Do you hire additional men at shearing time?"

"I don't employ any men."

"What?" Kurt asked, looking very dubious.

"The drovers are not my employees, they're my partners. There are four of them. Only Manuel and Ricardo are still bachelors, Juan and Enrique are married and have their own homes on the ranch."

"How much did each of them contribute to the partnership to get the ranch up and running?"

"Now you're thinking like a lawyer. They didn't contribute anything monetarily, but they've given me seven years of loyalty and sweat equity. Can't buy that sort of thing on the market, but I value that more than the few thousands they might have been able to throw into the common pot."

"Wow. You certainly don't fit the entrepreneurial mold as I learned it in business law."

"No, likely not, but I doubt that down the road any of the four will be suing me for millions like the members of the Hertz family seem to be doing to each other."

"Sounds like you keep up on the current business trends. I wouldn't think you'd have much time for reading the Wall Street Journal."

"Or enough intelligence to understand it if I did?"

"Rory," Marta warned.

"I didn't mean to imply any such thing, Mr. McCrea. It just seems like a pretty labor-intensive lifestyle. I'm quite sure you don't lack in intelligence."

"Sorry, Mr. Bancroft. All of my siblings, save for my younger sister, went to college and they often let me know they thought that my lack of schooling was a shortcoming, so I'm a bit sensitive when I think someone is selling me short because I lack a sheepskin with something besides wool attached to it."

"Do you ever regret not attending college?"

"Haven't so far."

Kurt changed the subject. "What do you do for fun? Golf? Play tennis? Hunt?"

"None of the above. I've hunted a couple of times, but it seems like a lot of work when frequently you don't get anything to shoot at. Tell your friend what we do for fun, Marta. Mostly it involves filling the big tub upstairs with hot water and lots of bubble stuff and. . . ."

"Rory McCrea! *Hush!*"

A grin wider than the Grand Canyon spread over his face as she blushed bright crimson.

"Oh, yeah, and she's teaching me to bowl," he finished up. "She beats me right regular at that."

Consuela, who was picking up empty plates leaned down to collect his and whispered, "Big dog house for you looking at her red face, Mr. Rory. *Muy rojo!*"

Dinner broke up shortly after dessert, and Kurt bid them both good night. As soon as the door closed on his sports car, Marta rounded on Rory.

"You just had to embarrass me, didn't you? How would you like it if I dragged out the intimate details of our life in front of your friends?"

"I don't think I'd blush the same deep shade of red as you did."

"You're impossible. Why did you feel the need to say that?"

"I don't know. I thought I was being pretty civil until he ventured into Wall Street territory. Then, I kind of thought he might be running a subtle put-down on me so he'd come off looking better to you. I wasn't in the humor to countenance that at my own table. But I apologize for embarrassing you." He pulled her into an embrace and kissed her lightly.

"I do think the tub thing is one of the activities I'd rate as the most fun, though. It's a hundred times better than swatting a yellow ball with a racquet, or walking for miles toting a golf bag and hunting for a golf ball that you sliced into the underbrush. Wouldn't you agree?"

"Well, yes. If you put it like that, I guess I'd rate the tub activities at the top of my list, too."

"So, now that Mr. Deep Pockets has departed, could I interest you in a little tub fun as the way to cap off a moderately stressful dinner?"

"Were you stressed by Kurt?"

"He did ask a passel of questions. I was beginning to think it was a modern form of the Spanish Inquisition."

"But you, in turn, didn't ask anything about his job."

"I really don't care about his job. He's a lawyer. A step above a car salesman in the trust category."

"Jack's a lawyer and you like him."

"Jack's a regular fellow. Kurt's a stuffed shirt."

"He isn't, Rory. He's nice once you get to know him."

"Maybe I'll warm up to him as time passes. Now that he's discovered where you live, I'd be willing to bet he'll find lots of excuses to drop in. I just hope he wears some older clothes in the future. I'd love to show him what fun sheep raising is in the dead of winter."

"I can't imagine him mucking out stalls."

"Me neither. Let me lock up, wife. Let's hit the tub for some fun. I feel the need to wash Mr. Bancroft out of my hair."

"I guess I should count my blessings. At least you didn't invite him to go out on the lawn for a few rounds."

"Not me, sweetheart. He's taller than I am and has a longer reach. Wouldn't be surprised if he hadn't trained a bit in self-defensive boxing during law school. I might not have the sheepskin with the gold seal on it, but I'm not stupid enough to challenge someone like Kurt to a boxing match."

He gave her a swat on the posterior and went to lock the mudroom door while she turned the lock on the front door. By the time he got upstairs, she was naked in the bathroom, sitting on the edge of the tub and filling it with steaming water and bath crystals.

"Stand up."

"Why?" she asked, standing slowly.

"Turn sideways."

She turned and blushed under his appraising once-over.

"You turn me on, wife. Just to look at you makes me hard as a rock. You're beautiful and I love the way you're rounding out. Only about three more months and we'll be parents."

"Will you still love me when my belly is a veritable forest of stretch marks?"

"Yes. I'd love you if you grew a beard and a mustache. I won't mind the stretch marks because I know what put them there. And I hope in the next few years to add more trees to the forest of them and more kids to our family. Every time I look at you, I get excited about the baby's arrival. Let's hop in the tub and discuss that. What are we going to name this incredible child?"

"Oh, I already know. If it's a boy I want to call him Jeffrey. And if it's a girl, Alyssa."

"I don't get a vote?"

"Are you one of those men who wants his firstborn to carry his name?"

"No. There's already a Rory Jon in the family. Another Rory would result in total confusion."

"Do you have names that you love? We could compromise. Or use your choices for middle names."

"Well, Maire is kind of Irish for Mary, so if it's a girl, can it be Alyssa Marie—an oblique honor for Mom? As for a son, Jack is probably my best friend outside of the family, so I'd like maybe Jeffrey John—JJ for short."

"Not Jeffrey Daniel to honor your black Irish father?"

"It might be best not to saddle the kid with the name of a man who couldn't hold a job. Jack is more my notion of an ideal guy than my elusive rogue of a father is."

"Are we agreed, then? Jeffrey John and Alyssa Marie?"

"I think so. Now that it's settled, lean back and let me feel you all over."

He started with her breasts, now slightly larger and more sensitive than before, and worked his way down over her belly, pausing to enjoy the movements of either Jeff or Alyssa. When he got below that level, she began to breathe faster as he touched the most sensitive spot on her body.

"Yes, ma'am," he whispered in her ear, "this sure beats tennis and golf."

"Mmmmmm," she purred as her climax sent her blood spiraling to her vagina. "Promise me, when I get huge and we can't make love in the missionary position anymore, that you won't forget this way of pleasuring me."

"We'll see."

"Let's change sides so I can show you that this is nearly as good as the other way."

She turned around and backed up to the other side of the tub, and he leaned back against her, gently bracing with his arms on the sides of the tub so as not to exert undue pressure on her swelling belly.

She teased his penis until he thought he would scream and it was only the thought of the drovers coming to see what was wrong that deterred him from giving voice to the steam of his rising passion. Cupping him, she began a slow stroking of his member and within seconds he erupted in a long ejaculation.

"And I thought masturbation was great," he told her, coming down from his high. "I'd much rather have you do it than me."

"The water is getting cold. Let's go to bed and pick up where we left off, okay?"

"Don't have to ask me twice."

He toweled her dry and she sprinted for the bedroom as he ran a dry towel over himself.

"No fair falling asleep before I get in there," he called after her.

"Not a chance. What's holding you up, slowpoke?"

Dawn again and bleating sheep. He turned over and pulled her to him. At least this morning the vacationing drovers would be back on the payroll. She mumbled 'good morning' as he began a slow circle of her clitoris.

"A short one before I have to brave the cold?" he asked.

"I thought you'd never ask. Is there time enough? I hear the sheep."

"The sheep be damned. I only have mine to feed today. So, yes, there's plenty of time."

"What about your breakfast?"

"Breakfast be damned, too. You're all I want to eat this morning."

"I'm not nearly as nourishing as oatmeal."

"That's where you're wrong, wife. I could live on your loving for years."

"I hope you always feel that way."

"Count on it, Marta."

It was nearly seven when he finally made it out to feed the sheep. When Ricardo raised his eyebrows and pointed at his watch, Rory told him to mind his own business in Spanish. The other drovers laughed. One look at Rory and they knew what had delayed him. His face wore the unmistakable look of a well-satisfied lover. The look persisted well into the morning. Even Consuela smiled and told him she thought he'd managed to sidestep the dog's house he'd flirted with the night before.

All morning, pouring over his ledgers, he couldn't wipe the look off his face. Even the rapidly depleting balances, sucked up by the purchase of winter feed, weren't enough to erase his smile. Life was good, even if the ledgers were inching toward red ink. Again.

Chapter Seven

When Marta got up the following Monday, Rory was already gone. She thought he'd be in for breakfast, but the morning went by and he was nowhere to be found. About six that night he came home, fed his sheep and the horses and finally arrived at the table for dinner.

"Where were you?" Marta asked.

"Butte."

"Why?"

"Maybe I was trying to talk your boss out of hiring Kurt Bancroft."

"Really?"

"No. I took a job at the feed store for most of December."

"Why?"

"You sound like the lisping inquisitor . . . minus the lisp. Christmas is coming and if I want to afford something nice for you, I need to earn some extra money."

"Oh, Rory, you don't need to do that. I've been splitting my checks between the joint account and my account and I have about $800 for shopping."

"I do need to do that. Your money shouldn't go for gifts for my side of the family."

"I might remind you that I have no side to my family, so why wouldn't it go for your side. Your side, since last June is my side, too."

"Sure, I guess it is, only I don't think you should have to foot the bill all by yourself."

"Are we that close to the bottom?"

"Will be once I have to buy hay again in January. With me working, I can afford enough of that, too, to last until spring thaw."

"But it makes you too long a day. You'll be exhausted and then you'll get sick because your immune system is all screwed up."

"It's part of the deal, Marta. I knew it would be rough when I bought the ranch, and it will be rough, lots of times. We've got a child on the way. I need to lay in something against the hospital charges when the time comes. I don't mind the extra work or the long hours. It's building toward our future. You won't be able to hold your job much longer, so I'd better pitch in now and feather the nest a bit for that new arrival."

"Ron said he'd like me to think about coming back in six weeks or so after the birth. He said he'd even let me bring the baby in with me so I could nurse. I'm thinking seriously about that. Until the baby is a few months old it will likely sleep most of the time and then I can get the work done."

"And after that?"

"If we still need the money I earn, maybe I can make arrangements with Dulce or Melinda to baby-sit. It's only for four hours four days a week. I would still do most of the child care."

"Sure, and the baby will be bilingual right from year one."

"Would that bother you?"

"Hell, no. When he or she gets to high school and has to take a foreign language, it'll be an easy 'A' for sure. I'm all for learning another language. Slowly, but surely, I'm picking up a bit of Basque. But Ron has to realize that if the baby is sick, your first responsibility is to our child, not him."

"I'll make him write that provision into the contract."

Tuesday afternoon, both Marta and Rory arrived home at the same time. Rory stood on the porch and took his boots off, emptying a bunch of hay from them.

"Man! They worked me like a dog today. We got in a huge shipment of hay from Utah. I must have bucked 500 bales up into the hay barn. I'm going to need a long session of back rubbings tonight."

He did look tired, so Marta offered to help him feed. When he protested he could do it, she insisted.

"Rory, don't be a stubborn goose. I can throw a flake of hay as well as you can, and I can mix the grain and fill the feeders, too. If we work together, we can be done in half the time and you can sit down and relax a few minutes before dinner."

He relented and she went in to change, coming out again in jeans, now with the zipper down to accommodate her expanding middle, covered by a couple of old sweatshirts of his that were big enough to accommodate her middle, too. Together in the darkness they worked side-by-side to feed the sheep and grain them.

It was very cold by the time they finished up and the wind was picking up. As Rory drove the wagon back to the barn, she snuggled behind him on the garden tractor's seat. Inside the barn it was a trifle warmer, and once he'd rinsed and stored the grain buckets he pulled her into an embrace. Her cheeks glowed pink from the wind and the cold.

"Thanks, wife. I appreciate all your help. I'll make a sheepherder out of you yet."

"Let's go eat. I'm starving."

"You're always starving these days," he told her with a grin.

They sat down to the warm stew and homemade bread Consuela dished up.

"Boy, Consuela, this really hits the spot on a cold night. Mutton stew. I'm glad you didn't fix salmon salad or potato salad. I need heat inside and out tonight."

"Mr. Rory, when did I ever make cold dinner on cold night? I always make warm in winter."

"What was that stuff you served on Sunday? Greens with bits of tomato and bacon and beets? Covered in vinegar?"

"You need vegetables that no have all the good cooked out of them. I look out for you. I feed what I know you need. Everybody needs green vegetables and red ones for the vitamins, too. You work hard. Need good nourishing."

"I'm not a big fan of stuff swimming in vinegar. Ranchers like ranch dressing."

"Should be called 'heart-attack' dressing. Vinegar good for keeping blood vessels open. Old people in the home I work at be still in their own homes they eat less ranch dressing and more vinegar."

"Nah. What they needed was more physical work. It's mental stress and strain that gives you heart attacks, not ranch dressing."

"Why take chance? Eat healthy, be healthy. Besides, I see you with money books and frowning. Is not also stress? So I fix greens and make the vinegar, no?"

"No."

"We see."

By this time, Marta was chuckling.

"Rory, don't you know you can't ever get in the last word with a determined woman?"

"You trying to tell me I'm not the king of my own domain? The prince of my own table?"

"Not as long as Consuela is the queen of your kitchen."

"I'm going to hide her vinegar bottle. I had heartburn all night after eating that salad."

They went to bed soon after dinner and Marta spent more than an hour rubbing tired muscles until finally she felt them relax.

"Rory, about the Christmas stuff. Last year my calendars didn't go over well with Aidan. What do you think I should get for everyone this year?"

"Hey, wife. Calendars are one of the most useful gifts you can give. How about ones in zippered pouches like you could carry in the car to keep all your appointments in? I've had one of those for years and it comes in very handy. Without it, I'd be lost. There's a place for telephone numbers and credit cards and money in the thing. Bet I use mine at least a dozen times a day. I think that should be your signature gift. After all, Aidan isn't around anymore to complain."

"Really?"

"Yes, really. I'd like a refill for mine. You don't have to buy the zippered pouch every year, just the insides . . . next year's pages."

"What else do you want?"

"I could use some new work boots. Mine are getting thin enough in the soles to feel the rocks through their bottoms."

"That seems like buying a woman a vacuum for Christmas. It smacks of work. Christmas should be about fun gifts—something frivolous."

"I am a working man, Marta. I like practical stuff. I have a whole rack full of ties I never wear. I'd rather have the boots."

"Speaking of ties, husband mine, Ron did hire Kurt and will likely offer him a partnership. There was a terrible blowup with Richard today. Rich got a notice he was being expelled from the law school for failing grades."

"That must have made for a pleasant afternoon at the old front desk."

"Yeah, it was kind of awful. I really felt sorry for Richard. He likes the out-of-doors and I heard him say he was going to switch to Forestry at college. It's not good when parents expect their children to follow in their footsteps, especially when the child expresses other interests. Two years and lots of money have been wasted trying to make Rich into something Ron wanted him to be."

"So, will Ron pay for the Forestry?"

"I don't know. Didn't sound like it, but maybe if Rich has to work to pay his own way, he'd be more serious about the classes he takes."

"So you'll be working with your old flame, huh?"

"Yes, and I'd appreciate it if you didn't get all nutty about that. It's a good job, the hours are good and the money comes in handy. He's nothing to me anymore. In fact, he's got a new girlfriend. Amber's quite the looker, so I doubt he'll be spending any time making cow eyes at a fat, pregnant me."

"Good. I'm the only one allowed to make cow eyes at you, you fat, pregnant beautiful woman. I've never seen you look lovelier. Pending motherhood becomes you."

"Flattery will get you everywhere. If he has this new girlfriend and you don't need to feel those jealousy twinges, do you think you could manage a social evening with them?"

"Doing what?"

"Kurt has four tickets for a concert in Missoula. The Montana Symphony is playing. It's part classical and part Christmas music. He asked if we wanted to go. I told him I'd have to ask you before I could say 'yes' or 'no.'"

"If I said 'no' he'd be classifying me as a poor uncultured slob again, so I'm obligated to say 'yes,' right? He's testing me like with the Wall Street Journal stuff. That boy will make a terrific lawyer. He sure can manipulate with the best of them. And he's smooth about it, too. Makes it seem like he's the big, openhearted good guy. Makes it very hard to say 'no' if you don't really want to fall in with the plan. I guess I'd better concur with Kurt's brilliant closing argument, and say a reluctant, 'yes.'"

"Oh, Rory. It'll be fun. We'll go have dinner and then enjoy the concert. You like music."

"Some of it—though I do think Beethoven's Fifth would have come off better if he'd indulged in a fifth of good Kentucky whiskey before scribbling notes on his parchments."

"You're terrible."

"When is this occasion?"

"Saturday night. Can you take off a bit early from the feed store?"

"I'll ask. Is this formal wear? Tux and starched shirts?"

"No, your suit will be fine."

"It'll have to be slacks and my sport coat. Jack borrowed my suit, remember?"

"Oh, that's right. Well, I guess your sports coat will be fine."

"Umm. In my sports coat, I'm going to look like a rube next to spit-and-polish Kurt. Maybe I should just wear jeans and a flannel shirt. Go total country."

"Rory, you could wear a burlap sack and still be the best looking guy in town, so stop it. You are not, nor will you ever be, the social inferior of Kurt Bancroft. He may have fancier duds, but you've got the aura. He'll never have the aura."

"The aura? Is that like a halo? I'm no angel, sweetheart."

"The aura is that inner self-confidence you exude. You're the epitome of the self-made man who's satisfied with his life and sure his life is exactly the life he wants to lead. It was what first attracted me to you. It wouldn't matter what you wore, that confidence comes shining out of you. You belong to no man but yourself. You answer to no man but yourself. You don't take a backseat to anyone. Not even Kurt."

"I answer to you. Are you sure my aura hasn't lost a bit of its luster since I got involved with you? Maybe turning into a tamed househusband has cost me a bit of that self-confidence."

"I don't believe that for a minute. You exude such an aura of iinner strength it makes me want to pant when you come into view."

"All right. I'll go and be my charming self. But it's at the end of a long, hard week, so keep a hold on my hand during the concert to keep me from drifting off into dreamland. I doubt I snore on key."

They met Kurt and Amber at a fancy restaurant in Missoula, getting there a half-hour late.

"Sorry Mr. Bancroft. I didn't get off work until two, then I had to shower and change. I held the pedal to the metal, but once I got to the city limits, I had to do the limit. Smokey was on my back bumper the whole way into the city."

"Kurt, please. Mr. Bancroft is too formal among friends. It's fine. I took the liberty of ordering wine. I hope you like wine."

"I like wine, but Marta will have to abstain due to the child she carries. What would you like, wife?"

"Hot tea, please."

"You think one glass of wine would harm the baby?"

"I'd rather not take the chance, Kurt. Hello, Amber. I really like the color of your dress. It does wonders for your eyes."

"Thanks, Marta. Everyone says it's a good color on me." Amber had been covertly eyeballing Rory since they sat down and turned from Marta to address him. "Mr. McCrea, what sort of work do you do?"

"I'm a sheepherder most of the time. I took a job at the feed store in Butte. Hay is going for $10 a bale this winter and I have almost 600 sheep to feed, so a little extra money will help out until we get spring grass again here or import some first cuttings from warmer states that will cost less. If we aren't standing on formality tonight, it's Rory, not Mr. McCrea."

"That must be a fascinating life. Sheepherder, I mean. Not feed-store worker."

Marta almost laughed. Amber was oozing charm in Rory's direction. It was all she could do not to whisper 'aura' in his ear. So much for him coming off second-best to Kurt.

"It has its moments. Yo, Kurt, I hear you managed to land a position in Ron Harrington's office. Marta says maybe a partnership looms. Congratulations."

"Thanks. I only got on because the son flunked out of law school. Guess Ron gave up his dream of passing the business on to his son after that."

"Better Richard fulfills his own dreams than Ron's dreams. Marta says he wants to go into Forestry."

"I guess. It's hard for me to understand why. He was given the golden opportunity to become a lawyer—all the bills paid, nice car, apartment on campus, and he pisses it away."

The waiter came and took orders. Kurt opted for braised salmon, Amber for chicken, Marta and Rory for prime rib. When asked about dressing for salads, everyone but Rory wanted balsamic vinegar.

"I believe my husband prefers ranch dressing," Marta told the hovering waiter, while giving Rory a wink."

"I do, indeed, Marta," he said, smiling at her. "In spite of Consuela's dire predictions."

"Who is Consuela?" Amber inquired.

"Consuela Mendoza is the best cook in Montana. She's part of my ranch staff. But she's worried about my arteries and wants to cover my salads with vinegar. When I insist on ranch dressing, she rolls her eyes and tells me I'm going to end up in the old folk's home in short order."

"I think you're a long way away from an old folk's home. I've been sitting here thinking you're one of the most virile men I ever met. You remind me of that cigarette cowboy."

"The Marlboro man?" Rory grinned and glanced sideways at Marta, asking, "Is that better than having an aura, wife?"

"About the same, I guess. Didn't I tell you?"

"Yes, but from you . . . well, you have a vested interest. I don't always know if I should believe it coming from you."

He turned back to face Amber. "Thank you," he said simply. Kurt, he noticed, was frowning.

At the concert hall, it was Kurt, Amber, Marta and Rory in that order in their seats. Rory relaxed and put his left arm around Marta's shoulders, and she reached up to squeeze his left hand. Meshing fingers with her, he whispered, "Virile, huh?" His reward was Marta's right elbow in his ribs. "That'll keep me awake for the next few minutes," he told her.

At intermission, they stood in a group in the lobby as concert goers milled around drinking wine and noshing on tiny finger sandwiches. Marta chose one with a chicken filling topped with an avocado purée.

"Hard to see how something the size of a butterfly wing would even begin to take the edge off a man's hunger," Rory observed. "You'd think a place as elegant as this could provide some hoagies or grinders."

Amber dissolved into a fit of giggles, and Kurt's frown grew deeper.

"I think they want something that doesn't splatter down over your shirt or go plop on your shoes. Something you can eat with one hand and not need two dozen napkins to mop up the mess," Kurt said in his best pedantic voice.

"I stand informed," Rory said. "Is yours any good, Marta?"

"Yes, it's quite tasty."

"Looks like something Consuela would set out for ant bait."

Marta knew Rory hated Kurt's condescension and was using sarcasm as a weapon against Kurt's little speech, so she put in a quiet request, "Don't, please?"

He acknowledged her request with a nod and felt her relax again as she leaned against him.

"Kurt, what kind of law will you handle in Harrington's office?"

"I don't know yet. *Divorces*? Business law is my specialty, so maybe some of that, too. And there are always the insurance cases and accident cases."

Rory caught the slight emphasis on 'divorces' and wondered if Kurt thought one day soon he'd be handling Marta's.

"Does that mean you have to chase ambulances and haunt the ER?"

"I think our office is above that sort of low-class operation, Rory. I know most folks think it's all lawyers do, but let me assure you, I'll have plenty of clients and more than enough billable hours without chasing anyone around for their business. You evidently don't have a very high opinion of me—or of lawyers in general."

"I wouldn't say that. One of my best friends, to borrow a trite phrase, is a lawyer. I think the world of Jack Strauss."

"Strauss from Boise?"

"One and the same."

"How do you know him?"

"Oh, we once toasted a few things together."

"Marshmallows at Boy Scout camp?" The condescension was back in spades.

"No. Not exactly."

"Jack was in an accident and his car caught fire. Rory managed to pull him out of it before it exploded," Marta explained.

"Ooh," Amber cooed. "Were you burned badly?"

"Jack got the worst of it. He was hospitalized for weeks and had lots of skin grafts to his legs. I had some superficial burns to my hands and arms—

not enough to leave scars—and I lost my eyebrows and singed off some of my hair. Could have been worse. I pulled him out and up the side of the hill about thirty seconds before the gas tank blew."

"That took a lot of courage on your part."

"No. It's what any guy would have done. I just happened to be the guy closest to the accident."

"You're far too modest. I bet Mr. Strauss is very grateful for your courage."

"Yeah, we've been pretty good friends ever since. He's done a lot of pro-bono work for me. Refused to charge me anything. Payback, I guess. But I do favors for him, too. His father recently died in Chicago. He and Connie were spending Thanksgiving with us, and he had to fly out right away and didn't have anything suitable to wear, so he's got my good suit and my dress shoes in Chicago."

"Thus the sport coat and slacks?" Kurt asked. "Connie? I didn't know Strauss was married."

Rory chose to ignore the remark about his sport coat and answered evenly, "He's not. But I think that may change shortly. Connie's a really nice woman and I think Jack's about to pop the question to her. Might have done it this Christmas but for having to sit shiva because of his father's dying."

"How do you know about sitting shiva? I'd have thought, with your name, you'd be devout *Roman Catholic*."

There was a sneer behind Kurt's voice when he said 'Roman Catholic' that further prodded Rory's growing dislike of Marta's friend.

"It'd be a dull world if all of us were WASPs, Kurt. I am Roman Catholic—the *devout* part might be debatable—at least to Father Leahy. We Catholics don't tend to study Judaism in catechism classes. The Pope, contrary to most people's thinking, doesn't control what we read or study outside the church. I read a lot of stuff on my own hook. I might have read about shiva sitting—in the Wall Street Journal for instance."

"Rory!" Marta warned again.

"Sorry, wife. A bargain is a bargain, but sometimes it's hard for me to hold onto my end of it."

"What bargain are you talking about, Rory?"

"Private matter, Amber. I think the second half is about to begin. Maybe we ought to reclaim our seats."

Following the concert Kurt suggested a bit of a nightcap at a pub near the concert hall, but Marta declined the invitation.

"Rory has to get up incredibly early, Kurt, so we should head for home."

"Could I come sometime and see your sheep, Rory?" Amber asked, batting her eyelashes in his direction.

"Sure. Drive up some summer day to the high meadows. That's when they look the best, right after they've been shorn and are still all white and clean. Maybe you could bring along some of those little butterfly-wing sandwiches. My drovers are always hungry for a mid-afternoon snack. I'd say maybe a couple hundred of those things might assuage their hunger."

"I will. I'll bring lots of sandwiches to eat. It was really nice to meet you."

"It was nice to meet you, too, Amber. Thanks, Kurt for the invite and the concert tickets. We'll have to do it again. That Mahler piece is one of my very favorites." Rory shook hands with Bancroft.

"Really? I'd have thought Fats Domino was more your style."

It was obvious that Kurt was more than a little rankled by Amber's adoration of the sheep man.

"Say, Amber, if you think Kurt is *virile* enough, bring him up with you to the sheep meadows. We could use a sixth for sheep dogging."

"What's sheep dogging?"

"That's where we chase the spring lambs down and tag their ears."

"Is it fun?"

"Yes, ma'am. I've only bruised my ribs twice doing that."

"Are sheep mean?"

"No, but they can kick like a mule when they're scared."

With that, they made their escape. On the way home to the ranch, Rory hummed the Mahler piece very loudly to keep from falling asleep. He stopped on the outskirts of Missoula and got a very large cup of coffee for himself and a medium-sized cup of tea for Marta.

"Keep talking to me, wife. I'm really bushed."

"I shouldn't talk to you at all. Why do you let people like Kurt get your goat? I get really uncomfortable, not knowing what's going to spill out of your mouth next."

"I know, and I'm sorry for making you feel that way. I don't suffer pompous asses gladly. You'd have thought Roman Catholicism was related to cannibalism the way he spit it out."

"Yes, and you're super touchy when it comes to condescension on someone's part."

"You noticed, huh?"

"It was like a red flag waving in the breeze on a mountaintop."

"More noticeable than my virility?" he asked, giving her a grin.

"Boy, was she ever impressed. I thought I might have to get her a bucket to drool in. But you notice that I didn't get my hackles all up about her fascination with *you*."

"You definitely paid attention in those classes where social deportment was taught. You're a lot cooler than I am when you're feeling threatened."

"Who said I felt threatened?"

"Hell, wife. *I* felt threatened by the vibes she was putting out. I kept thinking she was about to send you off with Kurt for that nightcap and invite me to go home with *her*."

"Well, I hope you weren't thinking about taking her up on that offer. You weren't thinking about going home with her, were you?"

"Oh, maybe the thought made a mad dash across my mind, but I rejected it," he teased.

"Maybe the thought of you sleeping on the couch tonight is making a dash across my mind right about now, Rory."

It was after midnight when they got to bed. He raised his eyebrows—his way of asking if she wanted to make love.

"Not until you've gone to confession. I'm not making love to someone who lets Amber types dash across his mind."

"Really. You'd shut me off for the next six days?"

"I would." She turned her back to him.

He nuzzled the back of her neck and massaged her breasts gently. When he ran his tongue inside her ear, he could feel her stiffness begin to melt.

"You're sure?" he whispered, slipping one hand down to rub her pubic area.

"No," she sighed, rolling over to face him. "There's never been a time when I could resist a virile man like you. Have at it, sheep man."

Afterwards, he lay on his back with her head cradled on his shoulder.

"You satisfy me, wife. Virile as I may appear to the fairer sex, you're the only one I love. If Amber types occasionally dash across my mind, you're the one who does the John Denver bit in it."

"John Denver bit? What's that?"

"You know—'You fill up my senses, like'" he crooned . . . "well, like no other woman I ever knew or none I'm ever likely to run across in the future. I love you, Marta."

"If she comes up to the mountain meadows, I hope you'll remember that." She nestled against him and was soon asleep.

Chapter Eight

"I had a visitor at the feed store today," Rory said over supper on Thursday night.

"Anyone I know?" she asked.

"Your old flame's main squeeze."

"Amber? What did she want?"

"Bird seed. And a bird feeder."

"And only you could wait on her?"

"That seemed to be her plan."

"So, *did* you wait on her?"

"Yes. I didn't have much choice. She came in on her lunch hour, which was also the lunch hour of all but Jay Hadley and me. Didn't think the boss would appreciate me calling him away from counting his profits to wait on Amber."

"Was she working her eyelashes like she had a tic in her eyelids?"

"Yep. Makes me wonder how she holds the lids up with all that black gunk on the lashes."

"Is this going to become a problem?"

"Not on my part. I couldn't vouch for Amber, though."

"There are times when I wish you were a little less virile looking, husband mine."

"Once the baby arrives and I have those bags under my eyes from lack of sleep and midnight feedings, maybe that'll put her off. Hard to look like the Marlboro man with saddlebags under both eyes."

"Well, just be careful. Women like that can wear you down."

"We're still going Christmas shopping Saturday? I took off. And I told Hadley I'd be gone to Idaho over the holidays, too."

"Yes, let's go and get what we need. If we wait until the last minute, the shelves will be empty."

"Butte or Missoula?"

"Missoula. Less chance of running into Amber in Missoula."

The next day, Rory and Phil Jordan were in the back of the feedlot unloading a semi-truck's worth of oats, bran, and bags of Equine Junior and Equine Senior alfalfa pellets. Rory had stripped down to his tee shirt because it was warm in the interior of the truck's trailer and unloading all those sacks was working up a sweat. It took them a good hour together to pile the last of the 50-pound sacks into the storage barn, and Rory was looking forward to a good cold drink of water.

Still carrying his flannel shirt, he went into the main part of the store and headed for the water fountain. Bending down to take a long drink, he finally quenched his thirst. As he stood up he flexed his tired muscles before turning around. When he did turn, she was there again.

"Run out of bird seed already, Amber?" he asked, putting on his flannel shirt and buttoning it up.

"I need something to feed wrens with. I was reading in my bird book and it said they liked to eat Niger seed, and that it took a special sort of feeder for that kind of seed."

"Niger seed is tiny and you need a feeder with small slits or you can use a mesh bag if the mesh is fine enough."

"Do you have either here?"

"Both, I think."

"Can you show me?"

"Yes. They're along the back wall."

He led the way to the feeders and pulled a mesh bag and a cylindrical tube down from the shelves.

"Which is better?"

"The mesh bag in the winter. Plastic tends to crack in freezing weather if any water gets in it."

"You have a very nice body. Strong. Muscular. I couldn't help but notice when you rolled your shoulders after you had a drink."

"Years of wrestling sheep tends to do that to you. I apologize for being half-undressed, but it was hot unloading the feed truck."

"Oh, no. You don't have anything to apologize for. I liked what I saw."

"Hey, McCrea!" Phil shouted.

"Yeah, Phil, I'm back here. What do you need?"

Phil came lumbering up with a clipboard.

"You remember how many bags of Equine Senior we unloaded? It says on the invoice there were 75, but didn't seem like that many when we were off-loading them."

"If you want to ring up Ms. Sykes' order here, I'll go count them again."

"Sure, okay. Just the mesh feeder?" Phil asked Amber.

"I guess I need the Niger seed, too."

"You want ten pounds or fifty, Amber?" Rory asked her.

"Fifty, if I can get you to load it so I can watch those muscles ripple again."

Phil, standing behind Amber, gave him a funny look and raised his eyebrows.

"Hey, Phil, can you grab a big sack of Niger seed and load it for her so I can count Seniors? I need to get out of here on time today."

"Sure, McCrea. Where's your vehicle, Ms. Sykes?"

"It's the navy blue SUV out front. See you around, Rory. And thanks for *everything*," she purred.

That remark sent Phil's eyebrows into orbit. Once he got the Niger seed loaded, he followed Rory out to the back barn.

"Hey, she's some chick. She got something for you? She sure was acting all chummy."

"She's the girlfriend of one of the lawyers who works in the same office as my wife works at. Marta and I double-dated to a dinner and concert last weekend with her and the lawyer."

"She knows you're married? Sure didn't look like it. She was putting the hustle on you big time. I could tell she would rather have had you loading her seed than me. Why do you have all the luck?"

"I don't know. My black Irish charm?"

"So, do you like her, too?"

"No, of course not. I'd rather not wait on her at all, but I can't afford to be nasty to the paying customers, no matter who they are. I'm married, Phil. I have a child on the way. There's no way I'm going to be interested in another woman."

"Still. . . ."

"There are 60 bags of Senior, Phil. They shorted us 15. Make a note on the invoice and let Mr. Hadley know."

"We have a 40-bale delivery of hay to the Coombs ranch still to go, Rory. You want to start loading the truck? I'll be out to help as soon as I tell Jay about the shortage."

"Sure."

He backed the flatbed truck up to the stacks of hay in the barn, then climbed up and started tossing bales down onto it. Phil reappeared and began arranging the bales Rory was tossing down. When all forty were on the truck, Rory jumped down and helped align the bales, tying the stacks down with flat nylon belts that he winched down tight.

"You know the way to the Coombs place?" he asked Phil.

"Yeah, sure. It's out on the Apple Valley Road about eight miles."

"If you know where it is, you drive."

They turned into the Coombs place and followed a long drive around to the back of a huge house and arrived at an equally impressive barn. A woman in her mid-thirties came out to direct the unloading. She wore tan jodhpurs, knee-high black riding boots and a thick gold sweater.

"Oh, good, you're here. I'd like the hay stacked in the loft," she said, pointing upwards. "You can drive the truck back in under the loft if that will make unloading easier."

"Yes, ma'am," Rory told her, motioning for Phil to back into the barn.

It was still a hard heft from the bed of the truck to the loft. Phil chose to stand on the bed and upend the bales so Rory, standing in the loft, could catch them with his hooks and drag them over the edge of the loft and stack them up in the back corner. The woman stood to one side observing the operations.

When the hay was all in the loft, Rory sat on the front edge of it and launched into space, landing squarely on both feet in the bed of the truck. He jumped down from that point to land on the floor of the barn a foot or two in front of the woman. He fished the invoice from his pocket, unfolded it and smoothed it out, then handed it to her.

"You're new, aren't you?"

"Yes, ma'am. I just started a couple of weeks ago."

"You're polite, too, and you don't complain about lofting the hay. The last delivery, the other guy didn't want to put it up there. Said he didn't want to get a hernia." She shot a glance at Phil and then turned to leave. "Come up to the house and I'll make out a check for the hay and the delivery. What's your name? I'm going to request you from now on."

"Rory McCrea," he told her, matching her long strides with his own.

"An Irishman?"

"Yes, ma'am."

"Come in for a moment. Would you like something to drink?"

"No, but thank you for asking."

"Have a seat, I'll be right back."

He eased into a kitchen chair and hoped he wasn't shedding hay chaff all over her spotless floor. He was looking at a shelf full of riding trophies when she returned.

"Here you go," she said, handing him the check.

"Thank you, and I apologize if I've gotten hay all over your floor."

"Nonsense. Think this kitchen has never seen a bit of hay on the floor? It's rare when there isn't hay on the floor. Do you have horses?"

"No. I raise sheep."

"Where?"

"South of Butte. I own the AmeriBasque Ranch."

"Then why are you slaving away at the feed store?"

"I'm about to be a father. Deliveries—for both hay and babies—are rather expensive these days."

"Well, congratulations. Is it going to be a son or a daughter."

"I don't know. All I know is it kicks like a mule."

"You haven't had a sonogram?"

"No, ma'am. The Irish like to be surprised."

"Well, I hope it's a good and healthy child, Mr. Rory McCrea. And thanks for lofting the hay."

"You're welcome."

"Jeez, McCrea. Were you holding a séance in there? Let's get back to the store. I still have to sweep up the back barn where that bag of oats split. You seem to gather up women like a magnet. What makes you so hot? They don't treat me that way."

"I don't know. You might try a few good manners and give them a bit more in the way of effort than they expect. She said the person who delivered her last load bitched about lofting the bales."

"I delivered the last load, and you're damn right I bitched. If she wants it in the loft, she ought to hire a couple of hands to put it there. Our job is just to get it to the barn and unload it, not to be sashaying those damn heavy bales all around Montana to suit some bitch of a woman."

"Maybe that's why you don't seem to attract the fairer sex, Phil. A bitch? I'd hardly call her that. She seemed very gracious to me."

"Yeah, well you were the one kissing her rich ass. Me, I got more self-respect than to fall all over her and do whatever she's snapping her fingers about at the moment."

Late in the afternoon, Marta came by the feed store. Phil was setting up a new window display with Christmas lights and a snowman.

"Excuse me," Marta said, "is Rory McCrea around."

"What do you need? I can help you," Phil told her, backing out of the window.

"I'd rather speak to Mr. McCrea."

Phil stood looking at Marta and shaking his head.

"Yeah, you and every other woman in Butte. What is it about that guy? That woman this morning and the broad we delivered hay to this afternoon too—they've all got the hots for McCrea. Now you. Well, he's busy loading up hay for a morning delivery tomorrow. He's out back and if I call him in, I'll be the one who ends up dancing on top of those towering stacks of hay bales and throwing them down on the truck, so if it's okay—just this once—let me be the one to help you."

"I really need to speak to my husband."

"McCrea is your hu . . . husband? Oh, geez, I'm sor . . . ry. I'll call him," Phil stammered. "The boss doesn't like customers out back when someone is tossing down hay bales. 'Fraid you might get hit if one rolls off the truck. I'll go get him for you."

"Thank you."

Rory came in brushing hay out of his hair and off his shirt and pants.

"Hello, wife. What do you need?"

"Rory, Bailey called the house and Consuela called me. Eric is going by air-evac to Denver Children's Hospital tomorrow at noon."

"Why? What's wrong with him?" A frown knit his eyebrows together.

"I called Bailey because Consuela doesn't always get things right. Bailey said Eric has been listless the past couple of days, so they went to the doctor's office this morning. The doctor put Eric in the hospital right away and they did some tests. He's got water building up on his brain and needs a shunt put in to drain it out, so they're sending him by helicopter to Denver for the procedure.

"Poor Bailey, she sounded scared to death. She wanted to know if you'd start right now and drive to Boise and bring Todd back with you so she and Michael can go to Denver to be with Eric. He'll be hospitalized about a week and she said Todd really likes you and she thinks he'd be happier with you than any of the others in Boise."

"Sure, of course I'll go. When you get home, call her and tell her I'm on the way and if I can't make it before she and Mike need to leave, have her leave Todd with Mom and I'll get him there."

"Okay. Sure you won't be too tired to drive?"

"No, I'll be fine. Worrying about Eric and Bailey will keep me focused. But see if one of the drovers can feed for me until I get back, okay?"

"Yes. Call me when you get to Boise, and please get a bit of sleep before you turn around to drive back."

"I will. Good thing I took tomorrow off for shopping. May have to delay that a bit."

"It might be fun to take Todd shopping with us—let him sit on Santa's knee."

"Yeah. Christmas is for kids, that's for sure. But Santa might not get to listen to any other kids' wish list. By the time Todd gets all his toys listed and I interpret his lisp for the Jolly One, it might be midnight."

"Bailey said Todd could stay until we go back for Christmas, if that's okay with you. I know you have to work, but things are slow at the law office, so when I told Ron about the problem, he gave me off until the New Year—with pay."

"Remind me to send your boss a case of good whiskey. That was damn decent of him."

"I just hope Todd likes me as much as he likes you."

"Sure he does. Keep the pancakth and thauthages coming and take him to the barn to feed the hortheth and you'll be his best buddy ever."

"I guess it'll be good practice for when we have one of our own. Well, I'd better go home in case there are any more messages from Bailey. Do you have your cell phone?"

"Yes. I'll see you late Sunday afternoon unless I call to say otherwise."

"Be careful."

"I will."

He pulled into Bailey's driveway at eight in the morning and let himself in when nobody answered his knock. Bailey was upstairs, frantically rushing around, gathering up clothes for Todd and filling a suitcase for Mike and herself for Denver. Todd was crying.

"How can I help, Sis?" Rory asked, making her jump.

"You scared me. Can you feed Todd some breakfast? He likes oatmeal and toast with peanut butter on it. I need to be to the hospital by ten if I want to go in the helicopter with Eric. Mike left last night to drive to Denver so we'd have a car if we have to stay a bit. Thank you so much for coming, Rory."

"Anytime, Sis. Hey Sport, let's go and eat. I haven't had breakfast either. Okay?"

"Yeth. I'm thad. Mama ith going away with Eric and I can't go."

"Well, Todd, you get to go away with me and go back to my ranch and help me and your Aunt Marta feed the horses. Don't you think that will be fun?"

"Yeth. But I want to ride in the helicopter, too."

"Maybe some day soon, I can get you a ride in one, but for now, why don't you stop shedding those crocodile tears and come and eat with me? Keep me company."

"Okay."

"You want a cup of coffee, Bailey?"

"No, but thanks, Rory. My stomach is in such a churn already I don't think it needs any more stimulation."

"Doctor say what caused the fluid to build up?"

"She said it happens sometimes when they bump their heads. Eric took a tumble down the porch steps in his walker. I just turned my back for a second to pull out another bag of groceries from the trunk of my car when he launched into space. I tried to catch him. I thought I'd broken his fall enough that he wasn't hurt too badly, but he'd hit the railing on the way down and had a lump right behind his left ear. Didn't seem to bother him for two or three days, then it was like he was in a daze. I don't mind telling you, Rory, I'm scared to death."

Rory came over and gathered her into his arms. "It'll be fine, Sis. Kids are tough and resilient. It wasn't your fault, if that's what's upsetting you. You do your best to protect them, and even so, they often find a way to negate all your precautions. Don't worry. Medicine is so advanced nowadays, those doctors can work all sorts of magic.

"I'll give you my cell-phone number and I want you to keep in touch. Let me know how Eric does with the surgery. Do you have someplace to stay in Denver near the hospital?"

"The Ronald McDonald House for the first couple of days, then maybe a nearby motel."

"You need money?"

"No, we're fine. We have good insurance, and the hardware store is going great guns. But thanks for the offer."

"Well, I'd better rustle up some grub for my favorite cowboy, right Todd?"

"Yeth."

"Rory, I know this is a huge favor Mike and I are asking of you and Marta, but everyone else is so wrapped up in their own lives and going forty directions at once with their own kids, that I thought Todd would get lost in the shuffle. When we were there at your place over Thanksgiving, Todd had such a good time and he truly loves you, so you were my first choice. I'm sorry to impose on you that way, but I didn't think I could worry about both my sons at the same time."

"It's no imposition, Bailey. I'm happy to lend a hand and glad you trust me enough to take care of Todd."

He fed Todd and gathered Todd's suitcase into his truck, then stowed Bailey's bags in the back and drove her to the hospital to catch the helicopter.

"Hey, Todd, maybe the helicopter pilot will let you sit in it while the nurses are bringing out Eric. Shall we ask and see?"

"Yeth, Uncle Rory."

Rory approached the chopper with Todd in his arms. The pilot was running his checklist when Rory tapped on his side window.

"You're taking his brother, Eric Innes, to Denver shortly and Todd wanted to ride in a helicopter, too. Is there a possibility of letting him sit in it for a few minutes?" Rory asked.

"Sure. Hi, Todd. You want to go around to the other side? I'll let you be my co-pilot for a bit. You can help me with my checklist, okay?"

"Yeth." Todd's eyes were bright with anticipation as Rory carried him to the right side of the chopper and opened the door.

"Here, Todd. Put on these headphones and you can hear what the nurses are saying about getting your brother ready to go to Denver."

He clamped the headphones on and Todd sat back in the seat, amazement lighting up his face. The pilot toggled a switch so he could talk to Todd on the headset.

"Say there, co-pilot, would you flip the switch to start the blades to moving?"

"Yeth. Where ith it?"

"It's that one right there," the pilot told him, pointing at a switch on the console.

Todd used both hands to turn it on. Above his head, the huge chopper blades began to slowly rotate. He watched in awe.

"Good job, co-pilot Todd. We need to let them warm up so when your brother comes on board, we'll be ready to fly. Can you flip two more switches, Todd?"

"Yeth, I can do it."

"Then I need you to do this one, and that one. The green one first. It turns on the lights to warn other pilots that we're coming near to them. And this one turns on the power to work the equipment that the nurses might need while we fly Eric to Denver."

The doors next to the helipad opened and a sedated Eric and a worried Bailey came up the ramp toward the helicopter.

"Hey, Todd, thanks for all your help, but I need your mommy to sit in that seat now, so we can get to Denver to help your brother. Here, I have some wings to share with you since you've been such a good co-pilot."

He pinned the silver wings on Todd's coat and Rory opened the door to haul Todd out and help Bailey in.

"Mama, I got to turn on three thwitcheth and make the bladeth go round and round. Look, I got wingth."

"Rory, it's no wonder our child loves you to pieces. Thanks for making it possible for him to ride in the helicopter."

"You and Eric have a safe trip. Here's my home-phone and cell-phone numbers. Let us know when you arrive and keep in touch. Reverse the charges so you won't have to hunt up any quarters for a phone, okay? And don't worry about the lisping inquisitor. I'll keep him busy and entertained so he won't feel like he's missing out on anything. Let us know how the surgery goes. I'll be praying for Eric."

Bailey blinked back tears and hugged Rory. "I'm sorry for all the times I let the others rag on you, Rory. You truly are the kindest-hearted of us all."

"Hey, now's not the time for that. You just take care—be safe and hopefully all will be well in time for Christmas. C'mon, Todd, we need to get in my truck so when the blades go really fast we don't get a face full of dirt."

He grabbed Todd up and sprinted for his truck at the edge of the heliport. There they sat and watched as the blades picked up speed until they were a blur. The helicopter lifted slowly off the pad and was airborne. Rory offered up a short prayer that the trip would be uneventful, then buckled Todd into his seatbelt and turned off the airbag on the passenger side.

"Let's go home, so you can help me feed the horses."

"Yeth. I like to give them oath."

They didn't arrive at the ranch until shortly before midnight. Rory carried a sleeping Todd into the house and while Marta put him into a day bed in the nursery across the bath from their bedroom, Rory retrieved Todd's suitcase and his teddy bear from the truck. When he got upstairs, Marta had Todd in the bathroom for a potty break. Rory found his snuggly pajamas and Marta helped put them on, then tucked Todd back into the bed and gave him his teddy bear.

"I'll leave the night light on in your room and one in the bathroom, Todd. If you get scared or need to get up to make pee-pee, just call me, okay?"

"Yeth. I love you Aunt Marta. And you, too, Uncle Rory."

With that and a goodnight kiss, Todd's eyelids fluttered closed and he was asleep.

Marta stood looking down on his angelic face for a few moments. Rory came up and hugged her from behind.

"Did Bailey and Eric get there okay?" he asked.

"Yes. It took them a whole lot less time than it took you. And Michael got there, too. He drove all night and got to Denver late this afternoon."

"Good. Bailey's going to need to lean on him. She was pretty upset. But, let's go to bed. I'm totally wiped out, and I have to go to work in the morning. Will you keep me posted if Bailey calls about the surgery?"

"Yes."

He fell asleep immediately and groaned when the alarm went off at five. After dressing, he looked in at Todd, who was sleeping on his tummy with the bear firmly clutched in one arm.

"Marta, Todd likes oatmeal and toast with peanut butter for breakfast, or pancakes and sausages with syrup," Rory whispered in the dark. "I'll be home soon as I can make it, but call me with any news about Eric."

"I will. Don't worry, Todd and I will be fine. I like to color, so I bought some coloring books and crayons for us to work on and I'll make a tent with some sheets over the card table. We can play cowboys and Indians."

"Just don't let him talk you into riding Domino or Jemima. At least not until I get home."

"I won't. You have a good day, husband mine."

He leaned down to kiss her and said, "Mine will likely be easier than yours, wife. Don't let Todd wear you to a frazzle."

"I won't. There are books to read to him if I need to sit a bit. We'll be fine. I love you."

"Love you, too, sweetheart. Call me."

At work, Phil caught him in the lunchroom over morning coffee and donuts.

"I hope I didn't get you into trouble, McCrea. How was I to know that woman was your wife?"

Rory frowned. "Marta?"

"The one who came in late Friday afternoon and asked for you. I thought it was another female who was panting after your body and maybe I might of said some things."

"Like what?"

"I think I said that that lawyer's woman had been here in the morning and she seemed a bit too interested in you. And I think I mentioned about the Coombs dame having the hots for you, too."

"Marta never said anything to me about any of that. We had a kind of family crisis, so she's probably forgotten all about it."

"Well that lawyer's woman called shortly before you got here and wanted to talk to you this morning."

"What about?"

"Wouldn't say. Seemed really put out that you weren't available."

"Hell, Phil. I'm too tired to think about anything like that this morning. That guy that was here last week decided on those pre-formed panels for building a barn with, so I'm trying to get as much of that into the trailer as I can. Jake was helping me, but those damn floor mats weigh a ton, so when it comes time to heave those on the truck, we're going to need all hands to accomplish the chore. I'll be out back loading. If she comes in, tell her I'm busy. Don't take any guff and don't be sending her out there where I'm loading."

"Okay, McCrea. But she ain't gonna like it one little bit."

"Makes no never-mind to me, Phil. I've got my hands full for the next few days. My nephew, who's only four, is staying with us while his brother has surgery in Denver. So if Ms. Sykes comes in and wants me, I'm not available, but if a woman *calls* on the phone, ask who it is and if it's my wife, come tell me because I'm waiting for word how Eric's surgery went. Okay?"

"Yes."

At one in the afternoon, Phil came out to tell him there was a call for him. It was Marta saying that Eric was out of surgery and doing well.

"Thanks, wife," he told her. Seeing Amber's car pull into the parking lot, he put the phone back in its cradle and escaped out the back door again. He was going to have to confront her and put it to her that he was happily married. Soon. But not today while his mind was still half asleep from the long weekend on the road. He was sure he'd need all his faculties on high alert when he confronted Amber. And he hoped, once things settled down a bit at home and Marta remembered Phil's remarks, that he'd already put the kybosh on whatever little game Amber was playing with him. He didn't want to have an Amber discussion with Marta while Amber was finding every excuse to visit him daily at the feed store.

Damn, he thought. *I need to turn down that aura.*

Chapter Nine

When Rory got home, Marta was sitting on the sofa and Todd was under the 'tent' in the corner of the living room. He poked his head out and Rory laughed to see him with a headband made from a paper sack to which several colorful feathers were stapled. Todd's face was painted with red streaks. Marta's waistband in her new stretchy pregnancy pants had a six-shooter crammed in it.

"You get right back into your tepee, Running Wolf, or I'm gonna have to plug you with my gun."

Todd snatched his head back in under the sheets and giggles erupted from within.

"I take it you had a bit of fun today."

"Yes and we made all of six trips to the barn to see the horses, too. At this rate, the doctor will quit crabbing at me about gaining more than a pound or two a month."

"Hey, Running Wolf, get your coat on and come with me to feed the sheep and the horses. Every Indian on this ranch needs to earn his keep by doing chores."

Todd scrambled out and came running, hitting Rory full force in the knees.

"Whoa, partner. Those knees are tired. Did you have fun today?"

"Yeth. Aunt Marta made me thith headdreth and thee made the tepee, too. I have bear inside, and my bow and arrowth. I thot bear tho I could make a thkin out of him and eat hith meat for dinner."

"Wow! I'll have to take you hunting with me. I never shot a bear, not even with my rifle. And you got one with your bow and arrows?"

"Yeth. But I didn't really thoot bear. I love bear. I was only pertending."

"Pretending is fun. I used to pretend I was Superman and I could fly around with my cape on."

"Aunt Marta, can I be Thuperman tomorrow? Can you make me a cape, like Uncle Rory wore?"

"I think I can scare up a cape, Todd, but you can't really fly, so don't be trying to do that by jumping off the porch or the steps or anything. Your mama wouldn't be happy if you got hurt."

"Okay. I'll only pertend to fly."

Outside, Rory took Todd's hand and they walked to the barn. It was cold and dark so Rory carried a lantern. He loaded the wagon with hay and grain for the sheep and settled Todd on the seat in front of him on the tractor.

"Can I theer, Uncle Rory?"

"Long as you don't steer us into a ditch."

Todd took over the wheel and turned it to go where Rory directed. He actually did a very good job of steering for a kid who could hardly see over the steering wheel.

"Don't touch anything while I feed the sheep, Todd. If the tractor gets broken, I would be very sad."

"Okay."

Rory made quick work of haying and graining the sheep, then let Todd drive them back to the barn where the lantern glowed in the doorway.

"Are you cold, buddy?"

"No."

"Well, I am, so let's feed the horses and get back up to the warm house. It smells like snow. If it snows, tomorrow night, maybe we can make a snowman."

"Can I give the oath to the hortheth?"

"Sure thing. Just one scoop for each."

Rory lifted Todd up while he dumped a scoop of oats into each horse's feed pail, then Rory tossed a big flake of alfalfa to all eight horses.

"One, two, three, four, five, thix, theven, eight," Todd counted. "I thought you only had two hortheth."

"No, Domino and Jemima pull the wagon, but these other horses are the ones we ride when we take the sheep up on the mountain. This one is my horse, and that one used to belong to your Aunt Kelsey, and the other four are for Manuel, Ricardo, Juan and Enrique. Where did you learn to count so good?"

"Mama helpth me and I watch Thethame Threet. The Count theth numbers every day. I can count to ten."

"You must be one smart kid."

"Yeth, thath what Mama tellth me. Where ith Mama, Uncle Rory? I mith her."

"She's in Denver. When we get up to the house, I'll show you on a map."

Dinner was corn dogs and macaroni and cheese. Todd's request left Consuela shaking her head. "He no grow he eat like that," she muttered.

They had ice cream and brownies for dessert, and Rory offered to give Todd a bath while the women cleaned off the table and did up the dishes. As he snuggled a sleepy Todd into his bed, Todd reminded him of the map Rory was going to show him.

"Stay in bed so your feet stay warm and I'll get the map."

Rory returned with a map of the United States and showed Todd where his ranch was and where Todd lived in Idaho, then took a ruler and a red crayon and drew a line down to Denver.

"Denver is where your mom and dad and Eric are. It's a long way. You know how long it takes to drive from your house to mine? Well it's more than twice that long to drive to Denver. That's why Eric and your mom went in the helicopter, so they could go quick."

"When will Mama come back?"

"Soon as Eric is better. Right before Christmas. You and me and Aunt Marta will go home to your house in time to open all your Christmas presents, okay?"

"Yeth. I like Chrithmith.

"Well, Todd, you had a busy day. I think you'd better get some shuteye, partner."

"Uncle Rory, I need bear."

"Is bear in the tent, still?"

"Yeth, he ith."

Once Rory retrieved bear, Todd was asleep in minutes. Rory pulled up an extra cover and turned out the light, then tiptoed down the hall and down the stairs.

"Asleep?" Marta asked.

"Yep. You must have worn him out."

"The feeling is mutual. It smells like snow. I dread the thought of having to cram him into a snowsuit and boots and mittens and stocking cap only to have to yank him out of it again because he needs to pee."

"The secret is to make him pee first."

"I've heard they don't need to until you get them all bundled up."

He sat down beside her on the sofa and pulled her close. "Thanks, wife, for looking after the lisping inquisitor all day. If you want to go up and soak in a hot tub, I'll be up in a bit to give your muscles a rubdown."

"That sounds heavenly, but I'm not sleepy yet. Thought I'd watch *The Nanny* before going up. Might get some childcare pointers. Want to watch it, too?"

"I'd better do up the books. Got the bank statement to reconcile. See if we have a few farthings left."

"Rory, that Phil you work with. . . ."

Oh, oh, Rory thought, *here it comes.*

"Is he married?"

"I don't know. Never asked him."

"He didn't want to go and get you when I came to the store. Does he shuffle all the hard work off on you?"

"I'm a bit younger than he is. I suppose he did more of the heavy lifting when he was younger, but now that he's in his forties—well, I don't mind. Some day I'll probably be deferring to some young buck, too and trying not to get stuck with all the heavy lifting."

"Do you like him?"

"He's okay. I mean, he doesn't ever tell me to do anything. He always asks. He's been there a long time and by right of seniority, he could likely boss me around, but he doesn't, so yeah, I guess he's an okay guy."

"What about Mr. Hadley?"

"The Big Cheese? He's okay, too. He pretty much keeps to his office unless it's really busy. The place does a land-office business and it takes some work to keep the store in supplies. Involves a lot of calling around trying to locate hay, especially in the winter. Jay's on the phone most of the day, so he doesn't harass us much. About the only time he's in a foul mood is when he's had a spat with Mrs. Hadley."

"Phil said all the women in Butte have the hots for you."

"I was wondering when you might get around to that. Phil apologized to me this morning for shooting off his mouth. He thought you were another of my 'groupies.'"

"*Do* women have the hots for you?"

"I guess some of them do."

"Do you encourage them?"

"No. If truth be told, it kind of embarrasses me. Makes me uncomfortable. I was just thinking today that I'm going to have to have a heart-to-heart with Amber and set her straight."

"Was she there again today?"

"No, but she called before I got to work and was miffed, Phil said, because I wasn't there to talk to her. When I see her pulling up, I go out the back and find something to do in the barn."

"What about the woman where you delivered hay?"

"The Coombs place? She was just glad to have someone polite who didn't mind hauling 40 bales of hay up into her loft."

"Was she good looking?"

"Yes, sure. In a rich sort of way."

"What does that mean?"

"Oh, you know. Expensive clothes that show off her figure to advantage. Probably a facelift or two. Silicon implants. Every hair in place and all of it welded down with hair spray applied by a Mr. Maurice or Mr. Alexander in some upscale beauty parlor."

"Do you find that attractive? You must have been looking at her pretty hard to pick up all that."

"I like women with fresh-scrubbed faces and soft hair and a smattering of freckles. I like women round with child who have peaches-and-cream complexions. I like women who are smart and hard-working and who have a sense of humor. That's the sort of woman I'm attracted to."

"Where does Amber fit into your scale? She's got soft hair and a good complexion."

"And all that stuff on her eyelashes, and her really annoying habit of coming into the store and commenting on my physique right in front of Phil."

"Well, I think I'm glad he's running interference for you. Otherwise, she might be offering herself up to you behind the hay bales."

"For that to happen, both of us would need to be willing and I'm *not* willing, so don't get that look on your face. Amber Sykes is an annoying but persistent customer. That's all she is.

"Our marriage is totally satisfying to me. You're more woman than I deserve. You beat all the others, hands down. You satisfy me sexually and in every other way, too. I have no reason to look outside this marriage for anything with anyone else."

"What about when we can't do sex because of the birth?"

"What? You think I can't do six weeks or two months without it? Up on the meadows in Idaho, I didn't have sex for 4-5 months at a time."

"Yeah, but I heard some stories about that, too."

"Like what?"

"How when you did come down, better not be a car on the highway in your way. That you went 120 mph in your rush to get to Boise to find a hot female and some sexual relief."

Rory grinned and shook his head. "Boy, I had no idea I'd become the stuff of legends."

"Well, weren't you hot to find a woman for sex?"

"Yes, sometimes."

"So, why do you think you might not feel the need while I'm not able to satisfy you? How do you know you won't be willing to take Amber up on what she's promising then?"

"I don't want to spend lots of time in confession?"

"Why do you always meet my serious questions with some sort of flip humor?"

"Because, Marta, you seem to always think the worst about me. Were you planning to take up with Kurt if I was laid up for a month or two?"

"*No!*"

"Why not? He's smart and rich and good-looking. Why wouldn't you consider him if I was incapacitated and couldn't perform for a few weeks?"

"Because I love you. I stood at the altar and promised to cling only to you."

"And I wasn't standing at the same altar promising the same things to you? I distinctly remember standing there. Don't you remember that?"

"Yes. But men are always more likely to . . . stray."

"Not this man, Marta. If you doubt everything else in the world about me, the one thing you can't doubt is my word. I promised to love you until death do us part. I intend to honor that promise. There will be no liaisons with other women. Not even if you *never* could have sex again. What makes you always question that?"

"My mother loved my father as much, or maybe more, than I love you. I guess I was about fifteen when I was on the school bus heading home and saw my father coming out of Tanner's Motel with a woman half his age. She was kissing him and he was returning her kisses.

"I was upset and when he went off for a business meeting, I asked Mom about what I'd seen. She got really sad and said she knew he was seeing someone else. It was like my entire world fell apart that afternoon on the bus. I thought they had a happy marriage, but I was wrong.

"If my father could do that—well, I suppose any husband is capable of the same sort of betrayal. And your mother took up with someone other than her husband, too, so marriage isn't always the lifelong commitment you would have me believe it to be."

"My mother had an affair with the man who turned out to be my biological father, but that never made me doubt your love for me, Marta. I'd never believe you capable of taking up with anyone else. I'd like the same degree of trust from you. I don't know what prompted your father to negate his marriage vows, but I'm not going to negate mine. You can take that to the bank. I love you, now and forever."

"Oh, Rory. My heart believes you, really it does, but in my mind I'm on the bus and he's kissing her and I'm scared. If you fell in love with someone else, I wouldn't want to live. I think that's why my mother died not long after that. Her heart was broken, and mine would be, too."

"Marta, stop it. I'm never going to do what your father did. I'm . . . *never* . . . going to do that to you."

He pulled her to him and lifted her chin with his hand until her eyes met his.

"Never, Marta. I will never love anyone but you. I may occasionally flirt. I might take a long look at a beautiful woman. I might even rate her on the scale of one to ten, but I'm in this marriage with you for my lifetime and yours."

He kissed her long and passionately, then told her, "Go take your hot bath and I'll rub some oil into those Todd-tight muscles."

"What about reconciling the bank statement."

"It can wait. You're more important. Now, go. I'll be up as soon as I lock up and check on Todd."

Good to his word, he massaged every inch of her with scented oil, and when she was warm and relaxed and smelled of apple blossoms he gently made love to her. When she tried to tell him she was sorry, he stilled her words with more kisses.

"You have nothing to be sorry for. I didn't know about your father. I can see how that would shake your faith, Marta, and I'm sorry your mother had to experience that, but that was them, and we are us and it won't happen to you. I'm a good Catholic boy. Marriage is for a lifetime. You're stuck with me."

"There's no one I'd rather be stuck with. Thanks for your understanding and your assurances. It might take another few years, but eventually I may get to the place where my doubts go away."

"I can wait. Goodnight, love."

"Night, Rory."

Chapter Ten

Fresh from his promises and assurances to Marta, Rory was in no mood for Amber when she arrived in the store the next day. She immediately sought him out and asked about something to keep her birdbath clean and free of algae. When he led her to the shelves that contained bottles to combat algae, she leaned against him and ran her hand down his back, ending up squeezing his left buttock.

"Phil," Rory barked. "Can you take over for me for a half hour. Amber and I are going for coffee across the street."

"Yeah, I can but. . . ."

"I'll owe you one, Phil."

"Okay, but what if your wi . . .what if *she* calls?"

"Tell her I'll call her back in half an hour."

Taking Amber's elbow, he steered her across the street to The Hen's House where they made tolerable lattes. He found a back-corner booth and installed Amber in it, asking what she wanted to drink.

"Whatever you're having is fine with me."

He came back with two big lattes and slid into the booth across from her. She took up her cup in one hand and slid her other one across the table to cover his.

"You are just the most delicious chunk of maleness I've ever known, Rory."

"Ms. Sykes. I'm going to put this very bluntly. I don't appreciate your coming on to me. I'm married to Marta. I intend to *stay* married to Marta. I don't want any side action. I don't want any romps in the hay with you or any other woman.

"I don't appreciate you coming to the feed store on a daily basis. I certainly don't appreciate your sexual comments or your touches or your innuendos. If

97

it persists, I'll file an order of protection against you and you'll have to stay away from me altogether. I don't mind serving you in the store as a customer, but anything further than that, I'm going to consider as harassment. Do I make myself clear?"

"What brought all that on? I thought you liked me."

"You'd be wrong on that score. I might have liked you as a friend, but when you pushed it beyond mere friendship, I stopped liking you at all."

Tears welled in her eyes, and she groped in her handbag for a tissue.

"You don't feel anything for me?" she asked, her voice quavering.

"No, I don't. And I never will. I love my wife. There's no room in my heart or in my marriage for anyone but Marta. That being said, I'm going back to work."

He picked up his cup and slid out of the booth while she continued to sit there in stunned silence. She watched him cross the street, sprinting between the cars and trucks. As if to signal the cold she felt inside, it began to snow. She finished her latte and went across the street to her car, then changed her mind and re-entered the feed store.

"Looks like I might need a snow shovel," she said brightly.

"They're on the back wall," Rory told her. "Pick the one you want and I'll ring it up."

When she came up to the counter, he rang up the sale and waited while she made out her check. As she handed it to him, she looked at him and said, "You may not think you like me, Mr. McCrea. But I've been around the block a few times and I know men. So, I'm prepared to bide my time. Marriages have been known to come apart. Maybe I can do a few things to facilitate that."

"It won't happen, Ms. Sykes. You can bide your time into eternity. I'll never be interested in you."

"We'll see, Rory McCrea. We'll just see about that."

Wednesday, the 20th of December, Rory got home about 5:30 to find Kurt's low-slung sports car in the front driveway. Opening the mudroom door and coming in through the kitchen, he saw Marta and Kurt sitting in the small breakfast nook at the kitchen table.

"Hi, Rory," Marta said. "Kurt stopped by so I invited him to stay for a cup of coffee and some fruitcake."

"Hello, Kurt. Are you one of those rare individuals who actually *likes* fruitcake?"

"It's not bad. Not something I'd ask for necessarily, but I don't mind a bit of it now and then."

"Sit down, Rory, and I'll pour you a cup, too. Something to warm you up. And some fruitcake, too, if you want it."

"Yep, cut me a huge slice. I ate lunch early and we had a dozen hay deliveries because Jay posted a notice that we will be closed Friday and not open up again until the 27ᵗʰ, so I'm starving."

"Tough day, then?" Kurt asked.

"Fairly rugged, yes. About emptied the barn of hay bales this afternoon. Must have moved a few tons between loading and unloading. I've got hay coming in here tomorrow as they're predicting snow and I don't want to be left hanging. That'll about end our hay supply at the feed store unless Jay can get another load in right after Christmas."

Marta set a plate in front of him and poured Rory a big mug full of coffee, then topped off Kurt's cup, too. She put the coffee pot back on its base and returned, placing another plate with several more slices of fruitcake on the table.

"Rory," Kurt began, "can I ask a serious question of you?"

"Fire away, Kurt."

Kurt frowned. "It might be best if I spoke with you in private."

"There are no secrets between Marta and me, so whatever you want to say, spit it out."

"Okay, but . . . a . . . twice in the last couple of weeks, I've obtained tickets to something. A Christmas Dance at the Elks Lodge in Butte. An ice-skating extravaganza in Missoula. Both times I asked Amber if she would like to go, and both times she told me she was interested in someone else and didn't care to go out with me. I don't usually ask who might have supplanted me, but she was acting so coy, I did ask. She said she had a thing for someone who worked in the feed store. She was crazy about him. She didn't or wouldn't name anyone and I didn't press. You work there. Do you know who she's seeing?"

Rory and Marta's eyes locked over the table's width. He shook his head in a barely perceptible 'no' but Marta's temper was already firing up. She looked loaded and she was gunning for bear.

"I believe Amber might just be in hot pursuit of my husband, Kurt. Rory said she's been in several times and always seeks him out."

"You?" Kurt asked. "You're seeing Amber?"

"I'm not seeing anyone, Kurt. Somehow she got it in her mind that I was interested in her. She's been to the store on lots of days and always wants me to wait on her. She's been a bit free with her hands, too, using the least excuse to rub my back or lay her hand over mine.

"Last Monday, she came in for algae treatment stuff for her birdbath. Behind the shelves, she started running her hand down my back and when she went below my belt, I took her by the arm and marched her across the street to The Hen's House, bought her a cup of latte and did my best to disabuse her of the notion that I liked her.

"Told her that her repeated advances at the store amounted to harassment and if she persisted, I'd be forced to get an order of protection served on her. I left her sitting there in the booth and went back to work. Next thing I know, she's in the feed store again wanting to buy a snow shovel."

"You must have done something to encourage her in the first place. Women don't just pursue a man for no reason," Kurt mused.

"I've done nothing of the sort. Other than be friendly at dinner and at the concert, I've never indicated anything else in the way of interest in her. But she thinks her feminine wiles will win me over, I guess. I have no interest in Amber. She's wasting her time if she thinks I'd ever be interested in her."

"That's not very complimentary to Amber. What's wrong with her? She seems like a nice woman and she's got looks aplenty."

"She's fine, Kurt, and she's pretty, too, but she's not my type and besides, I'm married."

"Don't make that condition sound like such an afterthought, husband mine. Maybe if you were more upfront about being married, you might find women less attracted to you."

"There's a wedding ring on my finger that I never take off, Marta. I am upfront about being married."

"Really? Is that before or after you flirt or give some female those long appraising looks? If a man gives me that sort of once-over, I would probably think he saw something interesting in me. Maybe that's why Amber thinks you've got the hots for her."

"Whose side are you on here?"

"Well, I just think you must have somehow put the notion in Amber's mind that you were interested in her."

Rory got up from the table and put his plate and cup in the sink, running water in the cup. Without another word he left the kitchen and went to his office where he pulled out the checkbook to write a check for the hay that would be delivered the next day. Closing his office door he leaned back in his swivel chair and tried to curb his anger. He didn't much hold with airing family problems in front of strangers, even if the stranger wasn't so strange to Marta. That she would accuse him of leading Amber on in front of Kurt sent his Irish temper into overdrive.

Once he'd cooled off slightly, he walked back through the kitchen and out the mudroom door to feed sheep and horses before dinner. Kurt, he noticed, stopped in mid-sentence when he appeared, and both Bancroft and Marta gave him a weak smile. That conspiratorial smile from each of them had his thermometer again threatening to shoot up to the boiling stage.

Anger, Rory noted, as he threw hay and grain in the wagon, always made feeding easier and quicker. There were no wasted moments when he was sore about something. He didn't linger to accommodate a sheep that came up for a scratch behind an ear. He didn't stop to rub a horse's nose or hang around the barn to chitchat with the drovers. It was like he was standing outside himself—looking at himself with clinical eyes when he was mad—observing the results of his anger.

The results of his anger were always the same. He turned inward and got quiet, and became extremely efficient at any task that happened to be at hand. His words were curt if he spoke at all, and he channeled his anger into movements that were both short and spare in nature.

Only the pell-mell sound of Todd's boots on the barn floor tempered his anger.

"Where you been, buddy?" Rory snatched Todd up and swung him around twice.

"I took a nap with bear," Todd informed him when he was again standing up.

"I'm tired, too. Could I borrow bear after dinner so I could take a nap?"

Todd frowned and thought that over for several moments before finally saying, "Yeth."

"You don't like anyone else to mess with bear, do you?"

"No. I love bear. I like hith fur. Ith thoft."

"Sure is. Say, how'd you like to go shopping with me and Aunt Marta this Saturday? I don't have to work, so maybe we'll go to the big mall in Missoula and you can sit on Santa's knee and tell him what you want for Christmas."

"I already thent Thanta a letter. I told him I wath good and I will leave him milk and two cupcakth. Do you think Thanta will know I'm here at your houth? How can I leave him milk and cupcakth here, Uncle Rory?"

The world is a scary place, even when you're four, Rory thought. He smiled down at the lisping inquisitor.

"Santa knows where you are, and besides, we'll be going home to your house on Sunday, the day before Santa comes, so you can leave him the milk and cupcakes at your house."

"Ith Eric all better?"

"Yes, he went home yesterday. I think he's better now. Your mama called last night to say he seems to be back to being Eric, and she said she missed you something awful, too, so you'd better hurry home to her so she can give you all the kisses she's been storing up for you while you were gone."

"How many kitheth did thee thore up? Can we go home now, Uncle Rory? I mith Mama really bad."

"I think she said she had 200 kisses to give you when you get home. You'd better stay with me the next four days and eat up lots of food so you'll be strong enough to hold up 200 kisses."

"Oh, Uncle Rory, kitheth aren't heavy. They are light like butterfly wingth. Mama theth that all the time."

"That's what she says, huh? Then I guess she's right."

Rory lifted Todd into the feed bin to begin filling the oat buckets for the horses. Marta came running down the hill and stopped breathless just inside the barn doors.

"Rory, is Todd here? I went up to check on him when Kurt left and his bed was empty."

"He's in the oat bin filling buckets."

"Oh, thank God. I didn't know what to think or where to imagine he'd gotten off to. I called all over the house but he didn't answer." She heaved a big sigh of relief. "Dinner will be served shortly, so hurry along with the chores, okay?"

"Yes."

His reply was clipped and she stood there a minute frowning. Without saying anything else, he turned his back on her and went to help Todd lift the buckets brimming with oats out of the feed bin.

"We'd better get a hustle on, partner. Dinner is waiting on us," he told Todd, pulling the small bundle of energy out of the bin and carrying him around to let him spill the eight buckets of oats into the horses' feed troughs.

In the kitchen, he held Todd on his raised knee while he scrubbed the pudgy hands clean under the kitchen sink's faucet, washing his own big mitts in the process. Plopping Todd down on his booster seat in the chair beside his, Rory sliced up Todd's chicken into bite-sized pieces and poured some gravy on his mashed potatoes. Todd dove in like he was starving and Rory had to smile as the small-sized fork made rapid inroads into the stuff on his plate.

"Don't forget the green beans, cowboy. You know it makes Consuela sad if you don't eat your vegetables."

Todd made a face, but dutifully speared a green bean and ate it.

That was the way conversation went all through dinner, like it was just Todd and Rory at the table. The drovers and Consuela kept glancing in his direction as Rory continued to ignore everyone but Todd. As soon as dinner was over, Rory picked Todd up and took him up for a bath and then played a game of Hi-Ho Cherry-O with him at the small table in his bedroom. After a couple of bedtime stories, he tucked a sleepy Todd in with bear and left the room.

He sat down in his office with a sheepherder's magazine and began reading about market trends and new feeding procedures. Marta appeared at the door and he glanced up, then returned to the article.

"Are you angry?" she asked.

He lowered the magazine to look at her.

"I was pretty steamed this afternoon. I've cooled down a bit now."

"Were you mad Kurt was here?"

"No."

"Well, what then? I sure don't like the silent treatment."

He didn't immediately reply.

"Was it something Kurt said?"

"No. Something you said."

"What?"

"I came home the other night and you were asking me about what Phil told you about the women who patronize the feed store. I told you something in jest about flirting with them or ranking them, or giving them a long look. I didn't expect to hear it being flung back at me in the form of an accusation this afternoon.

"I especially didn't expect you to accuse me of encouraging women to develop an interest in me in front of Bancroft. Some things are best not discussed in the company of strangers."

"Oooh. Touchy, touchy! But when you say 'I'm married,' like it was the last thing you'd think of when women come on to you, that didn't go over so well with me, either."

"It's not the last thing I think of. It's always front and center in my mind. That's what made your comment such a kicker. I *could* come on to them when they come on to me. I don't, but I could. Because I don't ever do what you were accusing me of, it frankly pissed me off that you *were* accusing me of that.

"It left me thinking—if you believe I'm encouraging such behavior on their parts when I'm not—why am I refraining? If you're going to believe the worst, why am I behaving like a choirboy? May as well do what you think I'm doing. Couldn't be hung any worse as a sheep than a lamb.

"And what's worse, when Kurt goes running to Amber to tell him about this afternoon, the news of our squabble will make her all the more aggressive because she'll think there's friction between us."

"It seems she'd have just cause to believe that, Rory. There is friction between us. You think I like hearing from Kurt that his girlfriend has the hots for someone at the feed store?"

"You didn't need to inform him it was me she was dogging."

"So, if this is our first major fight, I need to know how long your anger is going to be in play. Will you be over the silent treatment by breakfast? By the time we need to go to Missoula? Will you still be giving me those looks at the family's Christmas reunion?"

He smiled at her then. "I think I could probably nourish it until about bedtime. The Irish are quick to anger, but it never lasts for long. About the time I see you naked— between taking off your clothes and climbing into your flannel nightgown—it'll likely be quick to fade into nothing."

He stood up and walked to the doorway. Looking down into her eyes, he seemed to come to some sort of resolution. "Or maybe my anger is over now," he told her, tipping up her face to kiss her.

"I'm sorry for what I said," she apologized.

"I'm sorry for my anger, too. I'm going to print up a big sign to wear at work. *MARRIED TO THE WORLD'S BEST WIFE, NOT INTERESTED IN OTHER WOMEN* it will say. I'll wear it like one of those sandwich boards people parade around in to advertise stuff."

"Oh, Rory. Don't be a goose. Just maybe keep the flirting and those observations and rankings dialed back a bit, okay?"

"Yeth, I will," he lisped, Todd style.

Friday morning early, Rory went to feed and met the other four drovers in the barn.

"I've got 300 bales of hay coming in this afternoon. I'd appreciate it if some of you could help Phil and me unload it and stack it in the hay barns."

"When that store going to get squeeze tractor to unload?" Enrique asked. "Easier."

"I know. That thing can unload 50-60 bales at one time—unlike Phil and me. We can unload two bales at a time, but only if Phil's back doesn't hurt."

"We will be here when the hay comes," Enrique assured him.

"Thanks. I'll give you a Christmas bonus."

The feed store truck could only handle about 60 bales at a time, so they made five trips all told. It filled Rory with a sense of security to have that many bales in the barns, but it also depleted his bank account to a large degree. By the time the hay was all unloaded, all six of them were ready for a drink. The drovers piled onto the back of the hay truck and rode into Butte with Rory and Phil. They waited in the store for the last half hour before quitting time, then all six of them hit the tavern for dinner and drinks. Rory designated himself as the driver to take them home, so the drovers had a few *cervezas*, followed by more than a couple *margaritas*. By eight o'clock they were pretty well tanked and growing jollier by the minute.

"*Muy borracho*," Juan admitted, stumbling as he tried to get into Rory's truck for the ride home.

"*Espero su esposas no muy colérico esta noche*," Rory told Juan and Enrique. "I hope your wives aren't mad at me because you're drunk."

Back at the ranch, they disbanded and went their separate ways. Rory, being the only sober one in the bunch, was left to feed all 600 sheep and was treated to some very heated exchanges when he pulled up to feed Juan and Enrique's flocks.

Both Dulce and Melinda were yelling at their husbands in their respective trailers, but because they were screaming in Basque, Rory wasn't able to understand much more than the tone of their voices. As he began doling out hay and grain to the sheep, Enrique and Juan both came out and tried to help Rory feed if for no other reason than to escape the wrath of both their wives.

"*Muy mal*, no?" Rory commiserated.

Juan and Enrique grinned. "*Beber como una cuba—no vale la pena.*"

When Rory got back to the house, Manuel and Ricardo had stumbled up to their rooms and were flopped across their beds, snoring. He pulled the boots from their feet and covered them up with blankets. Marta arrived at the doorway just as Rory was tucking Ricardo in.

"Drunk?"

"Yep, pretty much so. Enrique and Juan's wives were reading them the riot act. Enrique told me it wasn't worth it—not worth all that yelling—to drink like a fish. Dulce and Melinda were both raising Cain, that's for sure. I'm surprised you couldn't hear it clear up here."

"Why did you let them get so tanked?"

"They worked hard this afternoon. It's almost Christmas, so I took them out for dinner and told them I'd stay sober so they could enjoy themselves. They took a bit more advantage of the 'enjoy yourselves' than they should have, but other than mad wives and sore heads come tomorrow, they'll be none the worse for wear in the morning."

"Are you still planning to go to Missoula tomorrow?"

"Yeah. Right after I finish feeding. Can you and Todd be ready by then?"

"Yes. I put him to bed early, so he'd be well rested by tomorrow. We'd better go early and shop fast as we have to come back and wrap it all so we can leave for Boise early Sunday morning. I need to get all Todd's clothes washed up and put back in the suitcase sometime tomorrow night."

"There never are enough hours, are there? Phil and I made five trips this afternoon and thank the powers that be, we didn't encounter any Smokies between here and the feed store in Butte cause we were pushing 80 mph most of the way both directions."

"I wish you wouldn't do stuff like that. I don't want to be like Kelsey. Learning you've been killed on the road."

"You'd miss me then—if I wasn't around?"

"Yes." Tears welled in her eyes thinking about the possibility.

"C'mon wife. Let's go to bed. It's been a long, hard day and I could use the rest."

On Saturday they set off early with Todd to shop in Missoula. Todd required a pit stop about halfway to the mall because he'd consumed four cups of hot chocolate for breakfast. The mall was teeming with last-minute shoppers. Marta suggested that they split up and she'd go one way while Rory and Todd went another. They tore their list in two and set off to shop, promising to meet in the central food court at one in the afternoon.

When they came together for lunch, Marta told Rory she'd found the cutest little shop in a far corner of the mall called Glo-Glass Ltd. run by a woman from Australia named Moraine Benny. She opened a box full of glass hearts each with a different inclusion inside that sparkled. There were pinks and reds, greens and turquoises and many shades in between. One heart for each of the women in the McCrea clan. Each heart was attached to a ribbon reflecting the same major color as the heart's inclusion.

"Aren't they pretty? Think your sisters and nieces will like them?" Marta asked.

"They're beautiful and very unique. I'm sure they'll be a hit."

"Good. Did you get the travel calendars for the men?"

"I did. Todd and I took them back to the truck already."

"What about for all the nephews?"

"Todd and I covered that base, too. The older ones are getting video games—the latest ones, so I know they don't have them already. The middle kids get some hand-held games that you stick a cartridge card into to play. And the youngest get Lego blocks or Lincoln Logs to build stuff with. For Todd, I got a Fisher-Price f-a-r-m s-e-t," Rory spelled out. It has s-h-e-e-p and c-h-i-c-k-e-n-s and h-o-r-s-e-s and p-i-g-s in it and a big b-a-r-n with some f-e-n-c-e-s and a t-r-a-c-t-o-r. I figured since he likes to help out at our place, he might have fun with that. For Kelsey's baby and Eric, I got some plush animals like bear to sleep with and a toy each with buttons to push to make bells ring or pinwheels spin."

"Did you get Kelsey something?"

"Yep. The requisite bottle of her favorite perfume."

"So, are we done, then?"

"No. I still need to get something for Mom and Walter. Mom said she could use a new warm robe, so maybe you'd help me with that one. I hate the looks I get while wandering around in lady's lingerie. And for Walter, there's a hand-sized drill that has lots of different pieces with it for sanding in tight places or creating designs in wood. Thought with his love of making lamps and stuff, he'd enjoy that more than a tie or a pair of socks. And then there's you. I still have to find something for you. If you'll take Todd in hand and hunt Mom a robe up, I'll get Walter's gift and yours."

"So why am I taking Todd with me?"

"Todd's not very good at keeping secrets. If I take him, your gift will never be a surprise."

After they ate, Marta started down the mall with Todd. Rory watched until they were out of sight, then headed for the store he'd seen that had what Marta had told him reminded her of her childhood. In a store with all sorts of breakable glass items he got her two gifts. The first was a snow globe with a small child inside making snowballs while standing next to an igloo. In one of their previous conversations she'd said her father used to build her an igloo in the winter. The second gift was a delicate, hand-blown glass swan barometer that could be filled with liquid. It would indicate the changes in weather and forecast approaching storms. It was also an item she remembered from childhood. Her mother had always had a similar glass barometer. He just hoped in the hassle of wrapping and sorting the gifts, it wouldn't be broken.

The last gift for Marta was something he couldn't keep secret. The padded-seat rocking chair for the nursery that he put into the truck's camper was not easily disguised. He tucked the well-cushioned snow globe and swan into an empty wooden box to protect them, then went back to get Walter's drill.

Rory made Marta and Todd sit down on a bench on the mall's concourse while he loaded the rest of the gifts into his camper so Marta might not notice the rocking chair. When he got home, he planned to do the unloading and take the rocker down to the barn. He would save it as a belated gift until they got home from Boise.

Heading back into the mall, Rory ran into a parade. Bunches of elves and St. Nick, too, were winding their way to Santa's House at the north end of the mall.

"Hey, Todd, don't you want to see Santa?" Rory asked when he located the bench they were waiting on.

"Yeth."

"Well, c'mon then. Santa went that way," he said, pointing down the long length of the mall.

"Maybe you can give Todd a piggy-back ride. I think both pairs of our feet are tired."

"Are you okay, Marta?" Rory asked, concerned that it was her pregnant state that was making her tired.

"I'm fine. Just the extra weight makes my legs tired quicker these days. It's not so bad where I'm walking on carpet or dirt, but these floors are hard as rocks."

"Do you want to sit here until I come back with Todd?"

"No, I want to see him on Santa's knee. Just don't march off like a house-afire, okay?"

"Okay, we'll just mosey along and you can sit down if you need to."

It took them about half an hour to reach Santa's House. Marta collapsed on a bench with a good view of the platform where Santa sat and pulled a disposable camera out of her purse. Rory and Todd got at the end of the line that had about 25 kids waiting to voice their fondest desires in Santa's ear. Rory took some good-natured ribbing about standing in a line full of children.

"What are you going to ask for? A Corvette? A Hummer?" one guy teased.

"Nope. I want a big set of Tinker Toys. I plan to build me a plane to fly in," Rory shot back.

"He likth helicopterth," Todd announced. "Uncle Rory let me drive a helicopter oneth when. . . ."

Todd suddenly got very quiet and hid behind Rory's legs. A worried frown creased his forehead. Rory noticed he was upset and that he kept looking at Santa. Rory wondered if Todd might be nervous about sitting on the Jolly One's knee.

"You a chopper jockey?" the guy asked, before Rory could ask Todd what was wrong.

"Nope. Sheep rancher."

"Then maybe you'd better be asking for a mild winter with lots of rain so the grass grows."

"Ain't that the truth," Rory said.

"Uncle Rory, Mama theth you're not thupothed to thay 'ain't.'"

"I stand corrected, Todd. 'Isn't that the truth' is better English. My apologies."

"A little grammar professor?" the guy asked, now grinning broadly.

"Yep. Appears so. For all his small size, he's got a mind like an elephant. He never forgets anything. Sometimes that's an advantage and sometimes it isn't."

"Have you been good, Todd?" the guy asked.

Todd didn't reply.

"The man is asking you a question, Todd."

"Mama theth I am not allowed to thpeak to thrangerth."

"You can if I'm here to protect you. Have you been good?"

"Yeth, I'm alwayth good. But I forgot about the thranger rule before. Will Thanta be angry, Uncle Rory? I thed I drove a helicopter. I didn't mean to talk to that man before."

"No, Santa won't be mad because you forgot the stranger rule. He knows I was here, and when I'm here, you can talk to strangers because I wouldn't let anyone harm you."

The frown disappeared from Todd's face, and Rory couldn't help but smile as Todd resolutely marched up to sit on Santa's knee. Midway up the steps, Todd turned around and asked in a loud voice, "Ith Thanta a thranger, Uncle Rory?"

"No, Todd, Santa is definitely *not* a stranger. And I'm still here to protect you."

Marta came forward and took several shots of Todd on Santa's knee. Rory moved off to one side of the platform and when Santa twice raised his eyebrows over one of Todd's lisped requests, Rory translated.

Todd gave Santa a huge hug. Santa admonished him to be a good boy until Christmas to which Todd solemnly answered, "Yeth, I will."

They left for home shortly after Todd's Santa visit.

After a late dinner, Rory bathed Todd and put him to bed, then went down to unload the truck's camper of all the gifts so he and Marta could wrap them. Before he went back in with the many shopping bags, he took the rocking chair down to the barn and hid it in the back corner of the loft.

Marta was asleep on the sofa when he finished bringing in the gifts. He pulled the afghan over her and let her sleep. Sitting at the dining-room table, he fell to the chore of attaching Christmas paper, bows and nametags to nearly a hundred gifts. He'd need to cull another bunch of aging ewes to sell for meat if he hoped to accomplish paying his Christmas credit card bills in January. Without Marta's savings, he would probably need most of the year to pay them off.

It was very quiet and Rory felt the tug of sleep, but he couldn't quit until all the gifts were wrapped and stowed in the camper again. He did up everything, but when he came to the box of glass hearts, he didn't know if Marta had chosen them specifically for each of his sisters and nieces or if any heart would suffice. Gently he shook her awake.

"Marta, did you have specific people in mind for each heart?"

She sat up and rubbed her eyes. "What time is it?"

"Nearly two."

"Oh, Rory. I didn't mean to leave all the work to you. I need to wash Todd's clothes and get them in the dryer, too."

"Consuela washed them and dried them."

"How? I didn't say anything to her about that."

"I called her while we were shopping. I hustled you out of the house so quickly this morning—uh, yesterday morning—that I knew you forgot about the clothes."

"Did I ever tell you what a sweetheart you are?"

"You might have mentioned it a time or two."

"Thank you for calling Consuela."

"You're welcome—but what about the hearts?"

"Yes, I selected them with specific people in mind. Let me put each one with its nametag, and we can both wrap. Unless you're sick of wrapping already?" she asked, noticing the huge pile of already done-up gifts.

"A cup of joe and I'll be ready to wrap. You want one?"

"No, but some hot chocolate would be nice."

"You got it. Sit down and start labeling which hearts go to whom."

It was almost four in the morning when he put the last of the presents into the camper and locked the door. Marta was already asleep when he crawled into bed, so he kissed her cheek and doused the lights. He'd told her they'd need to leave by noon, which meant he would only get about three hours of sleep. He had to feed, dispense gifts for the drovers and their families and make sure all the men had the schedule down for the three days he'd be gone.

He got up at seven and double-timed it through all his chores, then spent an hour giving presents to each of the drovers, their wives and children. Both Enrique and Juan invited him to share a drink of Christmas cheer, but he declined because he had to drive to Boise.

"*Más tarde*," he told them. "Later, when I get home again."

By noon they were on the highway to Boise. Todd and bear strapped in the back seat and Marta in the front. She held his hand for the first fifty miles.

"Are you sure you're not too tired, Rory?"

"I'm fine for now. And getting out every 80 miles so Todd can make yellow snow will probably keep me awake."

"He's sound asleep."

"We wore him out yesterday."

"Wasn't that just the cutest thing? Asking if Santa was a stranger halfway up the steps?"

"Yeah. There are times when I wish I had a video camera and could record things like that. We could have sent the tape to Funniest Home Videos and maybe won a fortune."

"Are you excited about seeing your family?"

"A little. It's not like they weren't all there at our place a month ago, but, yeah, it'll be good to see them again."

"Bet Bailey and Mike will be happy to have Todd back."

"I know. And you'll likely be happy to give him back."

"Oh, no, Rory. He's a really sweet child. I didn't mind keeping him."

"But you could use a break from all those trips to the barn, couldn't you?"

"Well, yes, but I'm losing my little hungry man. The pancake mix never got stale in the time Todd was with us, and we went through three bottles of syrup, too."

"I'm glad I'm not going to have to feed him as a teenager. I'd be standing on a corner in Missoula with a tin cup trying to keep him filled up when he's fifteen."

The trip was uneventful even though the roads were snow packed at the higher elevations. They pulled into Boise at 11 p.m. and Rory carried a sound-asleep Todd into his sister's house.

"I told him you had 200 kisses stored up to give him, so maybe you'd better ply him with those in the morning. And don't forget Santa's milk and cupcakes, too, or he'll be up at dawn worrying."

"Rory, I can't begin to tell you how much Mike and I. . . ."

"Could we hold off with all that, Bailey? Marta's asleep in the truck and I need to get her to the house and into bed. We'll see you tomorrow, okay? At the homestead?"

"Yes. Sean's moved in with his family out there, so that's where we're all going."

"Goodnight, Sis. Marta and I are going to miss Todd. The ranch will be awful quiet when we get home. Better chain him to you when we head back to Montana. I might be tempted to steal him from you."

Bailey stood on tiptoes and kissed his cheek. "See you tomorrow."

Maire had their bedroom all made up with the bed turned down when they came to the house. Rory carried Marta up the stairs and helped her undress. He pulled her flannel nightgown out of the suitcase for her and once she had it on he tucked her under the covers, then got in on the opposite side.

"No midnight Mass tonight?" she mumbled.

"Guess not. But maybe early Mass tomorrow."

"Oh, I hope not. I could sleep for a year. Goodnight, Rory."

"Night, love."

He turned out the light and fell instantly asleep.

Chapter Eleven

"Morning, Mom. I hope you don't mind me starting the coffee."

"Whatever are you doing up at this hour, Rory? You didn't get in till so late, I thought you'd sleep until noon."

"I have to get up every morning to feed sheep and horses. Hard to break the habit."

"Is Marta still asleep?"

"Yep. Dead to the world. She's had a rough couple of weeks chasing after Todd."

"That was so nice of you both, taking him in that way. I know it was a great relief to Bailey and Michael to know he was in good hands and safe while Eric was in Denver."

"It wasn't any trouble. Todd's a good kid. What are *you* doing up this early?"

"I'm cooking the turkey for Christmas. It's so huge, I have to get it in the oven by 8 a.m. or it won't be done in time to eat."

"Anything I can do to help?"

"Sure. After I make the stuffing, you can hold the bird up so I can cram the stuffing into it. With these old arthritic fingers, I can never get the legs out of the wire contraption to stuff the bird, and if I do get them out, then I can't get them back in again. And twenty-five pounds is more than I care to lift, so once I get it stuffed, you can put the turkey in the roaster and slide it into the oven."

Setting his coffee cup within reach on the kitchen counter, Rory volunteered to help make the stuffing, too. He sliced celery and diced onion while she tore bread into small chunks. In the roaster where the bird would go, he mixed the bread, onion and celery with a bit of milk to moisten it, then salted and peppered the stuffing, adding sage to the mix under the watchful

113

eyes of his mother. He rinsed the bird off in the sink, removing the giblets from the neck cavity and the neck from the inside of the bird.

"Turn the bird on its belly," his mom instructed.

When he did so, she stretched out the skin of the neck cavity, filling the hole with part of the stuffing, then securing the skin to the back of the turkey with two metal skewers.

"Now, roll it onto its back."

Rory flipped the bird over and held it, bottom up, while she put the bulk of the stuffing into that cavity. When she finished, he tucked the legs back inside the wire brace. Once Maire had removed the rest of the dressing from the roaster pan, he slid the bird into it.

"Take another two skewers and put one in each wing tip to hold the wings to the breast so they don't get too well done or burn. I'll make a packet with the neck and the giblets and the rest of the stuffing and we'll put it in the roaster with the turkey."

"How hot do you want the oven?" he asked, moving the rack to the lowest position.

"Oh, I like to start with 350° and cook it for an hour, then reduce the heat to 325° for the rest of the time. You have to leave it in a lot longer at 325, but it'll be falling off the bones tender for the longer, slower cooking. Bird this size, takes seven or eight hours."

"I thought you weren't supposed to stuff turkeys—something about the stuffing not getting hot enough or letting bacteria build up."

"I've been stuffing a huge turkey in this same way for almost 40 years, Rory. To date, I don't think anyone ever got sick eating one of my turkeys or the dressing. I guess it could be dangerous if you don't cook the bird long enough, but I've never had a problem."

"The voice of experience, huh?"

"I should hope so. Get me out the milk and butter, can you? I'm going to stir me up some yeast rolls."

"Good. I love your yeast rolls."

"Were the roads bad coming over?"

"Snow packed, but if you took your time and didn't get crazy, they were okay. There are always a few idiots on the road who want to be where they're going yesterday. Saw a couple of them upside down in the median, but most people were being cautious."

"I worry about you driving so far. I didn't realize what a trip it was until we came for Thanksgiving."

"Oh, it's not so bad. I've driven it so often, I think I could drive it in my sleep."

"Do you want some breakfast? There are eggs and bacon in the icebox."

"I can wait. Once Marta and Walter come down is soon enough. I might swipe one of your donuts, though."

"Help yourself. Walter likes the maple frosted ones, so don't eat all of those."

"Don't worry. I only like the glazed ones."

"The paper should be on the front walk by now. Walter would probably appreciate it if you fetched it into the house. He complains about the cold and his bad knees, especially when the steps and walk are icy."

"Sure, Mom. I can save Walter a trip. Ought to get you a dog that will bring in the paper."

"Oh, Lordy! No thank you. It's bad enough I have to stumble over and around Walter all day long without having to stumble over a dog, too, or clean up after one."

The porch thermometer read 4° and the snow was so brittle it crackled as he stepped on it. Clouds were piling up on the western horizon, threatening more snow before the day was over. Had it been warmer, Rory would have taken a drive up to the high meadows where he used to run sheep in the summers, but as cold as it was, he didn't want to chance getting stuck. You could freeze to death being foolish like that.

"Mom, how's Kelsey and baby Daniel?" Rory asked, laying the frozen paper on the kitchen table.

"Just fine, Son. Danny has already put on a couple of pounds. Kelsey said he's a good baby and only wakes her up a couple times a night. She'll be there for dinner tonight, I hope. Danny is the spitting image of Aidan—reddish hair already and his eyes are going to stay blue, I think."

"Was there some problem why she might not come?"

"Sean and Kelsey had some words. He told her it might be upsetting to the rest of the family for her to come—it would make everyone remember that Aidan was gone—cast a pall over the festivities. But I called her and said she was welcome to come and we'd all be a bit sad whether she came or didn't come. Kelsey was Aidan's wife and Danny is his son, so they're part of the family to my way of thinking."

"Sean's moved into the homestead? Was that what Bailey said? I was so tired last night, I don't know if I heard her right."

"Yes. Sean and Alice and their children moved in right after you and Marta got married and went to Montana. I don't think their kids were particularly happy to be stuck that far out of town, but Sean insisted that the homestead needed someone to live in it and keep it up."

"Sean has assumed Aidan's role? He's making the rules for the rest of us now? He's the one to decide who gets to celebrate the holidays at the old rancho? And Kelsey might not be welcome?"

"I think Sean fancies himself the new leader of the McCrea clan, yes. I don't think the rest of your brothers and sisters will let him get as controlling as Aidan tended to be. It might have been you filling that role, but you moved off so far away, it left a void when Aidan died."

"I wouldn't want that role, Mom. Not for all the sheep in New Zealand. I just hope Sean . . . well, I hope he's more benevolent than Aidan was. I never thought Sean had as nasty a side as Aidan. Sean can be full of himself, but he was never mean about it."

"I heard what you told him when we were there at your place. Love and harmony would prevail on your ranch. I wish it would prevail here, too. Never saw such a bunch for bickering over straws. There must have been some highly competitive genes in Patrick McCrea that got passed down into the ones he fathered."

"And that gene was missing in Daniel McIlvey?"

"I think so. You and Chris are certainly not cut from the same cloth as the rest. You and Chris have always been sweeter in nature. You two see the fun in life, not just the next chance to make a million dollars. You both got the sensible genes and the ones for humor. That's why Bailey chose to leave Todd with you and Marta. She knows you still can enjoy life—you're not so uptight about things."

"Meaning I'd rather play Hi-Ho Cherry-O with Todd than phone in my next stock purchase to my broker? Maybe if I had less of those sweeter genes and more of those competitive ones, I might be in better financial shape."

"Are things bad for you and Marta?"

"Things are tight. I took a job through the winter working at the feed store in Butte. With the baby on the way and having to buy hay, we're skating on pretty thin ice right now."

"Do you need money, Rory?"

"I always need money, Mom, but if you're offering me some of yours, I wouldn't take it. I'd thank you for the offer, but I'd decline it. All my life nobody in this family thought I could make a go of it without Aidan's hand in my affairs. AmeriBasque Ranch is my chance to show them they were wrong. I'd sooner eat beans seven days a week than take anything from any of you."

"Rory, I never thought that about you. I sometimes felt bad because Aidan got the land you wanted, but I know how levelheaded you are and you're tenacious, too. Where Aidan wanted the moon today, you were willing to put sweat and effort into getting where you wanted to be—even if it took years."

"It likely *will* take that long—decades, maybe. So, if you thought that, why did it seem like you were always siding with Aidan?"

"I always thought it was Aidan who couldn't make a go of it on his own. Yes, he acted like he was so smart and he did make good money, but he trampled on so many people to get where he got to, I knew someday his sins would catch up with him.

"I think he recognized something was lacking in himself. He adopted that know-it-all façade so nobody else would see he wasn't nearly as sure of his prowess as he'd like you to believe. That's why I felt I needed to bolster his ego and assure him he was just fine."

"Guess I didn't see it like that. Seemed to me you loved him more than the rest of us. Favored him. To my eyes, his ego outweighed his common sense—by far—even when he was a kid."

"I'm sorry if you thought I loved Aidan more than you. I didn't. I just saw you as a survivor with the ability to land on your feet. I worried that the first time Aidan encountered an immovable wall, he'd crumble like a clod of garden dirt and I knew he'd not be able to bounce back like I'd seen you do so many times.

"You always managed to make lemonade out of the lemons life handed you. If life had handed Aidan lemons like that, he would have sucked on them and the acid would have eaten him alive."

"When did you get so wise, Mom?"

"Oh, nearly 70 years of living. You tend to pick up a few tidbits of wisdom along the way. But, it's almost nine, and if we're going to get to the ten o'clock Christmas Day Mass, I suggest you wake Marta and I'll rouse Walter to get them started on the day."

"Rory?"

"Yep, it's me."

"What time is it?"

"Quarter to nine. Mom said for me to roust you out so we can go to Mass this morning."

"I'm still tired. Do we have to go?"

"No, rest if you want. I'll take Mom and Walter. You can lie here and smell the turkey cooking."

"Would you mind very much if I don't go?"

"Of course not. On Christmas, folks have the right to do exactly what they want to do. So rest while you can. I'll be back about noon, then if you want to go by Jack's place and say 'hello' we can do that."

"Maybe he'll be at Connie's place."

"So much the better. We can have a short visit with them both."

"I never realized how badly his legs got scarred in the fire. It was a real shock when he took off his trousers in our kitchen."

"Yeah, he got burned pretty good. I think he had something like15 skin grafts. Some they took from his thighs and his butt, so not only did he have the agony from his lower legs, but he couldn't sit down comfortably either. I'll never forget his screams while they were trying to cut away his pants from the burned flesh—or the smell of that burned flesh. Yuck! That's got to be one of the worst odors on this earth."

Marta was up and dressed by the time Rory, Maire and Walter returned from Mass. She'd cooked up bacon and eggs and made toast for their return and warmed it again in the microwave as they pulled into the driveway.

"Something smells good," Walter announced, coming through the kitchen door. "I'm *really* hungry."

"Good, Walter. Sit down and I'll serve it up."

"Looks like you've been busy, wife. I thought you wanted to rest."

"This little bit? Wasn't much of a chore. Not like fixing endless pancakes for Todd."

"This is a real treat to sit down to breakfast and not have to make it first," Maire said. "You found everything okay?"

"Yes. Hope you didn't mind me snooping in your refrigerator. I wasn't sure if you had some jam or not."

"It's really your icebox, Marta. It's just on loan to me."

"Please, don't feel that way. Rory and I are so pleased to have a place to stay when we come to Boise and I'm really glad to have you and Walter here to look after the house. Heaven only knows what it would look like if I'd had to rent it out. Renters don't always take such good care of someone else's property."

"Marta, Father Leahy sent his greetings after quizzing me up about why you weren't there. I told him you were great with child and rather tired, so he said he would forgive you for lying abed, since this is the season for celebrating another woman who was great with child."

"Does that mean I need to stuff a pillow under my maternity tops and waddle like a duck while I'm in Boise? I don't think I'm too great with child yet. I just started showing."

"Right. You haven't been able to fasten your jeans for six weeks now."

"Why don't you announce that to the whole of Boise, husband mine?"

He grinned at her. "Where shall I start? The steps of the Courthouse? The corner of Central and Main Street? Maybe hit the local radio station?"

"All three if you're so inclined. But don't be surprised if I let on like I don't know you at all."

"Hey, Mom, I'll do up the breakfast dishes and then, if it's okay with you and Walter, Marta and I might try to catch a visit with Jack Strauss."

"You don't have to do the dishes. Just go and have some fun while you're here. I have to stand guard over the turkey, so I don't mind rinsing off a few plates."

"What time are we due at Sean's?"

"I'd like to be there around 3:30 or 4."

"Okay, we'll be back by 3:00 to pick you up. Might have to move a few packages in the camper so the turkey will fit."

Jack was indeed at Connie's place when they stopped in. He looked pleased with himself and invited them in like he was quite used to being at Connie's house.

"I was hoping we'd get a chance to visit, Rory. You and Marta are a sight for sore eyes. While I'm thinking about it, I need to return a suit to you and an overcoat and some shoes. Sit down. Connie will be out in a minute. She's in the middle of whipping up a pecan pie."

Rory and Marta sank side-by-side onto the leather couch as Jack went up to retrieve Rory's borrowed clothes. When he came down again with everything but the shoes in plastic wraps from the dry cleaners, he had to root in the hall closet for Rory's suitcase and garment bag.

"Made yourself right at home, I see," Rory teased, as he went out to his truck with Jack to hang the clothes on the back seat's hooks. "I'll stick the shoes under the front seat if you'll give them to me."

Jack handed over the shoes and the suitcase.

"Did you get your mother settled?" Rory asked.

"Yes. It's quite nice, her apartment. They serve lunch and dinner every day, so I know she's getting proper nutrition and since the apartment held only a fraction of all the crap she'd accumulated, it seems really light and airy. I think she won't fall nearly as often with all the clutter gone.

"Because her memory is slipping, she didn't give me a hard time about tossing out the crap or giving it away. My sister lives close to Mom's new apartment, so she can look in on her and be sure she's doing well. How're things with you and Marta on the ranch?"

"Good. It's been pretty mild so far this winter. I'm working at the feed store in Butte to fill up the coffers. Marta plans to work until the first of March, so we're doing okay. Not great, but okay."

"Will she quit after the baby comes?"

"No. She said Ron offered to let her bring the baby to work so she can nurse. I guess he likes her work and was willing to make some accommodations."

"That's good, right?"

"We'll have to wait and see once the baby arrives. I don't want her to get so run down she gets sick. Her old boyfriend is a partner in the firm now, so if she wanted to stay home with the baby, that'd be okay, too."

"He's competition for her affections?"

"No, I don't think so. But he's got the fat wallet and the Ivy League education. If things get really tight at the ranch financially, the grass in Kurt's direction might begin to look greener."

"I don't see that happening, Rory. If any woman ever loved you with her whole heart, it's Marta."

"I don't know, Jack. Seems Kurt's current woman has got the hots for me, not Kurt, so that tends to complicate the scene a bit. Thought I might have to take out an order of protection against her last week. Once upon a time, I'd have been flattered, but since I got married, that sort of come-on by another woman just pisses me off. Her advances have caused a few sparks to fly on Marta's behalf."

"Ah, hell. Life is full of pitfalls. You can't help it if you're a babe magnet. Long as you just look and don't sample, there shouldn't be a problem."

"Marta suggested just last week that maybe I shouldn't look quite so often, so long or so hard."

"Geez, Rory. I just gave Connie the ring this morning. Maybe I ought to take it back if it means all my small pleasures—like eyeballing women—are going to be curtailed."

"Congratulations, Jack. I was wondering when you might work up the nerve to ask her to marry you. Have you set the date?"

"Not yet. June is the month for weddings, but it's Connie's busy catering season, too, so maybe late summer or early fall. Would you consider standing up for me as best man?"

"I would, yes. As long as you set a date long enough after the baby comes and I'm down from the meadows. Fall is when I'd be more likely to be able to take the time off."

"It kind of depends on Connie. She may not want to wait that long. "

"Sure, and I wouldn't want to get in the way of her decision. And I wouldn't be upset if you chose someone else to stand up with you if I can't be there when Connie wants to get married."

"You're one of my closest friends, Rory."

"Yeah, but if it's a Jewish ceremony, I'd probably need special dispensation from the Pope, or at least Father Leahy, to participate."

"We'll likely have an Episcopalian wedding since that's Connie's church. But she agreed to a Jewish ceremony, too. Guess you could take your pick if the Pope won't let you do both."

"Like I'm such a staunch Catholic I'd worry about what the Pope thought."

"We'd better go back in. If we leave the women with their heads together for too long alone, they'll have looked us up enough chores to last the week," Jack said.

"You're not even married yet and you're already learning the pitfalls."

They returned to the house and found Marta and Connie on the sofa looking at wedding gowns in a catalogue. Rory rolled his eyes at Jack and grinned.

"Well, Connie, are you going to let me see your dazzling diamond or not?" Rory asked.

Connie stuck out her hand and waggled her finger.

"Very impressive. I think Jack's got good taste in rocks and women both. I'm happy for you, Connie, but Jack's definitely getting the best of this deal. Good-looking woman, savvy businesswoman, and an excellent cook as well.

"Jack, if you come to the ranch and need dress clothes again, old man, you'd better have brought your own because within a year of being married to Connie, you'll be needing size 44s around the waist."

After an hour of chatting, Connie offered them a slice of pecan pie, but Rory and Marta both declined because of their pending dinner at the old homestead.

"We need to get going. If I know Mom, she's got the bird in its swaddling clothes and is standing on the porch ready to leave."

"It was good to see you both," Connie said. "I hope you'll both come for our wedding and bring the baby. Seeing your child might put the notion in Jack's mind that time's a-wasting. I want to have at least four, so the sooner he gets started, the better."

"Send him over at shearing time so I can work some of his spare tires from eating all those pecan pies off his middle. I promise to send him home with abs of steel."

"Jack told me about his shearing experience over Thanksgiving. I think I'd rather have the spare tires than have him bent over and hobbling from the physical abuse. Though the shearing doesn't seem to have left you all stove up."

"Did the first couple of years," Rory told her. "The first year, if I could have hired some of those Japanese women to walk on my back, I'd have shipped in a dozen or two."

It was on the dot of 3:30 when they pulled into the McCrea homestead. Only two other cars had arrived, a rental probably belonging to Chris and Ernesto, and Mike and Bailey's van. Rory and Marta carried in the turkey and some of the gifts, then Rory told Marta to save him a spot on the sofa while he toted in all the other presents.

Sean's kids, Annette, Sabrina, Nate and Riley, were nowhere to be seen, which, given previous Christmas' experience seemed odd to Rory. He was used to all the nieces and nephews crowding around, wanting to carry gifts into the house. After the third trip, they came down the stairs, their eyes red and their faces tear-stained.

"What's with the salt drops?" he asked.

"Our dog got in a fight with a coyote and came home all bloody. Mom tried to help him, but he just died. And Dad said we couldn't bury him because the ground's all frozen and all the company is coming."

"You'd feel better if he got buried?"

"Yes," Sabrina sobbed. "It's so cruel to just let Shiloh lie out there in the snow."

"C'mon, then. Go get your coats and hats and mittens and we'll give Shiloh a decent burial. I've got a pick and some shovels in the barn. Did Shiloh have a rug or a bed he liked to lie on?"

"He slept in the mudroom on a big pink blanket," Riley volunteered. "We could wrap him in that."

"Okay, you bring his blanket and we'll make him snug in it in the hole."

The kids scattered to get coats and Shiloh's blanket."

"Rory, I told those damn kids that dumb dog could wait until tomorrow. You don't have to do this now," Sean announced as the kids returned with their hats and coats.

"Wrong, Sean. I couldn't enjoy Christmas dinner or any of the festivities for thinking about a beloved dog left out there in the snow without a decent burial."

"Well, that's stupid. I'm not going to get all in a lather over a dumb dog."

"He's not dumb, Daddy. We loved Shiloh," Annette protested.

"Dumb enough to get all chewed up by a coyote."

That brought another freshet of tears from all four kids.

"Shut up, Sean. If you don't want to help, fine. But don't make the kids feel worse than they already feel."

"Ah, yes. Rory McCrea, the world's biggest bleeding heart."

"Yeah? Well at least mine is still pumping red blood, not ice water. Let's go, kids."

They followed him out to the barn where he located the pick and two shovels.

"Tell you what, guys. The ground outside is frozen, but here in the barn it's not all icy, so let's bury Shiloh in a corner of the barn, okay?"

"Okay, Uncle Rory," Nate said.

"Where is Shiloh?"

"On the other side of the house. Can you get him? It makes me sick to see him all covered in blood," Sabrina said.

"Sure. Riley, go fetch the pink blanket and I'll wrap him in that."

Rory came back with Shiloh bundled in the pink blanket, which he set in the corner near the stairs to the loft.

"Under the stairs the dirt isn't packed down so hard. Let's dig there. I'll loosen the dirt up with the pick and we'll pile it up over here until we get a big hole dug for Shiloh to lie in. Okay?"

He took off his sweater and hung it on a nail then plied the pick, making a square about four feet by four feet. Once the topsoil was loosened, he took the shovel and began to dig. In twenty minutes, he had a good deep hole dug and asked Nate to hand him the bundle with the dog in it. He placed the dog in the center of the hole and tucked the blanket firmly around Shiloh. He and Nate began shoveling the dirt back into the hole. When Nate got tired, Sabrina or Riley would take a turn, while Annette used a small garden hand spade to help. When the dirt was all filled in and level again, Rory found a small square of plywood in one of the stalls. He took a pint of white paint from the tack room and painted 'SHILOH' on the board, then placed it over the fresh grave.

"Give me all your hands," he told them.

Tucking two hands in each of his hands he bowed his head and they, following his lead, did likewise.

"Heavenly Father, who watches over all of us and all the animals, too, we're sending Shiloh to your Dog Heaven this afternoon. Please be sure he has a warm cloud to run and play on, a soft bed to sleep in, and plenty of good dog food to eat. Shiloh was a good dog and all these children loved him, so please, God, give Shiloh the same sort of love that Annette, Sabrina, Nate and Riley gave him.

"It says in Your Bible that not even a sparrow can fall from a tree that You don't know it and gather it home to be with You in Heaven, so we're sure you're gathering Shiloh into Your arms right now and we know he'll be even happier with You than he was on Earth. Keep Shiloh safe from harm. In Jesus' name we pray. Amen."

Four small voices each added an 'amen' to the prayer.

"Good job, guys. Now you have a Shiloh angel to watch over you." Rory pointed out the door of the barn to some fluffy white clouds on the horizon. "I think I can see him up there on that cloud right there, keeping his eye on you and wagging his tail."

"I see him, too, Uncle Rory. He's all better. He looks happy," Annette agreed.

"Yep, I think he's happy, too. Now, we'd better go in and eat before Grandma gets mad at us. She got up really early to cook that turkey."

The kids ran for the house to get washed up to eat while Rory stowed the pick and shovels back in the tack room. He was walking toward the barn door, pulling his sweater back over his head, when he ran smack into Christina, who threw her arms around him and whispered in his ear.

"What a dear, kind man you are, Rory. That was a beautiful thing you did for those kids, and that prayer was beautiful, too. I think you missed your calling. You should have become a priest."

"Oh, right, Chris. It took me hours to purge my conscience and my soul of all the women I'd romped in the hay with before Marta. That isn't a very strong selling point for the priesthood and celibacy."

"Well, it made those four kids a lot easier in both their souls and their minds to know that Shiloh wasn't lying out there all bloody in the snow until tomorrow. I could just strangle Sean. How could any father be that uncaring when he could see how upset they all were? You saw it in only a couple of minutes. I saw it that quickly, too. How could Sean not have seen it?"

"He saw it. He just chose to ignore it. You and I couldn't do that, but the sunburned Irish are adept at tuning out what they don't want to notice."

"I thought things might be different with Aidan gone, but I swear I do despair that anything will ever change. I love you, Rory, for easing the children's sorrow. Now come in out of the cold before you catch a chill."

"Yes, ma'am. That digging has put a powerful appetite on me. Best let all the serving dishes come to me last, as I'm likely to be scraping their bottoms onto my plate."

"After me, you come first," Chris challenged and took off running.

"I say we let Rory say the grace this year. I just heard him give a truly beautiful prayer out there in the barn," Chris said. "Will you say one, Rory?"

"It's not my house. It's not my place. The head of this household has always been the one to say grace at Christmas, Chris. I believe it's Sean's place to offer the grace at this table this year, since he's the one living here now."

Sean stood up and began, "Thank you Lord for all the bounty of this table. For this family gathered to celebrate the holiday and for all the gifts that grace the tree in the big room yonder. Oh, and thank you, too, Lord, for finally allowing Rory to recognize his true place in this family. Amen."

"And what exactly, Sean, do you think *is* Rory's place in this family?" Chris asked, giving voice to the question Marta was about to ask had not Chris beaten her to it.

"Everybody but you, Chris, knows that Rory thought he'd be the one to slip into Aidan's shoes after Aidan died. For years he was Aidan's protégé, so I guess it was only natural that he thought he'd be the elder statesman of the clan even though he's the *youngest* son.

"You heard him at his ranch before Thanksgiving telling us all how he expected us to behave. Telling us that his hired hands, for God's sake, were as much his brothers as we were, and that we had to suck it up and treat them with respect.

"Not only does he feel he can order us around at his place in Montana, but an hour or two ago here, in *my* house, he felt he could tell me to 'shut up' in front of my children and then told me I had ice water in my veins.

"Well, to that I say, *I*, at least, have *Patrick McCrea's* blood in *my* veins—a fact that neither Rory—nor you, Chris, either one of you, can lay claim to. So, when he concedes it's not *his* house or *his* place to offer up grace, he's right, being he's a bastard McCrea at best."

Marta saw Rory flinch and glance quickly at his mother. Saw Maire silently meet Rory's eyes. Understood the unspoken sympathy that passed between them in that brief moment's connection. Sean didn't notice the exchange, and went blithely on.

"You all noticed how he tried to take over after Aidan's funeral. Wanting Mom and Walter to sell this place. Wanting them to move to Montana with him so he could control the bulk of the money the sale of the homestead would bring. I'm grateful for that blessing as well—that you all were sensible enough to not fall in with his plan to rob us blind.

"And I have yet to see a farthing paid by him toward the upkeep of this place. All but you, Chris, and you, Rory, helped to pay the taxes last month so we could keep the place. I guess Rory doesn't really care about saving the old homestead since he still feels he was cheated out of his due when he didn't get to buy the biggest part of it to raise his sheep on.

"His lack of contributions toward keeping this place in our family doesn't surprise me. He never *has* paid his fair share of dues to this family. He always preferred spending his money on drinking and carousing in Boise."

"Whoa, wait just a minute, Sean. That's totally unfair! He *has* paid dues. It was Marta and Rory who took in Todd while Mike, Eric and I were in Denver. I didn't see you offer that bit of service.

"I saw your kids crying just an hour ago over their dog but it was Rory's heart that was pinched by their sorrow, not yours. It was Rory who buried Shiloh, not you. He's put plenty of sweat equity into this homestead. Maybe he hasn't contributed financially, but he gives of himself and he gives from his heart. And what do you mean, he's a bastard McCrea?" Bailey asked.

"You didn't know, Bailey? Your sainted Rory and your sister, Chris, were fathered by other than our father, Patrick McCrea."

"I don't believe that for a minute, Sean."

It was Rory spoke up in a quiet and tightly controlled voice after glancing again at his mother, who had flushed with color and lowered her eyes to her plate.

"He's right, Bailey. Chris and I are Mom's and Daniel McIlvey's offspring. I'm surprised you didn't know that," Rory informed her.

"Well, that doesn't change a thing. You're still a full brother as far as I'm concerned."

"Thanks, Bailey."

His mother still looked stricken because of his admission and he saw she was struggling with her emotions.

"Sorry, Mom. I didn't think it was a secret anymore. I thought they all knew."

She defiantly raised her head and looked at him with tears in her eyes.

"You don't need to apologize to me or for me, Rory," she told him. Then she glanced at each of her eldest children in turn, giving Sean a harsh and disapproving glare before telling them, "This is the last time this subject will ever come up again in my hearing. I want that understood—by all of you.

"I won't go into details, but Patrick was not Chris and Rory's father. However, they were both adopted by Patrick and raised by his and my hands, so as far as any normal, rational, *kind-hearted* human being is concerned, you're all equal members of the McCrea family. Now I suggest we eat before the food gets cold."

Sean opened his mouth to protest, but Maire smashed her coffee cup down at the head of the table with such force that the silverware jumped and rattled. "Not one word more, Sean. This was my home and Patrick's and if anyone has the right to make the rules here or say the grace, it should be me."

Bowls were passed and plates were filled in the tense silence that followed Maire's outburst.

"I thought you were famished, Rory," Chris said, noticing Rory's nearly empty plate.

"Kind of lost my appetite."

"Well, find it. I was counting on you to clean out the bowls so I didn't have to."

"Yes, eat up, Rory Owen McCrea," his mother admonished. "You will not make a mockery of all my hours of labor spent over this turkey dinner by passing up the opportunity to enjoy my efforts."

"Yes, ma'am," he told her, knowing when she used his full name, she was in no mood to brook a refusal. He set about cleaning out the bowl of potatoes and emptying the gravy boat over them. "Pass me more turkey, please, Chris, and some of those green beans in mushroom sauce, too. Marta, stand by with the Alka-Seltzer. Yes, Ernesto, I'd love two more rolls."

Marta noted that once more Rory had used flip humor to make light of a serious challenge to his place in the family. While she was glad that he'd not become angry enough to spoil the dinner, she wished he'd had enough of the put-downs to stand up in his own defense. He would need more than fizzy water after dinner. Between Sean's unkind words and the food he was packing away, she knew his stomach would be roiling later that night.

She was glad Kelsey had decided to pass on the dinner and just come for the opening of the gifts. It would have upset her to listen to Sean talk about Aidan and Rory in that manner. She bumped Rory's leg with hers under the table and was rewarded with a wink and a grin.

'Love you,' she told him in sign language, hiding her signing hand with her napkin.

"Glad someone does," he whispered back.

Kelsey and the baby came at 6:30 and that was the signal for bedlam to break out among the younger children. Presents were dispersed and piles grew in front of each family member. This year, there were even several gifts for Marta. When Bailey told Todd that the big box under the tree was for him from Rory and Marta, Todd's eyes lit up and he came over to where Rory was sitting on the floor to give Rory a big kiss.

"Better give your Aunt Marta one of your kisses, too, Todd. She helped me pick out your present and wrap it up."

"Yeth, I will. But you're in my way, Uncle Rory. I can't give Aunt Marta any kitheth. I can't reach her. You're thitting in front of her."

"So you want me to scoot my butt over?"

"Yeth, pleath."

Rory moved so Todd could get to Marta who was sitting on the sofa. Todd planted a big kiss on Marta's cheek, telling her, "I mith you, Aunt Marta. I liked to thay with you, and go down to the barn to see the hortheth."

"I miss you, too, Todd. I don't have anyone to color with or play cowboys and Indians with since you went home."

Gifts were opened and everyone seemed happy with what they got. The hearts were a bit hit with all the nieces who went around looking at all of them and comparing the colors and inner inclusions. Even the older females seemed taken by the uniqueness of the hearts. Todd was so excited about the farm and all the animals he did an impromptu jig around the Christmas tree, shouting, "It hath hortheth and theep just like at Uncle Rory and Aunt Marta'th houth."

Marta bent down to whisper in Rory's ear, "Well, husband mine, you certainly made a hit by choosing that gift. Thanks for sharing the credit for buying it with me."

"Hey, wife. We're a team. I don't choose, we do. I don't give, we do." He grimaced and rubbed his stomach. "You have any Alka-Seltzer? If you do, that'll be the best Christmas gift you can give me right about now."

"No, but maybe your mom has some. Or Alice might."

"It's okay. If you don't have some, I'll just tough it out. I'd rather do that than ask Sean or Alice for anything tonight."

Marta wrapped her arms around his neck from the back and gently kissed his ear. "Maybe we should go soon. You need a good night's sleep so we can head out tomorrow for Montana."

Once all the gifts were opened, Alice invited them all to partake of some cookies and eggnog. Kelsey edged around several people to bump up against Rory's shoulder. She opened the blanket on the bundle she was carrying to reveal the cherubic face of Daniel Aiden McCrea.

"Hey, Lass. Who's that good-looking kid you've got there? Faith and begorra, if he doesn't have red hair and blue eyes. There's no way anyone can look at Danny and be wondering about *his* father. He's a sweetheart, Kelsey. Just like his mother."

"Thanks, Ror. He's a good baby."

"Everything okay, then? Getting along all right?"

"Yes. Better than okay. Life is so sweet with this baby and my job, I couldn't ask for more. Well, maybe I could. I wish you and Marta lived closer. I miss talking to you, Rory."

"I'm only ever a phone call away, Lass."

"I know. But I'm aware that Marta has reservations about me, so I don't want to ruffle her feathers."

"I think she's pretty well over those reservations, Kels. If you need to call and talk, do it. She might want to chat with you herself—get some advice on child care along about March."

"Is that when she's due?"

"Yep. Timed it out so it'd happen between turning the sheep out on pasture—so I don't have to get up early to feed—and shearing, when I won't have time for anything but chopping wool. Had to count on my fingers to make sure the wee one would arrive at an opportune time. Only bad thing is—I'll likely have to plan all of our kids to arrive in March. It'll break the bank buying all 15 kids birthday gifts in the same month."

"Oh, Rory! What a bunch of bull you can spit out. That's one of the things I miss the most—your totally warped sense of humor."

"That's me. Adolphus Q. Jokester."

"Are you really planning on 15? I bet Marta will have something to say about that. Where is Marta, by the way?"

"I think she went upstairs with all the nieces to help them tie on their hearts."

"They're beautiful. I love mine. It's my favorite color."

"Yeah, she had definite ideas in mind and she knew exactly what color to buy for everyone. Her law assistant's mind shows through. She's very observant. Totally detail oriented."

"Speaking of details, am I mistaken, or is there a bit of an undercurrent of tension present tonight."

"Don't be looking under rocks unless you want to get bitten by a snake, Lass."

"There is, isn't there? I felt it as soon as I walked in the door."

"Can't fool you, can I? Never could." He gave her a rueful smile. "Sean felt the need to out Chris and me as 'bastard McCreas' at dinner. It upset Mom."

"And you as well?"

"Yeah, a bit—mostly because of Mom. My gut is doing the cha-cha-cha right about now."

"I thought they all knew before now. It shouldn't have come as a surprise. It's obvious that you and Chris don't share anything with the rest of them—not hair color or eyes or skin tone—not to mention personalities."

"Bailey didn't know, and I think by the way their mouths dropped open that Clancy and Colton didn't either. Maybe it was only Sean, Aidan and Maeve who knew the score. I felt really bad for Mom. Chris and I won't ever think less of her because of her relationship with McIlvey, but I sure would be hard-pressed to vouch for the rest of them."

"I'm sure your mom loved him in her way, so she shouldn't feel bad about having a couple of reminders of her love for McIlvey. I've often wished I had a reminder of my love for a certain bastard McCrea."

"Never more than I used to wish it, Lass. Funny how life turns out, sometimes."

"Yes, and I guess I'm starting to believe that the Man upstairs is wiser than we mortals about such things."

"Yeah, I'm of the same mind. We could have. God knows how often I wanted to. But now, since Marta, I'm glad it never happened. I hope you won't take this wrong, Kelsey, but she's the best woman for me. I don't have words enough to tell you how much I've come to love her. We have our differences on occasion, but I'd be lost without her."

"I could never be offended by your love for your wife, Rory. Marta *is* the best thing that ever happened to you, and well I know that. It's just the tiniest corner of my heart that still wishes we could have been lovers—that I could have had what Marta and you have now."

"I don't think lavender eyes would go so well with red hair and freckles," he told her, backing away from any more intimate discussions.

"You're right. Well, I'm going to take my leave. Danny will be screeching for his dinner shortly, so I need to go home. If I feed him here, he'll fall asleep in the car and be up all night. Take care, Rory and tell Marta I said goodbye."

"You, too, Lass. And you can tell her yourself. She's coming down the stairs, now."

"Hi, Kelsey. Aren't you going to let me see your bundle of joy?"

"Yes, certainly. Rory was just saying you're going to have your own bundle in March."

She unfolded the blankets again and Danny took the opportunity to stuff a fist in his mouth.

"Oh, oh! I know that sign. I just told Rory goodbye because I need to get Danny home before I nurse him so I can put him in his crib right after. Otherwise, he'll be up for hours."

"He's a sweet child, Kelsey. He must be so much company for you."

"Yes. I'd feel Aidan's loss a lot more if I didn't have Danny."

The look that passed between Kelsey and Rory said she would miss him a lot more, too, if not for Danny. Fortunately, Marta's attention was totally absorbed by the baby and she missed the look and Rory's small smile in answer to it.

"Well, wife, maybe we ought to see if Mom and Walter are ready to go, too. That Alka-Seltzer is sending out siren calls that keep getting louder by the minute. I'd like to walk Kelsey out to her car if you don't mind. Would you be willing to find Mom and see if she wants to go back home?"

"Sure. I can do that. You and Kelsey didn't get much of a chance to visit tonight."

"It's not that. I just want to be sure she doesn't slip and fall with Daniel. The temperature is dropping and what was slush is now probably ice on the walk. I'd let you walk her out while I find Mom and Walter, but I don't want you to slip and fall, either," he told her, patting the bulge in the front of her.

Beside the back door of her SUV, he waited while Kelsey strapped Danny into his car seat. When she stood up to face him, he hugged her and kissed both her cheeks.

"Thanks, Lass, for still loving me with that tiny piece of your heart. You'll always inhabit a tiny corner of mine as well."

She laid her head on his chest and heard his heart beating steady and strong.

"You'll never know how much knowing that has shored me up since Aidan died. Before he died, too. How much knowing that will always—oh, Rory—I've got to go before I start crying. Have a good New Year. I love you."

"Love you, too, Lass."

She slid into the car and started the engine, pulling away from the drive quickly and without looking back. He stood in the snow on the lawn and watched the taillights disappear into the darkness before turning to go back in. The feeling of melancholy he'd so often fallen prey to in those summers up in the meadows away from her stole unbidden over him again. It didn't get a chance to last for long.

"Hey, husband mine. The troops are assembled and ready to roll," Marta told him.

His depression lifted immediately in the face of her high spirits.

"Good. Let me start the truck and warm it up. Can't be giving Junior chills or he'll be kicking both of us all night."

With Walter and Maire snuggled in the back seat and Marta sitting against him in the front seat, he pulled out of the drive to head for home in Boise.

"Good thing it was light still when we came to Sean's. With all those gifts in the back, the weight would have made the back of the truck sag so much my headlights would be pointing at the clouds, not the road."

Walter laughed and agreed that he and Maire would have added to the problem since they both ate plenty at dinner.

"Mom, I'd like to apologize again for. . . ."

"There isn't any need for that, Rory. It had to happen sooner or later. But I meant it when I said that was the last I wanted to hear about it—including from you."

"Okay."

Rory punched the radio on and they sang Christmas carols the rest of the way home. Maire and Walter apologized for being tired as they opted for an early bedtime.

"It's okay. Marta and I are going to bed, too. Right after I get some antacid in me."

In the kitchen, he dissolved two tablets in water and downed the drink, making Marta shudder.

"I don't know how you stand that stuff."

"It makes me burp and gets rid of that big bubble of gas pressure under my sternum. No matter how bad it tastes, the alternative is a night's worth of tossing and groaning. Better a small misery than a huge one. Let's go to bed."

As they nestled, the wind came up to whistle around the eaves.

"Thank you for the snow globe and the swan. You remembered. You never forget things I tell you, even said in passing. That's one of the things I love most about you."

"After Sean's little opus at tonight's dinner, I could lie here awake for another hour or two if you wanted to enumerate all the other things you love me for. I could use a few more positive words."

"Why don't you ever speak up and give him back what he's giving out? You always do that humor bit. It doesn't make for such a good defense."

"You think I should have cleaned his clock right there at the table? Shoved his face into the mashed potatoes? I thought it was neither the time, nor the place, Marta. I could see how upset Mom was and I didn't want to add to her discomfort."

"I know. You always think of others first, and I'm glad you kept your cool, but someday in the near future, you need to sit down with all your siblings and clear the air. Tell them in no uncertain terms you won't accept their rancor toward you and Chris any longer."

"One-on-one? It'd probably get me a bunch of bruises if I took them all on at once."

"You're doing it again."

"Ah, wife. I long ago learned that you can't change people's minds. It's foolishness to try. So, what's to be gained by confronting them? Nothing. They are what they are and I am what I am. Like oil and water, the twain shall never mix."

"That makes me incredibly sad, Rory, to hear you say that."

"Me, too, Marta. But that's just the way it is. Better we both learn to accept it."

She rolled to face him, tears streaming down her cheeks.

"I'll never accept it. It's so *unfair!*"

"Hey, no more salt drops—they're positively forbidden on high days and holidays. I love you even though you feel the need to do your Amazon woman on my behalf."

"I love you, too, Rory."

She snuggled against him and was soon asleep.

Chapter Twelve

As the lights of his pickup swept across the entry lane to his ranch, Rory noticed their AmeriBasque sign was missing. He slowed down, looked out the side window and saw it lying about 10 yards away in the roadside ditch.

"Wow! Looks like someone must have had an accident and took out the sign and the posts, too. Hope nobody was hurt. Remind me in the morning to fix it."

"Don't you have to work?"

"Oh, yeah. Well, tomorrow night then, unless I can con some of the guys into doing the repairs."

Up at the house, Enrique was hammering new boards onto the porch stairs. The ones he'd removed were broken and splintered.

"What the hell happened?" Rory asked. "The sign at the end of the lane looks like someone pulverized it and now the stairs? Did you have a sheep stampede or something?"

"No. I think a drunk driver. I hear a big bang and I get up to see, but all I see is red lights going down the lane. Then, I hear another big bang. Maybe that was the sign. I not quick enough to get plate number, but I see the color. Red car. Close to ground."

"Some fool kids out on a lark maybe. Too much red wine or cold beer."

"You no think it was on purpose?"

"Why? Something make you think it was?"

"These steps. Look like someone tried to do on purpose. See here where the tracks back up and come forward again."

It did look a bit like someone had made a second run at the stairs.

"Maybe we'd better call the sheriff's office. You're sure of the color and size of the car?"

"Yes, the size for sure. Maybe the color was reflection of the lights in back."

The only one Rory knew who owned a car close to the ground was Kurt Bancroft and he couldn't imagine Kurt coming around to do that sort of damage. He quickly decided to go into Butte early enough to check out Kurt's sports car before work.

He was up early and fed, then kissed a sleeping Marta before he left for work.

"I can fix breakfast," she mumbled, rolling over in bed and rubbing her eyes.

"I need to get going, and you need to rest in. It was a busy week, so sleep while you can. I'll call you later, okay?"

"I can pack you some lunch."

"Consuela did that already. Just sleep until noon. I told Consuela not to bother you until then."

"I feel guilty sleeping when you've been up and fed and are going off to work. You're as tired as I am."

"I'm not pregnant, so if I'm missing a few winks of sleep, it only affects me, not Junior. Sleep. That's an order."

"Aye, aye, Admiral. What do you want for dinner?"

"Lasagna? Salad? Garlic bread? A cold beer?"

"Okay. That sounds good."

"See you about six."

When he didn't come home at six, Marta started pacing the floor. The roads were worse in Montana than they'd been in Idaho and all day it had spit snow off and on. Finally, she could stand it no longer and called Rory's cell phone number. He didn't pick up until the seventh ring.

"Are you okay?" she asked. "Where are you?"

"I'm fine, but I won't be home until about nine. Can you get Ricardo to feed for me?"

"Yes, I can ask him. Why won't you be home?"

"I'll explain when I get there. I'm at the police station."

"Did you have an accident?"

"No. I have to go talk to the Lieutenant now. Don't worry. I'm fine."

Telling her not to worry only increased her sense of foreboding, so she was relieved when she saw lights coming up the lane a bit past nine. He pulled around to the back of the house and parked between the sheepcote and the mudroom. He was wearing a deep frown when he came into the kitchen but quickly erased it when he noticed her watching him.

"Keep my dinner hot? I'm starving."

"Salad may be a bit wilted and the garlic bread is kind of crusty, but the lasagna is none the worse for wear."

"Good. Hope there's a lot left."

Marta dished up a huge square of it and filled a basket with the garlic bread. The salad came out of the refrigerator all crisp and cold and not in the least wilted. Marta set that and a bottle of ranch dressing in front of him, too, then went to the refrigerator again for a frosty bottle of beer. She sat down and watched him wolf in about half of everything before he slowed up enough to ask her if Ricardo had fed.

"Yes. He fed. Now are you going to tell me why you were at the police station?"

The frown returned and he took a big swig of his beer before he said, "You know how the sign and the steps were all smashed last night? Well, Enrique said it was a small car—low to the ground. Only person I know with a car like that is Kurt, so this morning I went into Butte and went past the law office looking for his car. Didn't see it.

"I stopped in the office and asked Ron where Kurt lived. Said I'd left something of mine in his car when we went to Missoula for the concert and I hadn't had time to get it back over the holidays. Ron gave me Kurt's address and I took a short jaunt over to the apartments where he lives. His little car was parked under the covered garages and it had extensive front-end damage.

"I went from there to the police department and explained about Enrique seeing the little car and how the sign and our steps were all pulverized, possibly by a car belonging to Kurt. They said they'd check into it. After that, I went to work."

"I can't believe Kurt would do something like that, Rory."

"Wait, it gets better. Lieutenant Coburn called sometime around one to say they'd impounded the car—that Kurt had called it in as stolen early this morning. Said they'd check out our sign to see if they could match the paint scraped off on the sign to the car's paint damage. Called me again just at quitting time to say they'd made a match.

"They had Kurt in Coburn's office asking him what he knew about the sign and the steps. He was adamant that the car had been stolen. The Lieutenant took me down the hall and asked me if I knew Kurt and if he had a problem with drinking. I told him I only met the guy a couple of times but he didn't seem like an alcoholic."

"I don't think he is, either."

"I got the feeling the police don't believe the car was stolen, so then they wanted to know if Kurt and I had any unsettled grudges or problems between us. I told them, 'Not on my part, but I can't speak for Kurt.' because I wasn't sure if maybe Kurt was pissed at me because of Amber or something."

"Is he being held? If they charge him, it could mean the loss of his law license."

"They let him go on his own recognizance. They said they were dusting the steering wheel and the doors for fingerprints and they'd let me know if something turned up. I was just leaving when Kurt said he'd be happy to pay for the damages even though he hadn't caused them. I thought that was sort of weird. Why would you offer money if you weren't involved, somehow?"

"Did Kurt advance any thoughts on who might have stolen the car?"

"None that I heard. Hey, this is really good. Is there more lasagna? With all the police stuff, I didn't get either breakfast or lunch today."

"One more small piece."

"Bring it on."

"You don't suppose he was in the car, but not driving?" Marta asked, serving up the last piece of lasagna.

"That doesn't make much sense, either. Who would be driving if not Kurt?"

"Amber, maybe. Wasn't she upset when you told her to stay away from you? What if they were out and she had a few drinks and took it in her mind to get even with you?"

"I doubt Kurt would let even Amber abuse his car like that."

"If they do get the prints and can't match them, you ought to get her prints on a cup of coffee and let them see if hers match what they find on the car," Marta said.

"Run that past me again. Did I just hear you suggest I invite Amber to join me for coffee?"

"Well, sure, in the interest of solving this case."

"I think I'd rather let the police gather her prints. Don't want to start something up with her again."

"Whatever, but someone should fingerprint her. Was she in the store today?"

"Not that I saw, but I was out back most of the afternoon, unloading hay."

"I have to go back to work tomorrow. I'll keep my ear to the ground. If Kurt was involved, he may let something slip in the office or act guilty."

"Just don't open your mouth and accuse him of anything or ask him about the accident. Someone who would trash a sign and our porch might have enough of a screw loose to want to up the ante by trying to injure a person next."

The phone rang in Rory's office and he went to answer it while Marta rinsed off his dishes and put the lasagna pan in the sink to soak. He didn't come back and didn't come back, so she finally went to stand in the doorway of his office. He was making squiggles and squares on a notepad, the phone pressed to his ear.

"Yeah. Amber Sykes. I don't know where she lives. She was dating Bancroft until she decided she fancied me more."

He drew a series of exclamation points on the pad while he listened.

"No, sir. I didn't encourage that at all. She's been coming into the feed store almost every day. I told her if she persisted in harassing me, I'd get an order of protection against her."

He glanced up at Marta and shrugged his shoulders.

"No, Lieutenant. I don't know any other females Kurt might be involved with. Did he say he'd given Amber a key to his car?"

He listened for another two minutes and then hung up the phone.

"What was all that about?"

"Lieutenant Coburn said they lifted four good prints from the car that didn't match Kurt's prints. Said they were narrower and possibly belonged to a woman, so they called Kurt and asked if there was a possibility of a woman having access to his car. He said Amber had borrowed it one afternoon because her car was in the shop for a timing-belt change.

"Coburn thinks she may have had a key made to the car while she was using it. But what still doesn't fit is the late report of the car being stolen. It was already back in the carport at the apartment shortly after the police got a call reporting it stolen, so either Kurt saw it was gone before it got back or he's trying to cover his ass by reporting it stolen when it really wasn't."

"The plot thickens," Marta said.

"I don't want you going in to the office tomorrow. Call in sick or something."

"Rory, I can't do that. I've been gone for two weeks already. My desk will be piled to the sky with work."

"Better that than have Amber waylay you."

"So you think it was her?"

"I don't know what to think. Coburn is going to her house to get her prints and ask her some questions. If she's out to do me harm, she might just take it in her mind to get to me by way of you. I wouldn't have thought her to be squirrelly. Did she strike you as someone with problems?"

"No, but anyone who continues to chase someone after they tell her they're not interested—well, sometimes people are obsessed. Like John Hinckley with Jodi Foster, and they do things to impress the one they're obsessed with. He shot Reagan. If Amber's obsessed with you, who knows what she might do. Maybe it's you who ought to call in sick."

"But what if it's like Hinckley? He was obsessed with the actress, so he shot the President to impress her. What if Kurt is so obsessed with Amber he's out to impress her by wrecking our ranch? I really don't think you should go to work until this is straightened out."

"Oh, Rory. Nobody is going to do me harm in a law office on Main Street."

"Bet Reagan and his bodyguards would challenge that statement, Marta. I don't want any harm to come to you or the baby. Stay home, okay? Humor me?"

"And would I be safer here? You'll be gone all day."

"Here, at least, the drovers are around. All of them are crack shots with a rifle. They can hit a coyote several hundred yards away. I can warn them to be on the lookout for anything or anyone out of the ordinary."

"You don't think that sounds the least bit paranoid? Who's going to protect you at the feed store if Kurt comes gunning for you there?"

He sighed, acquiescing to the logic of her argument. "Okay. I guess I am being a bit paranoid. Go to work if you want, but let me be the one to drop you off and pick you up. If you have all that work piled up, it shouldn't matter to Ron if you go in earlier than one o'clock. Come with me in the morning and you can eat breakfast at The Hungry Hen, then take my truck to work. You can pick me up after I finish and we'll go home together. The roads are bad and I don't want to take the chance of anyone trying to run you off the highway."

In the morning, he drove her to Butte and pulled into the feed store's back lot at 7:30 a.m.

"C'mon, I'll buy you breakfast."

He took her hand and led her across to the restaurant, where he ordered two specials for them to eat.

"Morning," the waitress greeted them, turning over two cups and asking if they both wanted coffee.

"Hot tea for me," Marta requested.

"Coffee is fine with me," Rory told her.

Breakfast was served just as his cell phone rang. He fumbled in his coat pocket to extricate it.

"Hello?" There was a brief pause during which time, Rory ate his sausage.

"They did, huh? Well, maybe I'm not too surprised. She made a rather veiled threat when I told her there was an iceberg's chance in hell I'd ever be interested in her." He listened again then said, "I could—maybe over my lunch hour. About one, then?"

He punched the 'end' button and flipped the phone closed.

"It was her?"

"They think so. She denies it, of course, and Kurt has ridden in like the white knight to represent her. He won't press charges for her taking his car, Coburn said. They want me to come down and press charges and give them a damages figure for the cost to replace the steps and the sign. He must have it bad for her if he's willing to overlook the damage she inflicted on his car."

"Do you think it's wise to press charges?"

"Yes, I do. I want it on the records, so if she gets a slap on the wrist, and decides on a repeat performance it won't go as easy a second time. Besides, nobody who is that warped should get off without at least being forced to pay the damages."

"How much do you think it will cost to replace the stairs and the sign?"

"Couple of thousand?"

"Really?"

"No. But isn't that what people do? Jack the cost way up to reap a bit of extra cash?"

"Are you planning on doing that?"

"Of course not. Not that I couldn't use a couple of thousand. You don't know me well enough to know that?"

"I thought it was kind of out of character, but I thought, too, you just might be mad enough to want to soak it to her. I'd be tempted to teach her an expensive lesson, not just try to recoup the money for the materials and the labor to make the repairs."

Since he'd need his truck at one to go down to the station, Rory dropped her off at the office. Kurt's SUV was in his parking space, so Rory got out and walked Marta in. The door to Kurt's office was open and he got up when he saw Marta and Rory.

"Marta, it's good to have you back," Kurt said. "Rory, can I speak to you privately for a minute?"

"Sure, if you make it quick. I'm already late for work."

Kurt showed him into the office and shut the door behind them.

"I'm really sorry about the mess this has become. I don't know what got into Amber. I'm not going to press charges on account of my car. I need to know if you are."

"Yes, I am."

"Would you reconsider that? I think she was really depressed and took some medications. I don't think she was thinking rationally the night it happened."

"I want it on the record, Kurt, against the possibility of further incidents. The only way I'd not press charges is if she'd agree to check herself into the mental health facility in Missoula to get her head straightened out. The next time it might be something not as easily replaced as a few boards and posts."

"If you press charges, she'll go to trial. In her fragile state, do you really want to testify against her?"

"Meaning what? If I do, her obsessions may escalate?"

"It might happen. She's very upset that you don't like her like she likes you."

"Then, with the previous case on the files, the next time, she'd get prison time, wouldn't she? But if I don't press charges, she could do it again and the results would likely be the same—a fine and damages, or maybe some community service? She needs professional help, Kurt, before someone gets badly hurt."

"Then, I guess you'll do what you feel you need to."

"Yep, I guess. And this further warning—should anything happen to any of my family members or my drovers, I would . . . well, let's just say nothing better happen. If you're representing her, you make that clear to her. If anything happened to Marta or our baby, or the drovers and their families, I'd be willing to spend my life in prison to make sure whoever harmed me or mine never lived to do it again."

"You surely don't mean that."

"I most assuredly do mean that, Kurt. I care that much about Marta and our future child. I care about my drovers and their families like they were my family. I don't want Amber anywhere near my land or my wife or either of our places of employment.

"My rifle will be loaded and always close at hand to assure that compliance to my request. I've got to go, but you tell her for me to keep her distance if she wants to live to see thirty."

"I could report you for making threats like that."

"Like me, Kurt, you'll do what you think is necessary."

"Hey, McCrea. You think you can just stroll in here at noon?"

"Sorry, Mr. Hadley. That woman who comes in here all the time spent the evening after Christmas Day plowing up some property on my ranch. I had a meeting with her lawyer this morning and over lunch I have to hit the police department to file formal charges against her."

"That blond that keeps coming in and calling and asking for you?"

"Yes, sir. I may have to file an order of protection against her which means you'd either lose her as a customer here or me as an employee if you wanted to keep her business."

"Women!" Hadley shook his head. "They're all nuts!"

"I think this one may be certifiably so."

"Well, take whatever time you need. How much damage did she do?"

"Took out the sign at the end of our lane and broke up the stairs leading up to the porch. And she did it in her former boyfriend's car that she 'borrowed' for her project. I'm just glad I wasn't home when it happened or Ms. Sykes might be wearing a total body cast about now."

"Well, there's a sacked-feed truck to unload, so maybe you'd better hustle if you need off at lunch."

"Yes, sir, and thanks for letting me take the time."

Out back Phil was sitting on a bale of hay waiting for him to help unload. Rory opened the door of the semi and jumped up into the interior.

"Hey, Phil, drag that flat dolly over here so I can pitch the sacks onto it."

Phil got up reluctantly and doused his cigarette, then hauled the dolly beneath the trailer's door. Rory began pitching out the sacks and didn't halt until the dolly was filled to overflowing.

"Cripes, McCrea. We'll never move this thing. You made it too heavy."

Climbing down from the trailer, Rory took hold of the handle and began to tug it in the direction of the storage shed. Phil was surprised to see the dolly move—enough surprised that he stood watching until Rory suggested he get on the back end and push.

"Christ, man. You must have had a double bowl of Wheaties this morning."

"No, just a bit of extra adrenaline."

"What are you pissed about this morning? Your wife?"

"No. You know that Ms. Sykes that's been dogging me lately? She did a number on my stairs and sign posts at the ranch two nights ago."

"I thought she *liked* you."

"Yeah, she does. That's the problem. When I told her I wasn't interested, it's like she slipped a cog. I'm going to press charges against her this afternoon. Hope that convinces her I meant what I said."

"Either that or it'll drive her further around the bend. Jesus! And to think I was resenting the fact that all the dames want to be tight with you. Maybe it's good I'm such an ugly son-of-a-bitch. Nobody never did nothing like that to my place."

At one, Rory was ushered into Coburn's office. Papers charging criminal trespass and damage had been drawn up and awaited his signature. He took the pen and signed in triplicate.

"You realize this will require you to testify when her case comes up for trial, don't you?"

"Yes. Her lawyer suggested she's maybe not in her right mind and if I testify she may be further induced to try something else. What's it take to get an order of protection against her? And what rights do I have to protect my wife and unborn child or my drovers and their families if she shows up with the intent to do harm to any of us?"

"You can petition the courts for an order of protection."

"Would it make an exception if she wanted to purchase goods at the feed store where I work?"

"I don't know. Usually it's all-inclusive—no contact in person, by phone or written correspondence, but you'd have to ask the judge about that if you didn't mind her coming into the store."

"I don't want her coming in, but it's not my place to deprive Mr. Hadley of business because of my personal dislikes. He might just decide he'd rather have her business than employ me. What about being allowed to protect me and mine? The ranch is a far piece off the beaten path. It takes a long time for the law to get there."

"The new law says you don't have to wait until a perpetrator is inside the house and threatening you. If you reasonably believe lives are in danger, you can use deadly force without fear of repercussions anywhere on your property. But, if you're any good with a weapon, I'd suggest you try to incapacitate, not kill."

"Thank you. I don't know what to expect from her. She's not rational. Ten minutes after I told her in no uncertain terms I wanted nothing to do with her, she was back in the store telling me she could wait for me to change my mind."

"Typical stalker mentality."

"You'll let me know when to show up for court?"

"I will, Mr. McCrea. And I'll have my men keep an eye out for any irrational behavior on her part, too."

"Thanks, Lieutenant, and it's Rory. There are so many McCreas in my family, you use that name and between my brothers and my nephews, dozens of us jump up."

"Okay, Rory it is. I'll give you a call when the case comes up. And I'm Paul if we're going to be on a first-name basis."

"I appreciate all your diligent work, Paul. You guys are good."

"Well, it helps when there's someone to point a finger in the right direction."

Ten days later, on the 6th of January, Coburn called to say the hearing was scheduled for the 10th at 10:30 a.m. Rory got up that morning and bundled his work clothes into a roll and dressed instead in slacks and a sports coat, knotting a tie beneath his chin.

"I forget how handsome you are when you get all gussied up, husband mine," Marta told him over breakfast."

"I didn't know handsome was a function of what I wore. You're beautiful no matter what you put on," he teased.

"You are handsome all the time, it's just when you take the time to shave that close and put on your finery, the good package takes on an even greater luster."

"A ten, maybe?"

"At least. Are you nervous about the hearing?"

She noticed he wasn't eating much. The scrambled eggs hardly had a dent in them.

"I don't think that's the word for it. I don't like being the one that maybe puts a young woman in a cell. On the other hand, I also don't want her to think she can just trash this place because I'm not returning her affections."

"You're too kindhearted, Rory. I wouldn't have any problem sending her up the river for 20 years."

"Twenty years? It's not like she's going to end up in Sing-Sing in solitary. She may get a month or two—just long enough to hone a real grudge against us."

"Well, we'd have a month or two of peace, in any event. She brought it on herself, so I don't think you need to feel bad about the consequences."

"Yeah, I guess not. I'd feel better if she'd agree to get some help, though. I would retract the charges if she'd do that."

"Has she given any indication she'd be willing to get help?"

"Not that I know of. I laid out that thought to Kurt, so I guess if she'd decided to accept that offer, he'd have called before now. Guess I'd better go. I'll probably be late to supper tonight. I'll need to make up the morning off. Everybody and his cousin is low on hay so we'll be delivering after dark I bet."

"Call and tell me what happens?"

"I will if I can."

He tossed his work clothes in the passenger seat and left for Butte. The hearing was being held in the judge's chamber and he got there 15 minutes before the scheduled 10:30 start. Kurt and Amber were sitting on one side of the judge's desk. Rory took a chair in the back of the room in front of a wall full of law books. When the judge entered, Kurt and Amber stood up, so he followed suit.

"Mr. Bancroft," the judge acknowledged Kurt. "You're here representing Ms. Sykes, I take it?"

"Yes, your Honor, I am."

"And you, young man, I presume, are the complainant."

"Yes, sir," Rory said. "Rory McCrea."

"Well, since the damages as listed on your complaint, Mr. McCrea, amount to less than $1000, this complaint can be heard as a civil case. Does the accused wish to enter a plea at this time?"

"She does, your Honor. My client wishes to plead 'not guilty' at this time.

A look of incredulity spread over Rory's face.

"Ms. Sykes would like a trial by jury. She feels there are circumstances that caused her to participate in the damages to Mr. McCrea's property. She would like to file a counter claim. She'd like to charge Mr. McCrea with alienation of affections at this time and she further suggests he's the cause of her damaging his property—that his decision to end the affair that he'd encouraged for weeks left her so upset she was not in her right mind when she went to his ranch and caused the damages to his property. We're prepared to file those counter charges at this time, your Honor."

"Kurt, you've got to be kidding," Rory protested rising to advance on the judge's desk.

"Mr. McCrea. Please resume your seat. Mr. Bancroft is perfectly within his rights to so file on behalf of his client."

"Your Honor, never for one second did I *ever* encourage any affections from Amber Sykes. There *never* was any affair and I greatly resent that charge being lodged against my name or my person."

"You'll have your day in court, Mr. McCrea."

"How does my complaint against Ms. Sykes for criminal damage get turned into me on trial? I haven't done anything to have to be tried for."

"Evidently Ms. Sykes believes otherwise. I'll set a date for the trial and let all the parties know by the end of the week. For now, you're all free to go."

Kurt gave him a grin that said, 'We have you by the balls, now.'

Furious, Rory left the chambers and went straight to the office of Lieutenant Coburn.

"Paul, got a minute?" he asked, leaning against the doorframe of Coburn's office.

"Sure, Rory. You look like the Mad Hatter. What's up? She got off with nothing but a fine?"

"Hell, no. She wants a trial by jury. She's filed a counter charge against me for alienation of affections. Claimed that my breaking off the affair was the cause of her actions—that she was so distraught she wasn't in her right mind."

"You're pulling my leg, right?"

"I'm deadly serious. The judge is going to call with the date for a trial. That means I'll have to hire an attorney to defend me against her charges. I'm already up against it financially. I don't have the money for an attorney."

"How's your credit?"

"Maxed out. I'm in hock to the bank big time for the ranch. I don't have a credit card because I can't afford to be tempted to use it."

"I don't think I can ease your mind, Rory. I'd suggest you find a lawyer and make a deal with the devil to pay him over months or years if you need to. I'm really sorry to hear it turned out like that.

"If it's any consolation, I'd be willing to testify on your behalf as to the mental state of Sykes, but with the understanding I can't speak to what transpired between you two before I got involved in the case, as I wasn't privy to your private conversations. I only know what you told me, which is, of course, hearsay, and won't be permitted in court."

"*Nothing* transpired between us. She's spinning a fantasy in her head. What worries me is that she'll come off as the victim to a jury and I'll end up paying all the court costs and have to pay for the repairs to my place, too. Not to mention what the trial and the notoriety will do to my wife and my marriage as well as my name and standing in this town."

"You could drop all charges and see if that would make her drop hers."

"Wouldn't that be like admitting she was right in saying we were having an affair? Thanks, but I don't want any tongues clacking over that notion. I'm the innocent one here—why am I being made to feel like I'm guilty of something?

"I've got to get to work. But thanks for your help, Mr. Coburn. Guess I'll see you in court."

He was still furious. His anger was so overwhelming it persisted all afternoon. He loaded and unloaded hay with a vengeance that left Phil standing to one side of the hay truck watching in amazement. What normally would have taken until 7 or 8 p.m. was all done by 6:30.

"Hey, McCrea, I don't know what's stuck in your craw, but be careful driving home. The roads are bad and in your foul mood, it wouldn't be good to be goosing the gas pedal like you manhandled those bales all afternoon. You're about to be come a daddy, so drive careful, okay?"

"Yeah, Phil. I hear you. See you tomorrow."

He didn't drive at seventy, but he pushed sixty in spite of the snow. Marta knew it had not gone well when he slammed into the mudroom and stormed into the kitchen.

"Rory, what?"

"Not now, Marta. Maybe not tonight. Maybe not in the next month. Let's just eat. Don't ask me, please."

"Okay. Sit down and I'll dish up the stew. Consuela made crusty French bread, to go with it. You want coffee or beer."

"How about arsenic?"

"If you don't want to discuss it, then don't be saying stuff like that."

"Sorry."

He forked in the stew without another word, and then ate apple pie. When he'd finished he said, "I need to make a call, Marta. And I'd like to make it in private, so don't be putting your ear to the office door, okay?"

"All right." The look that crossed her face told him that his request had hurt her. There had never been secrets between them and he regretted that he didn't have enough control of his anger yet to tell her why he was mad. He needed Jack Strauss' advice before he could consider calming down.

In the office he called and got Jack, which was unusual. Usually it was his answering service that picked up.

"Jack, it's Rory."

"Hey, old man. To what do I owe this honor?"

"When I tell you, you might not think it's an honor."

"Problems? Spit it out, Rory."

An hour later, what he'd spit out had Jack volunteering to defend him against Amber's charges. The knot in his gut began to slowly unwind. While he was still upset, he finally felt he could relate the day's events to Marta without shouting and cursing. She was sitting curled up under the afghan in his chair near the fire when he came out of the office. The hurt was still evident on her face.

"Hey wife, come sit with me on the sofa. I'm sorry about being short with you. I need to tell you about this morning."

She got up and came to sit with him, tossing the afghan over both their laps. He told her what had happened and let her explosion that followed carry on unabated because he knew exactly how she felt, having been ready to explode all day himself. Once she calmed a bit, he hugged her to him and said, "No matter what gets alleged in court, I want you to know I never encouraged her."

He blinked hard not to let the tears flow, his anger giving way to the sorrow that the accusations would put Marta through. "I'm not your father. Riding on a bus, you'll never catch me kissing other than you as lover to lover.

"It's going to be ugly. She'll try to make it sound like I was in her pants twice a day for weeks. I want you to promise me that you will not believe a word of what she says. I could never do that to you, Marta. I know you've wondered in the past, but I *couldn't* do that to you. I have not *done* that to you."

"Who were you calling?"

"Jack. He's coming to defend me at no charge. I hated to ask him—well, I didn't get a chance to ask—he volunteered, but we can't afford to pay a legal beagle here in Butte."

"Come to bed, Rory. I can only imagine what a disaster today was for you. And I'll be there in court every day to support you. I believe you. I know you didn't have any sort of relationship with Amber."

"Kurt tried to warn me."

"Shhh." She wrapped both arms around him and kissed him gently all over his face. She hadn't seen him that shaken since he'd had to go identify Aidan's body in the morgue.

"You're not like my father. I know that. I know you wouldn't do that to me. I know you love me to the exclusion of everyone else. You're Rory McCrea, the kindhearted, steadfast sibling. You aren't capable of deceiving those you love. So have no fear, husband mine. I know you're innocent of her charges."

"Oh, Christ, Marta. I was so afraid it would make you wonder and worry—that it would dredge up all your doubts again. I'm so sorry it's come to this. Even if *you* don't doubt me, I'm sure there will be others who do."

"It doesn't matter about anyone else, love. I don't doubt you and that's all that counts. Come to bed. I could stand a reaffirmation of your love. Come, make love to me?"

He picked her up and carried her up the stairs to their bedroom, where he made sweet and gentle love to her.

"Thank you," he told her, pulling her against him.

"No, thank you, husband mine. Go to sleep. It will all seem like a fading bad dream in the morning."

"Remind me of that over breakfast," he told her, giving her one last kiss.

Chapter Thirteen

After a restless night, he got up at five and went slowly to the barn to begin mixing sheep feed. The problem of Amber Sykes and an upcoming trial filled his thoughts. What if Jack were involved in something in Boise and couldn't get to Butte? What if Amber had some sort of 'evidence' that he didn't know about. He didn't put it past her to have broken into his house before wrecking the steps. What if she'd taken something intimate—a pair of his boxer shorts to prove that he'd had some sort of relationship with her?

"*Hola*, Señor Rory. *Trabajar en fecha a hora*," Ricardo observed. He and Manuel began hauling out buckets to mix feed in.

"Yeah, I'm working early. Couldn't sleep. Might as well get up and work. *No duermo bien.*"

The drovers looked at each other and it was Manuel who asked, "*Problemas?*"

"Yes—*sí. Una mujer. Loco en la cabeza.*"

"*Una mujer en la automóvil?*"

"*Sí*, the woman in the car. *Dice estoy enamorada de ella.*"

"*Es verdad?*"

"No, it's not true. I'm not in love with her. *No enamorada! Tengo una esposa. Enamorada mi esposa solamente.* I have a wife and I'm in love with her. Only her!"

Both men rolled their eyes and shook their heads but fortunately didn't ask any more questions. Nor did they speak of the matter during breakfast as the scowl on Rory's face served as a warning not to bring the subject up again.

He was early to work at the feed store, too, arriving well in advance of Phil. He picked up a box of horse worming tubes and began stocking the

148

shelves. After that, he took the push broom and swept all the aisles until Jay Hadley made his appearance.

"You're here early," Jay said. "This going to be another day you need to take some time out of for personal reasons?"

"No, sir. Just couldn't sleep last night so I got up early and was done with my sheep feeding earlier than usual. What's on the agenda for today?"

Jay checked the roster. "Two hay deliveries so far—ten bales on one and twenty-five on the other. An order of sacked alfalfa cubes going north to the Bar-Q-Bar ranch. Maybe wait until it gets a little warmer to load. Don't want you sweating loading the hay and then standing around in this -10° heat wave we're having. This afternoon it may get downright hot. Get up to zero, maybe."

Rory wasn't sure whether dusting shelves and rearranging items was preferable to loading bales of hay, but it was a trifle warmer inside, so he decided it wasn't beneath his dignity to go up and down the aisles flicking the feather duster around. He was way in the back corner of the store straightening cans of cat food, when he smelled a musky perfume.

"Mr. McCrea. I was hoping to find you in this morning. I need a dozen big salt blocks loaded in my truck."

"Yes, ma'am, Ms. Coombs. Are you parked around back?"

"No, but I can be."

"Sure, if you'll pull through the gates on the right side, I'll meet you out there and load you up."

He pulled on his coat and leather gloves and went out the back door to wait for her. When her truck appeared, he indicated she could back up to the nearest storage bin. She got out and opened the tailgate of her camper.

"Might be better if you wait in the truck, ma'am. Mr. Hadley doesn't like customers standing around out here, and besides, it's still pretty cold this morning."

She returned to her seat, but left the door open, sitting sideways on the bench seat to talk to him while he loaded the salt.

"You have any of those mineral blocks?"

"Yes. Couple of different types. Horse? Cow? Sheep? Deer? Which do you need?"

"What's the difference?"

"Makeup varies. I'll pull the brochures with the contents listed. What are you feeding?"

"Horses and cattle. But there are deer that come to the salt licks, too. I always feel bad for animals when it gets this cold. Putting out some sweet-feed blocks or mineral blocks makes me feel like I'm helping them survive the harsh weather. I suppose your sheep like it cold with all that wool on them."

"They don't mind the cold as long as they've got a bit of shelter from the winds that rip through."

"So, you build shelters for them?"

"Yes. There are six sheepcotes already built and a couple more started. It's too cold to mix mortar now, but we've gathered enough rocks to complete the other two when it gets warmer."

"When do you find the time? You work here all day. That doesn't leave many hours for construction projects, I would imagine."

"I've got drovers—four of them. I pay them for the hours they spend building around the ranch. I can pitch in on Sundays—it gets accomplished."

"So, if you need more sheepcotes, does that mean you're planning on increasing the size of your herd."

"Flock? Yes, that's the general idea. Increasing the number of sheep."

"Is there a limit to what you can increase to?"

"Yes. I figure about 1000-1200 is all I would be able to feed on the land I own or lease. We're only about a fourth of the way to that number."

"How many do you have now?"

"Six hundred, more or less."

"Isn't that halfway, then?"

"No. Next fall about 200 will go to slaughter for the meat. The older ewes that are past their breeding prime. I want to cull them out before November's breeding."

"Does it bother you to send them off to be killed?"

"A little maybe. Hard not to have some feelings for them after you've nurtured them from tiny lambs, and spent all those years shearing them each spring. But old sheep are prime targets for predators and I take a bit of comfort in knowing that a quick death at the slaughterhouse is preferable to being dragged down by a coyote or a wolf or a mountain lion. How many mineral blocks do you need, and which ones?"

"Give me four for deer and a half-dozen each for the horses and cattle."

"Yes, ma'am. Is there someone on your end to unload all this?"

"Me."

"If it's not real busy, I could maybe come put them up for you at the ranch."

"You'd do that?"

"Yes. You're one of the store's best customers. We'd like to keep it that way."

"You might inform your cohort of that desire. I never met any man who complained more and did less than he does."

"He's not had such a good or easy life. I think he's got aches and pains on top of his aches and pains."

"Well, it shouldn't bother his aches and pains to be courteous or civil. He's like a bear with a sore paw. I hope his working with you will allow some of your courtesy to rub off on him."

He closed the camper door and told her he'd meet her inside to tote up the bill. When she came in, he quickly added up all the various blocks and handed her the invoice. She took it and made out her check. Phil had arrived by that time and was looking over the roster of deliveries to be made.

"Hey, McCrea. When do you want to get started loading?"

"Jay said to wait until it warmed up a bit. If I go out with Ms. Coombs to unload her order, think you could manage the store on your own for an hour?"

"Why would you want to unload her stuff? It's not our delivery, is it?"

"No, but it's slow this morning and those salt blocks are heavy."

"Aren't you already having problems with females? Why would you want to let yourself in for more? I see the way she looks at you—like you were some Greek god walking."

"Can it, Phil. She's a good customer. Let's keep it that way."

"Sure, sure. Do what you want. I can manage here."

"Thanks. I'll tell Jay."

Jay also wanted to know why Rory was volunteering to unload for Ms. Coombs.

"She spends a lot of money here. It makes for good business relations, Jay. If it were jumping this morning, I wouldn't go, but it's deader than an Irish wake, so Phil should be able to handle the load."

"Ah, hell. Go on, then."

"Thanks."

He climbed into his truck and followed her out to the ranch and unloaded all the blocks into her barn.

"Come in and sit down for a cup of coffee. I've got leftover fruitcake and I'd be happy to have someone eat at least part of it."

"Thanks. I like fruitcake and coffee sounds pretty good about now. It's warmed up to all of a $-4°$ according to the thermometer at the barn."

She heated coffee and sliced some fruitcake. He enjoyed both.

"You said last time that you were about to be a father. Has it happened yet?"

"No, ma'am. Late March is Marta's due date. Sometime around the 27th."

"Are you excited?"

"Not yet. When I'm grabbing her suitcase and the contractions are two minutes apart, then is when I'll probably get excited."

"So giving birth is old hat to you? You have other children?"

"No, but I have about 21 nieces and nephews, a couple of which I was around for the initial appearance of. And I've probably assisted a hundred sheep with difficult deliveries, too. Guess that takes some of the excitement out of it. Well, I'd better head back to the store. Thanks so much for the warm up and the fruitcake."

"Thank you for coming out to unload the blocks. It would have taken me a lot longer than it took you. I'll probably need another delivery or two of hay before the end of March, but if I don't see you again, good luck on becoming a father."

"I'll probably need some luck. You don't have to diaper sheep, and none of my siblings ever invited me to clean the bottoms of their offspring, either."

"Manners, a good work ethic and a sense of humor, too. I hope you are employed by the feed store forever."

"That's not likely. Beginning in April, there's shearing, and after that, it's up on the upland meadows all summer."

"Doesn't your wife miss you—won't she, especially when the baby comes?"

"Yes, some. But I come down frequently. The drovers and I rotate days off for family matters."

"Well, thanks again."

"You're welcome. Give a call when you need more hay."

"Only if you'll deliver it."

Lieutenant Coburn had called the store for Rory while he was gone, so Rory took the message out to the back barn and called from there for a bit of privacy.

"Lieutenant Coburn, please," he told the woman who answered.

She connected him after a brief wait.

"Paul, it's Rory."

"I'm glad you called. One of my men said Ms. Sykes was in The Sports Shop trying to purchase a gun."

"What kind of gun?"

"Small pistol. He didn't specify the type."

"Did they sell her one?"

"No, there's a waiting period, and when my man told the owner that the woman was involved in stalking, the owner decided to deny the request. But that doesn't mean she might not try again in some other town or city where they don't know her. I can put a notice on the ATF site that dealers have to check. It will show a 'don't sell' if she tries to get one someplace else. That should put a stop to a legal purchase, but it won't prevent her from going to a gun show where they don't always check . . . getting one there."

"Do whatever you think will deter her, Paul, and thanks for the head's up."

All the rest of the afternoon he worried about the safety of Marta and the rest of his ranch personnel. Loading and unloading hay, he came to the conclusion that he'd better teach Marta how to shoot and buy her a gun. Or sign her up for a concealed-weapon class. He knew she'd tell him he was being paranoid again, but with the possibility of a loony Amber with a gun, Marta's safety was not something he felt should be left to chance.

She could tell he was worried when he was quiet at dinner. Waiting for Manuel and Ricardo to leave the table before asking questions of him, she was surprised when he suggested they both sign up for the weapons class.

"What brought that on, Rory?"

"Coburn called to say Amber was trying to buy a gun. I just think I—we—should be ready for the eventuality that she somehow lays claim to one."

"Maybe we should just move away. Go back to Idaho."

"And do what?"

"Raise sheep, of course."

"Where?"

"We'd buy a ranch."

"We'd need to sell this one first. I don't think we'd ever clear enough to get out of debt on this mortgage, let alone sign up for another one."

They spent a quiet New Year's Eve at home. The roads were bad, with the temperatures hovering in the minus degrees. Enrique invited Manuel, Ricardo and Juan to his place and when Rory fed that evening, the party was already in full swing. Enrique had invited Rory and Marta, too, and Consuela, but only Consuela went, and she didn't stay for long.

Rory and Marta toasted the arrival of the New Year with a mug of hot chocolate topped with whipped cream. Consuela had gone to bed long since.

"Does this mean we're turning into a boring old couple?" he asked. "It's kind of a far cry from last year's celebration."

"I suppose it is sort of tame, but you're tired and I'm pregnant, so it didn't seem to make much sense to go out for drinks. You'd likely fall asleep and I can't drink because of the baby. Better we stay home. Listening to that wind howl, I'm glad not to be out there on those icy roads with all those who have been drinking."

"What kind of resolutions are you making for the year?"

"I'm going to have this baby and I'm going to lose the weight I've gained. I'm going to not eat dessert after the baby comes. What about you?"

"I'm going to learn how to change diapers and get up for at least half of the midnight feedings."

"You've been sleeping poorly for the last several days. If all you plan to do is toss and turn all night, I might let you have *all* the midnight feedings."

"I'm sorry. Have I been disturbing your sleep? I could sleep in one of the other rooms."

"Oh, no, you don't. I wouldn't be able to sleep at all if you weren't there to keep me warm. Are you upset about something?"

"Just worried. Afraid the other Amber shoe is going to drop and I won't be ready for what she springs on us next."

"Rory, you've got to stop that kind of worrying. You don't want to end up with ulcers. It sounds like the police are keeping tabs on her, so maybe you should relax."

"Yeah, maybe. It's not going to stop her from trying something anyhow, so it is kind of a waste to keep stewing."

"How about we cap off this fantastic celebration with a hot shower and hit the sack?"

"Not a hot bath?"

"The doctor said it would be better from now on if I showered. He doesn't want me sitting around in a pool of water that may contain some harmful germs. And besides, it's getting kind of hard to lever myself out of the tub now that my girth is growing by leaps and bounds."

"I hadn't noticed," he said, giving her a grin.

"Liar. I've put on eighteen pounds and it's all middle."

"No it's not. Some of it ended up here," he said, cupping her breasts.

"Careful. They're a bit tender these days."

"How about your lips? Are they okay?"

"Yes, of course they are."

"Good," he said, dragging her into an embrace and bruising them with several kisses. "Happy New Year, wife. It's a year full of promise. A new child, hopefully some good fleeces to sell at a good profit, more lambs, and a wife I can make mad passionate love to again along about June."

"I've enjoyed the gentle loving. Do you miss the other?"

"Sometimes. Sometimes I'd like to grab you up and ravish you, and now I have to restrain those urges so as not to cause harm to Junior. But I don't mind the gentle type of loving, either. However, I'm not looking forward to curtailed relations while you heal up from the delivery. I find it pretty hard to keep my hands—and other things—off you."

"Even now when I resemble the Goodyear blimp?"

"Even now. Ever. Always. You're one chunk of desirable woman—whatever your shape."

She blushed and ducked her head so he wouldn't see how much his evaluation pleased her. "I'm still an eleven or a twelve, then?"

"Fifteen, at least. You might even be a twenty. Pregnancy has given you a glow and made you even more incredibly beautiful. I wouldn't have believed you could become prettier than you were the day we married, but you have."

She stood on tiptoes and kissed him warmly. "If that's Irish blarney, I hope you never stop dishing it out."

"It's not blarney, Marta. Every day I love you more. I can't imagine my life without you in it. You have no idea how content I've become, waking up with you beside me in the mornings and knowing you'll be there when I hit the bed that night."

They shared a hot shower and Rory soaped her from the crown of her head to her toes, using herbal shampoo and vanilla-scented soap.

"Thanks, husband mine. It's getting harder and harder to reach my feet," she admitted as he wrapped her in a huge towel and began to rub her dry.

"My pleasure, wife."

He unwrapped the towel and stood looking at her, watching her belly bump as the child within kicked. Looking up again, their eyes locked and he smiled at her. It was a look so filled with love that it made her shiver.

"You're cold. Here. Jump into your nightgown."

"It wasn't the temperature that gave me chills, Rory. It was the way you were looking at me. If ever I doubted your love, that look would have removed the last vestiges of my doubts."

She stepped toward him and traced her hand from his lips downward, noting with her fingertips the width of his chest, his flat and muscled stomach, the way the fine line of black hair arrowed down to his pubic area where his manhood rose in response to her touches.

"You best quit that, love. The desire to ravish you is about to overpower me."

"Let's go to bed, Rory. Let me see what I can do to relieve your desires."

She hung her nightgown back on the hook behind the door and went naked to their bed. Beneath the flannel sheet and goose-down comforter she ministered to his need and he to hers.

For the first time in many nights, he slept without tossing and turning, and woke at dawn. He rolled to his side. Bracing his head with a hand, he looked down on her. Her cheeks were pink and her hair tousled on the pillow. She looked content—as content as he felt. Before he got up to feed, he lay back down and offered up a prayer that the newly minted year would keep both them and their child safe. For truth, he knew he'd die if he didn't have her beside him.

Chapter Fourteen

The court sent notice that the trial instigated by Amber Sykes would take place on January 24th. They sent notice in enough time for Rory to touch base with Jack and for Jack to clear his schedule and hop a short flight into Missoula where Rory picked him up on the 22nd. Driving back to the ranch, they discussed the possible arguments and counter arguments that might arise during the proceedings.

Marta was waiting with a big dinner when they arrived. She hugged Jack and thanked him for being willing to come and act as Rory's defense counsel. Shortly after they ate, Jack and Rory moved to Rory's office to refine the arguments, telling Marta they'd talk to her in the morning and advise her of their strategy in case she got called as a witness.

"Go to bed, wife. Jack and I may be up a long time."

"Jack's room is the same one he had when he was last here," she told Rory, standing on tiptoes to kiss him. "I'm going to watch the 10 p.m. news before I go up, but I'll keep the volume down. Will you want coffee or hot chocolate?"

"Can you pour some coffee in that carafe thing so it'll stay hot? Otherwise, I may be nodding off in an hour."

"I can do that. And there's a bit of pie left if you get hungry."

She went to the kitchen to make a fresh pot of coffee, and tapped on the office door when it was ready.

"Cups, sugar, creamer, pie. Anything else you need?" she asked.

"Can't think of anything," he said, giving her a hug and a brief kiss.

It was long after midnight when he crawled into bed and then it was up to feed and resume the discussions with Jack early the next morning. By mid-afternoon, Jack folded his notes into his briefcase and said he was sure they'd covered everything he could think of.

156

"I'd like to meet with Lieutenant Coburn, Rory. Can we buzz into Butte and spend a few minutes with him?"

"Let me call and make sure he's going to be in his office."

"Marta, sweet thing that you are, could I trouble you for a sandwich or some cheese and crackers? I ate so much at breakfast, I wasn't hungry for lunch, but now I'm beginning to feel a tad empty. And I'm not sure when we might get back from Butte."

"Of course, Jack. Chicken or beef?"

"Chicken's fine. Little lettuce and some mayo on it?"

"Coming right up."

Jack followed her into the kitchen and sat at the table in the alcove while she made him a sandwich of chicken and Rory one with roast beef.

"Who ever would have thought his complaint about the posts and the steps would end up like this?"

"That's what keeps me in business."

"Well, not at the rate you're charging us. I'm so grateful that you're willing to be here to defend him. I really feel like we ought to pay you something."

"You have. You're giving me free room and board in one of the nicest places on earth to visit. Please don't sweat the small stuff, Marta. I like you and Rory and that's what friends do, they look out for each other."

"You're a sweetheart, Jack. Rory has been beside himself. First he was in a rage that she turned the tables on him, then he was frantic that we'd get stuck with some huge lawyer fees and court costs, and now he's worried wondering what she's going to come up with next."

"I've got to say, that husband of yours provides me with some really unusual cases to ponder on. None of that old boring crap with Rory."

Rory, off the phone, came in and sat down to eat his sandwich. "Coburn can see us at 4:30. I was thinking, it'll be late when we get done, so maybe we ought to stay in Butte and eat dinner. Marta, would you like to ride in with us and eat, too?"

"No. I would, but I feel kind of tired. You both go ahead and have a boy's night out. I have a good book started, so I plan to eat early and then curl up with that."

After a brief meeting with Coburn, Rory and Jack hit the bowling alley for a couple of games before heading off to dinner at the steak house.

"I'm glad Marta didn't come, Jack."

"You want her well rested for the trial tomorrow?"

"No. She always creams me at bowling. And then she tries hard not to gloat, but that tiny smile keeps tugging her lips up at the corners. It's hard on my ego to go bowling with Marta."

"I know what you mean. She used to tell me things in the office when she worked for me and if I chose to ignore her advice, it usually turned out badly and she'd treat me to that little smile, too."

"She is a formidable woman."

"Yes, she is, but she's also so damn cute with her pregnant belly leading her around like that. You're a fortunate fellow, Rory McCrea. Not every pregnant wife handles that state as well as Marta seems to handle it. She just gets lovelier every time I see her."

"She sure does. That's what makes this court thing so ironic. If she were acting like a harridan, Amber might have a leg to stand on, but Marta's just been fantastic. Happy and healthy and content."

"Good. That'll be points in our favor with the jury."

When court took up at ten the following morning, Kurt Bancroft stood up and said, "I call Rory McCrea to the stand."

Rory rose from beside Jack Strauss at the defense table and walked to the witness chair, pausing to take the oath to tell the truth before sitting down. After a brief smile at Marta, who sat in the first row behind Jack, he focused his attention on Bancroft.

"State your full name for the record, please," Kurt began.

"Rory Owen McCrea."

"Mr. McCrea, what sort of relationship did you have with Amber Sykes?"

"None."

"You never spoke to her?"

"Of course I spoke to her. We went to a concert in Missoula with Ms. Sykes and you. We ate dinner together. I spoke to her then."

"And since then, have you spoken to her?"

"She's come into the feed store a few times, so yes, I've spoken to her on those occasions."

"Have you ever been alone with her for any length of time?"

"No."

"You didn't, within the last month, invite her for coffee at The Hungry Hen?"

"I did. But only. . . ."

"Just a 'yes' or a 'no' will suffice, Mr. McCrea."

"Yes, then."

"And how long was that meeting?"

"Ten minutes maybe. Fifteen at the most."

"Did you or did you not spend time with her in the Hadley store?"

"I did. She's a custom. . . ."

"'Yes' or 'no' will do."

"Yes."

"Do you harbor any warm feelings for my client?"

"No."

"You weren't flattered, then, when we went to dinner and the concert when she expressed some interest in you?"

"No more than any man would be."

"You're married?"

"Yes."

"Happily married?"

"Yes."

"You've never been interested in another woman?"

"Not since I got married, no."

"How long have you been married?"

"Just about eight months."

"And you've never been attracted to another woman in those eight months?"

"No."

"You've respected the marriage vows you took then?"

"Yes."

"And would it be fair to say you expect others to respect those vows you took?"

"Yes."

"And would it also be fair to say you respect the marriage vows of others in your acquaintance?"

"Yes."

"Did you or did you not have a relationship with Kelsey McCrea?"

"Yes. She's my. . . ."

"Your 'yes' will suffice, Mr. McCrea."

"Have you ever kissed Kelsey McCrea?"

"Objection." Jack countered.

"Your Honor, the question goes to establishing the parameters of Mr. McCrea's assertion that he is faithful to his vows and the vows of others."

"I'll allow it. You may answer the question, Mr. McCrea."

"Did you ever kiss Kelsey McCrea."

"Yes."

"Kelsey McCrea was your brother Aidan's wife, was she not?"

"Yes."

"Was she married to him at the time or times you kissed her?"

"Yes."

"So the fact that she was married didn't deter you from kissing her, did it?"

"No."

"How long did your relationship with her last?"

"Seven or eight years."

"Other than kissing her, were you ever intimate with her in other ways?"

"No."

"Remembering your oath, did you or did you not spend a night in bed with your sister-in-law while she was still married?"

Rory was about to say 'no' when he remembered the night of the storm when Kelsey was still weak and recovering from the loss of her baby—the night he'd crawled into bed with her to comfort her while the storm raged around his cabin at their Idaho ranch. He was both chagrined and amazed that Kurt had somehow managed to find out about that. He must have been talking to Kelsey, and it angered him that Kurt had gone so far as to investigate his relationship with her or involve her in the current situation. He wondered how many of his siblings Kurt had contacted and which of them might have added a few logs to Kurt's prosecutorial fires.

Remembering his mother's admonition that honesty was always best, he answered truthfully.

"Yes. One night."

"So one might reasonably conclude that you weren't opposed to playing around with a married woman?"

"We weren't playing around."

"You've admitted to being in bed with her while she was still married to Aidan, your brother."

"Yes, but we weren't playing around."

"Shall I extrapolate from that that you were seriously involved—seriously intimately involved?"

"I was only in bed with her because. . . ."

"You're excused, Mr. McCrea."

He got up slowly and though his facial features remained unchanged, Marta could tell how frustrated and angry he was by the way his hands had balled into fists. Jack patted his arm and smiled to let him know they'd get their chance.

"I call Mr. Phillip Jordan to the stand."

Phil came forward and was sworn.

"You work with Rory McCrea at Hadley's Feed Store, do you not?"

"Yes."

"How long have you worked together?"

"Since November, I guess."

"As part of your duties, you both travel together to ranches to deliver hay and other items?"

"Yes."

"Can you tell us about those deliveries?"

"What's to tell? We load the truck, drive out to wherever we're supposed to unload it and we unload it."

"And Mr. McCrea shares equally in those endeavors?"

"Rory? Yeah, sure. Rory's a good worker. He never shirks his fair share of the work, either loading or unloading. He does more than his fair share lots of times."

"And how does he treat the customers?"

"He's polite to everyone. Lots better than me."

"Is he equally as polite to men as he is to women?"

"I guess. But seeing as how we most often deliver to women, I'd say he's especially polite to them."

"Does he ever flirt with female customers?"

"If he does, he's not obvious about it. But all the dames seem drawn to him."

"So are you saying he flirts 'clandestinely' with women?"

"I don't know what that means."

"Does he wait to flirt when you might be otherwise involved so you wouldn't notice? Have you ever turned around suddenly and caught him flirting?"

"No, I don't think so. Course, he was in the house at the Coombs ranch for a long time, but since I wasn't inside there with him, I don't know what happened."

"How long was he in the house?"

"Seemed like a long time, but maybe it was 15 minutes. Twenty minutes, tops."

"Who was in the house when McCea was inside?"

"Mrs. Coombs."

"Only her?"

"I guess. Didn't see anyone else but her."

"Has she shown any special interest in him since that time? Or he in her?"

"He volunteered to help her unload the salt blocks she picked up at the store."

"When was that?"

"Right after the first of the year. A couple of weeks ago."

"Was that part of his store duties?"

"No. We only unload if *we* make the delivery, not if the customer comes in on his or her own to pick up supplies."

"Do women seem to like Mr. McCrea?"

"Yes, he seems to attract them like soda in a can attracts hornets."

"Does he encourage them in their interest?"

"Objection," Jack said. "Calls for a conclusion by the witness."

"Sustained."

"Let me rephrase the question. Does Mr. McCrea go out of his way to service female customers."

"Objection."

"What is the nature of your objection, Mr. Strauss?"

"May I approach the bench?"

Judge Halloran motioned both lawyers to the bench.

"Sir, I feel the word 'service' may be construed by the members of the jury as my client having sex with them. Most of the rural population speaks about a stud 'servicing' a mare or a bull 'servicing' a cow. I believe the term to be prejudicial."

"Step back."

Both lawyers returned to their tables.

"The jury is not to take the word 'service' in any other context than that it means to wait on customers," Halloran instructed.

"Mr. Jordan, does Mr. McCrea go out of his way to wait on female customers?" Kurt asked.

"He always seems happy to wait on women."

"Do women request that he wait on them or prefer him over you to fill their orders?"

"Yes."

"You may step down."

"I call next, Amber Sykes."

Amber was dressed in a navy suit with a mid-calf-length skirt. Beneath the jacket she wore a light pink blouse with a jabot that filled the V at her neckline with ruffles. Her lipstick and blusher were in shades of pink with light gray as her eye shadow. The overall effect was one of a demure and beautiful young woman.

"Ms. Sykes, when did you first meet Mr. McCrea?"

"Last fall. When Rory and his wife went to a concert with us."

"Meaning you and me?"

"Yes."

"And do you know why McCrea and his wife were invited to go to the concert?"

"I believe his wife works in your office and you were friends with her a long time ago. You had four tickets and so you asked her and Rory to accompany us."

And the four of us went out to dinner prior to the concert?"

"Yes. At a fancy restaurant in Missoula."

"Did you notice anything about that dinner?"

"Rory—Mr. McCrea, he kept smiling at me and seemed to be paying more attention to me than to his wife. I thought he was incredibly good looking."

"Before the evening ended, did he offer you an invitation?"

"Yes. He said when he went up to the high meadows with his sheep, I should come up to see his flock then."

"Why do you think he wanted you to come up to the meadows to see the sheep? Why didn't he invite you to see them at his ranch?"

"He said the sheep would be clean and white after shearing in the spring, but I think that was just an excuse. I think he wanted me to come up there because he wanted to meet me someplace where his wife wasn't hovering about."

"And so, you thought perhaps he was more than casually interested in you?"

"Yes. And when I wanted something at the feed store, he acted all pleased to see me, too."

"But then, he invited you for coffee and told you he didn't ever want to see you again?"

"Yes." A tear dribbled down her cheek. "It came as such a total shock after all his attentions prior to that day. I was totally upset. He got up and walked out on everything we'd been building toward and I was just crushed. I think I went a bit crazy. His not wanting to see me when it had been going so well between us, well, it just devastated me."

"Thank you, Ms. Sykes. Your witness, Mr. Strauss."

"Ms. Sykes, in what way did Mr. McCrea's supposed attentions manifest themselves?"

"Oh, you know. Smiles. Long looks. A hand on my back guiding me to the items I was looking for in the store. Once, he came into the store all sweaty and he had his shirt off. He knew I was standing behind him and he flexed his muscles to impress me, then he blushed when he turned around. But I could tell he was showing off his body for my benefit."

"Has he ever done more than that?"

"No, but I could tell he wanted to. It was just that there were usually other people around in the store, so he couldn't do what his eyes were telling me he wanted to do."

"What color are McCrea's eyes, Ms. Sykes?"

"Objection. Relevance?" Kurt asked.

"If Ms. Sykes spent all that time gazing into Mr. McCrea's eyes as she'd like to have the jury believe—if he spent so much time that close to her—she should know the color of his eyes."

"I'll allow it."

"What color are Rory's eyes, Ms. Sykes?"

"Blue. A heavenly shade of blue."

"I'd like it noted for the record that Rory McCrea's eyes are lavender, not blue. Has Mr. McCrea, outside of that one time he asked you to accompany him when he bought you coffee at The Hungry Hen, ever invited you out? Or even asked where you live?"

"No."

"He's never asked where you lived or expressed any interest in visiting you where you live?"

"No, but I felt that he was leading up to asking. Or maybe he already knew my address. It's on the checks I wrote at the feed store."

"Did he ever, in your presence, spend time looking at the address on your check?"

"Yes, every time, and he'd always ask me for my phone number and write it on the check, too."

"So when he told you in no uncertain terms he didn't want to see you again, you were angry?"

"Yes, and hurt, too. I'd been feeling the vibes he was putting out, so it came as a real shock when he said our affair was over."

"How do you define 'affair' Ms. Sykes? Doesn't an affair usually connote sexual intimacy?"

"Objection. Leading the witness."

"Sustained."

"Have you been sexually intimate with Mr. McCrea?" Jack asked, rephrasing the question.

"Not yet, but I felt it was only a matter of time."

"You're excused."

She exited the witness chair, dabbing her eyes with a tissue, and reclaimed her seat behind the table to the left of where Rory sat.

"I call Jay Hadley to the stand," Jack said.

"Mr. Hadley. You heard Ms. Sykes make reference to my client looking at her residential address on her checks and asking her for her phone number, too. Was that standard practice at your business?"

"Yes. My employees are to check all addresses, and if there isn't a phone number listed on the check, they are to ask for one. Or if the address is a post box, they're to get a physical address."

"So, there would be nothing unusual about Rory McCrea asking her for a phone number or physical address?"

"No. In fact, if he hadn't done that, he would be in Dutch with me. I've been stiffed a few too many times, so I don't put up with my employees being lazy in that regard."

"You may step down. I now call Lieutenant Coburn to the stand."

"Lieutenant Coburn, you're an employee of the Butte police department, are you not?"

"I am."

"When did Mr. McCrea first contact you?"

"December 27th. He reported that someone had damaged both his sign on the highway and the stairs leading up to his porch."

"Was he the one that witnessed the damage?"

"Only after the fact. I believe it was one of his drovers that had seen a low-slung sports car going down the lane after the drover heard the crash associated with the destruction of the stairs."

"Did Mr. McCrea indicate to you anyone he thought might have been responsible for those damages?"

"Yes. He said the only person he knew that had a sports car like that was Kurt Bancroft."

"The same Kurt Bancroft as is sitting over at that table?" Jack asked, pointing in the direction where Kurt and Amber sat.

"Yes."

"What further information did you have on that car?"

"Mr. McCrea said he'd gone past the apartments where Mr. Bancroft resided and noticed extensive front-end damage to Mr. Bancroft's car. And on further checking, I discovered Mr. Bancroft had, just that same morning, reported his car stolen."

"Stolen? Even though it was in the garage at the apartments where he lived?"

"Yes."

"What did you do then?"

"On Mr. McCrea's suggestion, I impounded the car and checked the car to see if the paint from it matched the damage to McCrea's posts and stairs."

"Was it a match?"

"Yes."

"What occurred next?"

"I asked Mr. Bancroft if there was any way anyone had access to a key to his car and he told me that he'd loaned the car to Ms. Sykes some time previously while her car was in for repairs."

"Then what did you do?"

"I had the car dusted for prints. We got four good prints that did not match with Mr. Bancroft's."

"How did you come to fingerprint Amber Sykes?"

"Well, Mr. McCrea said he felt she might be responsible for damaging his property and the fingerprints were small, like a woman's prints, so we checked it out."

"And?"

"The prints were those of Ms. Sykes."

"Your witness, Mr. Bancroft."

Kurt rose and stated, "I told you she used the car when her car was in the shop. Why did you then conclude the prints were from the night of the damage and not from the day she borrowed the car?"

"The prints were fresh, not smudged, which made them look to be of recent origin, and because of Mr. McCrea's suspicions it was Ms. Sykes who damaged his ranch."

"No further questions."

"I recall Rory McCrea to the stand."

"Mr. McCrea. Mr. Bancroft has suggested that you are not above stretching the truth when it comes to keeping vows. Have you, since your marriage, ever cheated on your wife with another woman?"

"No, I have not."

"In the matter of your sister-in-law, Kelsey McCrea, please elucidate more about your relationship with her."

"My brother, Aidan, raised Black Angus cattle. We were joint owners, together with Kelsey, of Star Sheep and Cattle Company. I was the sheep man, and Kelsey also preferred sheep to cattle. In the seven or eight years of working together with the sheep, I came to be very fond of Kelsey. I thought of her as the ideal woman. She was beautiful, strong, good with sheep, and had a good sense of humor. She was easy to talk to about anything. I admired her spunk."

"And you kissed her?"

"Yes. A total of three times, I think."

"And you spent a night in bed with her?"

"Yes. One night fully clothed. It was after Aidan's abuse caused her to miscarry. She was still weak and upset and vulnerable. There was a really bad electrical storm and she hated storms, so I lay down beside her to soothe her fears and give her comfort."

"You had no sexual thoughts on that night?"

"Oh, I wouldn't say that. But she was married to my brother, and while I might steal a friendly kiss on occasion, I wasn't into cuckolding my brother. What I mostly felt for Kelsey was the same sort of love I feel for my sisters. With an added need to protect Kelsey because Aidan could be a mean son-of-a . . . well, let's just say he had a pretty volatile temper."

"Redirect, your Honor," Kurt said, rising.

Jack relinquished the floor for the moment.

"The reason Kelsey McCrea aborted the fetus she carried was because of Aidan's assertion that the child was yours, not his, wasn't it?"

"She didn't abort the child. She lost it because Aidan twice kicked her in the stomach after hitting her so hard in the face she fell out of her chair to the floor."

"Because he suspected the child was yours?"

"Yes, that's what he accused me of on more than one occasion."

"Was it true?"

"No. I've never slept with Kelsey that way. I've never been intimate with her."

Jack took over again as Kurt sat down.

"Did you invite Ms. Sykes up to the meadows to see your sheep?"

"Yes. She professed an interest the night we went to dinner and the concert, so I invited her up to see them come summer."

"Why not invite her to the ranch?"

"The sheep in winter, before shearing, are dirty and matted. After shearing, they look white and clean. I learned in 4-H that to impress a judge, you'd better present a sheep that looked like it had been bathed six days a week and twice on Sunday. If somebody wants to see my sheep, I'm going to suggest a time when they all look their best."

"So it wasn't that you didn't want her to come where Marta, your wife, might be observing the meeting?"

"No, sir. Marta and I have no secrets. Had the meadow meeting occurred as fact, not just invitation, I probably would have set it up for a Monday when Marta is also up in the meadows."

"Were you flattered by Ms. Sykes obvious attentions?"

"A little, maybe. Ms. Sykes is an attractive woman. I think most men would be flattered if an attractive woman paid them some attention."

"But you had no intention of returning her attentions?"

"I am always willing to acknowledge a woman's finer points, but not to the extent of doing anything but look."

"Why do you think Ms. Sykes filed this 'alienation of affections' charge against you?"

"Objection. Calls for a conclusion by the witness." Kurt put in.

"Overruled."

"I think she's built up a fantasy in her mind about us as a couple and when I said it would never happen, I think she was so angry she took it out on my property and when it looked like that wasn't going to change my mind, she decided to file suit."

"Redirect, Mr. Bancroft?" Jack asked.

"No, not at this time."

"Then I call Marta McCrea to the stand."

Marta came forward touching Rory's hand as she passed him on the way to the witness chair.

"State your name for the record, please."

"Marta Lansdorf McCrea. *Mrs.* Rory McCrea," she said, emphasizing her marital status.

"You're married to—well, of course you are—you just told us that. What kind of husband is Rory McCrea?"

"He's a good man. A man who works long, hard hours. He's loving and kind and funny. He's gentle and he's devoted to me and awfully good to his friends and his extended family as well. In the McCrea family, most of them refer to him as the kind-hearted McCrea. Not all of his siblings are as considerate of others as is Rory."

"Were you aware of his feelings for Kelsey McCrea prior to your marriage?"

"Yes. I knew he loved her. But since we've been married—well, I know she'll always own a small part of his heart, but I also know that Rory loves me and would never betray our marriage with anyone else."

"What makes you so sure?"

"Oh, I won't say he doesn't appreciate a fine female—we have a standing joke and a rating system about that. I won't say he never looks or flirts—he does. But he never does either seriously. Most often it's with a grin like he was sharing his penchant to eye a good-looking female with me. I've never felt he was seriously looking or that I should be upset if he does look."

"So you trust him implicitly?"

"Yes. I have no doubts about Rory."

"Even about his relationship with Kelsey?"

"No. Not even about that. Maybe at first I did, but not now."

"What made you get past your doubts?"

"Rory tells me daily in so many ways that he loves me. And he's honest to a fault. He has a highly developed sense of integrity. It's not in his nature to lie, even when telling the truth makes life hard for him."

"You heard Mr. Jordan say Rory goes out of his way to wait on the female customers. How do you feel about that?"

"It goes with his chivalrous nature. He's always been someone that wants to help and protect the weaker members of society. He'd be the same with a crippled man, or an old man who couldn't lift heavy things. I think he carries more of the heavy work at the feed store because he knows Mr. Jordan is not as young, nor as strong, as he is."

"Do you believe your husband was carrying on a clandestine affair with Ms. Sykes?"

"No. Not for a moment. He would never be able to hide it from me were he doing so. We've only been married a short time, but if you look closely at Rory, you can read his emotions in his eyes and in his body language like he was an open book. He couldn't hide something like an affair from me. I'd know in a minute if he was serious about anyone else."

"I have nothing more, your Honor."

"Redirect, Mr. Bancroft?"

"Yes. Please. Can any one individual *ever* be totally sure of someone else's intentions or interests, Mrs. McCrea?"

"I think, when two people share a life and a bed and a deep and abiding love, they come to the place where they *can* be totally sure, Mr. Bancroft. As you can see by my girth, I share a life and a bed and an abiding love with Rory. Outsiders may nourish doubts about us, but both of us are totally sure of the love that stands between us. I love my husband. He loves me.

"It's a faith born out of mutual respect for each other and absolute faith in each other. I love my husband, Mr. Bancroft, and that makes me quite sure he's never encouraged the likes of Amber Sykes to engage in any sort of behavior I'd find fault with."

"Nothing more, your Honor."

"I'll entertain closing arguments at two this afternoon," Halloran decreed.

In Kurt's summary, he tried again to paint Rory as a philanderer. Rory never changed expressions as Jack had warned him that any displays of emotion would surely be noted by the jury. Instead, he sat sideways in his chair holding hands with Marta across the rail, quietly squeezing her fingers that were meshed in his.

Jack rose and faced the jury and in a very eloquent speech, portrayed Rory as a warm and loving husband, which he'd seen with his own eyes on more than one occasion. He said that this trial was the result of spite, not only on the part of Mrs. Sykes, who had made up a relationship in her mind that wasn't borne out in reality, but also on the part of her lawyer.

Jack alleged that the 'alienation of affections' charge might have been lodged more on Kurt's behalf, since Amber had decided she preferred Rory's attentions to his, Kurt's. That if the truth were to will out, Mr. Bancroft felt a large degree of animosity toward Rory McCrea because Amber was no longer interested in him. He called the charge a 'nuisance' charge and not one that any rational person would take seriously and asked the jury to find for Rory and assess awards for property damages and the responsibility for court costs to Ms. Sykes.

The wait was short. In two hours, the jury came back with a decision in favor of Rory. Judge Halloran assessed damages at $2500 for the destruction of property at the ranch, and further assessed $5000 in court costs, stating that he also believed the case to be a frivolous waste of the court's time.

Marta came whirling through the opening in the rail to grab Rory in a huge hug.

"Our honor is restored," she told him.

"Yes, and it's because of your testimony, Marta. Thanks for putting your faith in what we share so eloquently."

He grinned down at her and kissed her button nose.

"I say a celebration is in order. I'll stand for dinner at the steak house."

"Good," Jack said. "I'm always starving after a trial like this."

Chapter Fifteen

Amber still came to the feed store with much more frequency than Rory thought necessary. He was always polite, but avoided being alone with her in the back aisles of the store. There was little he could do about the way she watched him. *Like a robin eyeing a fat worm*, he thought. It got to the point where his senses went on high alert before she actually appeared inside the store. "Cosmic vibrations," he told Marta. "I swear the gods are trying to warn me."

For Valentine's Day, Rory took Marta out to dinner and was surprised to see Kurt and Amber a few tables away. He purposely sat with his back to Amber and let Marta face her so Amber wouldn't have reason to think he was looking at her or making any sort of eye contact.

"Are they a couple again?" he asked Marta in a low voice.

"I guess. He doesn't discuss his love life with me, but he's twice brought her to the office on their way to somewhere else. She always looks daggers at me. She's creepy."

Marta delivered all that with her hand partially covering her mouth. Rory noticed and asked, "You talking like that because you think she reads lips?"

"You never can be too careful when dealing with weird people, husband mine. Whenever she comes in the office, I have this overwhelming urge to get up from my desk and hide in the restroom."

"Same as my cosmic vibes at the feed store?"

"Yes. I think so. You remember me telling you that you had an 'aura' about you? Well, she's got one, too, only hers is an evil one. She just emanates something that scares me."

"I doubt she'd be foolish enough to try anything again. Those fines Judge Halloran assessed should have convinced her that she'd better be on her best behavior. What do you want for dinner?" he asked, opening the menu and studying its contents. "And don't be telling me raspberry jelly and cornflakes, either."

Late in her pregnancy, Marta had developed some strange cravings and twice he'd caught her mixing raspberry jelly into her bowl of cornflakes and milk. Whole raspberries he could have understood, but not the jelly. When she told him she couldn't find raspberries in Butte in the dead of winter, he brought home several bags of frozen berries for her cereal.

"I want a great big juicy hamburger—no, a cheeseburger with bacon and onions on it."

"Heartburn City, here we come. And fries?" he asked, grinning at the scope of her appetite.

"Well, of course, fries. And some of those good onion rings, too."

The waitress appeared in time to hear fries and onion rings.

"My wife would like a huge cheeseburger with bacon and onions on it. And the fries and onion rings, too," Rory related to the Sherman-tank of a waitress who stood looking at him and scribbling on her order pad.

"I got the rings and fries. And you, doll?" she inquired in a voice Rory was sure had been coarsened to a scratchy rasp by years of cigarette smoking. The fingers wrapped around her pen were yellowed to a pumpkin shade.

"Ham and Swiss on sourdough and a side of your cowboy beans, I guess."

He folded the menu and handed it to her. "And coffee for me. Tea, Marta?"

"No. I want a strawberry milkshake."

He frowned but kept his own counsel. His mother had often said that pregnant women shouldn't eat strawberries or the baby might be born with a strawberry birthmark. It was likely an old wives' tale without a shred of science behind it, but it crossed his thoughts anyhow.

"A strawberry milkshake, too, for my wife," he told the waitress.

"Sweetie, we can make vanilla, chocolate or mocha, but there ain't strawberry one in the entire state of Montana in February."

"Chocolate, then, with lots of whipped cream."

Rory saw the waitress glance at Marta's ever-expanding middle and roll her eyes.

"She's eating for two," he volunteered, hard pressed not to laugh out loud.

While they waited for their dinners to be served, Kurt and Amber got up to leave the restaurant.

"Evening, Marta. Rory," Kurt said.

"Kurt. Amber," Rory responded.

"Looks like we both had the same inspiration for VD."

"Seems so, Kurt. Did you enjoy your dinners?"

"Yes, I think we did, didn't we, Amber?"

"It was delicious, Kurt. And Kurt was so sweet all day. He got me flowers and candy and this little gold heart," Amber said, holding out a chain bearing a gold heart with a diamond in the center. "Isn't it just beautiful, Marta?"

"It's lovely, Amber," Marta agreed.

"So, are you two doing anything after dinner?" Kurt inquired. "We're going to the movies."

"I think Marta said we should go bowling."

She shot him an alarmed glance. Bowling, with her belly protruding like a beach ball? Then she noticed the look in his eye and knew he was being facetious.

"Yes," she agreed. "When I'm not pregnant I always beat Rory at bowling. So he thinks this may be his last chance to recover some of his pride." She was rewarded with a grimace and a 'touché, my love' look from Rory.

"Mind if we come along and watch?" Kurt asked. "I'd like to see Adonis here taken down a peg. Wouldn't you, Amber?"

"I think my husband was pulling your leg, Kurt. After dinner, we're going home. Rory promised me a back rub with some good lotion. The winter and this pregnancy have made my skin all dry and my back aches something fierce by the end of the day. Sorry to disappoint, but I'm not up to rolling my usual 290 on the alleys tonight."

"Will you be in the office tomorrow?"

"Yes. Why do you ask?"

"Ron is out until next week, so I thought you might be taking a few days off, too. There's not much to do with him gone."

I have the Clemmons brief to work on, and the Heidiger case as well. I think I can stay busy."

"Okay. Enjoy your dinner. C'mon Amber, the movie will be starting soon."

Amber fell in behind Kurt, letting one hand trail across Rory's shoulders as she passed his chair. He gave no indication he'd noticed, and refused to look in her direction or to acknowledge the small smile—a smile he could see out of the corner of his eye— that she was wearing.

After they'd left the restaurant, he said, "She just never gives up, does she?"

"No, and that's what worries me. The whole time she was standing there she had eyes for only you—like she was in some sort of trance."

"Suppose Father Roberts does exorcisms? Maybe we could hire him to drive her devils out."

"Don't tell me stuff like that, Rory. I won't be able to look at Father R. without laughing come Sunday."

"If you laughed, you might finally have something to confess the following Saturday. Bless me Father, for I have sinned. Last Sunday I snickered in the middle of your sermon and I am guilty of not taking communion because all I could think about was you in your cassock in a frenzy, driving bad spirits and the very devil out of Ms. Amber Sykes."

"Oh, Rory. Don't make me laugh or I'll pee my pants right here in this restaurant."

After dinner, they strolled, hand-in-hand through the business area, looking at window displays. It was cold, but the wind was still, and Marta said she thought she'd better walk a bit after her enormous dinner. A corner video-game arcade was open and Rory steered her inside. At a game called "Bowl-O-Rama" he produced some quarters from his pocket and invited her to play against him. With a glint in her eye, she took him on.

"Sweet leapin' leprechauns!" he cursed. "I can't even beat you on a damn machine."

"Why do you let yourself in for these drubbings? I would have thought by now, you'd have learned you can't beat me at bowling."

"One more game?" he asked, shoving four more quarters into the slots.

"Okay, but don't say I didn't warn you."

By this time a small cadre of local teens had gathered to watch the match up. When she creamed him a second time, there were snickers and pitying looks.

"Okay, wise guys. I'll pay the tab if any of you think you can do better," he said, challenging the entire group.

One lanky boy with a shock of unruly hair and a mild case of acne took him up on the challenge. Rory put in another four quarters and the game was off and running. It didn't take Marta long to pulverize that kid's ego, too.

"Geez, Mister. She like that on the real alleys?" he asked.

"Yep. She wipes up the floor with me every time. I've never beaten her— not one single time."

"Maybe you ought to sign her up for the pro-bowler's tour. She could make money. You could be her manager. If you're that lame, you'd need some sort of job while she pulled in the big bucks."

"Now there's a thought. What do you say, wife? Ready to hit the big time?"

The guys were all looking at Marta's middle and smiling.

"Looks like she's carrying her bowling ball with her already. All she needs is some shoes and she'd be good to go," one of the older boys teased.

"Looks like you mighta been doing something besides bowling with her, man." This from a cool dude in a leather jacket who sported hair in various shades of blue and green.

"Careful, cowboy. I don't appreciate hearing stuff like that when there's a lady present. Someday you want to have a woman as cool as mine on your arm, you'd better clean up your act."

"Yeah, cowboy," the rest of them chimed in, elbowing their friend. "Have some manners, woncha?"

"Hey, mister. Care to try a game against me?" the leather-jacketed one asked. "You're such a pussy, I bet I can beat you twice as good as she did."

"Twice as well, maybe?"

"What are you? The grammar coach? Are you gonna play or not?"

"Sure. Put your money where your mouth is."

The kid slipped two of his quarters in the machine. Rory added his own two. His score at the end was 180 to the kid's 142.

"Looks like the pussy can beat you, and my wife can beat me, so how does it make you feel to know you're not as good as me and you sure as hell aren't as good as her? What shall I call you? What's weaker than a pussy?"

The kid's eyes narrowed and a hand went into his jacket pocket. Rory heard the snap of the switchblade's blade opening and was ready when the kid lashed out with the knife, trying his best to cut Rory's face. Rory was amazingly quick, seizing the wrist of the kid's knife hand and twisting his knife arm up high behind the kid's back. He jerked up harder and the kid screamed and dropped the knife.

"It's best not to mess with a sheep man, son. I might be a pussy at bowling, but I've had years of building muscles while wrestling sheep. You try that again, I'll break your arm off at the shoulder."

For emphasis he wrenched up on the arm again and the kid sagged to his knees.

"Now, pick up your knife and fold it up and don't take it out of your pocket again."

The kid's fingers grabbed the knife and Marta held her breath, afraid he was going to come up with it swinging.

"Fold it up," Rory said again in a deadly quiet voice. "Good. Now put it away."

As soon as the kid put the knife in his pocket, Rory stuck out his hand.

"No hard feelings?" he asked, ready to shake hands and make peace.

The kid stuck out his hand and Rory shook it.

"What's your name?" he asked.

"Why? You gonna report me?"

"No."

"It's Little Joe Sanchez."

"You going to school?"

"Nah. I dropped out my sophomore year."

"Working?"

"When I can find work."

"What kind of work do you like to do?"

"Whadda ya care? It ain't like you're going to offer me a job."

"You might be wrong. As you can see, my wife is pregnant and she's due to deliver the end of March. I've got about 600 sheep that will need shearing in April and the early part of May. I could use some help. You're stocky, and you might make a good sheep-shearing man. If you think you can cut the mustard, I'll put you on the payroll. Give me your address or your phone number so I can get hold of you when the time comes."

"Is that a pussy job?"

Rory grinned. "Son, I guarantee you 'pussy' is not a name you'll apply to that job after you shear the first sheep. You want a trial or not?"

"Yeah, I guess. You got some paper? I'll write my numbers down."

Rory walked over to the desk where the arcade manager sat and asked for a sheet of paper and a pen. The kid followed him over and wrote down two phone numbers and an address Rory recognized as belonging to one of the seedier areas of Butte.

"First number is my old man's. He sleeps days, so don't call there before 4 p.m. The other number is my sister's. Probably better to try that one."

"Okay. Tell her I might be calling, so she'll know."

"Yeah, yeah. You won't call. Nobody calls me."

"I will."

Rory fished in his pocket and pulled out his wallet. "Here's my card, Mr. Sanchez. Between now and April, I suggest you start lifting some weights. Even a good-sized *lamb* weighs in at 150 pounds or more."

On their way back to the restaurant parking lot where they'd left the truck, Marta used the time to give Rory an earful.

"He could have killed you. Why did you bait him like that?"

"I don't know. Saw a little of myself in him when I was his age, maybe? Recognized that bantam rooster stance—the one where you're trying your best to let on like you have the world by the tail when inside you're scared shitless? He's a kid screaming for someone to care about him. It struck a chord."

"Why does it have to be you who cares? What's wrong with his parents or his sister?"

"Kid like that has probably been fending for himself for years. Parents drink. Sister has a kid every ten months and has her hands full without taking him on, too. He doesn't have the education he's already realized he needs to get a good job. He's too proud and stubborn to go back to get one. He probably feels a lot like I did when all the sunburns rubbed my nose in their college sheepskins and told me I'd never make it in the world."

"I don't think I'd feel safe with him running around the ranch."

"He'll turn out to be the best sheep-shearing man in Montana, next to me and the drovers. You watch. He'll never admit it, but as soon as he gets it down how to shear, and he gets the praise from the five of us for doing a good job, he'll be so grateful for all the attention, he'll be the first one to the barn in the morning and the last one to leave at night. Think you could put him up in a bedroom for the shearing season?"

"Oh, Rory, no! We'll have the baby and I'd be afraid. Anyone who'd pull a knife over such a little thing. . . ."

"Okay. I'll see if I can find a small travel trailer for the incorrigible one. Would you like to lay a little wager? I say he'll become one of my best hands. You want to take the opposite view?"

"Definitely. He won't last a day."

"Five bucks? Ten?"

"That's a pussy bet, Rory," she told him with a grin. "A hundred."

"You're on."

Chapter Sixteen

At 7 p.m. on March 31st, Rory called Boise to talk to his mother.

"Mom? It's me, Rory. You're a grandmother. Again."

"Marta had the baby? What is it?"

"It's a girl. Seven pounds, four ounces. Her name is Alyssa Marie. We used all the letters in your name and just rearranged them for her middle name."

"How kind of you. Is Marta okay?"

"Yep. Tired of course, but fine. They'll be coming home in the morning."

"I'm so happy for you both. Was it a hard labor?"

"Not on me."

"Rory Owen McCrea. How dare you joke about what has to be a woman's worst pain? When did she go into labor?"

"A bit after 3 a.m."

"And when was the baby born?"

"Right on the dot of 5:30 this afternoon."

"Well, that's not too long a labor for the first baby."

"Felt like forever to me."

"Would they let you stay with her all through it?"

"You don't think I'd have let them toss me out, do you?"

"Well, in my day, it was a whole different ball of wax. Just when you could have used a husband's strength, they sent him to the waiting room to read magazines."

"Mine wouldn't have been around anyhow, Mom."

"Patrick was there. Maybe not Daniel, but Patrick was there."

"I guess I'm glad of that. I wouldn't have missed Alyssa's birth for the world, so it's kind of hard for me to understand how good old Daniel could just walk away and not be there for mine—or Chris's."

"It was kind of a hard situation. Patrick wanted you to be *his* son. And he didn't want the competition for your love that Daniel might have provided. So, that was the agreement they struck. Daniel would give up all claims to you and Chris, and in return, Patrick would be responsible for raising you both."

"Well, what was is what was. Can't change it now."

"Do you still regret that you never knew Daniel?"

"Yeah, Mom. Sometimes. It'd be nice to have a point of reference for some of what's inside me. I have the pictures, so I know about the outside things, but I'll never have a chance to know the other stuff."

"Sometime soon, before I die, if you want to sit down with me in some private place, I'll tell you all I know about Daniel."

"Hey, I thought you said you didn't want to hear any more on the subject of Daniel McIlvey."

"Maybe I owe you and Chris a bit more. I just don't want the rest sitting around hearing it and condemning me because I dared to love more than one man."

"Have they done that since Christmas? Condemn you?"

"Not directly, but there's an undercurrent. I feel that they wished I'd stopped with the first six of them—never been involved with Daniel."

"I'm kind of glad you pressed on. Hey, Mom, it's been good talking to you, but I'm behind on my chores, so I need to get my sheep fed. We'll send you a picture or two when we get them developed, okay?"

"I'll look forward to it, Son. Tell Marta I'm so happy for you both."

"Mom, can you do a favor and call the rest of them and spread the news? I've got shearing coming up this week and I won't have time for playing the town crier. And Marta will likely be tired as I am by day's end."

"I'd be happy to tell them, Rory. Congratulations, Son. I just know you'll be the best father ever."

"I hope so. Don't want to raise any juvenile delinquents."

He fed in the dark and when he got back to the house, the phone was ringing.

"Hello?"

"Rory, your mom just called with the news. I'm so happy for you and Marta."

"Thanks, Lass."

"Is she cute?"

"I think so, but then I might be a tad biased on the matter."

"Does she have dark hair and lavender eyes?"

"Try no hair and who knows what color eyes. She had them all squinched up at the indignity of having to make her way into the world. What she has is a very lusty bellow. No way I'll be able to sleep through her demands for 2 a.m. feedings."

"Your mom said you named her Alyssa Marie?"

"Yes."

"How did you come by that name?"

"Marta liked Alyssa. I turned Mom's name around from Maire to Marie."

"Are you disappointed it's not a boy?"

"No, sure *not* disappointed. Just glad she has all eight fingers and toes."

"Rory. Have you been drinking? Eight fingers and toes? Is she missing some?"

"No. She's just perfect. I wanted to see if you were paying attention. I know how women get when they discuss babies. All kind of fuzzy and dreamy. You'd think, after as bad as labor is, you guys would be angry when you talked about babies. Not want to sign up for any more of them. But, no, you're all smelling the baby powder and those curdled-milk spit-ups and half wishing for another one in the next nine months."

"I swear, Rory. You must not do anything much but sit on your heels observing people. There's not a man in my acquaintance that would have characterized women that way. At least not with that much observational accuracy. Just the other day a woman came into the boutique with a new baby and you're right, I smelled the powder and was wishing for a brother or sister for Danny."

"Hey, Lass. I wondered when Danny was born why you chose that name for him. I assume you know about Daniel McIlvey being Chris's and my father."

"Yes, I knew. Maeve told me not long after you learned it from your mother. Danny's named for him."

"Why would you want to give your son the same name as a man who, at best, was not a very good example of what most parents would want their child to be like?"

"Rory—you don't know why?"

"No."

"I couldn't very well call Aidan's son 'Rory Aidan McCrea' now could I? That would have sent seismic shock waves through the McCrea clan. I wanted to name him that, but I knew I couldn't, so I did the next best thing. I named him for your father."

"Why?"

"Because Daniel McIlvey gave the world you—so I thought it would be a fitting tribute to name my son for a man who *fathered* the one man I will always love and respect—you."

There was a very long pause and finally Kelsey spoke up, asking, "Are you still there?"

"Yes."

"Did I shock you into silence? Are you upset that I named Danny for your real dad? You do understand why I couldn't name him Rory Aidan, don't you?"

"Yes, I understand that."

"Are you upset?"

"No. I'm honored now that I see your reasoning. Makes me feel a bit better toward my father, too."

"Rory, I know you love Marta—especially now, but you've got to know that I love you, too. You used to call me your 'ideal woman' and it always made me feel so special. You have the gift of making women feel loved and appreciated. That's a rare thing, Rory. I hope you never lose that quality.

"I wish I were the recipient of your love. I know I can't be, but that doesn't prevent me from wishing it were so. Every time you hear me call Danny by his name, know that it stands in place of yours only because I didn't have the courage to call him Rory."

"Discretion is the better part of valor, Kels. But thank you for coming as close as you dared."

"My will says Daniel would go to you and Marta if something happened to me—with the provision that Marta agreed, of course. You're named as his godfather. In many ways, I think of him as the son you and I would have had, had life worked out differently."

"I'd be happy to claim him as my son, Lass, but I'd also as soon not—for the not wanting anything that bad to happen to you."

"I'd just as soon it didn't happen either. Will you give your new daughter a kiss from her Auntie Kelsey? And give Marta one from me, too. I'll be sending gifts as soon as I can get into town to find some. Is there something Alyssa is in need of?"

"I think Marta said something about some kind of sacks that tie at the bottoms?"

"Not sacks like feed store sacks, Rory." He could hear the amusement in her voice and finally she chuckled out loud. "S-A-C-Q-U-E-S. They're buntings for babies. They keep the baby's feet warm, but you can untie them and pull them up to change diapers. I'm sending Marta and the baby a gift and I'm going to find you a book about raising children." She laughed again. "Sacks. You're hopeless."

"Not only hopeless, but tired, too and shearing starts as soon as I bring Marta and Alyssa home. I've got a call to make to a young stud that I hope will help with shearing, so, it was good to talk to you, but I'd better make that call before it gets much later. Love you, Lass and thanks for naming him Daniel."

"Bye, Rory. Send lots of pictures of Alyssa. I'm dying to see what she looks like."

"Let's trade. I'd like to keep up with the progress of your almost Rory son, too."

"Will do. Love you."

"Love you, too, Lass."

He dialed the father's number first, it being late in the evening.

"Hello?"

"I'd like to speak with Little Joe Sanchez, please."

"You a cop?"

"No, my name's Rory McCrea and I'd like to hire Joe for my ranch for a month or two. To shear sheep."

Rory had to hold the phone at arm's length as the elder Sanchez bellowed for Joe to come to the phone.

"Hello?"

"Little Joe?"

"Yeah, who wants to know?"

"Rory McCrea, the sheep man. You got some muscles built up? Ready to go to work?"

"Really. You really want to hire me? What's it pay?"

"I pay apprentices a basic $100 per month and I provide room and board. There's a bonus of $4.00 a sheep that you shear without ruining the fleece. Ruined fleeces cost $4.00 out of your basic pay for each one I can't sell. Interested?"

"Yeah, I guess. How do I get there?"

"Be at the video arcade in two hours. I'll pick you up there."

"What do I need to bring?"

"Clothes for a week. Whatever personal items you want. No boom boxes or loud music, but a radio is okay if you play it low. TV reception sucks here unless you have a big antenna or a dish. Some books if you like to read. Basic stuff like soap and toothpaste."

"And where am I staying?"

"There's a furnished travel trailer behind the shearing barn. It'll give you some privacy. But no smoking, candles, or open flames. I can't afford to have you burn the place down. Agreed?"

"Okay, I guess."

"Two hours. Be there."

Rory stopped at the hospital to visit a minute before visiting hours were over. Alyssa was sleeping in her plastic bassinette, a finger in her mouth.

"They say when you can leave tomorrow?"

"I have to check out by 11 a.m. Why are you here so late?"

"Had to call the world and let them know the good news. That took a few hours. And I'm picking up Joe Sanchez at ten tonight to take him back to the ranch. So I thought I'd just drop in and make sure nobody had stolen my two favorite girls before I collect Joe."

"Is there food in the little trailer?"

"Yeah. I picked up some stuff on the way home this afternoon. Dulce made some enchiladas for him to heat in the microwave, and there's some soda in the fridge. Should hold him a day or two. At least until he sees if he likes the job well enough to stay."

"Better put your $100 in the chipped tea pot in the kitchen so when he leaves tomorrow, I can collect my wager."

"I'll do it tonight, soon as I get home. I'd better not leave Little Joe waiting. He's about half convinced I'm funning him. I'll be here about ten tomorrow. I'm sorry that shearing is going to use up many of my hours for a month or more, but Dulce and Melinda are just dying to see the new babe and even Consuela had a gleam in her eye, so I don't think you'll lack for help around the house."

"I just want to be home with you. I hate even one night in a strange bed."

"I'll miss you, too. Get some rest, wife. I doubt either of us will get much of that from this point on—at least not for a good stretch."

"Night, husband mine. And thanks for giving me such a beautiful child."

"Any time, love. Long as it gets born in March."

Little Joe was standing just outside the arcade with a plastic sack full of his essentials.

"Man, I thought sure you weren't coming. I was just about to leave for home," Joe told him, throwing his gear in the back seat and climbing into the front one.

"If you're going to work for me, we need to arrive at some understandings. I keep my word and if, for some reason I can't keep it, I'll always call and tell you I can't. I have four drovers and one of the drover's sons that shear with me. We're partners in the ranch, and as such, I expect you to treat them with respect. Bernardo is about your age, but he's been in the sheep business a long time and knows the ropes.

"From time to time, all of them will give you orders. I expect you to comply with their directions, same as I'd expect you to comply with mine. You do a good job, and they'll all be your friends. You screw up or get a smart mouth, and I don't think you want to find out how they'd treat you then.

"I'm giving you a good opportunity to learn a trade that will make you some serious money if you do it well. I don't often take chances on strangers. I hope you will remember that and not let me down."

"Why me? Why are you taking a chance on me? I was ready to rearrange your face that night in the arcade. Nobody calls me a pussy and walks away whole."

"Let's just say I like scrappy kids. You reminded me of myself at your age. A chip on my shoulder big as a boulder and ready to dare anyone to knock it off. Someone gave me a chance, so I thought I'd maybe do the same for you."

"So, what should I call you?"

"Well, not Rory, that's for sure. Either Mr. McCrea or you can call me 'boss' like Bernardo does."

"What about the others?"

"I doubt they'll object if you call them Señor whatever. Might not even mind you calling them by their given names long as it's respectful when you call them."

"What *are* their names?"

"Enrique. He speaks pretty fair English. Juan is getting better at it, but he lapses into Spanish when he can't remember the English words. Ricardo and Manuel speak mainly Spanish or Basque.

"If they don't want anyone to know what they're talking about, they all speak Basque. Even I only know a few words of that, so they can discuss whatever they want to in that language and I'm none the wiser. Sometimes, when we all sit down to play poker or when we start kicking a soccer ball around or playing football, they speak Basque so they can gang up on me."

When they got to the ranch, Rory parked up at the house and walked Joe down to the trailer.

"You're plugged in, so you have heat from the electric wall heater. There's food and sodas in the refrigerator. The toilet is connected to the shed's septic system. The only thing you lack is hot water for showers. You're welcome to use the one off the mudroom up at the house. The sheets are clean and Consuela will change them every week—or oftener as the weather gets hot or you sweat on them after shearing. You can use the washer if you need to wash your clothes. Just ask Consuela to show you how it works."

"Who's Consuela?"

"She's my chief cook and housekeeper. She's another one you should treat with respect. And it goes without saying that my wife deserves the same degree of respect as you'd give me, understood?"

"Yes, sir, boss. Do I start tomorrow morning to work?"

"Yep. Bernardo will show you how to mix sheep feed and you can help feed my sheep since I have to go to Butte to bring my wife and my new daughter home from the hospital. If you have questions, Enrique is in charge whenever I'm off the premises."

"What time do I start?"

"We generally hit the floor running about 5 a.m."

Joe rolled his eyes. "That's pretty early."

"Yes. Not all the year is so labor intensive, but shearing is a long, hard pull, so the sooner we get started in the morning, the more likely it is we get to eat dinner about eight or nine at night. Once my wife feels more comfortable around you, you're welcome to eat at the table up at the house."

"She's not comfortable with me? Why? I didn't do nothing to her."

"Anything to her. I think she was a bit off put when you came at me with your switchblade."

"Would it help if I apologized to her?"

"It might. But words are cheap, so maybe let your actions do the talking for a bit until she stops thinking of you as Joe the Ripper."

"It was you I came after. How come you're not like her—afraid of me?"

"I believe in giving second chances. But not thirds, okay? You'd better get to bed. You have an alarm clock or should I bang on the door in the morning?"

"I don't think you have to worry. I'm so nervous I don't think I'll get a lot of sleep."

"There's nothing to be nervous about. Just be willing to listen and learn, that's all that's required of you. If you don't think you can hack the job, all you have to say is 'I'd like a ride back to Butte' and I'll take you back anytime you want to leave."

"Uh, thank you, boss man."

"See, that wasn't so hard. Goodnight, Joe. See you in the morning."

"Yes, sir."

"Hey, that's even better. I think you'll work out just fine, Joe. And if you save half of what you earn each month, if or when you decide to leave, you'll have a bit to hold you until you can find another job."

Rory didn't get to the shearing until mid-afternoon, once he was sure Marta and Alyssa were settled in. By the time he changed clothes and went to the barn he could already see that Joe was not thinking of shearing as a 'pussy' job.

"Bernardo, show Joe how to run a wooly in here for me to shear."

"Yes, boss."

Rory stripped down to his bare chest in anticipation of the sweat shearing always produced. When Joe and Bernardo came back in dogging a sheep, Joe's mouth dropped open.

"Boss, you think I'll get a chest like yours shearing sheep? Damn, I'd be the envy of every guy on my block in Butte if I get built like you. Are all of them built like that?" He gestured at the drovers.

"Yes. Shearing is no game for pussies. Grab that stool over there and come and watch how it goes. Tomorrow, I'll help you shear your first one, but late this afternoon, I want you to be able to tell me how the order goes in clipping, so pay attention to details."

"Yes, sir."

Rory had to smile as Joe went to collect the stool. Marta was going to lose $100. And he was going to gain it, along with a kid he knew would turn out to be as good, if not better, at shearing than he or his drovers were.

Chapter Seventeen

In the morning, Rory and the drovers all arrived at the barn at about the same time. They quickly mixed feed for the sheep and distributed hay to the various cotes. As they were returning to the shearing barn, Little Joe was sweeping up the shearing areas.

"Thanks, Joe. You showed a bit of initiative sweeping up. I like working in a clean area. Now, are you about ready to try your hand at shearing?"

"No time like the present, I guess, Mr. McCrea. I'm as ready as I'll ever be."

"Okay. Yesterday you watched me shear four or five. What's the first step?"

"Get a sheep into the shearing pen?"

"Yep. But they're all in their sheepcotes. Which sheep are you going to bring down to the shearing barn and how are you going to get them here?"

"I don't know. I didn't see any of that yesterday. All I did was go with Bernardo and get one from the pen outside this barn."

"We work the cotes from the farthest to the closest, which means we start with Juan's sheep up there on the hill past the big house. We use the dogs to drive the sheep down to the pens outside this barn. The dogs work on hand signals and whistles. Come along and watch them."

As the drovers set up to shear, Rory and Joe walked up to get Juan's sheep. The dogs, sensing action, danced and jigged beside them. With a couple of short whistles and a sweep of his arm, the dogs entered the cote and began herding the sheep toward the opening. Nipping and darting, Speedo, Punk and Sophie soon had the whole flock headed in the right direction. Joe watched in amazement.

"Them dogs get transplanted with people brains?" he asked. "They're too smart for dog brains."

"No people brains, but they are bred for this kind of work. Some of what they know comes by way of their genes and some is from long hours of training. Part instinct, part intelligence and repetition. And rewards. You like praise for your work? The dogs like treats for theirs. In the barrel in the barn are dog biscuits. Put a few in your pockets so when the dogs do what you ask, you can reward them."

The dogs prodded the sheep into the corral nearest the shearing barn, then came and sat down expectantly at Rory's feet. He flipped each of them a couple of biscuits and gave them the signal to lie down.

"Well, Joe, go fetch whichever sheep you'd like to start on."

Joe came back dogging a smaller ewe and managed to maneuver it up to the pen where Rory waited. He got the sheep inside without a problem on his first try.

"Good, Joe. Now what?"

"Lay out the equipment to shear with. Shearing scissors, swabs for cuts and a cloth to bundle the hide in."

"The fleece in. We aren't skinning sheep, just shearing them. Okay, then what?"

"You grab the sheep and start shearing."

"What part gets shorn first?"

"The chest."

"Right, except it's called the brisket. But first you have to get the ewe in position. Come over here beside me. Now, slip your left thumb in her mouth and grab a handful of wool on her right hip."

"Will she bite?"

"Not if you slip your thumb in behind her front incisors."

Joe hesitantly ran his thumb into the corner of the ewe's mouth and grabbed onto the wool of her right hip.

"Yeah, just like that. Bend her head over her right shoulder and swing her toward you."

"Good. Now lower her to the ground gently. You'll need to move back as she comes to a flat position. Now, kneel on your left knee and put your right leg over her, there, right in front of her back legs. Okay, you're ready to start clipping the brisket. Here are your shears."

Rory ruffled his fingers through the wool and indicated where Joe should clip, then, using continuous instructions and by lending an occasional hand, he led Joe through the clipping.

"Boost her into a sit, Joe," he instructed, "so you can get to the off side."

Rory took hold of the sheep and showed Joe how to accomplish it. He let Joe continue to clip. Forty-nine minutes later, the sheep was shorn and driven out to the outer corral again.

"I'll do the next three," Rory volunteered.

Three of them were done in the time it had taken Little Joe to do his one.

"How long did it take you to get that fast?" Joe asked.

"Most of my first summer, part of my second." Rory grinned over at Joe. "Ready for your next one?"

"Sure, boss."

"Go fetch one, then."

This time Joe brought back a slightly larger ewe and quickly had it in position. Rory sat on the wall of the shearing station and let Joe progress without offering any help. Only when a nick happened, did Joe stop his efforts and look up helplessly.

"Sorry, sheep," he said.

"Happens all the time, Joe. Swab it with iodine and it'll be fine."

Rory resumed his seat and let Joe finish the sheep up. There were two ragged spots, but otherwise, it was a good job.

"Ready for another one, or are you tired?"

"I'm not so tired, but my hand is burning from working the clippers."

"Let me take the others, then. You can dog sheep for a bit or just watch."

Rory took the next six or seven, showing Joe how to prevent the ragged spots.

Over the next six weeks, Joe became better and better at shearing and seemed to have caught on to many of the other chores as well. Rory had invited him to join Ricardo and Manuel at the table for dinner close to the end of April.

Joe dressed in his best shirt and jeans for the occasion and came to knock on the mudroom door. Marta, startled by the knocking, opened the door with caution.

"Mrs. Boss," Joe began as an alarmed look crossed Marta's face, "I want to say how sorry I am for pulling my knife on Mr. Boss back there in Butte. Mr. Boss has been very good to me and I want you to know that I appreciate this time I've spent here and I hope you can forgive my younger and stupid self about the knife thing. Mr. Boss asked me to come to your house for dinner tonight, and he's the boss, so I am here."

"In this house, I'm the boss. There will be no knives, no swearing. You will be on your best behavior. This ranch is a place of peace and harmony and I will not endure any fighting or bad behavior at my table. If you understand that, then you are welcome to sit at the table and eat. Do you understand?"

Joe gave her a heartbreaker of a smile and nodded in the positive, so she let him in. Dinner was a peaceful event with Joe darting glances at her to see if he were behaving correctly. He ate and listened to the conversation, seeming to be in awe that families actually conversed over dinner. When Alyssa cried and Marta picked her out of the bassinet, another smile broke over Joe's face.

"Can I hold her?" he asked. "I liked to hold my sister's kids. I'm done eating and if I hold her, you can finish your food."

Marta looked at Rory with doubt, but he nodded it was okay, so Marta reluctantly handed the baby to Joe. Joe pushed his chair back from the table and settled Alyssa on his lap. His knees rocked slowly back and forth and Alyssa got quiet and smiled at Joe. He cooed at her and hummed a song and her eyelids grew heavy and finally closed.

"You seem to have the magic touch, Joe," Marta told him. "She's been fussy all day, but now she's sleeping like an angel."

"She's a pretty baby. Nice eyes. Like Mr. Boss's."

After that, Joe was a regular at the ranch table.

The first week of May, with shearing almost at an end, Rory had come up to his office for more tally sheets for Bernardo. Fleeces were piled high and Bernardo and Joe were employed washing them and putting them out on racks to dry. Bernardo was charged with keeping a running count of all the fleeces.

While Rory was rooting in his desk drawer for the sheets, the phone rang.

"Hello?" he answered.

"Have I reached Mr. McCrea?" a decidedly Scottish voice asked.

"You have. Mr. McDougal?"

"Yes, McDougal here. Have you fleeces to sell again this year."

"We're in the middle of shearing. Another 70 or 80 left to clip. I figure the rest of the week and we'll be done. Another few days to get them all washed, dried and bundled. Should be completely done around the 20th of May. After that, I'll have some to sell."

"Would you be of a mind to sell me your lot again?"

"Yes, sir. I'm sure we could work out a deal."

"Without going through the auction market this time? I so liked the quality of your fleeces, I'd as soon not have to compete on the open market for them. I'd like to come in, at your convenience, of course, a few days in advance of the 20th. I'd like to bring three or four of my mill hands to help pack the fleeces up and make them ready to ship. I'd like to take them with us when we return to our mill. Are there lodgings near your ranch?"

"You're welcome to stay at my ranch. We have plenty of room."

"I don't want to impose."

"It's not an imposition, sir."

"All right then. Of course, I'll be happy to pay the standard lodging fees."

"Guests at the ranch don't pay lodging fees. We'll be happy to have you and your men. If I don't have to rent a vehicle to deliver the fleeces to the Denver airport, I'll be saving enough money to feed you for a week."

"Expect us May 16th or 17th, then."

"I'll look forward to your arrival."

"How many fleeces do you estimate you'll have available?"

"I should have 560 top quality, like last year; another 20 good quality, but not top; and 12 fair fleeces. You can take the 32 I'd consider not top quality if you want, or you can decide to just take the 560. Or any part of them you need."

"I'd like as many as you can provide. What reason do you offer for the lesser-quality fleeces?"

"I took on a young man. He's learning to shear. The first dozen he did have a few ragged spots. The next twenty were better, but still not of the quality I'd feel good about offering as tops."

"Well, thanks for being so forthright about the quality. The reason I like dealing with you is your honesty. You don't misrepresent the quality of your fleeces. There was not one that I bought last year that fell below your high standards. Set aside those done by your new man and I'll have a look. I have little doubt they'll still be better than 90% of the fleeces offered by any other rancher in your country."

With a light heart, Rory went back to the shearing barn, and handed the tally sheets over to Bernardo. He told the men that the same buyer was coming to buy all the fleeces this year again, and that set off a round of rapid Basque and big smiles.

"Can we have a meeting in my office tonight after we finish?" Rory asked.

"Yes, we meet with you," Enrique said.

"We'll quit tonight at six so you can eat. Come to the office around 7:30."

Over supper he told Marta about the Scottish contingent coming on the 16th or so and that they'd be staying at the ranch. A frown creased her forehead, but she didn't say anything. She was quiet all through dinner and seemed somewhat annoyed when he announced he was having a meeting of the drovers right after dinner.

In the office, he expounded a bit more about the arrangements with McDougal, then turned to the summer and what to do about moving the sheep up to the meadows.

"Bernardo, are you wanting to become a drover—go up to the meadows with the sheep this year?"

"No, Boss. I have been saving my money. I want to go to the junior college this summer and take some classes so in the fall I can go to the university. I want to become a CPA."

"Well, great, Bernardo. You're really good with numbers. Your tallies are always right on. I think you'll make an excellent CPA. Maybe when you get done, you can do my taxes every year. I'd trust you more than the guy in Butte."

Bernardo grinned and agreed to take Rory on as his first customer after graduation.

"Any of the rest of you have something else to do this summer, or can I count on your to move sheep around the meadows?"

The four drovers all said they were looking forward to time on the mountain. Only Joe was quiet. With shearing coming to an end, he thought maybe his employment was also about to end.

"Joe, do you have plans for the summer?"

"I don't know."

"Are you open to spending the summer up in the high meadows? Learning to ride a horse and becoming a drover along with the other men?"

"Would they let me do that?"

"What do you think, guys? Could you use an extra hand? I could use a bit of time off this summer to help Marta with the baby."

"*Sí*, Boss. We like Joe. He works good. He will make a good drover. We teach him to ride. He can use Señora Kelsey's horse, no?"

"Sure. That horse is getting fat standing around. It'll be good for her to work a bit. Joe, if you're going to be a drover for AmeriBasque, you need a start on your own flock of sheep. When the ewes begin to deliver their lambs, we'll pick out a dozen new lambs from my flock and they'll be yours from then on.

"If you decide to continue to work here, we'll help you in the fall to build a sheepcote for your flock. Each of the drovers has a different ear-tag color so we know what sheep we each own. Mine are silver, Enrique's are yellow, Juan's are brown, Ricardo's are red, and Manuel's are green. You have any objection to blue?"

"No, I like blue just fine, but you can't just give me lambs."

"Hey, I'm the boss. If I want to give you sheep, I can give you sheep. But if you'd feel better about it, I'll take a percentage out of your summer wages to pay for them and I'll make you out a bill of sale in September saying you own them free and clear."

There ensued a short conversation in Basque with all heads nodding in the positive when it concluded.

"We each like to give Joe three our lambs, too," Enrique said. "Make big flock for him. No charge, our lambs. Free."

"You trying to guilt me into making mine free, too?"

Their smiles said that was exactly what they had in mind.

"Okay. Mine are free, too. Think you can handle 24 sheep, Joe?"

"Yes, sir. Thank you, all of you. *Gracias!*"

The meeting broke up on that note, the men and Joe scattering to their various rooms and homes. Marta was engrossed in a novel, Rory noted. She was lying on the couch with an afghan over her. Alyssa was asleep in the wheeled bassinet. There was a small fire burning against the chill of the late April evening.

"Good book?" he asked, sitting down at her feet.

"Yes."

"Did you go to the doctor today? And the pediatrician?"

"Yes."

"What did they say?"

"The baby is fine. All her tests are okay and she's gained two pounds."

"And you? Are you fine, too? It's been a long time."

"He said I was okay. But if you're asking if I'm up for sex, I'm not. And I might not be up for it for a long time."

"Do you want to give me a reason?"

"I'm tired, Rory. And all you do is make me more work."

He frowned and asked, "In what way?"

"Well, first you invite Joe to the table. I'm surprised you didn't give him a bedroom up here, too. That makes extra work for Consuela or me—or both of us."

"I can un-invite him, if you want."

"Oh, yeah, sure. Make me out to be the ogre that tosses him out into the cold."

"He'll soon be up on the meadows."

"Like that will make a whole lot of difference. One more packet of frozen meals to make, or bigger amounts."

"No, it'll be the same. I was planning on Joe taking some of my time up there so I could stay here more and help with the baby. I know I haven't been much help during shearing, but in another week or two, I can do more to help you."

"Is it your idea of helping to saddle me with another five or six men for a week? You didn't even ask me if I wanted to run a bed-and-breakfast. You just took it on yourself to invite them like I didn't even need to be consulted."

"Marta, Mr. McDougal pays far more for our fleeces than anyone else I've run across. There's no place close to put him and his men up. It's only for a few days."

"Yeah. A few more jobs. A few more days."

"If you're so worn out, maybe you ought to quit working at Ron's office."

"Oh, sure. And when the fleece money runs out and you're hiring two or three more street waifs, how do you plan to pay the bills?"

He could see that she wasn't in the mood for anything but arguing, so he decided to end the conversation right then.

"I'm going to bed. I'll carry Alyssa up. This conversation isn't getting either of us anywhere tonight. Soon as shearing is done, we'll sit down and discuss it further. If you need more help around the house, I'll hire someone."

He stood up to leave, hurt by her indifference to his request to resume intimacies, but determined not to give vent to what he was thinking on that score.

"Maybe you should hire someone to take care of your other needs, too."

Stung by the suggestion, he replied with some heat, "I'd rather not have to do that, Marta."

"Why not? For as much attention as you pay to me, I feel like someone you hired."

He sat back down and said, "What brought all this on, Marta? There's got to be something more to it than what you've said so far. Is this a postpartum depression or something?"

"No! At dinner you talk to Manuel and Ricardo and Joe. You hardly say word one to me. You get up and go to work. You come home and hold meetings. You spend all the damn day at the barn. You sleep like the dead. You never hear the baby cry. I thought parenthood meant both of us—not me on duty 24/7 all alone."

"Marta, that's unfair. You know how much work shearing is. I'm tired when I go to bed."

"And I'm not?"

"Yes, I'm sure you are. Give me a poke and I'll get up with the baby if you've pumped some of your milk into bottles. I'm willing to get up at night so you can rest. I know it's been hard for you. C'mon up and I'll give you an all-over rub with that good lotion, and I *will* get up with Alyssa if you'll wake me when she cries."

He took her hand and tugged her to her feet. Carrying the bassinet he followed her up the stairs, where he set the baby down in her usual spot next to Marta's side of the bed.

"Maybe if you'd put her on your side, you might be able to hear her when she cries."

He went around to the bassinet and lifted it up, then moved it to his side of the bed. He went into the bathroom and got the lotion, determined to re-awaken some passion in her. When he came back to the bed, she was wearing her flannel pajamas and when he raised the lotion bottle, she shrugged.

"I'm tired, Rory. I'd rather go right to sleep," she told him as she rolled over to face away from his side of the bed.

He had no problem hearing the baby crying as he didn't sleep much that night. He alternated between feeling some sympathy for her burdens during the shearing time, and being miffed that she thought her burdens that much greater than his.

He had a very hard time understanding her suggestion that he hire someone to take care of his needs. Of all she'd said, that worried him the most. Lately, she was not the same Marta who got upset if he flirted with another woman. He knew childbirth changed women, but he hadn't expected the180° turn she'd done on him. All he hoped was, with a night or two of good sleep, she might be more receptive to him in the future.

Alyssa cried at 3 a.m. and he gently lifted her out of the bassinet. He sat on the edge of the bed and rocked her, humming to her and looking at her in wonder. Even in the soft light from the bathroom, she was beautiful. She watched him, a dimpled smile curving her heart-shaped mouth.

"Say, there, daughter mine," he whispered. "Let's go down and warm you some dinner. Your mama is tired and I haven't been very good about sharing these nighttime meals. It's time for you and I to get better acquainted. So you be really quiet and I'll fix you a nice warm drink and then we'll rock a bit and get a fresh dry diaper."

He padded softly down the stairs and filled a pan with hot water, settling the bottle in it while he held her in his other arm. Twice he refilled the pan until the bottle of Marta's milk was warm to the touch. He tested the milk against the inside of his wrist then went into the living room and sat down in the big padded rocker to feed her. She drank greedily and twice he pulled the nipple from her mouth to burp her. When the bottle was empty, he set it on the edge of the hearth and gathered up the afghan. Sitting down again, he covered his bare legs with the blanket, wrapping Alyssa in it, too. He rocked gently and soon she was asleep again.

It was the dampness of a very wet diaper soaking into his tee shirt that woke him with a jerk. The suddenness of his movement startled the baby and she let out a wail.

"Your plumbing seems to be in good shape, daughter mine," he told her. He put her down on the sofa and went to find a diaper. There was a box in the corner on the table, so he picked one out and went about exchanging a wet one for a dry one. *At least,* he thought, *these go on with sticky tabs. I don't have to worry about sticking you with a pin.* When she was changed, he got a fresh sleeper out of the laundry basket in the kitchen and changed her into that. Carrying her back upstairs, he sat in the rocker up there until she went back to sleep, then put her back in the bassinet. Changing his undershirt, which now felt uncomfortably damp and cold, he crawled back into bed for the hour of sleep he'd enjoy before dawn called him to the shearing barn.

Marta wasn't up when he left, and the pattern persisted for the rest of the shearing time. He got up at least once a night to feed Alyssa, allowing Marta to sleep. By the next-to-last day of shearing he was running on not much more than adrenaline he was so tired.

"Consuela, can you make rooms ready for our visitors? I don't want Marta having to do anything she doesn't volunteer to do," he told his chief cook.

"Sure. I take care. You in dog house again?"

"I don't know. With the shearing I couldn't help out here much. She got run down. Tired. I don't know, Consuela. I'm not very experienced with women's moods after giving birth."

"She need you to love her. Tell her you think her still pretty. How you say? Desire her?"

"Desirable?"

"Yes. Sometimes, with this. . . ." Consuela patted her stomach. "It look like meat you pound with hammer to make tender—no make you feel desirable those marks."

He thought about that on the way down to the barn where the last few sheep waited shearing. He'd just tackled the first one at 8 a.m. when a big van pulled into the yard, and came slowly down to the shearing shed before halting. Doors slid open and the McDougal contingent spilled out. Rory finished the sheep he'd started while McDougal and his crew looked on. When he boosted the shorn sheep down the alleyway, he dried the sweat from his face and put his shirt back on, then extended his hand to Archibald McDougal.

"Mr. McDougal, sir. Welcome to AmeriBasque Ranch. I trust you had a good flight and found us without too much difficulty."

"Yes, Mr. McCrea. Your directions and map were very well wrought. Very nice setup you have here. Let me make introductions. This is Ian Caldwell, my chief mill foreman. And Roddy Matthews, Tom Cunningham and Andy McIntyre. Men, this is Rory McCrea."

They each stepped forward and shook hands. Then, Rory spoke a few words in Spanish and all of the drovers came to line up.

"And this is my crew," Rory said. "Enrique Laboa is my top drover. This is Juan Zalbide, Ricardo Aulestia and Manuel Olaziregi . Bernardo, here is Enrique's son and my chief tally officer. He plans to go to college soon to become an accountant. And this is my newest shearing man, Joe Sanchez."

"You have an excellent crew here, Mr. McCrea. I'd like to take a look at your fleeces now if I might. You spoke of some 30 you didn't feel were quite up to your high standards. Let's start with those, if we may."

"Yes, sir. Joe, pull your fleeces, please."

Joe wasn't sure he wanted to pull his. He was aware that Rory didn't think his work measured up and that had been reinforced by Mr. McDougal's comment about substandard fleeces.

"Joe—your fleeces?" Rory said again, giving Joe an order via the tone of his voice.

He went to the back shed as Rory and the Scots followed along. Joe pulled out all of his fleeces, laying them out on the wide table one-by-one for inspection. He was nourishing a bit of anger that Rory had singled him out first, sure he'd make a poor impression that might color the way the rest of the sale went.

"Mr. Sanchez," McDougal began after inspecting all 32 fleeces carefully. "Mr. McCrea is correct that these fleeces have some minor flaws. In anyone's barn but his, your work would be deemed excellent. With the exception of the two you indicated were your first efforts, your work is well above reproach. I see no reason to turn down a single one of them."

Joe's mouth fell open and he shot a swift glance at Rory to see his reaction. Rory was grinning like a proud father. He gave Joe a brief nod of congratulations. It was the first time anyone in his life had ever found anything he'd done worthy of congratulations and his chest constricted so tightly he could hardly breathe.

"Gather up your fleeces, Joe, and store them back again. Can't have them gathering dust before they get shipped. You learned well. You did well. You'll be paid well, and you have a job shearing for me as long as you want one. Now get your fleeces out of the way so we can spread out the others. Then, you might want to hang around and listen and learn about evaluating them."

"Yes, sir," Joe said, "and thank you Mr. McDougal. You, too, Mr. McCrea."

Joe gathered up his shearing efforts and carefully wrapped them in cloth bundles again, all the time trying to keep his feet—the feet that felt like they should be dancing on air—on the ground.

"Bernardo, bring your tally sheets, then go and count what's still left to shear, please."

As each drover pulled up bundles of fleece to spread out on the inspection table, Bernardo added the totals of those shorn against the 45 yet to do, dividing the fleeces by color ties into the correct pages for each of the drovers. McDougal was also complimentary of Bernardo's facts and figures.

"You must be very proud, Mr. McCrea. As usual, your fleeces are of the highest quality. You have an absolutely magnificent crew. How long will it take you to finish the rest of those unshorn?"

"Tomorrow, noon to 2 p.m.?" He consulted with the four drovers in Spanish and they nodded that they could have the rest shorn by that time. He knew they could finish the rest that day if not for the need to entertain the Scots and have dinner at a sensible hour, not at the 9-10 p.m. hours a long day of shearing often entailed. Today he intended to knock off at 4 to give the drovers time to shower and dress for dinner. Consuela had been warned to be on the lookout for their arrival and have a dinner in mind that could be put on the table by 6 p.m. regardless of when McDougal's group arrived. He sent Joe on the run to tell her they were here.

"May we wander about the place a bit?" McDougal asked. "I'd like to see your setup."

"Yes, sir. Bernardo, can you do the tour-guide bit?"

"Yes, boss." Bernardo shelved his tally sheets and tucked his pencil behind an ear and came forward to give the Scots a tour of the ranch.

"I'd show you around myself, but if I want to meet tomorrow's noon deadline, I'd better finish up as many sheep as I can this afternoon. When you're done looking, come back to this barn and I'll go up to the house with you to introduce you to my wife and see you get settled in so you'll all have a chance to freshen up before dinner."

"I'm quite sure we're in good hands with Bernardo, here. Carry on, Mr. McCrea."

Rory was sweating profusely when the tour concluded, having shorn five sheep in the time they were wandering around the ranch. Twenty-one of the forty-five remaining sheep were now devoid of their wooly coats, leaving twenty-four to do.

"We'd like to watch for a moment or two, if that's possible," McDougal said.

"It's fine with me. Bernardo, fetch the long bench for our guests."

Bernardo came back with the bench and carefully dusted it off. The men sat down to observe a shearing.

They watched two that Rory did, speaking low among themselves. When Rory looked up in question of their mutterings, McDougal spoke.

"They were just comparing the American way of shearing to our way. It has some similarities and several differences. They were just saying your way seems more efficient."

"Neither I, nor the Americans can take the credit for that, sir. This is Basque shearing we practice here. My drovers were the ones with the expertise. I learned everything I know from them. If this way is more efficient, it's Basque efficiency that makes it so."

McDougal smiled, thinking to himself that it was the way McCrea was willing to give praise and tribute to his men, rather than taking the credit all to himself that made his operations efficient and his fleeces the highest quality. Men worked gladly for an overseer who was that willing to share credit and financial gain with the men. It was obvious that his men held him in high regard and therefore did their best to perform at peak levels.

"Let me go sponge off and I'll see you get settled, sir."

He hit the trough out the back door of the barn, using a horse-washing sponge to wash the sweat off his torso and dunking his face and head into the cold water. He hand-combed his hair back off his forehead and put his shirt on.

"Ready?" he asked.

"Lead on," McDougal said. "I'm looking forward to seeing the inside of an American ranch house. It looks huge from out here."

He almost led them around to the mudroom entrance, catching himself at the last minute. He took them up the front stairs and opened the door into the long hallway. Marta stood just to the left in the entrance to the living room.

"Marta," he said, taking her hand and drawing her to stand beside him. "This is Mr. Archibold McDougal. His mill foreman, Ian Caldwell, and Roddy Matthews, Tom Cunningham and Andy McIntyre. My wife, Marta, and behind in the bassinet, our daughter, Alyssa."

"Hello, and welcome. Would you like a drink of something first, or would you prefer to go to your rooms and freshen up first?" Marta asked. "Please make yourselves at home."

"Perhaps it would be best to go and wash up a bit. It was a long flight and a long drive. If it's not too much trouble."

"No, of course not. Come with me, please."

Each of them picked up a suitcase or bag and tramped up the stairs following Marta. Rory went to the kitchen to be sure Consuela was on track with dinner. It smelled like a roast cooking already, and she gave him a peek into the oven. The roast was in a huge enameled pan, with potatoes, carrots and onions surrounding it. It made his mouth water and he remembered he'd had no lunch.

"Serve at six? *Seis?*" he asked her.

"Yes, I be ready then."

"Good. You're the best, Consuela."

"I no want to be in your dog house, Mr. Rory."

He dashed upstairs for a quick shower and a change of clothes, then came down to find some bottles behind the bar in the corner of the den. He rarely drank anymore, so he hoped they didn't ask for anything too exotic.

One-by-one, the Scots came down to join him at the bar. Most of them requested Dewar's and Rory was happy that he'd picked up a bottle of that. McDougal, when he appeared, asked for soda water with lemon.

"Do we have a lemon, Marta?" Rory asked.

"Yes, I think so. In the refrigerator in the kitchen."

About that time Alyssa let out a cry and Marta hurried to comfort her while Rory went to the kitchen in search of a lemon.

"Damn good of you to put us up here," McDougal said on his return. "And if that smell is any indication, supper will be something to write home about. Your wife is most gracious, too. She must have gone to considerable effort to make us welcome. The rooms are spacious and inviting."

"My wife has many talents," Rory agreed. "She turned this place into a home. It was pretty run-down when I bought it. She's very good with paints and fabrics. If I showed you photos of before and after, you'd find it hard to believe how much she's accomplished in the last year. She's more than my right arm."

He knew she was listening while she fed Alyssa, so he didn't say more than what he felt was the truth. He quelled the urge to give her more of a build-up, knowing instinctively she'd reject even his mild accolades if she thought he was trying to butter her up.

Up until the birth, she had been his right arm and maybe most of his right leg, too. Now, he wasn't so sure how she felt about being valued in that way. As he poured a second round of drinks he found himself wishing everyone gone from the ranch so he'd have the time and the privacy to attempt to get back to their former relationship. His thoughts were interrupted by Marta herself.

"Rory, can you look after Alyssa while I shower and change for dinner?"

"Yes. Sure." His eyes met hers and he hoped his look conveyed his love and thanks for the effort she'd put forth to make the Scots welcome. She turned away, not acknowledging his unspoken message and went up the stairs to their room. She only came back down when Consuela announced dinner.

The drovers, Bernardo and Joe took their places at the table, each across from one of the McDougal men. Marta presided at her end nearest the kitchen while he took his seat at the other end opposite her. She played hostess, making sure each man was served and that each had ample opportunity to sample seconds. Rory carried on desultory dinner conversation with McDougal, who was seated on his right while worrying about Marta. She was brittle tonight, not her usual warm and sunny self.

After dinner McDougal and all the rest of his men and Rory's crew thanked Marta for the excellent repast, and asked her to convey their appreciation to Consuela as well. Marta did as they asked, then, soon after, said she was going up to put Alyssa down for the night. She didn't return for the rest of the evening.

The men swirled their after-dinner brandies and discussed sheep and the making of wool materials, until some of them began to openly yawn.

"You must be very tired," Rory said, taking pity on them. "Feel free to go up at any time."

It was all the invitation most of them needed. Only Ian Caldwell and Archibald McDougal remained.

"Mr. McCrea, might we go into the privacy of your office and discuss payment for the fleeces?"

"Wouldn't you rather wait until tomorrow when you're rested? And when you can see the final fleeces that still are on the sheep?"

"I have no qualms that the quality of those fleeces will be at the same level as are all the others. I'm always more generous after a good meal and my brandy. It would be to your advantage to deal now, unless you're too tired."

"No, sir. I'm fine. This way, then."

He led them to his office and when they both sat, he came around behind his desk and sat quietly, waiting for McDougal to open the negotiations.

"I paid you what last time?"

"You paid $50,000."

"For how many fleeces?"

"A few less than 300." Rory opened a ledger. "Ten less than 300, to be exact."

"And this year you have just short of 600?"

"Yes. Counting the best ones at 560 in number and those of slightly less quality at 32, there's 592 altogether. And I don't expect top dollar for the 32."

"Nonsense, Mr. McCrea. I count all 592, which is slightly more than twice what I bought last time. Would you be happy with twice the dollar value? $100,000 for the lot?"

Rory smiled and shook his head. "I'd be overjoyed to have that amount, Mr. McDougal. But because you're bearing the cost of boxing and shipping, I'd be willing to take $90,000 for them all."

"I appreciate that offer, Mr. McCrea, but my shipping costs will be more than offset by the fact that your fleeces are so clean and free of debris that it will save hours of preparation on my end before milling. I insist on paying the full $100,000. I want you to never *think* about selling your fleeces elsewhere unless I'm forced to forego purchasing them because of a downturn at the mills. So, I'm willing to pay more for an exclusive right to your fleeces."

"Then I accept your most generous offer. And I'll hold myself and my men available to help you pack up the lot. Thank you very much."

Ian Caldwell handed McDougal the briefcase he carried and from that, McDougal produced his checkbook.

"Will you want to hold shipment up until this clears the bank?"

"No, sir. I do believe your credit references are of the same high quality as you keep telling me our fleeces are. I'd be happy to hold the check until your return to Scotland is finalized and all the boxes arrive in good order."

"Just out of curiosity, may I ask how you will divide the money with the youngest of your men? With the young man who's learning to shear?"

"Since you made no distinction in the price you're willing to pay for his fleeces, he'll be paid the same price per fleece as I pay the other drovers or what I take for myself. It'll be divided by number of sheep shorn and each will get the same amount based on the number of sheep they own."

"But your young man doesn't own any sheep, does he? He was shearing your sheep, isn't that correct?"

"Far as I'm concerned, he sweat so much over the 32 he sheared, I figure he owns them by way of that sweat equity. He'll get full value for his 32."

"Good. I wondered how that would work out. He looked so relieved when I said his fleeces were excellent that I hated to think all his hard work would be for naught financially. Well, Rory McCrea, it's late and I'm sure you'll need to get up early to meet the noon deadline, so if it's all right with you, I suggest we retire. Then, tomorrow, while you finish the final shearing, we'll be about crating what's already set to go."

"Goodnight, then, sir. Mr. Caldwell. Breakfast is around eight in the morning. Enjoy that before you come down to begin packing. It's still a bit chilly at six."

"Thank you. We'll do as you suggest, though at six it's likely the same as our noon in Scotland. But a damn sight drier. If my big markets weren't scattered all across Europe, I'd be tempted to move my mills here just for a glimpse of sun more than a dozen days a year."

Chapter Eighteen

The drovers were again very pleased with the price of the fleeces. Joe Sanchez, when Rory handed him a check for $5,408 for his thirty-two fleeces was speechless.

"Those sheep I did were *your* sheep," he protested, trying to hand the check back.

"You earned them, Joe."

"What should I do with the money?"

"Bank whatever you can get along without. Someday, you may want to buy yourself a sheep ranch. If you get in the habit of saving what you can, you'll have the money for a place of your own."

"I don't never want anyplace but here, Mr. McCrea."

"Don't *ever* want," Rory corrected. "You want to be a big sheep man you need to remember your English lessons. There might come a time when I lose this place, so it would be well to be prepared to go it on your own."

"Why do you say that?"

"I might lose the place? Because I owe so much on the ranch that if something were to happen, I might go under."

"Like what might happen?"

"Lots of years of no rain. Hay so expensive I can't buy enough of it for winter feedings. Sheep diseases wipe out the flocks. There are a hundred things that could go wrong."

"Then I'll put the money in the bank and if something goes wrong, I'll give it back to you."

Rory was touched by Joe's benevolence.

"Joe," he said, "let's just cross our fingers and toes and hope nothing that bad happens, okay? But thanks for your offer to help out. I knew you'd make me glad I hired you on."

As soon as the fleeces were on their way to Scotland, the drovers set about teaching Joe how to manage Kelsey's horse. He took to it quickly and by the first of June, the long drive up to the mountain meadows began. Rory spent four days establishing the camp and making sure all was in order before coming down the hill again. In all the time since Alyssa's birth, he'd not had the space or privacy to try to work out the problems with Marta, but he was bound and determined to do so the following weekend.

When Marta left on Tuesday for work, he volunteered to keep Alyssa at home with him, telling Marta he wanted to catch up on his bookkeeping. As soon as she was on her way, he put Alyssa in her sling and settled it against his chest and went to see Melinda.

"Melinda, I need a favor."

"Of course, you marvelous man, you. Thank you for so much money. We paid most of the trailer off so our monthly payments are now much less. What do you need?"

He was glad her English was much better than any of the rest of them.

"I don't know if you've noticed, but Marta. . . ."

"*Triste, no?*"

"Sad? Yes. I don't know what to do to make her happy again. I'd like to take her away for a weekend, but with the baby. . . ."

"I would take care of her for you. I miss having a baby in the house. I like one to care for I can give back." She grinned and asked, "This weekend?"

"Yes, if you'd be willing."

"Don't give it another thought. I will take her starting Friday at lunchtime. That way, you can go whenever your wife gets home. Usually she's early to get home on Fridays."

"I'll be happy to pay you."

"No. I don't want your money. Just plenty of *leche por la niña.*"

"Thanks, Melinda. I'll have Marta make you a good supply."

The next stop was in the kitchen where Consuela was paring potatoes to put into her shepherd's pie.

"Hello, Mr. Rory. Did you have good walk?"

"Yes. Consuela, you have a sister in Boise still, no?"

"*Sí.* Lucinda."

"How would you like a week off to visit her?"

"How I go? Your missus no can do all the work by self."

"I'll help her. I need some time with her all alone. Can you be ready tomorrow, Wednesday, when Marta goes to work? I can drop you at the bus depot and get you a round-trip ticket for Boise. You can call your sister now and see if that's okay with her."

Giving him a doubtful look, she wiped her hands and went to the phone to call. He took Alyssa into his office and put her down in the small mesh-sided playpen with its mobiles and assorted rattles.

Consuela leaned on the doorframe to inform him of what she'd found out.

"My sister say she can meet me in Boise. Bus arrives almost midnight, but Lucinda's man, Diego, can come to pick me with her."

"Good. I'll call now and reserve a ticket for you."

He called and used his debit card to reserve a ticket for Consuela. With the drovers up on the mountain and Melinda willing to care for the baby and Consuela gone, he hoped to get Marta to agree to forego working on Friday and go with him to Missoula for a weekend getaway. If she wouldn't leave Alyssa behind, then at least he'd have her alone in the house for some serious talking. He knew he couldn't go on like they'd been with each other. He was sick about the silences and scared about her refusals in bed. He needed his woman back.

On Wednesday, he drove Consuela to the bus station, and got her the tickets at the counter, then waited until she'd boarded the bus, admonishing her not to forget to return. He drove home again and when Melinda came over, he gave her two of the four bottles of milk Marta had left him in the refrigerator, subbing two empty bottles he'd purchased in Butte at the dollar store for the ones Melinda took. The two empties he put in to soak in the dishpan in the sink.

By the time Marta got home, all the bottles were soaking, empty.

"She drank all four in the time I was gone?"

"Yes. Maybe you'd better leave me a couple more for tomorrow."

"Six? And feed her myself, too? I think it may be time to start mixing some of my milk with formula if she's going to be that hungry. The pediatrician said it was okay to do that if I ran short."

"Should we try that? Do you have any formula?"

"Yes. I bought a can when he told me that, just to be prepared. Let me go pump a half a bottle, or maybe a full bottle and divide it into two then we can add formula to make two of them full. If she tolerates it okay, I'd be tempted to go with formula and get these breasts to dry up. They leak at the worst times."

She went to the kitchen and pumped while he finished up the paperwork in his office. Alyssa slept in the playpen. He hated being that devious about the milk, but if Alyssa didn't take to the taste of the formula, he might not be able to take Marta away for the weekend.

Marta mixed formula into her breast milk and when Alyssa cried, she tried her out on the mixture. Alyssa, whom Rory had shorted two bottles that afternoon, drank the formula down without a peep. And she slept better that night, too. In the morning, her diaper was full of a bit looser stool, but it wasn't like diarrhea, so Marta pumped another bottle's worth of breast milk and filled three bottles one-third full, using formula to make up the rest. Off she went to work, beginning to see some light at the end of the breast-feeding tunnel. Rory gave those three bottles to Melinda, and made up two with formula only. Alyssa, he was happy to learn, was pleased to drink them both without complaint.

Friday, Marta came home at 3:30. When she went up to change, he slipped out to get the flowers from his truck. Ringing the doorbell, he waited while she ran down the stairs to open it, calling his name.

"Rory? Where are you? Why didn't you get the door?"

She opened the door and there he stood, flowers in hand.

"Marta McCrea. I've come to ask you out for a weekend away from all your concerns," he told her handing her the flowers.

"Where's the baby?"

"She's with Melinda. Melinda volunteered to keep her so we could go to Missoula and spend the weekend together."

"Oh, Rory. We can't do that. What about feeding her?"

"I gave Melinda the bottles you made with your milk mixed with formula. I fed Alyssa only bottles with formula and she didn't turn a hair. She drank them with relish, so I think you can safely go. She's not going to be hungry. Why don't you go up and pack a small bag with some of your prettiest things and I'll wine you and dine you. I'll even take you dancing."

She frowned and he was sure she was on the verge of telling him she didn't want to go. He stepped through the doorway and tipped her chin up to meet his eyes.

"Please, Marta? I want you back. I want my wife back. My best girl back. My love back."

She pulled out of his arms and crossed her arms over her chest. She stood there a long time considering. Then she turned and went up the stairs. He waited in the foyer, not sure what she'd decided. She might just as easily be getting into bed as filling a suitcase. He'd about given up hope when she appeared at the top of the stairs with her case. He smiled at her, his heart lifting again. She came slowly down the stairs and when she reached him, he took the suitcase and set it on the floor. He tipped her chin up and kissed her gently.

"I love you, wife."

"I should put these flowers in water. Where's Consuela?"

"In Boise, visiting her sister."

"Really? Why? Is her sister ill?"

"No. I thought she needed a break. And I wanted you all to myself. Alone."

She snorted at that.

"It's true. I've missed you every day and every night for a month, Marta. I need you to talk to me. To tell me what's wrong. To love me again. I just need you. I've been really upset because we've . . . drifted apart."

"You could have fooled me," she said, her response one of hopeless resignation.

His heart constricted. Truly worried now, he asked, "Why would you say that? Come in here and sit down and tell me. Is it something I did? Or said? Or didn't do or say? I don't know how to fix it if I don't know what I did wrong."

He took her hand and led her into the den to sit on the plaid sofa. He put his arm around her and pulled her up snug against him.

"Tell me what's wrong."

She pulled out of his embrace and turned to face him.

"We had a baby and I had so many hopes and dreams of what those first few days and weeks would be like. But you dumped me off with Alyssa and hardly got us settled before you took off for the barn."

"I didn't have much choice about that, Marta—no shearing—no money coming in."

"I was scared, Rory. I've never had a baby before. I was afraid I'd do something wrong and she'd get acutely ill or die. You came and you went, hardly stopping to ask me if I was okay. You assumed, with Consuela here, you could trust her to give me advice and support.

"What I wanted was *your* support. *Your* arm around me in the mornings when Aly cried that funny cry I wasn't sure was normal. But you were at the barn. And even when you sat down to eat, you were all full of plans for the next day and extending invitations to Joe to eat with us and invitations to the Scottish men."

"I was preoccupied, Marta. Much too preoccupied . . . I realize that now."

"If you stopped to say anything to me at all, it was to ask me to make sure everyone *else* in your sphere of concern was taken care of. But other than inquire about whether I wanted to resume having sex with you, you didn't seem to care if *I* was taken care of."

"Why didn't you. . . ."

She gave him a look that said she didn't want to hear any of his excuses—wasn't willing accept even part of the blame for his lack of support. He left his question hanging and closed his mouth as she went on.

"My life changed 360° while yours went on exactly the same as always. It was like I'd done my wifely duty and given you a child to assure everyone of your ability to produce one and then you stopped considering my feelings totally."

He shook his head in the negative direction and said, "No, that's not true, Marta. Even in the middle of shearing all those sheep, I never stopped loving you."

Her face said she wasn't buying it.

"I was scared that now I wasn't pretty enough, or slim enough to hold your interest anymore. My breasts are sore and swollen and they leak. My stomach looks like a roadmap of Germany. My eyes have black circles from lack of sleep and from worrying that you hated me now. I kept thinking about the Ambers and the Ms. Coombs with every hair in place and me with my shaved pubis and I just couldn't gather up the will to let you see me naked. Since sex requires that state of undress, sex was out, too.

"I wanted you so much to be tender and caring and assure me I was doing things right, being a good mother, and you weren't there. Not *once* were you there for me."

He swallowed convulsively and buried his face in his hands. He didn't raise his head for the longest time. Finally, still not looking at her, he apologized

"Marta, I'm so sorry," he said, his voice muffled and full of agony.

For the first time since she started in enumerating his shortcomings, she softened.

"Rory. . . ."

"Everything you said is true. I've been so wrapped up in shearing, I didn't stop to think what I was doing to you. If I could take time back and do it over, I would. I felt like half my heart and most of my soul was missing when you wouldn't talk to me or didn't want to snuggle."

He was so contrite, her anger and resentment began to diminish as his words continued to pour out.

"As far as holding my interest, you've never, *ever* been more beautiful to me. Stretch marks, shaved, bald, wrinkled, old . . . whatever . . . to me you'll always be the most beautiful wife God ever created. I love you, Marta. Please, don't ever let me forget to tell you that—don't ever go around with your feelings hurt because I have forgotten. Tell me if you feel I'm ignoring you, and please accept my sincere apologies for doing so these last few weeks."

He couldn't look at her, so great was his remorse. Finally, she turned his face toward her.

Tears spilled down over his cheeks and he made no effort to staunch their flow.

"Rory . . . please don't. . . ."

"I'm so very, very sorry, Marta."

"I'm sorry, too, Rory. Half the time I was as angry at myself as I was at you. I know that shearing is hard work. I tried to tell myself that you weren't ignoring me on purpose, but I guess the hormones got in the way of my common sense. I love you but at the same time, I was horribly afraid you might find someone who was prettier and more full of life.

"Never, Marta. I'd never do that."

"I was so tired and I was sure my inability to bounce back to my former size and state of mind was driving you away, but I just couldn't seem to help myself. Thank you for the flowers, by the way. They're lovely."

Running his sleeve across his eyes, he said, "You're welcome, wife."

He pulled her over to sit on his lap and took her face in both hands. He started with her forehead and kissed her gently. Then he slowly worked his way down her nose, kissing the tip of it before moving on to kiss cheeks and ears and her neck under her ears.

She relaxed against his guiding hands and allowed him to move her face at will until he brushed a kiss across her lips. She gave a small moan of pleasure and his kiss deepened until he was kissing her with a good deal more pressure. His tongue sought entrance and she allowed him access.

"I want you, Marta," he whispered.

She wrapped her arms around his neck as he lifted her from the sofa and carried her up the stairs. In their bedroom, he slowly undressed her, taking his time, tasting and kissing every part that he exposed—the swollen and leaking breasts, her slightly rounded belly with the stretch marks on it, the shaved pubis that was just beginning to grow a fine silky stubble.

Looking her in the eye, his fingers touched her most sensitive spot and he was rewarded with her shiver of pleasure. He continued his massage of that area until she reached up and began to fumble with the buttons of his shirt. Stopping his exploration of her momentarily, he quickly climbed out of his clothes. She took hold of his rising member and ran her fingers over the sensitive tip until she heard his ragged in-suck of air.

"Make love to me, Rory," she told him in a breathless whisper.

He lowered her to the bed and covered her with his body. She raised her legs to circle him and allow him entrance. Smiling down at her, he gently entered her, watching her face to be sure he didn't hurt her in an area so recently healed.

"Don't," she said and he withdrew immediately.

"No, I didn't mean 'don't' that way. Don't hold back. It's okay. It doesn't hurt anymore."

"You're sure?"

"Yes."

He re-entered her, still being gentle, and began a slow building toward a release, which came sooner than he wanted it to.

"Sorry," he apologized. "Couldn't help it. It's been too long."

He tried to withdraw but she locked her heels behind his back and wouldn't let him. Gradually he grew hard again and when she began to rock up to meet him, he plunged downward to meet the upward thrusts of her hips. In less than five minutes they exploded together and Rory was glad the house was empty of anyone who might have mistaken their cries of pleasure for yells for help.

He carefully rolled off her to lie on his side. He maintained his closeness to her, unwilling to lose the contact of his flesh with her flesh—unwilling to sever the bond of love and trust that was again starting to blossom between them. She searched out his hand and meshed her fingers in his.

He was quiet for a long time, savoring what had just occurred after so many weeks without her closeness.

"Thank you, wife," he finally said. "You're the sweetest, sexiest woman I've had in a long, long time."

"I'm getting cold," she said.

"Me, too. Lay still, I'll get the blanket."

Sitting up, he reached down and grabbed the comforter at the bottom of the bed. He dragged it halfway up, but stopped short of covering her with it. Smiling, he looked down at her naked body with an appraising eye.

"Don't, Rory," she said, trying to yank the blanket up to shelter herself from his gaze.

He caught both her hands in his, preventing her from accomplishing that mission.

"Please, Marta, let me look at you. I don't ever want you to hide yourself from me. Maybe you don't feel as beautiful since the baby came, but to me you're a hundred times *more* beautiful. You're not just *my love* now, you're the mother of my child, too.

"All the things you counted off as reasons I might not feel the same way about you—the swollen breasts, the stretch marks—are exactly why I love you even more. Like a pear or an apple, you're all the sweeter for having matured and ripened."

Her eyes met his with such a look of gratitude he felt himself becoming aroused again. Smiling down at her, he gently cupped each breast in turn, then squeezed one of her nipples.

"Does that hurt?" he asked, catching the drop of milk that dripped on the side of his thumb. He licked it off with his tongue. It was such a sensual thing to watch she felt herself growing hot.

"It's tender, but you didn't hurt me."

"And this?" he asked, circling the aureole with his tongue.

"Mmm. That makes me feel all shivery."

His finger trailed down between her breasts, coming to lightly trace some of the stretch marks on her stomach.

"Looks more like Hungary than Germany to me. Makes me "Hungary" for more of you."

His voice grew sexier and deeper as he traced the marks with his tongue, edging ever lower until he reached the destination he was aiming for. Gently he tongued her until she came in a shuddering orgasm.

She thought he'd stop, but he didn't. The heat started building in her once more. He teased her pleasure spot until he felt she was mere seconds away from another one. Only then did he enter her and share the explosion that followed.

"That was wonderful," she sighed. "Are you ready to quit now?"

"I guess. I don't want to wear out my welcome, love."

"Like there was even a remote possibility of that happening, husband mine."

"So, do you want to spend the rest of our romantic weekend here, or go to Missoula?"

"What would you rather do?"

"I asked you first."

"I don't want to waste time driving to Missoula. I want to stay here and feed you grapes like we were at a Roman orgy. Since you think I'm still beautiful, I want to dance naked in your arms with only the blaze in the fireplace to light the room. I want to wake up in your arms and I want you to make love to me hourly."

"Tall order, that last request," he said, grinning at her.

His grin morphed quickly into a more serious demeanor as he looked earnestly into her eyes.

"I missed you so much, Marta. I don't ever want us to drift apart again. Promise me you'll always let me know if you feel I'm neglecting you."

"I will, Rory. I'll kiss your ear and that will be a sign that our love needs our attention. If *you* feel neglected, you can kiss my ear, too. Agreed?"

"Yes, and once again, I apologize for not recognizing your need for my support. I would be devastated if you ever left me. I can't imagine my life without you in it."

"Or me, you in mine. Let's go naked to the kitchen and make hot chocolate with marshmallows and scads of whipped cream on it."

He put on several dreamy CDs while she put the kettle on to boil. While they waited for the kettle to whistle, he steered her around the kitchen in a slow waltz punctuated by kisses. He was almost sorry when the blast of steam exiting through the kettle's spout interrupted his dance with her.

Instead of sitting down at the table to drink the chocolate, he leaned against the counter and pulled her back to lean against him. With every sip of the chocolate she felt him harden, so when he carefully took the hot cup from her hands and set it well back on the counter next to his, she knew what was coming. Without a word he lifted her to sit on the edge of the counter and entered her again.

Ten minutes later he lifted her down and gave her back the now lukewarm cup of chocolate. When she finished the last swallow, he licked the remnants of whipped cream and marshmallow from her upper lip, then waltzed her toward the stairs and did a credible imitation of Fred Astaire, that time going up the steps, not down.

She giggled.

"You don't like my Fred?" he asked.

"No, I was just thinking I'll have to bleach the kitchen counters before Consuela comes back. She'd die if she knew what we were doing in there."

"Yep, I'd be in her dog house for sure."

They tumbled into bed wrapped in each other's arms and finally succumbed to sleep.

Chapter Nineteen

Rory continued to be much more attentive to Marta through the summer. The realization—the fear—that he might have lost her never completely left his thoughts. He alternated work up in the meadows with days at home, eager to chart the progress of his new daughter and keep the bond between himself and Marta strong.

Marta blossomed under his attentions. She regained her verve for life and seemed happier than ever. More relaxed about Alyssa, too, she began to enjoy her daughter and looked forward to the time when Alyssa would walk and talk.

Over the Fourth of July, Marta took a week off from her job and they went to Boise to show off Alyssa.

"It takes almost as big a truck to tote all the stuff for a baby as it takes to move 300 sheep," Rory told his friend when they stopped to visit Connie and Jack. Connie was getting excited about their upcoming marriage in September, but not so excited that she didn't spend a good hour rhapsodizing over Alyssa.

"Oh, Marta, she's just precious. Look at her mouth—it's a perfect heart shape. And her hair is going to be black like Rory's and her eyes may be his eyes, too. But she definitely has your cute button nose and rosy cheeks. I want to steal her."

Jack rolled his eyes, recognizing the fact that he'd soon be married and, if Connie had her way, the father of several children.

"I'm not sure I'm ready for kids," he lamented. "I don't want to share Connie with some little snot-nosed brats."

"Jack!" Connie warned. "Don't make me have second thoughts. Get over here and hold this little angel and see if she doesn't steal your heart."

Jack dutifully went over to the chair and picked up Alyssa very gingerly. Rory had to laugh at his reluctance.

"Don't you be grinning that way at me. You come from that enormous family. I doubt there was ever a time when there wasn't a baby around. You're used to them. All I had was one sister and she was two years older than me, so I don't have any experience with kids this young. Do you have to change her?" he asked Rory.

"Sure. Since Marta's still working in the afternoons for Ron, I get to take care of Alyssa. I could hardly leave her wet and messy until Marta got home. Not only would that be hard on the babe's backside, but Marta would kill me if I left the chore for her return."

"What about Consuela? You could get her to change those diapers."

"Consuela's not going to raise my child, Jack. Nor is anyone else. Once in a while, Melinda will baby-sit, but our children will not be wards of the daycare system."

"I suppose the baby means we can't go out together for dinner, then?"

"Of course we can. Alyssa is adept at handling social situations. Most of the time she's totally bored by them and goes right to sleep. Where do you want to eat?"

"Well, not McDonald's Play Land or Chucky Cheese. I don't know if babies are welcome at the Renaissance."

"Call and ask," Rory told him.

Jack came back and said if Alyssa was quiet, it would be fine, but if she set up a squall, they would be moved to a private room.

"Either way, we can eat there. Why not go the private-room route to begin with?"

"Okay, I'll make a reservation for tonight. What time?"

"Marta?"

"How about 7 or 8, Jack? Rory and I have some other stops to make this afternoon."

"That okay with you, Connie?"

"Sure, Jack. Let's do eight."

After Jack confirmed a reservation for four at 8 p.m., Rory and Marta gathered up Alyssa and took off to stop and see some of Rory's siblings.

At Bailey's house, Todd and Eric were playing in the sandbox while Bailey relaxed on the lounge, taking in a bit of sun. Todd recognized Rory's truck and started jumping up and down, yelling, "Ith Uncle Rory!"

Todd came barreling through the gate and ran headlong into Rory's knees.

"Careful, Dude. Don't knock me over and spill my baby girl on the sidewalk."

"Can I thee her?"

"Sure, but let's go sit on the porch out of the sun."

Marta brought up the rear, lugging the diaper bag, and asked Bailey if she could warm a bottle for Alyssa.

"Not till I get a look at that sweet little bundle of joy," Bailey said, snatching Eric out of the sandbox and brushing him off. "Todd, you and Eric can look, but don't touch. Your new cousin is just tiny yet and I don't think she wants to be covered with sand."

Rory sat down in a lawn chair on the porch and unfolded the blanket from around Alyssa. Bailey got a dreamy look in her eyes and Rory was reminded of a conversation he'd had with Kelsey about how women forgot the pain of childbirth the minute they saw or smelled a baby.

"Oh, she's just dear. I'd so like to have a girl. She's got your hair and eyes, Rory. But thank St. Patrick, she's got Marta's nose."

"Can thee play, Uncle Rory?"

"Not yet, Todd, but maybe by next summer. She might be big enough to like to splash in your wading pool then."

"What *can* thee do?"

"She can eat and sleep. She can smile and coo. She can make messes in her diaper."

"Theeth not potty trained yet? Eric is almoth potty trained."

"I think potty training comes later in life. Alyssa is only three months old."

Marta came back with a warm bottle. Todd wanted to know if he could feed Alyssa.

"Okay, buddy. Sit on my lap and I'll help you hold her so you can give her the bottle."

Todd didn't hesitate a moment, crawling rapidly up to sit on Rory's lap. Once he got settled, Marta handed Alyssa over, trusting Rory to be sure she didn't fall off Todd's small lap. Todd took the bottle and touched the nipple to Alyssa's mouth. Alyssa began sucking motions with her lips and tongue and that gave Todd the giggles.

"Hey, Todd, don't tease her. Feed her. Put the nipple of the bottle in her mouth. Gently!"

Rory guided Todd's hand to insert the nipple and Alyssa drank with gusto.

"See this mark that says '6' Todd? When she drinks the milk down to that mark, we have to stop and make her burp, okay?"

"Yeth. Why doth thee need to burp?"

"So she won't get a tummy ache."

"Can I fix you two something to eat, too?" Bailey asked.

"No, thanks," Marta told her. "We just ate with your mom and Walter, then we had a strawberry sundae at Connie and Jack's place. Unless you want something, Rory?"

"Nope. I'm stuffed, too."

In half-hour visits, they managed to hit the rest of the McCreas before five in the afternoon. Rory asked if Marta thought they'd have time to visit Kelsey, who didn't get off work until five, but she suggested that he wait until the next day. She said she and Connie had talked about getting their hair done and having a facial in the morning.

"So, if you want, why don't you take Alyssa out to see Kelsey and Danny while Connie and I get the treatment? Kelsey won't be working tomorrow on the Fourth."

"You don't want to go with me?"

"No, I trust you," she said, giving him a wink, "and I'd love to get my hair cut and have a facial. I haven't had time to pamper myself like that since March."

"That place is open on the Fourth?"

"Connie said they're open until noon. Then they close for the parade that starts at one. She made the appointments, so I guess they don't celebrate by taking the whole day off on the Fourth in the beauty business if it falls on a weekday. If you come back to Connie's by 12:30, we can get a good seat for the parade."

"Okay. It's a deal. Will I recognize the 'new' you? Please tell me you won't come out with fire-red hair all stood up in spikes."

"Oh, Rory. Don't be a goose. I just want to trim the split ends and have one of those soothing masques applied. I want to be pampered."

"Pampered? I can think of some other ways to pamper you that wouldn't include putting green gloop all over your face. Maybe later tonight? After dinner?"

"Sure. You could use warm chocolate instead of avocado. That tastes better when it comes to removing it."

"You just be sure nobody in that salon is licking anything off you, wife. I claim all of you as my exclusive tongue territory."

Dinner with Jack and Connie was delightful. Alyssa slept through both dinner and dessert allowing conversation to ebb and flow with no disruptions at all. Marta looked devastating in her spaghetti-strap sundress and Rory had a hard time concentrating on what was being said for thinking how very beautiful she was.

After dinner, on the way back to his mom's place, he told her as much.

"I could scarcely tell you what got said, Marta. You just look fantastic tonight. I couldn't take my eyes off you and I didn't catch half of what Jack was prattling on about because I couldn't drag my eyes away from you.

"I'm going to have to bring you some burlap sacks home from the feed store to wear so I won't have to keep saying, 'Huh?' like some sort of retard because I'm not paying attention to what anyone's saying."

"You didn't look so bad yourself. You should wear those lavender shirts more often. And thank you. It's nice of you to notice when I get dressed up."

"You don't have to get dressed up for me to notice you, love. Even in a burlap sack, I still wouldn't be able to take my eyes off you."

It was really late when they got back to the house, but once Alyssa was fed and diapered and tucked in to her portable crib, Rory made love to Marta very quietly, so as not to disturb the baby or his mother and Walter.

Rory called Kelsey about six in the morning to see if she was going to be home.

"I sure am. You get yourself out here pronto. I'm dying to see Alyssa and I want you to see how big your nephew has grown, too. I bet he'd make four of yours."

"Nine too early?"

"No. That's halfway through my day. I've got stollen and I'll make fresh coffee, or tea if you prefer that."

"Coffee is fine. See you shortly, then."

Connie beeped her horn out front and Marta came and gave Rory a quick kiss before heading out for her spa treatment.

"Alyssa is still sleeping. Keep an ear peeled for her, okay?"

"Will do. Enjoy your mud pack or whatever."

"Mom, do you need anything from the store? I need to pick up another can of formula for Alyssa before I go to see Kelsey."

"I could use some more cola. I thought we might have a picnic in the back yard after the parade. I think we can see the fireworks they set off at the football field from there. That way it might not be so loud it would scare the baby."

"Need anything else? Charcoal? Napkins? Onions?"

"Onions? Don't they give you heartburn?"

"Sometimes, but what's a burger without onions?"

"Well, I don't want to be the one to cause your midsection any misery."

"Ah, hel . . . heck," he corrected, "they only give me grief if I'm already in a stew about something else."

"Should I take that to mean you're on a good roll?"

"Yep. It was bad for a while there. I thought maybe Marta was going to take the baby and kiss me goodbye. Or more likely just forego the kiss and leave."

"Why would she ever think of doing that? She loves you."

"Yeah, but I got all wrapped up in shearing. I didn't realize how much I was ignoring her needs. She had this idyllic picture in her head about how it would be after she came home with Alyssa and I didn't measure up. For six or seven weeks I was hardly around enough to play a bit part in that picture.

"We kind of got to be at odds with each other. She wouldn't say what was wrong and I wasn't paying enough attention to pick up the clues that something *was* wrong. Got so bad in June, it finally was like there was a huge chasm standing between us.

"Thought I was going to lose her for a bit, there. Scared the sh . . . crap out of me, Mom. I couldn't have eaten onions in May or June. Probably couldn't have even smelled them then. Even without onions, my gut felt like someone had run a rusty dagger in it."

"But it's better now?" Maire asked with concern.

"Yes. Finally I sent everyone out of the house and we sat down to mend fences. When she told me how she felt—well, I felt really bad for doing that to her. *Really* bad."

"Rory, I can't believe you'd deliberately hurt her. Surely she must have known that."

"No, it wasn't a sin of commission—to borrow a cliché from Father Leahy, but it sure was a sin of *omission*. Either way, I hurt her badly. Fortunately, she was kind enough to forgive me and I'm being very careful not to omit anything ever again.

"If you'd have told me back in my wilder days how much I'd come to love one woman, I'd have laughed in your face and sworn it would never happen to me. But the thought of losing Marta—I just can't imagine I'd ever recover from that.

"I'll be back in a jiffy if you'll listen for the baby."

"I can do that. It's been a long time since I've listened for a baby. More than 25 years. A quarter of a century. I wish I were young enough to have another one now."

"Don't you be getting all mushy on me. I swear, there must be a gene that turns women all soft in the head whenever they encounter a newborn. Kelsey and Bailey and Connie—and now you—are all reduced to Pablum when it comes to babies.

"Is there something in baby powder that deletes the memories of giving birth or taking care of helpless babies and makes you all yearn to have one underfoot again? Didn't you have enough of babies and diapers to last a lifetime with the eight of us, Mom?"

"I thought so at the time, but reflecting back, those times were some of the best years of my life."

When he returned from the market, he made up two bottles and put enough diapers in the bag to last until after the parade, then strapped Alyssa in her carrier and took off for Kelsey's house.

She was waiting in the kitchen and the smell of stollen warming in the oven made his mouth water. It also brought back memories of the winters when she'd make it, knowing he'd be hungry and cold after feeding in the pre-dawn hours.

"Hey, Lass. I thought stollen was for frigid mornings."

"It's usually made as a Christmas pastry, but nothing says you can't make it at other times, providing you can find the candied fruit, or are smart enough to freeze some of the fruit when it's available in the winter. Oh, let me look at her," Kelsey demanded when he set the carrier with Alyssa in it on the table.

Rory pulled aside the light blanket that had shielded her face from the sun when he carried her in.

"She's beautiful. Oh, Rory. I see Marta across her cheeks and her mouth and nose. Does she have your eyes?"

"I don't know. You'll have to see for yourself when she wakes up."

"She's going to have dark hair—probably black like yours. It always gets darker as they get older. Danny started out with hair like corn silk, but it's getting darker and redder as time goes on. She's truly beautiful. You must be so proud."

"I sure am. Speaking of babies, where's Danny?"

"Still asleep. You ready for some stollen? I know you're ready for coffee."

"Yep, I'd like some of both."

He was eating his second slice of the pastry when Alyssa woke up. She didn't cry, but when he leaned over her to let her know he was there, she gave him a goofy grin.

"You must spend a lot of time with her. So many men are strangers to their children in the early years. Lots of kids actually scream bloody murder when their fathers come into view because they don't know them. But she knows you. Look at that smile—it's your grin, Rory. It just hasn't got the wicked bit behind it yet. I hope it stays sweet and doesn't turn devilish like yours."

"At least not until she's old enough to go to confession."

"Look, her eyes *are* lavender, or almost that color. She's black Irish, just like you."

"With a healthy dose of German Fräulein thrown in for good measure."

"Marta's German?"

"She's a Lansdorf. I think that's German, isn't it?"

"Yes, probably. I hope the Irish side is dominant. I like Irish poets better than German beer meisters."

"Well, I don't know about that. I think I prefer a good cold brew to one of those poetry slams where earnest young men get up in those French berets and make lousy verse."

"Have you been to a poetry slam?"

"There was a five-minute TV spot on one held in Missoula one night. Pathetic is the only word that comes to mind. Do people actually *pay* to see something like that?"

"Yes, they do. And states hold contests to send the best to Washington for the finals."

"Well, then, maybe that's something to recommend them. Those slams kind of remind me of floor debates in Congress. All the over-emoting and posturing that goes on in both places."

"So, how's life in Montana?"

"Pretty good. Sold the fleeces for big bucks to the same mill in Scotland. Hired me a new kid to shear and sent him up the hill, through the long grass, to apprentice as a drover. He's riding your horse who was getting lazy and fat from lack of employment."

"How did you find him?"

"He pulled a switchblade on me one night in an arcade in Butte."

"And you hired him?"

"Yep. Against Marta's dire warnings. He's turned out to be damn good on the clippers. His first two fleeces were a bit ragged, but they got steadily better as time went on. I paid him full price for all 32 of them."

"Wow! He must be good."

"Yep. Even McDougal thought his fleeces were better than 90% of those he'd looked at when touring other ranches."

"How's Marta? She didn't come with you?"

"No. She's fine—better than fine, actually. Connie set up a facial thing at some spa, and a haircut, so she said she felt like pampering herself and went there this morning."

"Things are okay with you two?"

"Yes. Sure are. I was just telling her last night that she looked so ravishing during our dinner with Jack and Connie I found it hard to keep my mind on what Jack was saying."

"Or your hands off her when you got home?"

"You know me, Lass. I like to ravish ravishing women."

At that juncture, Danny let out a bellow and Kelsey went to fetch him. Alyssa was busy watching the sunspots that a birdbath outside the kitchen window was reflecting onto the ceiling above the table.

"Here he is," Kelsey announced, plopping Danny into his high chair. "Danny, can you say 'Hi, Rory' to your uncle?" she asked, pouring him a bowl of Cheerios.

It came out as 'WaEr,' but Rory could recognize it as a damn good attempt. He had to tease Kelsey a bit though, asking her if some foreign DNA had crept into either her or Aidan's genes somewhere back a ways.

"I wondered if he'd end up like Todd, with a lisp. Are Bailey and Mike at all concerned about the lisp?"

"Not yet. Maybe when he starts school. Don't they have a speech therapist now in the grade school? I think it's cute."

"Yes, but not everyone has your patience to try and understand him."

"It was so funny right before Christmas when we kept him while Eric was in Denver. We went to Missoula to the mall and Todd wanted to sit on Santa's lap. He got halfway up the stairs and turned around to ask, 'Ith Thanta a thranger?' I guess Bailey had told him he couldn't talk to strangers. I think everyone in the line and all the parents understood Todd. They all laughed like they understood him."

"You like Todd, don't you?"

"He's a sweet kid. All the McCrea kids are sweet. It's only when they grow up they get mean."

"I'm trying not to paint Aidan that way to Danny. I don't want him growing up thinking ill of his father."

"No, I agree. There's nothing to be gained by that. But maybe you'd better restrict his associations with Sean, because it seems like he's getting to be nearly as bad as Aidan was."

"What's he done now?"

"He was giving me grief again about not paying my fair share of the taxes on the old homestead. I told him I'd give him $1000 toward his damn taxes if he'd like to kick in the $6900 that my place's taxes amount to every year."

"Wow! How can you pay that much?"

"Well, not by buying a new ski boat, that's for sure."

"Yes, it does seem like if you can purchase one of those, you should be able to manage the taxes, doesn't it?"

Alyssa switched her attention to Danny who had finished his Cheerios and was banging his bowl on the tray of his high chair. Rory picked her up out of her carrier and propped her up on his lap so she could see Danny better.

"Baba," Danny announced.

"Yes, baby. Her name is Alyssa. Can you say that?"

"Baba."

Rory couldn't help smiling and Kelsey bristled up.

"I venture to say yours won't be any better at names when she's his age, Rory McCrea, so wipe that grin off your face."

"I wasn't laughing at Danny. I was remembering what Mom said about Aidan trying to say stuff when he first started talking. He couldn't say 'b' very well. There was a book about a dog that chased off a burglar, only Aidan always wanted Mom to read him the book about a 'gurglar' so maybe Danny has inherited that from Aidan."

"Oh. Okay, then."

"You aren't going to be one of those overprotective moms are you? The kind that tackles the kid on the opposing soccer team if he manages to kick Danny in the shin during a skirmish?"

"He's only got me to protect him, Rory."

"Better plan on letting him spend summers at my place then so I can prevent you from making him into a mama's boy."

"Only if you'll send me Alyssa so you can't turn her into a drover," Kelsey shot back.

"You don't seem to be mellowing much with the passage of time, Lass. Still full of fire and brimstone? Hot lava bubbling inside?"

"If I don't stand up for Danny and me, who will?"

"No prospects on the horizon?"

"I haven't been looking."

"Why not? It would make life easier if you found someone."

"I have. He's not available," she said, giving Rory a pointed look. "I doubt very seriously there's anyone else in the world that could measure up to you."

"Ah, Lass. Don't be using me to prevent you finding love again."

"Can't help it, Rory. I do measure everyone against you. Sometimes one of them has one or two of your good traits, but not the whole package."

"Well, don't give up. I used to measure all the women I went out with against you, too. And look what happened. I found one. Now, I'm not saying Marta is the same as you—she's not. You still have some good points she doesn't have. But she had lots of similar traits and some extra features you didn't have, so it was easy to fall in love with her."

"What kind of traits does she have that I don't?"

"She's a lot more practical than you. She sees a solution to problems that neither you nor I would have thought of in a million years. On the other hand, she's far more vulnerable than you ever were. She never thinks she's good enough. She worries about me cheating on her. I was surprised when she suggested I come see you without her. It has to do with her father, whom she caught messing around with a woman—not his wife—when Marta was about fifteen.

"I can see something like that might make her wary."

"Everybody comes with some sort of baggage, Lass. The trick is to look past the baggage and find the good things. I hope you'll try that. It'd make me sad to think you'd pass up a warm and caring guy because he wasn't me."

"Maybe you're right. Del's been coming around for months. He's really quite nice, and I like him. But he ain't you."

"What do you like about him?"

"He's kindhearted. He's got a good sense of humor. He likes Danny. His kisses don't set me a-jangle like the rare ones you gave me, but he's nice."

"Give it a shot, Kels. Took me a bit to get over comparing Marta to you, too, but after a bit I came to love her more than anyone, even you. Still do. Always will. I'm sure of that finality, so there's no reason to be waiting for me. Give Del a chance."

"Maybe I will."

"Good. What time is it?"

"It's 11:45."

"Holy mackerel! I'm supposed to pick Marta up for the parade at 12:30. I'd better get cracking. Are you going to take Danny to the parade?"

"Yes. Del's picking us up in about ten minutes."

"Maybe we'll see you there. Come introduce Del. I'd like to meet him."

"Maybe I will. You've got one sweet child, Rory. And I'm truly glad for you and Marta. Forget what I said. I have no intention of coming between you guys. I just will always love you."

"Love you, too, Kelsey lass. Just not in the same way I love Marta and Alyssa. Take care now, and keep in touch. I enjoyed the pictures you sent of Danny. Maybe not so long from now, you both can come spend a week at the ranch. Alyssa is at kind of a disadvantage. She doesn't have all those cousins so close at hand to play with."

"I'm sure Danny would love it."

Rory strapped Alyssa into her carrier and kissed Kelsey on both cheeks, giving her a warm hug. He kissed the top of Danny's head, too, before leaving.

On the drive back to Boise, he wondered what Marta would look like after her spa morning. If she was even prettier, he knew he wouldn't see much of the parade.

Chapter Twenty

After their small vacation in Boise, Marta went back to work and Rory alternated between the upland meadows and the ranch. In the middle of September, he was up on the mountain when an arctic blue norther rolled in resulting in four bone-chilling days of heavy frosts. That storm precipitated Rory's decision to move the sheep back down to the ranch earlier than he'd planned.

Their drive down was even worse. The entire time the drovers were moving the sheep lower, they were hit with freezing rains and 35 mph winds. By the time the sheep were safely in their sheepcotes, every one of the men had bad colds and sore throats. Their ailments quickly spread to Marta, Consuela, Alyssa and the rest of the residents of the ranch. Alyssa made two trips to the pediatrician for earaches. For most of the rest of the week, no one felt really in fine fettle and Marta missed several days at work, while taking care of a fretful baby and a sick husband.

When he'd recovered enough to stop running a fever, Rory signed on at the feed store to work again for Jay Hadley. During the summer, the store's heavy deliveries of hay slacked off to the point that Phil could manage very well on his own because most of their clients' stock was on pasture in the warmer months. With the sudden downturn in temperatures, and the killing frosts, requests for hay deliveries picked up again, so Hadley was happy to have Rory back on the job.

Amber Sykes resumed her frequent visits to the store as soon as Rory was again employed there.

"That woman hasn't been in here but maybe twice all summer long," Phil related. "Now you're back, ain't hardly a day goes past she's not in here for something."

Rory, still coughing, was not much in the humor to wait on her, but she always managed to come in when Phil was at lunch or out sweeping up the storage areas so he was forced to take care of her requests. She was again attempting to lure him into the back corners of the store where she proceeded to stand too close, or lay a hand on his arm.

Twice Rory told her he didn't appreciate her attentions, but she didn't back off at all. He related Amber's attempts to be chummy to Marta and asked her what she thought he ought to do.

"She had words with Kurt a couple of days ago, and stormed out of his office, so I guess if she's mad at him, she's back to dogging you. I don't know what you should do, Rory. Maybe cough on her and with any luck she'll take pneumonia and die."

"If I thought I was still contagious, I'd give that a try."

"She sure doesn't hesitate to let me know she harbors no good will toward me, either. I try to take a break when she comes in, either going to the lunchroom and having a piece of fruit or going to the restroom. I thought I'd given her enough time to leave on Wednesday, but when I returned to my desk, she was still talking to Kurt.

"The look she gave me would have curdled milk. And when I sat down to pick up where I'd left off on typing Ron's brief for the Cutter case, I couldn't find the pages I'd already typed. I looked everywhere—but they were gone.

"When Kurt went to the police department to meet with a client who'd been charged with drunken driving, I went in to empty his wastepaper can, and there were all my sheets, ripped and crumpled in it. She must have grabbed them the minute I left my desk and took them into his office to mutilate.

"I don't know if Kurt abets her behavior, but he sure didn't say anything to me about the missing pages. There was no way he couldn't know she was destroying two hours of my work. So, I think he must be encouraging her to make my life miserable."

"If it isn't one damn thing, it's another. I'd file one of those harassment things, but with her screwed-up head, she'd likely have me back in court defending myself again. Just try to keep out of her way. Heaven only knows what she's capable of."

One week to the day after their conversation, Rory was in his office when someone rang the doorbell. It was already dark and he was waiting for Marta to get home for dinner.

Consuela yelled from the kitchen, "I no can get door, Mr. Rory," so he got up and went to see who was on the porch.

"Mr. McCrea?" the uniformed Highway Patrol officer asked.

"Yes."

"Does your wife drive a Honda Civic?"

"Yes."

"I'm afraid there's been an accident. Witnesses said they saw a dark blue or black SUV force the Civic off the road about six miles north of here."

Rory's mind raced to think what the road was like that distance away and remembering about the trees and the rather steep drop-offs that bordered the highway in the vicinity, he felt his stomach turn over.

"My wife?" he asked, dreading to hear the answer.

"Not good, I'm afraid. They had to use the power jaws to extricate her from the car. The helicopter took her to Missoula to the trauma unit there at the hospital downtown."

"But she's alive?"

"Yes, but I don't know for how long."

"Can you take me there? If you run lights and siren, I could be there sooner than if I have to go the speed limit."

"I'm heading that way. Can you leave now?"

"Yes, sure. Let me get a coat and tell Melinda to come and mind the baby."

He grabbed his coat and put in a call, telling Melinda that Marta was in an accident and asking if she could take Alyssa for the night.

"Yes, I'd be happy to do that. Is Marta okay?"

"I don't know. I don't think so. But the police are here and I have to go. They're giving me a ride to Missoula. If I need to come home, maybe Enrique will come and pick me up?"

"Yes, sure. Call us when you find out how she is, okay?"

"I will."

He went to the kitchen and told Consuela he was going and explained about Melinda coming to get Alyssa. Then, with his heart constricting in his chest, he climbed in with Officer Horton for a very fast ride to Missoula.

"You have any idea who'd want to run your wife off the road, Mr. McCrea?"

Rory closed his eyes and shuddered. Amber drove a dark blue SUV.

"The witnesses said the plate number began with 485 J something. Does that ring any bells with you?"

"No, not the plate number, but my wife has been on the receiving end of some mean behavior by a woman—an Amber Sykes. She drives a dark blue SUV. I've never noted the plates, but you might want to check that first."

Officer Horton picked up his mike and called dispatch.

"Sue, can you run the make, model and plates on a Ms. Amber Sykes from . . . 'she live in Butte?' he asked Rory, who shook his head 'yes' . . . Butte."

Sue came back, "Amber Sykes is registered in a 1998 GMC Jimmy, dark blue, license 485 John Boy 6."

"Thanks, Sue."

Even running lights and siren, it still took much too long for Rory's liking to arrive in Missoula. Horton dropped him off at the ER door and went to find a place to park his car.

"I think my wife was brought in about an hour or so ago by helicopter—Marta McCrea?" he asked the receptionist.

"We got a patient by helicopter, but none of the paperwork has come to my desk yet, so we didn't have a name. If you'll sit over there, I'll see if I can find out something more positive to tell you."

"Thank you."

He couldn't sit. Pacing the length of the waiting area, he felt sick. When Officer Horton came in and looked at him under the lights, he, too, suggested Rory sit down.

"Do they know anything yet?" Horton asked.

"The receptionist went to check. Said they got a patient by chopper, but she didn't have a name or anything yet."

"You look like you could use a cup of coffee, Mr. McCrea."

"No, I don't want anything—not till I find out how Marta is."

"You look kind of like you're going into . . . well, you're really pale—the coffee might help."

When Horton came back with the cup of coffee, Rory was sitting down and even from halfway across the room Horton could see him shaking.

"Take it easy, sir. I'm sure someone will be here to talk to you in just a minute or two."

He handed Rory the coffee and Rory took a swallow, not even noticing how hot it was or how it burned his mouth and throat.

"Thanks. If it *was* Amber Sykes that caused Marta to go off the road, what will happen to her?"

"Attempted vehicular manslaughter? I'd say 25-50 years. Tell me what sorts of things she's been doing to your wife."

"Marta said she gives her dirty looks when she comes to the office where Marta works. She's dating one of the lawyers in that office. Last week, she took some work Marta had typed up and ripped it up while Marta was in the lunchroom. And it's not the first problem we've had with her. Some while ago, she came to our ranch and plowed over my sign on the highway and did a number on my front stairs, too."

"Why?"

"She accused me of flirting with her and having an affair. It's not true, but she dragged me into court on the charge of alienation of affections. Judge found in my favor and gave her a big fine. She's always hanging around the feed store in Butte where I work. I don't think she's right in the head."

"You sit tight, sir. I want to go out to my car and relay what you told me. See if they can locate her and her vehicle. I'll be back."

"Mr. McCrea, I've just been to the Level I trauma ER. The doctor in charge of your wife's care said he'd be out in approximately 60-90 minutes to talk to you."

"You don't know how she's doing? Did they tell you anything at all?"

"No, nothing about her condition. But they have the best team in the state in there, so please be assured that everything possible is being done for her."

"Can I go back and see her—just for half a minute?"

"No, I'm sorry. I know they won't let you in her cubicle. Maybe it would help to make the time seem shorter if you filled out some of the paperwork. I think, given the severity of her injuries, she'll go to the intensive care unit. It would facilitate things if you'd give us some information."

She put together a packet of questionnaires on a clipboard and handed it to him.

"If you have any questions, just ask me," she said, giving him a small consoling smile.

He looked at the first page without seeing anything of what was written there. His thoughts kept going back to that morning. Kissing Marta goodbye and telling her that Consuela was making potato soup with cornbread for dinner, along with pork chops. Teasing her that he'd heard what he thought was 'da-da' out of Alyssa the night before. His shaking got worse when he thought about that and he finally returned the clipboard to the receptionist telling her he couldn't begin to fill out any paperwork until he knew how Marta was doing. She slipped out from behind her counter and sat next to him, the clipboard on her lap.

"What's your wife's full name?" she asked. "I'll write because you're shaking so much that if you did it, I probably wouldn't be able to read it."

"Her name is Marta Lansdorf McCrea."

"Her age?"

"Twenty-seven, almost twenty-eight."

"Her birthdate?"

"November 18th uh . . . 1979."

"She's married of course. Your full name?"

"Rory Owen McCrea."

"Date of birth?"

"April 23, 1977."

"Her social security number?"

"I can't remember it right now. 270-49-88 something, something, I think."

"Do you know yours?"

"Yes. 274-15-0337."

"Do you have insurance?"

"Yes. Farm Bureau and State Farm—I don't know—and Blue Cross."

"Do you have your Blue Cross insurance card?"

"Maybe."

He rooted in his wallet and finally produced the plastic card.

"Let me take that and make a copy for our records. I'll be right back."

She sat down again and handed back the card. Turning over a page, she took the pen up again and asked more questions.

"Religion?"

"Catholic."

"Do you want me to put in a call to Father O'Brien? He might be able to offer you some comfort."

"Or give my wife extreme unction? Is that what you're leading up to?"

"No. I don't know your wife's condition, so I would hardly ask you if you wanted me to call Father O for that. I just thought you might like someone to come and lend you some support. I didn't see anyone else here to support you, that's all."

"Sorry. Not right now. Maybe after a bit, but not yet."

"I have to ask these questions, but again, I don't know her condition, so remember these are just standard, okay?"

"Yes."

"Do you know if your wife had signed any paperwork saying what she would or would not want done for her or to her medically in the case she was unable to speak for herself?"

"I don't know. Maybe, if it's standard, she might have signed something like that when she delivered our child."

"Where did she deliver?"

"In Butte. At the hospital."

"When?"

"End of March, this year."

"I can check with medical records there."

"Would she prefer a private, semi-private, or ward bed if and when she gets out of ICU?"

"I don't know. Is all this really important right now?"

He was shaking badly again, she noticed. She excused herself and went down the hall. When she came back, she held out a warmed blanket and when he didn't take it from her, she unfolded it and wrapped it around his shoulders.

"Is your wife allergic to anything—food, or medications?"

"Not that I know of."

"Who is her physician?"

"Dr. Martin Feldman."

"What sort of physician is Dr. Feldman?"

"OB-GYN."

"Do you know his phone number?"

"No, not off the top of my head."

"I think that gives me something to begin a record for your wife with, Mr. McCrea. Will you be the responsible party if your wife can't sign all the legal sheets about her care and confinement?"

"Yes. Of course."

"Then, do you think you can sign here, and here, and here again?"

He took the clipboard and scribbled his signature in three separate places.

Minutes passed like hours. He sat with his eyes closed dreading what the doctor would say when he finally came out to talk. Officer Horton came back in and sat down next to Rory.

"Sorry, sir. When I went out to relay what you told me about the woman, I got another call about a minor accident on the freeway. I had to ask them to call another unit. You hear anything yet?"

"No."

"Shouldn't be much longer. The Highway Patrol in Butte is going to check out the Sykes woman. I asked them to page me here if they found out anything. I'd like to hang around to find out the extent of your wife's injuries, if I might. I want it on my records if I have to go to trial about the accident, and I'd just as soon hear it from the doctor's mouth as get it after a dozen people have passed it on and just as likely screwed it up. Would you mind if I waited with you?"

"No. I'd be glad for your company."

"What do you do for a living?"

"Raise sheep."

"Big operation?"

"We run about 600 currently. Hope to end up with about double that."

"You have some family you want me to call? Someone who would come and sit with you?"

"My family members are all in Boise."

"What about someone from your home here?"

"They'll help me most by staying on the ranch to take care of our baby and the sheep. Excuse me, I have to find a restroom."

"There's one right around the corner."

He was sick, pitching up everything he'd eaten all day and maybe some of the previous night's dinner as well. He rinsed his mouth and ran a paper towel wetted with cold water over his face. He was about to open the door and return to the waiting room when Horton came to get him.

"Doctor's waiting to talk to you."

Rory closed his eyes and offered up a brief prayer that the news would be better than what he feared it would be.

"You okay?" Horton asked.

"No, but that doesn't matter now. I need to know how she is."

"Mr. McCrea, I'm Michael Trask, chief of the ER trauma unit. Why don't you sit down and I'll tell you about your wife's condition."

Rory sat down and shook all over.

"Your wife is in critical condition, Mr. McCrea. She has a fractured femur, four broken ribs, a punctured lung leading to a pneumothorax—that's air in the pleural cavity. All those injuries are fixable. What most concerns us is the severe blow she received to her head resulting in some swelling of her brain. She's in a coma and at the present time, I can't offer any estimation when, or if, she'll come out of it. We're monitoring her inner- cranial pressure closely. If the swelling gets worse, we may have to make a small opening in her skull to relieve it."

"Can I see her?"

"The nurses are cleaning her up now. If you'll go up to the intensive care unit on the 7th floor, you can see her when she comes up, okay? Should be another 30 minutes or so."

"Thank you."

Trask went back in the direction of the ER and when Officer Horton turned back to ask Rory what else he could do before he left, he noted that Rory's eyes swam with unshed moisture. Horton wasn't sure if he was more upset now because he felt relief that she was still alive or because of renewed worry about the seriousness of her condition.

"I know you're scared, Mr. McCrea, but she has youth going for her, and you going for her, too. I see lots of accidents. The injured ones with someone who loves them always seem to do better than those who have nobody in their corner.

"Now that you know something, is there anyone you want to call? There's a room about twenty yards down that hall that has a phone. If you don't have a quarter, I can give you one. If you make collect calls, you can use it over and over."

Rory rooted in his pocket and came up with six or seven quarters. He ran his sleeve over his eyes and took a deep breath before he spoke.

"I've got some. Thanks for everything, and please—I don't care if it's day or night— let me know if it was Amber Sykes who did this to Marta. If I'm not at the ranch, I'll be here, or my housekeeper, Consuela, will know where I am."

"Whenever I know anything, you'll know it, too. I'll be pulling for her."

"I appreciate that. It was kind of you to stay."

"No problem."

Rory found the room with the phone and went in and locked the door behind him. It was almost 10 p.m. and he debated if his mother would still be awake, but he didn't want them to learn about Marta in the newspaper or on TV. He put a quarter in the phone and got the operator.

"Ma'am," he began, "my wife has been in a serious accident and I need to make several calls to Boise, Idaho and have you charge my home phone number."

He related the number to be billed and waited while she checked it against the name he'd given her, then gave her his mother's number. When Maire answered, he didn't know how to break the news to her.

"Mom? It's me, Rory."

"Is everything all right? You don't sound like yourself."

"No, Mom, everything is not all right. Marta's been in a serious accident. She has broken bones and a collapsed lung and a bad head injury. She's in a coma and the doctor just said he can't tell me when, of if, she'll come out of it. Mom, I'm so scared."

He got out only a few more words and then he choked up.

"Rory Owen McCrea, you get hold of yourself. I know you're the softest hearted of all my children, but it will do nobody any good if you fall apart. You've got to be strong for Marta's sake, so you buck up right this minute and you put on your brave face, even if you don't feel brave."

Sniffing back the moisture he said, "Mom, can you call all the rest of the family? I think Marta could use all your collective prayers. I know I could use a few, too. Will you ask Father Leahy to say a special mass for her?"

"I will do that, and more than that. I want you to call me every day and I'll pay for your calls. I'd come to be with you, but Walter had a small stroke—a TIA, they called it—and I'm kind of afraid to leave him alone."

"I don't expect you to come, Mom."

"What about Alyssa?"

"Between Dulce and Melinda she'll be okay, I think. I'd better go, Mom. They said I could see Marta when they take her up to the intensive care place."

"You be strong, Rory. I know you're very upset, and I know how much you love her, but she doesn't need to see you bawling like a baby when she wakes up, and Alyssa doesn't need to see that either or she'll be scared."

"I know, Mom. I'm sorry for falling apart. It's just that for hours I didn't know if she'd even survive. I still don't know, but at least she is alive for right now. I'll call you in the morning if I know more by then. Take good care of Walter, too. Bye, Mom."

She was bruised and very still when they allowed him in to see her. Her face was swollen and tubes ran everywhere. He put on his brave face while his heart did several untimely contractions. A nurse bustled in to check the drip flowing into Marta's left arm.

"Is there anything I should do?" he asked her.

"Are you her husband?"

"Yes. Rory McCrea. Marta is my wife."

"In coma cases, I think it helps when someone close to the patient talks to them about normal, everyday things. I've seen people wake up after three or four months and tell their family members that they remember someone talking to them while they were in the coma. So, I suggest you hold her hand and talk to her about whatever you'd tell her if she were awake and sitting across the breakfast table from you."

"I need to leave you numbers where I can always be reached."

"You just sit and hold Marta's hand and when I get done building her chart, I'll come in and get all that kind of information from you. Don't be afraid to talk to her—just don't talk about the accident—talk about happy things."

"Thank you."

He sat down in the bedside chair and took her hand. Rubbing it gently, he told her about how the day had gone and that Alyssa seemed to really enjoy the rice cereal they had started her on.

"That cereal fills her up, Marta, and because you gave her some last night before bedtime, she slept until almost seven this morning. I wonder why they don't suggest feeding kids that right from the start? It would be lots easier on new parents if babies weren't up a dozen times a night squalling for more teat or another bottle.

"Consuela's soup sure smelled good, and she was whipping up a big batch of cornbread to go with it, too. You hurry up and get better and I'll have Consuela make more of both. It's a good meal on a cold and blustery night.

"I talked to Mom tonight. She sounded good, but she said Walter had a small stroke—nothing too serious, I guess. Didn't sound like she was overly concerned. He must be in his early 80s by now. Still making those lamps out of old branches and parts of bushes and trees. He showed me some of his work last July when we were over there.

"He's got one piece that he's carved to look like a swan with a very graceful neck. I told him he ought to try placing some of his stuff in the art museum or else try to sell some of it at the swap meet. He said he was afraid he'd get so many orders he wouldn't be able to fill them."

The nurse came in again with several more forms to fill out and sign, and he gave her a list of his numbers at the same time. He'd just settled down again in the chair when she told him that they preferred him to wait in the ICU waiting room and they'd allow him in every hour for five minutes. When he shook his head, indicating he didn't want to leave, she told him he'd be able to spend more time with her once she was stable and she got moved to a regular room, but for now, they needed to be able to monitor her closely without having to move him out of the way.

"It's really best for Marta. Looking at you, it's probably a good idea if you go home and get a good night's sleep so if she does wake up tomorrow, she won't be staring at a zombie. I promise to take good care of her for you and I'll call you right away if there's any change in her condition. The front desk called up to say there's a man by the name of Enrique downstairs waiting for you. Go home, Mr. McCrea. There's nothing more you can do here tonight."

He didn't want to leave, but Enrique took one look at him and said it might be best to go home and at least shave and shower and change clothes.

"No es muy guapo esta noche," Enrique said, enough worried about the pale man who stood before him to forget his English.

"Okay. Maybe you're right. I'm going to need my truck if I come back, so let's go home so I can sleep a few hours and then I'll clean up and come back here tomorrow."

When he got up the next morning, Alyssa was crying. He changed her diaper and hurried to the kitchen for a bottle to warm. He took her into his office and propped her up on his knees so he could phone the hospital while he fed her the formula.

Assured that Marta's condition was critical but stable—there had been no further increase in pressure in her head—he felt a little ray of hope. He put Alyssa in her playpen and gave her some plastic keys to play with while he phoned Jack's office. Amanda Reagan answered.

"Ms. Reagan, this is Rory McCrea. Is Jack around?"

"Hi, Rory. How's that baby girl?"

"She's good. Growing. Said 'da-da' last week."

"How are you and Marta? Jack said you'd been here for the Fourth of July."

"I'm fine, but Marta was in a bad accident last night and isn't doing so well. That's why I wanted to speak to Jack."

"Rory, I'm so sorry to hear that. Is there anything anyone can do for you or Marta?"

"Pray."

"Can we send cards or flowers? Where should we send them?"

"She's in intensive care. No flowers allowed in there. Why don't you wait until they move her to a regular room, then I'll give you the name and address and room number to send cards to."

"Well, you tell her I'm pulling for her. Here's Jack, now."

"Rory. You in trouble again?"

"Yeah, Jack. Trouble like I've never seen before."

"What's up? Another woman making eyes at you?"

"Marta's in intensive care. She was in a really bad accident last night. She's in a coma."

"Rory, I'm sorry as all hell. Here I'm making jokes and you're probably at your wit's end with worry. What happened?"

"Highway Patrol said witnesses told them a dark-colored SUV deliberately ran Marta's car off the highway. They got a partial plate number. Looks like it was the Sykes woman's SUV. I don't know if they found her or her car yet, but if she did that to Marta, I don't ever want her to see life outside the prison walls again."

"That's understandable, Rory. I'm sure. . . ."

"I called for two reasons, Jack," Rory said, cutting him off. "One, I want to know if you'd be willing to prosecute the hell out of her on my and Marta's behalf if she did it, and two, because of the situation here, I'm not going to be able to be your best man. I'm sorry about that. I was looking forward to your and Connie's wedding."

"Rory, don't give it another thought. And yes, I'd be willing to rep you in any case against Sykes. I'll be gone for two weeks beginning October 21, but I doubt the wheels of justice will grind that quickly. If she's up for bail, try to get to the hearing for that and tell the judge why you think it shouldn't be granted."

"I don't know if I can do that, Jack. Marta's nurse said I should talk to her every day about normal things. I'll have to split my time between the ranch and the hospital in Missoula. It's going to be a nightmare."

"Do you want me to come over there now?"

"No. There's nothing you could do. You're terrified of babies so you wouldn't be any help with Alyssa."

"No, but I could hold *your* hand. Help you over the rough spots."

"Mom told me to suck it up and put on my brave face, so that's what I'm trying to do. Thanks for the offer though. I'll be thinking of you on October the 20th. I hope you are as blessed with Connie as I am with Marta. Say a lot of prayers, Jack—both Marta and I can use them."

"Call if you need me to come, Rory. I'll wait to hear from you."

After that, there were many calls from all his siblings. Christina called the last of them all.

"Oh, Rory, you must be devastated. Your Marta—I know how very much she means to you. Is there any news this morning?"

"Just that she's stable and her brain seems to not have swollen any more overnight. She's still in a coma, Chris. I totally lost it last night I was so scared. Mom gave me what for because I was crying when I called her. But she's had a long life and Marta's life is barely getting started. It's not fair. Alyssa and I need Marta to be here."

"I know, Rory. We're all praying for her, and you, at our house."

"Mom told me to put my brave face on. I don't feel brave, Chris. I feel like I was six again when lightning struck the barn and set the silo on fire. Then I was terrified that we wouldn't be able to get the cows and horses out in time, or the mother cat and her kittens in the loft. However petrified I was back then, multiply that feeling by a thousand, and you'll have some idea how petrified I am right now."

"Rory, I can shut up my shop and come to be with you."

"No, Chris. There's nothing you could do here. You've got kids in school and Ernesto sometimes gets called out to the lab in the middle of the night. I appreciate your offer, but your family needs you there. Just keep Marta in your good thoughts and prayers."

"Well, you be sure to let us know how she's doing. And take care of yourself, too. It won't help Marta if you don't stay well."

In the following days, Marta showed no sign of coming out of her coma. She had surgery to repair her broken leg and the tube they'd put in for the pneumothorax was removed a day after the surgery. Rory was working at the feed store days, and spending every other night at the hospital in Missoula, so he could take care of Alyssa on the opposite nights.

He was just getting Alyssa settled in her high chair for some rice cereal when the doorbell rang. Enrique had taken Consuela to Butte to the market, so Rory went to answer the door. There on the porch stood Kelsey and Danny, surrounded by suitcases, bags and infant paraphernalia.

"Lass, whatever are you doing here?"

"I took a leave from the boutique, Rory. I want to help you out. I know you wouldn't ask me, so I'm volunteering. Danny and I have come to stay until at least the end of the year or until Marta wakes up and can come home. You need someone to look after Alyssa and you, just like I needed someone to look after me when I lost the baby. I didn't have to ask you for help, you were just there. You didn't ask me for help, but I figure, turn-about is fair play. I'm here to help, as long as you need me."

He caught her in a huge hug.

"Saints be praised, Kelsey. You couldn't have come at a better time. Between working and worrying about Marta and Alyssa, I'm finding it harder and harder to keep my brave face on. Come in, Lass. I was just about to feed Alyssa her breakfast. How did you get here?"

"We drove. Didn't you see my car?"

"No. God's honest truth, I'm so tired you could drive over me with it and I'd probably not notice it."

"Where's Consuela? Shouldn't she be feeding Alyssa?"

"Enrique took her to the market. The place looked like Mother Hubbard's cupboard because I haven't had time to go to the store on my way home from work. She'll be back in a couple of hours. Want some coffee? She did make some of that fresh before she left."

"Sit down and feed your daughter before her cereal congeals from turning cold. I'll get the coffee. You want a cup?"

"Yes, definitely. Cups are in the cupboard over the canisters."

"You want more than coffee? Are there some eggs and bacon?"

"I don't know. The larder is about empty. If anything like that exists, it's in the refrigerator. Hey, Danny, looks like you're ready to take off and walk."

Danny was levering himself up on Alyssa's high chair and looking like he'd love some of her rice cereal.

"Yep. He's been pulling himself up on chairs and table legs then taking a couple tottering steps before he falls down. Child Protective Services will be checking me out for all the bruises he's been creating."

She lifted up Danny's shock of red hair to expose a purple bruise of a couple of inches right next to his hairline.

"Coffee table," she said. "I'm splitting garden hoses to use to cover all the sharp edges with. My house looks like those bumper cars at the fair."

"Has Danny had breakfast?"

"Yes. He ate two pancakes about an hour ago. Not that he'd be opposed to helping Alyssa with her cereal, too."

"Make him a bowl if you want. Or there's instant oatmeal in packets in the pantry."

"C'mere, kiddo. Let's put you in your booster and mama will give you Fruit Bites."

Kelsey went to foyer where Rory had stowed her bags and returned with a plastic booster seat and a small individual box of Fruit Bites. Danny fell to eating like he was starving. Kelsey poured milk in his sippy cup and set it next to his bowl of cereal, then got out three eggs and a package of grated cheese and made Rory an omelet and some toast.

With Alyssa watching Danny, Rory was able to enjoy a good breakfast for the first time since the accident.

"You have to work today?"

"Yes. Jack's been letting me come in at noon so I could get some rest. I don't get back from the hospital until after midnight, usually. Where should I put your stuff?"

"I didn't bring a bed for Danny, so if it's okay, can Danny sleep in the room that Marta decorated for Alyssa and use her big girl's bed? That bed is close enough to the ground if Danny rolls out of it, maybe he won't break anything. Is Alyssa sleeping in her crib in there now?"

"Yep. She outgrew the bassinet about a month ago."

"Can I have the room across the hall from the nursery? That way if they cry in the night, I'll hear them."

"Sure. I'll go take up your stuff, then I'd better head off to the job. Hadley's been so nice about the work, I don't want to take advantage of him by being late."

"Go. The platoon is here. I'll take care of everything."

He went to put his dishes in the sink and once his hands were empty, he caught Kelsey in a hug and kissed both her cheeks.

"Thanks, Lass, for coming, and for staying, and for breakfast."

"Well, you just tell that wife of yours to get a hustle on and come home soon. I'm sure after a couple of days with two toddlers, I'll be more than ready to relinquish the job of minding both of them. Leave me the numbers for your work and your cell phone. I'll probably have loads of questions, like where to find more diapers for Alyssa or what she likes to eat in the way of baby food."

"She loves puréed pears. And applesauce, but not peaches. She gags on chicken and spits out carrots. It might be too early yet for puréed meats. Green beans are good, but they make her stools an ugly shade of putrid Army green."

"Are you going to Missoula tonight?"

"No. I've been going every other night so I can spend time with Alyssa. Tonight is a home night."

"So, you'll be home for dinner?"

"Yes, about 6:30 or 7."

"Okay. Don't worry about a thing."

"I wish I could take you up on that order, but. . . ."

"I know. As long as Marta is in a coma, you can't do other than worry. I'm sorry, that was a poor choice of words."

He smiled a small sad smile and she knew how much he hurt inside and how very worried he was about Marta.

"Rory, she'll be fine. I just know it in my bones."

"God, Lass, I hope so. She just lies there. The bruising has faded and her leg and ribs are mending, but even when she opens her eyes, there's no one home in there. It's really hard to make happy talk every other night when I don't know if anything I say gets through to her. I'm really tired, but I dread crawling into bed night-after-night without her. It breaks my heart. I want her back, Kelsey."

"You'll have her back, Rory. You just have to be patient. And strong."

"You must have been talking to Mom."

"Yes, she called me and told me how upset you were. That's when I decided to come. I'll be here to take care of things so you can concentrate on Marta. I'll even get up and feed your sheep so you can catch a bit more sleep."

"You don't have to do that, Lass."

"I want to. It'll be like old times. Tell the drovers to show me what you feed and I'll be more than happy to do that."

"Did I ever tell you how much I love you, woman?"

"Not as often as I would have liked to hear it. Or had you mean it in a way other than the way I know you mean it now. Go, get ready for work."

"Okay. But thanks, Kelsey."

Officer Horton stopped by the feed store a week after Kelsey had arrived to say they'd stopped Amber Sykes trying to cross the border from Arizona into Mexico and told him she was being extradited back to Montana and her car was impounded for shipment back as well.

"How's your wife?"

"Still in a coma. Thanks for asking. And double thanks for letting me know that you caught her. My friend, Jack Strauss, said if there's a bail hearing, I should show up and put in a bid for no bail. Will they let me know, do you think, if there is a bail hearing?"

"I'll tell the prosecuting attorney that you'd like to be notified. They'll probably call me to put in my report at the same time, so I'll call you, too, just to be sure."

"You guys have risen a good bit higher in my estimation since Marta's accident. I didn't always think so well of you when you were handing me a ticket for speeding. You guys are always all business when it comes to writing up tickets. Made it hard to believe you had a heart. I know better now.

"Thanks for all you've done for me. I appreciate the time you took to stay with me the night of the accident and your willingness to keep me posted on what's happening now. Next time you pull me over for 80 mph in a 60 zone, I'm going to say 'thank you, officer' instead of grumbling under my breath."

"Well, there are those two parts to our mission statement. To 'protect' means we have to hand out those tickets to protect the rest of the people on the roads from the speed demons, but there's also the part about to 'serve' which means when a tragedy occurs, we try to put ourselves in your place and help out however we can. We have wives and families, too, so we know how we'd feel to be told that someone we love has been injured or killed."

"I hope to hell nothing like happened to Marta ever happens to your wife or your family. Let me know if there's a bail hearing. And thanks again for all your kindnesses."

"I'll do that. I hope your wife soon comes around."

"Me, too. Thanks."

While life didn't exactly smooth out into a comfortable routine, with Kelsey in charge of the household, Rory had a bit less to worry about. Alyssa certainly took to Kelsey, and with Danny to entertain her, she seemed more content. Kelsey also got on okay with the drovers, being an old hand with the sheep. She helped with the breeding and with the fall inoculations, doing about as many as Rory would have done, had he been able to devote the time to the autumn chores.

Rory took to coming home after work every night, and eating with them, then going to Missoula to sit with Marta into the wee hours of the morning. He'd return about 4 a.m. and catch some sleep, rising at 10 to eat and get ready for work. It didn't matter to Marta, he thought, when he came to be with her, but he felt he should at least be there for dinner at the ranch to give Kelsey time to relax for a few moments without worrying about Alyssa or Danny.

Kelsey was an early riser and always fixed him a good breakfast, creating banana-nut loaves or pumpkin bread in addition to making bacon and eggs or sausage and pancakes. He'd lost about 15 pounds since the accident and she seemed hell bent to put the weight back on him.

All of October went past with no noticeable change in Marta. Each morning, Kelsey's eyes inquired silently about her condition and it was with sadness he'd tell her, "No change."

When it came to the start of November, Kelsey asked him what to do about the upcoming holidays and what degree of celebration he'd feel comfortable with. She said Chris had called to ask if he would welcome her family for Thanksgiving to make it a bit more festive.

"I don't mind Chris and Ernesto and their kids, but nobody else. I'm strung out so far I'd probably snap if Sean said one word crosswise to me. I wouldn't want to be held responsible for my actions if he goaded me right now. I can't deal with everyone this year, Lass. Can you call and tell them all that I'm sorry, but I can't be a genial host right now."

"You aren't worried that if you invite Chris and her brood, the rest will be mad?"

"Chris always knows what to say to make me feel better. And Ernesto, too. She's not going to be on my case prodding me about this and that—things she'd do better or differently.

"I'm a whole lot more comfortable with Chris and you than I ever was with the rest of them. I just can't take a slew of advice about what I should be doing now. Sean will want to worry me about how I hope to pay for the hospital bills. And Maeve will suggest that maybe if I brought Marta home to familiar surroundings, she'd wake up sooner. I'll miss the kids, especially Todd, but it'll be better if I don't have to explain the situation with Marta to a dozen and a half of my nephews and nieces."

It was nearly ten at night when he got to Marta's room on the second of November. The nurse who'd taken care of Marta in ICU was getting a cup of coffee in the cafeteria when he stopped in to grab a cup himself.

"Mr. McCrea. How are you holding up?"

"Not so well. My brave face is getting harder and harder to put on the longer this coma lasts."

"No change at all?"

"No, not so far."

"You must be exhausted."

"I'm too tired to notice. This coffee is about the only way I can function."

"You don't have any help or family to give you a break?"

"Yes. My sister-in-law came to stay. She's been taking care of our baby, and that's been a real boon. At least I get 5-6 hours of sleep most nights. You don't really realize how much your wife does until she's not there. When she wakes up, I'm going to appreciate all her efforts a lot more."

"Well, I hope it happens soon. They've been doing physical therapy haven't they? To keep her arms and legs from atrophying?"

"I guess. The bill I got yesterday had those sessions listed. I'm not here in the daytime, so I hope they aren't charging me for something they aren't doing. Her doctors keep saying something about no decerebrate movements so far and that's a good sign. I don't know what that means."

"Decerebrate movements of the hands mean they rotate outwards. Instead of the palms facing the body when the arms are lying next to the body, the back of the hands face the torso. It's a sign of worsening brain functions. That she isn't exhibiting them *is* good news."

"Thank you. I wish they'd clue me in when they toss around all that medical jargon. I'd worry less if I knew what they were talking about."

"Yes, the medical profession is guilty of not explaining a lot of stuff. It's like a closed society and you need to know the lingo to be a member. They talk like that on purpose to keep the hoi polloi out. They like to keep the common folk in awe of their superior knowledge. But us nurses have our feet planted more firmly on terra firma, so if you want to know something, ask one of us, okay?"

"Yes, thanks for the tip."

Upstairs, he sat down beside Marta's bed and took her hand, the palm of which was warm and definitely not rotated outwards.

"Hey, Marta. We're almost to Thanksgiving. I wish you'd wake up and give me the best reason ever to be thankful. Only Chris and her family are coming this year. I can't deal with the rest of them and all the kids. You know I get on famously with Chris, so I don't mind her. She's the only one of all of them that always is on my side—she's always supportive, and I could use some support right now.

"Kelsey is going to cook a turkey and make pies. She's been so much help while you've been here—I can't begin to tell you how much of a load she's taken off my shoulders. You might laugh if I told you I didn't give one sheep a shot this past week. She got out there and rolled up her sleeves and inoculated every one of mine herself. And she's been fantastic with Alyssa. All the stuff I'm not so hot at, shampoos and wiping snotty noses—she does without a murmur.

"But as much help as she's been and as much as I appreciate her help, she's not you. God, wife, how I miss you. You have to wake up. I can't face Christmas and shopping at the mall without you. It would just be too incredibly sad. You always know what to get all my sisters and nieces when I don't have a clue. And you're the one who can make the Christmas tree look terrific even when it's all spindly and misshapen.

"Please, Marta, wake up. I need you so much."

On the fifth of November, Rory took Kelsey and the children to church. After the mass, they ate lunch in Butte and Kelsey asked if she could go to see Marta in the afternoon.

"Sure, Lass. Maybe it would help if she heard someone's voice besides mine. Just keep all your words on the happy side—they said not to talk about anything down, like the accident. I'll keep Danny and Alyssa if you want to go. Maybe by dinner, I'll have him walking like a pro."

"Don't count on it, Rory. Just make sure he doesn't kill himself falling into something hard and unforgiving, like the TV console. He missed hitting that by millimeters yesterday."

"Ah, hell, Kelsey, a guy needs a few scars to brag on in first grade. Stitches are even better."

"Don't you dare let him need stitches, Rory McCrea."

"I'll do my best, Lass. Give my love to Marta. Tell her I'll be there about eight tonight."

Kelsey returned in time for an early dinner. Danny had remained unwounded in her absence, but Alyssa was fussy, having missed her afternoon nap.

After eating, Rory got Alyssa ready for bed and tucked her in. Danny was in the bathtub getting dinner washed out of his hair and ears.

"Rory," Kelsey called from the bathroom. "I didn't want to say anything in front of Manuel and Ricardo or Consuela, but while I was at the hospital, I heard the nurses discussing Marta with her doctor. They were telling him she'd exhibited much more movement the last two days than usual. I didn't hear the doctor's comments, so I don't know if that's a positive thing or not. But you might ask her nurses when you get there."

"That's what the ICU nurse told me. She said the nurses were more likely to tell me things in words I understand. I will ask one of them. But don't get up your hopes. It's probably a new concoction they fed her through the tube that gave her gas cramps or something."

"Wouldn't that be positive? If she was beginning to feel pain?"

"Is it ever positive to feel pain?"

"I don't mean to upset you, I just thought it might signify some increased awareness on her part. You'd better get going if you want to arrive before the 8 p.m. hour I promised her you'd arrive at."

"Yeah, right. Like she'd know."

"Rory, don't get discouraged. She's going to come out of it."

"Your faith must be a hell of a lot stronger than mine, Lass."

It was dark and cold on the drive to Missoula. The melancholy he had occasionally suffered from settled in his mind like the cold settled in his bones—setting up for a long-term stay.

In her room, he didn't bother to turn on a light. She wouldn't know anyhow and he thought the blackness suited his mood a lot better than the glare of the fluorescents. He pulled his chair close to the bed, took her right hand in his left and laid his head on the bed. Tired to the very core of him, he didn't say anything, but dozed fitfully.

"Rory?"

He knew he was dreaming. In his dreams he often heard her call his name.

"Rory, is that the harvest moon?"

His head jerked up off the bed and he looked out the window. A huge yellow-orange moon was inching up over the mountains. He closed his eyes and began to shake, afraid to look at her.

"Rory? Is it the harvest moon?"

It was all he could do to speak.

"No, love, it's the shepherd's moon. Oh, God, Marta, how much I've missed you."

Her eyes were open and shining in the light from the moon.

"Where are we?" she asked, looking at her surroundings for the first time in many weeks.

"You're in the hospital in Missoula, Marta. You had an accident in September, coming home from work. You've been in a coma."

"But the shepherd's moon comes in November. I remember your story. I've been here for months?"

"Yes. You had all of us worried sick."

"I don't feel bad. I feel fine, I think. Oh, no! The baby! How is Alyssa?"

"She's fine and she'll be ever so happy to have her mama back."

"When can I go home?"

He stood up on legs that felt like jelly and took a few deep, steadying breaths. He felt lightheaded and still very afraid.

"You just stay still until I can get the nurse and your doctor to check you out. I don't want to take any chances of you lapsing back into a coma. If they say you can go home, I'll take you the minute they say you can go. Lie still, and I'll be right back."

He bent down and kissed her gently, then quickly went in search of her nurse.

"Mr. McCrea, are you okay? You look like you saw a ghost. Oh, no! Is it your wife?"

She stood up and began moving rapidly toward Marta's room with Rory in lockstep behind her. She turned on the lights and Marta flung an arm up over her eyes to shield them.

"Can you turn the lights down?" she asked.

"Mrs. McCrea, it's like a miracle. I'll turn them down as soon as I check your vitals, love, but I need to see your eyes."

Shining her penlight into both eyes and watching the pupils shrink as was normal, the nurse said, "Good! PERL."

"What does pearl mean?" Rory asked, worried again.

"It means, you dear soul, that her pupils are equal and reactive to light. P-E-R-L."

She turned down the bright lights and made a swift call from the bedside phone.

"Dr. Trask, you might want to come up to room 715 if you can. It seems that Mrs. McCrea has awakened from her long sleep." She turned to Rory and told him, "Trask is on his way. Whoa! Mr. McCrea, please sit down, before you fall over."

He half fell into the bedside chair as a dozen interns along with Dr. Trask and Marta's neurologist poured into the room. The neurologist did a brief evaluation, then asked questions about the year and what the names of her family members were.

"That's my husband, Rory. And I have a daughter, Alyssa. And there's Consuela and Enrique and Manuel and Ricardo and Juan and Dulce and Melinda and Rory has lots of sisters and brothers and their kids. There's Todd. He lisps. Do I really need to name them all? I want to go home and if I have to name them all, I'll be here for two more days.

"Oh, and it's November of 2006. I know it's November because that's the shepherd's moon. Rory has a beautiful story about the shepherd's moon."

"Well, Marta McCrea, it seems like all your faculties are intact. If you'll agree to stay one more day for some cat scans and an ECG, I think your husband might be able to take you home tomorrow evening."

"Good. I want to go home. Rory, don't leave until I can go with you, okay?"

"Not a chance, love. You couldn't blast me out of here with twenty tons of dynamite."

He got the small photo album from the desk in the corner of the room and held it open so she could see the pictures he'd taken of Alyssa.

"Oh, Rory. She's grown so. What did I miss? Start at the beginning and tell me everything."

About six in the morning he finished telling her all that had happened while she lay sleeping. About Kelsey coming with Danny to help out at the ranch. About Jack suing Amber and her insurance company and winning a big award from them. About Officer Horton's testimony and his kindnesses after the accident. About Amber never being able to harm her again.

"They sent Amber to jail for how long?"

"Forty years, with no possibility of parole. But the part that will make the most difference is the $6.5 million settlement for your injuries and your pain and suffering. As soon as the insurance company pays, I can clear the hospital charges and pay off the ranch. We can put money away for Alyssa's education—for all our children's educations—and still have enough to share with the drovers."

"That's a lot of money, Rory."

"Yep, it is, but it can't touch how much you're worth to me, Marta. It isn't nearly enough for the hell you've been through."

"You kind of look like you've been in hell right along with me, husband mine."

"You took a few off my lifespan, wife."

Breakfast arrived and she ate like a bear coming out from hibernation.

"While you're polishing off your toast, I need to call Kelsey and tell her the good news. She'll be worried when she discovers I didn't come home last night."

Marta tossed him a saucy look and asked, "She wasn't sharing a bed with you while I was gone, was she?"

"No, definitely not. But she was an enormous help with Alyssa, so I hope you can find it in that somewhat jealous heart of yours to thank her."

"I was just teasing, Rory. I'm really grateful that you had her to help you out."

"She taught Alyssa to say 'mama' and got her to eat carrots. But she drew the line at trying any potty training, no matter how long you were in a coma, so I'm really happy you woke up. I'd be a complete disaster at potty training."

The tests showed Marta to be well, and save for an aching leg when the weather changed, she had no residual effects from the accident. The entire family again came for a rip-roaring Thanksgiving celebration, there being so much to be thankful for that year. After many requests, Rory again told them the story of the shepherd's moon, ending it with a quiet prayer of thanks for the moonbeams that shone the night Marta had awakened from her coma.

When the feast and the celebration were over and the ranch house was quiet, Marta took Rory's hand and led him up the stairs.

"Make love to me," she urged. "We've got a couple of months to make up for."

Rory knew that life's frequent distractions might soon make the accident and Marta's long sleep and her recovery distant memories, but before he went to sleep, he vowed to never let a night go by without thanking God for his wife—and for the light of a shepherd's moon. Maybe the same angel who'd told the wise men and the shepherds to go to Bethlehem for the birth of the Christ Child had been the one to whisper in Marta's ear that it was time to make the trip back from her comatose state—to follow the shepherd's moonbeams and come back to him.

There were no moonbeams that night, it being the dark of the moon by then, but the room was lit well by the sparks given off by two people who were very much in love.

—End—